Lead,
Kindly Light

Mark Scrivenger

"FIVE STARS"

Mark Scrivenger's *Lead, Kindly Light* is a novel that grips from the very first page, pulling readers into a world as brutal as it is breathtaking. Set in the raw, unforgiving landscape of Van Diemen's Land, the story unfolds with a rare blend of emotional intensity and historical authenticity. Scrivenger crafts characters whose lives are marked by suffering, resilience, and unexpected tenderness, weaving their experiences into a narrative that feels both intimate and expansive.

Tom's storyline quickly emerges as the most compelling, distinguished by its depth, tension, and emotional weight. As the narrative develops, the meticulous detail and structural foresight embedded within Scrivenger's writing become increasingly evident. Each character's journey gains greater significance as the connections slowly draw together, culminating in a conclusion that not only promises to mesmerise—it succeeds.

Lead, Kindly Light ultimately transcends its brutal setting to deliver a deeply human story – one that confronts suffering while illuminating the quiet but persistent forces of love, resilience, and transformation. Through Tom, Grace, Marianne, and the many lives that intersect within this unforgiving world, the novel reveals the extraordinary complexity of ordinary people shaped by extraordinary circumstances.

Scrivenger's meticulous historical detail, emotional depth, and flashes of unexpected humour work together to create a narrative that is as immersive as it is affecting. By the final page, the story

lingers not only for its vivid portrayal of a harsh era but for its exploration of the enduring hope and compassion that can emerge even in the bleakest of places.

Mary Anne Yarde

Some characters in this story were real people, some with their surnames changed slightly. Others are invented. Some events were real. Some are not. How the real occurred is plausible guesswork; others are pure imagination. Together, they make a work of historical fiction.

This work pays its respects to the original owners of the land whose story it shares, the Muwinina and Mumirimina people, most of whom did not survive British colonisation, and the Wadawurrung people of the mainland.

We acknowledge the Tasmanian Aboriginal community as the continuing custodians of lutruwita (Tasmania) who have survived invasion and dispossession, and honour Aboriginal Elders past and present.

Editing and design by Anna Scrivenger

CONTENTS

CHAPTER 1

Hobart, October 1830

"Stole silver spoons from your sister? Nice lad. Mam loves you still, I wager."

The Chief Assessor looked up from his papers at the young man who stood before himself and his fellow Assessors of The Colonial Board of Assessment. The records, as usual, were impeccable. Measured before the voyage at five feet seven and a half inches - taller than most - and a shoemaker. The records did not show he was well-built, with grey-blue eyes and a prominent nose that suggested the face was not in balance, though it was complemented by a strong chin and a broad neck. Nor did it mention his dark brown hair, dented by a slight wave as if suddenly upended. A man capable of good work, should he choose it, or should he be forced to it ... and there were compulsive ways to ensure that he did. It was recorded that at the time of sailing, he was twenty-three. This personal information was set out, as was the reason he was before them: robbery in a Lincoln street, found guilty, sentenced to death, but commuted to transportation for life.

Amazing, the Chief Assessor muttered to himself, what His Majesty wanted to know – or us to know – about the debris he sends us. Wants to know too, whether there is anything these wretches can do to be of use in his Colonies before they die. Another boatload of them now arrived from the Mother Country to assess. Better get on with it.

"We see you are here for robbery. Here to stay. Not good at villainy are you? We do not see the good ones."

"Where is this place?"

"Hobart Town."

"What! Where is that?" He looked about for some clues on what it meant. Nothing. Just a dark room with men opposite. What then? He had no experience to help him.

"Van Diemen's Land. One early matter to stick to your skull is that you are not to speak unless replying to a question, or you are invited to speak, and every person you reply to must be addressed as 'Sir', or 'M'Lady', or 'Madam.' You understand?"

"Yes."

"Yes, what?"

"Yes, I understand."

"Yes. What!" The voice raised.

"I understand! What more do you want?"

"Dear God!" he muttered to his other Assessors. "Do they only send us the imbeciles?"

The young man looked at the bare planks of the floor between them.

"Hobart is a prison, of sorts." The Assessor immediately regretted being imprecise in speaking to this character, but now he had to continue.

"His Excellency Lieutenant Governor Arthur is in charge of all and everything. Everyone. His finger is on every pulse. He will know the colour of your hair, the length of your stream when you pass water, and where you do it. He has two magistrates to run the courts, and busy they are.

"Then there are the officers and the lower ranks, to guard and administer, as we do. Next are free settlers, who came of their own free will – for reasons best known to themselves – to this godforsaken place.

Seeking their fortune, they say, though what they expect to find out here..."

He glanced at the young man's coarse, stained linen shirt. Or what had once been a shirt. "And at the very bottom of the pile, on a pile of filthy ordure, are the prisoners, who you will recognise as they will be dressed in such savage rags as you. So there is no mistake that you are unworthy of human intercourse. The only wretches beneath you are the Blacks – savages who never even had the wheel. The Good Lord only knows how they survive and He is not saying; though they survive when you would not. Perhaps the Blacks are ahead of you."

He paused to take a deep breath. The air smelled of sweat, and of the dust that was swirling in a shaft of pale light streaming in from the small side window.

"You will not speak to any of those above you unless you are asked a question or it necessitates a reply, when you will finish with "Sir," or address a lady as I have said. Although, it is impossible to envisage a circumstance whereupon you could come into contact with a lady. Now, I have enlightened you about your status as a denizen of the dung heap and I am an officer. So, what do you call me?"

The young man felt his temper rising. "Sir."

"Very good. We have made a little step forward. Now, what is your name?"

"Tom, Sir."

"Tom what? Is it Thomas?" The Assessor knew anyway.

"Thomas, Sir."

"Do you have another name besides Thomas!" the Assessor almost shouted.

"Thomas Sir Scrimshaw."

His interlocutor was turning puce, and another Assessor took over.

"How old are you?" He asked in a more even tone.

"I was twenty-three when I came from court. I had my birthday on the boat here, so must be twenty-four. Didn't get a birthday glass though; think I should have one now I'm here eh? Must be ale somewhere hereabout?"

"Forget something?"

"Sir?"

This is not a place of celebration, Scrimshaw."

"Could do with some, Sir."

"I do not think your insolence is very helpful to your position," the Assessor returned, sharply, "You have a trade or occupation?"

"I was a shoemaker before I was grabbed by the law." A pause. "Sir."

"How long?"

"Many a year, after some little schooling. Must be ten or so year. Sir."

"You can cut?"

"Depends on what you want cut... Sir."

This was not a particularly satisfying reply. "Anything else?"

Scrimshaw thought for a few moments. On the transportation vessel, he had been – because young and strong – pressed into helping the ship's carpenter with repair work on the voyage. As well as being one of a motley heap of convicts in the hull, he had seen, briefly, a few officers with women who must be their wives, including one so lovely he stopped his current work to soak in her blonde beauty, until he was curtly reminded of his task by the carpenter.

"I did some work with the carpenter on the ship... Sir. One of the stairs broke, and then we had some wet inside the hull. So I jus' helped get her shipshape in order that we might get here and enjoy the sights... Sir."

Not that he had seen any sights except the sea. The *Southworth,* under master John Coombs, had docked in Hobart shortly after dawn, and after four cramped and endless months at sea her cargo of fetid prisoners was promptly disgorged blinking onto bleak, muddy shores to be seen by the Board for assessment prior to the next stage of induction into their future lives. Or deaths. For who here would care either way?

This assessment had not gone well, and both sides were irritated, although all the authority rested with the Assessors. The Chief Assessor was still glaring at the shoemaker, or carpenter, or whatever he was.

"We will tell you what will happen now," said the Assessor. "These are the Orders of His Excellency. You will take your possessions with you and be escorted by a guard to Ordnance to receive your uniform as a prisoner. That uniform will be washed on Mondays and Fridays, and you will wash weekly with tallow soap to cleanse your miserable body as far as possible, although you will never wash away the sin that will forever curse you.

"Your uniform garments will be replaced every six months. You will work in whatever capacity we decide, from sunup to sundown, on six days. And on the Sabbath you will attend Church to repent your sins. If you are discovered out after hours without permission or authority, you will be severely punished. You will have breakfast before you start work, and dinner at one o'clock.

"After leaving Ordnance, you will go to the prisoners' barracks. You will start work today on the public works, namely the wharf, until we determine your future work, which we expect will be in two days after we have finished all our assessments.

"It would be in your interests to work as a shoemaker in the Colony, but you have not helped yourself with your insolence and attitude. So, it may be that hard labour will be beneficial for your future, however long – or short – that may be. When you lift your head up, in the Town, see the gallows swinging and think upon how you would measure. Now go."

Thomas Scrimshaw picked up his bundle of possessions, such as they were after the privations of four months under sail from England, and left through a door indicated by a guard. Outside, another escorted him to Ordnance across a roughly cobbled courtyard, not in the traditional sense of supplying weaponry and armaments, but for convict uniform. Still slightly unsteady and swaying from his re-acquaintance with terra firma, Thomas stepped towards another door and muttered to himself as reassurance.

"Dead? Not yet. Not while you lot live."

Tom, to be so called henceforth, had an expectation that the garments, whatever they were, would be a reasonable fit, and that an experienced tailor or similar would size him up and dole out whatever he was required to wear. Motioned inside the door by the guard, before him was a counter with two men dressed in grey behind it, and behind them wooden bays with a jumble of oddly-coloured clothes. A man dressed in this curious outfit was leaving through a door at the side. Tom barely had time to absorb what he saw when a voice shouted.

"Here, you!"

He turned to see items of this clothing thrown at him.

"Put them on. Now."

He found himself with a new jacket, trousers, waistcoat, shirt, cap and, finally, a pair of boots. His eyes opened further to behold the yellow and – was it grey? – of his new attire.

The jacket was buttoned-up from waist to neck with an attached stiff collar. The left half of the jacket was yellow, the front of the left arm and leg and the right side of the back in yellow, the opposite sides in black, or was it a grey, a dirty grey? There were, he noticed, arrows imprinted on the garments. *What are these for?* he wondered, *I can tell which way up it all goes.* Not sure how to address this man, he stabbed at the arrows.

"Property of the King. So are you." He guffawed. "Very fine colours, too. Easier to keep an eye on you and what you are up to."

Having changed, as ordered, he realised the garments were of very coarse, rough cloth – uncomfortable, and meant to be. Waterproof, and meant to be. It felt like he was wearing carpet. He stared at the boots.

"Socks?"

"Socks?" shrieked the man. "*Socks?* You think it's a palace? Get on with it! Your feet will learn. A new set of this fine wear every six months. Now piss off."

Another convict shoved him across towards the door as the next man awaited his arbitrary collection.

His feet felt as if hungry rats were in a small, rough sack. As a shoemaker, he would have to have a look at these boots and see what could be done to improve things.

"Don't much fancy this place," he muttered to himself, realising that being overheard by the guard shepherding him across yet more cobblestones to yet another door was not helpful. Then, inside, a corridor, second door along, a large room, filled with wooden slatted bunk beds with a blanket on each bed and very small windows, stoutly barred.

"Put yer bag there. Yer bed while yer here."

Tom obeyed.

"Now come."

Although the day was young, Tom suddenly felt old. His experience of the morning on land might as well have been on the Moon. Was he? He trudged after the guard, across cobbles and courtyard, and out of the barracks. He suddenly realised, now out of the enclosures, that it was quite foggy and he could not actually see much at all. Was the Moon like this?

He was taken down to a wharf under construction. Black water lapped against the roughly hewn rocks, added to from a huge pile by grunting men dressed like himself. In the fog, he could make out the shadowy shapes of boats at anchor on water and two more moored at another completed wharf.

"Another one fer yer."

The guard turned and left to go through the routine with another new inmate.

A man, in grey, motioned to the pile and other prisoners struggling with a large rock, working out how to move it from the pile to the wharf area and to tip it in; a steady procession of men involved between the pile and the water. A routine soon settled in, which numbed him from the cold fog to some extent, and the itchy clothes were also heating him.

There was nothing to look at. Fog and labour and rocks. A splash! A cry. Labourers ahead of him looked into the dark water. A man, his yellow jacket eerie and shimmering in the little dark waves, thrashed frantically. Then he was not, the weight of his fancy uniform and water-filled boots pulling him under. All stopped, watched and then resumed their living labour. His had ended.

A meagre dinner was distributed on the dot of one o'clock; one of his fellows said it was like a clock. The Governor saw to it. Then it was back to work until the air cooled and sharpened as the day crept towards its end, and as the weak sun went to an easy rest and darkness became the sentinel, Tom and his band of not-so-merry men edged slowly to their barrack beds. They retired silently – partly on fear of breaking the order, partly as too tired for anything.

A new day dawned, and men with it. Breakfast was a gruel without taste; mere fuel for labour. Outraged skin swathed in carpet-burns as the day edged in step with their labour. Heads down; this was punishment, not an opportunity to enjoy any sights. What sights might there be?

A couple of hours into work, hauling and heaving boulders and lesser rocks into position to resemble an embryonic wharf, there was a different sound from scraping boots. Horses. Such a change from footfall; a sound that had rung daily through most of his life but that he had not heard or seen since... was it Sheerness? Lincoln, even? Well, leaving old England anyway.

It was a sound that belonged to a different world; his home and his youth, both lost forever. He looked up, half-expecting to glimpse the slight form of his mother across the street, waiting for the horse to pass, or one of his sisters – probably Margaret, knowing his luck – the one with the spoons. Or without them, now.

His father had something to say about that... He could get around his mother, being the baby of the family, but when the constable came for him his father had cast him out then and there, and his ties to the rest of the family had unravelled.

This was not Lincoln. Their imagined forms faded back into his memory, and the familiar streets of the home he'd likely never see again were nothing like this desolate place.

This sound rang out from an unadorned carriage with two dark, mud-spattered horses picking their way along and sometimes across the pitted track. As the carriage passed his reluctant detail, he saw an extraordinarily lovely young woman inside, riding as a passenger. As she gazed out at her surroundings, their eyes briefly met. He felt a shiver run down run up and out of him, but she was gone; the horses moved her away.

Ah, that bastard yesterday, saying that him seeing a lady to address was impossible. But he'd seen one already; that was the first part accomplished! Had he seen her somewhere before? What was she doing out here?

Reality tapped him on his shoulder, and it was back to scratched back, hands, rocks. Their ignored struggles, few words exchanged amid the bustle of others along the roads, the servicing of the boats at the wharf, tenders from those out at anchor in this wide, dark, hostile water; this was his life now, new but here. He had expected to be hung and dead by Easter, but now it was October, and he was yet alive, if a little disorientated, with plenty of fight left in him.

He was still uncertain whether these others were men on the Moon and that pale circle was where he had arrived. The Moon was best seen in the dark, but he had also seen it in blue daylight sometimes. He had sailed in and on pale and dark blue for many months. Was it the Moon he had reached, by way of all those dark nights sailing towards it through the inky blackness? How could he be sure? Were ladies on the Moon all beautiful?

Dinner was as announced, stuffed in by dirty fingers with a glance at the dark green hills across the water, and a quick look behind him away from the water, announcing more hills rising steeply into a mighty black lump where the top was beyond his eyes. Were there giants here, too?

The men's pace dwindled slightly in the afternoon as weariness overcame them. It was heavy work. As the sun dipped, they left the wharf and took a slow walk, more a hobble in the darkening sky, and Tom collapsed on the low wooden bed, wrenching his unbearably salt-stiffened shoes off as he did. He kept his clothes on for warmth, aiding the one blanket despite the irritation and scrape every time he turned in the night.

The next morning at breakfast, as he dreaded another day with his dour boulder companions, he heard.

"Scrimshaw!"

He looked up. A guard was looking for him.

"Here."

"Here what!"

"Sir."

"Get your bag. Your assessment has been decided. You are assigned to Mr Gellibrand. His man will collect you shortly. Come back here with it."

Tom limped off to pick up his small bag and returned.

"Outside."

As ordered, he did so.

Presently, a man rode up on a horse.

"Thomas Scrimshaw?" the man said, glaring at him.

Tom nodded. It was safer than the Sir business.

"Good. You're ready. I'm Samuel, to you. Mr Gellibrand's supervisor. I'll be reporting to him on your work and attitude. And it had better be good. Follow me."

They set off, the horse walking, Samuel astride, a man in his forties solidly built with thinning curly, dirty blonde hair, dressed in grey, with Tom limping along as best he could.

He could look around now. To his right the wharves and harbour busy with boats, the widening expanse of water; too wide to be a river, he thought, but it seemed to funnel from the big hills, and there was a whiff of the sea from wind coming up over the water.

Across the expanse, a dark, blue-green canopy cloaked the hills, except where there were patches of flat light green, on which appeared to be embedded little squares of tobacco-stained teeth. Had there been a fight between the giants here and these teeth were the loser's loss? Where did they live?

He looked to his left. Up to the great hill, up and up? Was it the bedding, a great blanket thrown over a sleeping giant? Another under that canopy? So much, so strange.

Not only did his eyes absorb the surroundings, but he sensed different smells. In looking around, he saw human and animal waste on and by the rutted track and dumped haphazardly, often only detected by walking in it. The odours of putrefaction blended with wafts from a rotting corpse hanging lopsidedly on a gibbet. He closed his eyes. There were strange non- animal scents too, with trees and shrubs he had never seen; did they have weird smells as well?

There were other people directing themselves on the road, and rows of houses of similar colour and shape and design as back in Lincoln, and blocks like those teeth across the water. Were they actually houses, of sorts? Roads going off at right angles to this main road along the water, other roads running off these side roads to serve houses perched on the hillside, as if too exhausted by their efforts to climb any further and here they rooted.

Shops, too, with ladies going in and out, merchants showing signs of their wares. There was more going on in this peculiar place than he had realised – it was a small, hilly town with a fine, clear harbour, and perhaps not as wild as it had seemed. Now, he had time to lift his head, carefully to not trip and fall in his hated boots, and risk landing in the waste. They lurched along the road as he absorbed this place, where he was destined to spend the rest of his life.

Samuel was watching him closely. "You heard of the Convict Bank?" he said eventually.

"A bit... Sir."

"Mr Gellibrand agrees with it. Work well and hard, and he will reward you with small sums put into your account there."

Thomas raised his eyebrows doubtfully, and Samuel nodded in confirmation.

"He's a fair man, you understand. A barrister. Believes in Trial by Jury, though the Governor doesn't – he wants things done his way, the only way. The Governor watches everything. Helps the settlers, though not Mr Gellibrand. Buys land himself, the Governor. Mr Gellibrand doesn't get on with the Governor, really... Lots of legal stuff. Beyond me."

He pointed to a building they were passing with a large green door, with windows on either side and green window surrounds, with bars on the windows. Its sign read BANK, which Tom understood, having some reading ability. He smiled just a little; *are the bars there because of me? To keep us in or out?*

Samuel continued: "You have an account at the Convict Bank. You had one in England too, if you didn't know – money in from calculations made of the work you did in the hulks or as required. It is already transferred here. It's set up that you might have hope of supporting yourself one day. You get sums added depending on your work to help you settle here and contribute."

Settle here? Tom thought. *Here?*

But he had money! That was a turn-up for the books. "How do I get to it – the Bank... Sir?"

Samuel erupted with a cross between a snort and a laugh. "Do not trouble your thick head about that. Only the Governor can approve money coming out. He does it sometimes, if one of you lot has been on good behaviour for a long time – a very long time – and is coming up to the end of their sentence. I believe you're here for life. It'll be a long wait." He laughed again, without mirth, and shook the reins so that the horse increased its pace, and Tom stumbled in trying to keep up.

A few yards further on, Samuel added."You will be based at Derwent Park, the Master's residence. He has other properties, so if needed you will go to one or other. It's within my obligation to advise him of need and report to him on your effort. So do not make my life more difficult, in your own interests. Understand that I am your real master. Mr Gellibrand likes to see his men before they come under my eye."

They moved on in silence, and Tom was pleased to see various signs outside buildings; inns and public houses. Here at last were some welcoming similarities to Lincoln. He tried to put out of his mind the inconvenient fact that his sentence for robbery came directly as a result of drinking in such an establishment. There was one, he saw, with the painted sign of The Red Lion. Good.

Larger houses appeared, with more land around them. Samuel turned left into a muddy drive lined with small trees. English ones, he recognised, but looking lost, scrawny and unhappy out of old England. At the end, a three-storied house of the same smooth, honey-coloured stone, or tobacco colour as he knew it. It became more impressive as they got closer, and as they reached it Samuel stopped, pointed at Tom, then at the large door and dismounted. He turned to Tom.

"You don't know where or what you are without me. Run away? Where to? And if you get lost, which you will out here, the Blacks will spear you. I hear they eat white men, even dirty ones. You're young and beefy enough; and be a change from kangaroo. You're not going anywhere, see? Just here."

Tom saw the point of the first assertion, but just here? We'll see about that later, he thought.

Samuel went up steps to the heavy front door and banged a large brass knocker. The door was opened quickly by a middle-aged woman (another female!), and there was a brief exchange of words. She left and returned with a man of medium build with slightly receding sandy hair, a slight paunch and reddish cheeks from happy acquaintance with culinary and vinous pleasures. Aged about forty, he was dressed in the type of silken and embroidered finery Tom had seen very occasionally in Lincoln.

This man came carefully, almost elegantly, down the steps. Gellibrand, Tom presumed.

"Your name?"

"Tom. Tom Scrimshaw."

"What!"

"Err… Tom… Thomas Scrimshaw… Sir."

"I do not wish to be encumbered with the inadvertence of your memory, as even a limited brain of the sort which brought you here should remember the simple sound of 'Sir.' You are to work for me, here and elsewhere, under the supervision of Samuel, who will report to me on your character. To encourage you as a contributor to the wellbeing of the Colony in earning your own way, I will make a modest contribution to the Convict Bank. It will be some recompense for His Majesty in facilitating your removal here at his expense."

Tom thought he would prefer no contributions either way, but held the utterance.

Mr Gellibrand, as a barrister, warmed to his own eloquence.

"The colony is ruled – ruled, I say – by the Lieutenant Governor. Not a man to brook dissent, which is a matter of great sadness to those who believe the people should have a voice in the courts at least, if nowhere else. You will have been apprised of the working and eating rules on your arrival, and on attending Church on Sundays to contemplate the iniquities which brought you here and in the hope of making you a better man.

"I must, however, drip some raindrops to dampen this glow of optimism. The Governor has a pessimistic view of man and his redemption, despite his fine rule. His views on womankind are not vouchsafed to me, nor anyone I warrant. Whether he is right or wrong with this modicum of optimism, we shall see with you. Let it not be wasted.

"Now, Samuel will take you to where you will stay while assigned to me, and may you use your time propitiously in accordance with the rules and your own disposition within them. You understand."

 It was not a question, but a demand.

"Yes... Sir."

With that, Mr Gellibrand turned and went inside, and the door was closed behind him.

Samuel motioned Tom to follow him across a courtyard surrounded by stables, carriages and carts to another structure – a barn of two floors, with the smell of animal feed wafting from the upper floor. Having halted, Samuel opened a door, which had a square cut in it for light and air, and pointed inside an almost impenetrable room. When his eyes adjusted, it had a wooden slatted and framed bed, with a blanket, a bowl, a glass and a bucket. More of the same. At least he was spared a rolling hammock, wherever this place was. A Colony?

"Put your bag down. Breakfast is gone. Dinner at one. Work to do. On the wall."

Samuel could be a man of few words.

They left this small room, enough for a bed and the floor for the rest, to go back across the courtyard to Samuel's patient horse, which he mounted and spurred forward. Tom knew enough to know to keep up as well as he could over this undulating ground, and did so in silence. They went to a field at the side of the main house, then uphill into another field where a wall with scattered stones nearby had partially collapsed and needed maintenance.

Another man, dressed like Tom, was close by and bent to pick up a large stone. He carefully edged it onto a gap in the wall.

"Over there," commanded Samuel, pointing to an area some thirty yards away, in similar need of attention. "You can see what is to be done. I will return later to see how you work."

Suspecting correctly that Samuel would halt the horse by the side of the house to check on what work was being done, Tom had moved to the pile of stones and bent to grapple with the first one. His feet chafed. He wondered whether, now his own socks had worn out on the voyage, it would be better to loosen his bootlaces or have them tighter. Chafing or blisters? Or both? He believed it was deliberate to have prisoners wear out their own clothes, such as there were, to add to the rough miseries on arrival.

He mouthed an obscenity and worked on the wall. He juggled the first stone carefully into place, followed by another, recalling the skills honed in the past two days on a larger scale, down at the jetty. Turning for another stone he heard a dull thud, as the first, nudged by the second, fell to earth, followed by the second.

Samuel, watching from afar, smiled; he knew that wall building was a backbreaking, scratching, bruising skill needing practice. There would be plenty of that. He turned the horse towards another part of the park.

When Samuel had gone, Tom picked his way carefully across the paddock. To his left lay the sleeping giant he surmised to be sleeping under this dark grey-green cover with a strange odour from it – or was it from the giant? Everything, everyone was smelly. How long before the sun slid behind this bulk; is that when the giant woke up? The land curled fearful in the dark?

He walked painfully towards the other stone toiler, who bent to pick a stone without looking at him. Tom grunted. The man took no notice, and placed his stone in a gap. He seemed to measure the spot mentally, and it sat as if designed for the spot. Straightening up, he at last turned to survey Tom. He was about a decade older and gave no particular indication of interest in this newcomer. A man of medium height and weight, with light brown hair, a lined, tanned face from exposure to the elements, and gnarled hands from working with stones.

Now he, Tom, had to make the running. Now not just obeying orders, he felt less sure on what to do. But he needed to say something to close the gap between these two men dressed as one.

"Tom. Tom Scrimshaw. Been here a few days." He blurted out.

The man grunted.

Another attempt. "Took a few things; thought they needed freeing up."

"Lots of us did," was the response, then the man looked at him and introduced himself: "Alan, great wall builder.

"Like the uniform? Tells us apart from the others who like it here. They call us Magpies, though I never seen a half-yellow magpie. We're more like that thing young kids get with yellow eyes. It used to be duck trousers. Both for us sent here, and those who weren't sent. Trousers that were tough, lasted. Sort of canvas. But then they decided they couldn't have us looking like them, so got us these coloured monsters all the way from England so they could keep us apart. Keep us at the arsehole end. The Irish get all-yellow ones... I don't know which is better."

Tom smiled at the thought. Alan looked at Tom as if he might know all this with a nod but then, realising Tom was young and new, he added. "Magpies to them, Slops to us who wear them. Makes us brother crims."

Alan glanced towards the house. "Better get on with it. Sam's alright sometimes, but don't let the matey bit fool you. He works for the house, not you. What he decides, BigHouseMan says yes to. There's plenty of thieves, too, in this den. 'Tis a strange place. Very strange." He paused. "But then, so was home."

He shrugged and turned back to his wall, ending the conversation. Tom turned and picked his way back to his expectant stones.

The sun slowly edged across the sky, flickering light off trees, stones, and the big house. An old cart pulled by an old horse with an ancient driver in blue garb came very slowly into view. Horse and driver knew the routine, possibly the cart too, in its own way. Alan stopped as it approached and called to Tom, gesturing at the arrival. They both moved towards the cart.

The driver gingerly got down, went around to the rear and produced two bowls and four chunks of bread. He deposited all this on the bumpy ground, grunted, re-mounted the cart, flicked the reins and the little group moved slowly away without a word. Alan picked up a bowl and two hunks of bread. Tom took the rest, recognising the method of the barracks, with a delivery change.

The bowl contained a pound of meat, as ordered by the rules. It was indeterminately beef or mutton, perhaps also some onion or some turnip for some touch of taste, lukewarm from its trip to the field. Ravenous, Tom tore into it, one hand steadying the bowl, the other grasping the meat and plunging it into his gaping mouth, and dunking bread in the stew while chewing. When gorged, he wiped the bowl clean with the bread remnant, and then licked the fingers of both hands. He looked across at Alan, who was still eating and using a fork to spear the bowl contents. When he'd finished, he still had one piece of bread. How was this?

A *fork*? Ah, yes, he too had a fork and spoon in his possession, although knives were not permitted. He should remember that for tomorrow, for breakfast, a thing called 'hominy', he had been told by a longer-serving convict at the wharf, was made of corn cooked over a fire.

There were no pockets on or in the Magpie. Nothing could be hidden, unless you shoved them down a boot. His feet were now blooded, literally and figuratively. If it hurt too much, back to fingers. Fingers were both friends and enemies; friends to have kept him alive, to do things, protect him; but enemies that got him into trouble and brought him here. What of the bread, though?

"Haven't eaten all y'bread. Don't want it?" Tom asked hopefully.

Alan grunted. "I'll have it later. We'll have nothing now till tomorrow morn. And I'll be hungry long before then."

Ah. Tom saw that now. He felt starved in the two days in the barracks when he was wharf building. There were things to learn, and Alan was teaching some of them. The cart returned to collect the empty bowls, and quietly departed. Nothing was said, just come and go.

The two men resumed their afternoon toil and finished as the sun bade farewell, too. Samuel trotted up, looked at Tom's work in particular, and rode away. The two men were left to walk wearily back to their tiny dark rooms, Tom more so, as less inured to this labour.

As they trudged, Alan spoke. "Been here a lot longer than you. You learn things as you go, lots learned from others before you and it makes this lousy life a bit better. Pass it on to the new boats."

Tom realised this meant him and he replied: "Learned some already from you on eating; forks, and keeping some back for later. I learned stuff from Sam, too. Not all good. He told me about the Convict Bank and said I can't get to it and never will. Bastard laughed."

Alan stopped and turned to look at his young, temporary, companion.

"I was told that, too. But it's not true. I was told by our side it's not true. They want us to think that. If we knew we could get all our money, the bank would be cleaned out, and the town and inns bloody. The Governor wants to be seen to make this hole a credit to him. They say he keeps telling London how good he is, in making this a fine prosperous Colony with his settlers. '*His*,' mind you. Has to be done by commerce. Shops and businesses need customers. They need money. And where's there's a big pile of money doing nothing? Our bank."

Alan grunted as he continued. "We can't get it officially, but we *can* – unofficial – like. Can get it in little bits so we can spend it in little bits, which helps the Governor."

He grunted again. "Different commerce to that which got us lot here. It goes in the day you set foot here, from what you had when you got on the hulk before the transport sail and what you earned on the hulk. I was told you get a penny set aside from every shilling they say was the value of the work you did there. No idea how they work it out. There's an official on the boat who has it, and it's transferred when you land here. I was told that the official is called Surgeon-Superintendent, and looks after us. Remember one on my boat." Tom recalled the name too, but had no cause to meet him, and he was thankful for that.

Alan went on. "He also looks after our money. Our health." There was a sour laugh.

Tom hoped his work on the boat had earned some money too, but he remembered Sam saying he wouldn't get it.

Alan continued. "Can't say it's not smartly done. This surgeon hands over your record to the bank. Your name, ship you were on, the money you have. Then, after you're sent to work, like for Gellibrand here, his name and address as your Master is put on the record. Whatever you have, and who and where you are, is here already.

"The bank has a system worked out; makes it easier for them. You go in. They tell you that any attempt to get money which isn't yours, isn't in your own account, will be reported and you will be hanged. You are told to watch the gibbets, there's always a new face, or a face what was. Then they ask your name and boat, and Master. After all the time on the bloody boat, its name stays on your brain. They know it anyway. And your Master. If you can't remember the name as a new boat, give a description of where you are."

Tom had already forgotten the name of the man in the big house, but could say it was big, on the edge and had a driveway of English trees, and give some description of the man. But he clearly heard the warning on execution. Having avoided that fate in Lincoln, he was not going to risk another go. He reckoned others would be careful as well. He'd seen gibbets; not all were successful.

"Most in this dump can't read or write, but reckon we all know about money and sums. Our grandparents, and theirs and theirs, couldn't read and write but worked, had little businesses and kept themselves and families alive. Otherwise we wouldn't be here."

Tom thought of his father with money on the kitchen table, moving it around with mutterings on what was going where.

"The Governor wants trade with our money, too. He says we're not slaves. Could've fooled me. But he makes the settlers we work for pay something into the Bank for our work. Not free labour, like a slave. But it depends who you get. Some are more bastards than others. The Governor's eyes are everywhere. But one of them is blind to us taking little sums to help businesses – and his reputation in London, if not here. Frightens the shit out of us with the rules, and forgets them when it suits him. But you can buy extra bread from the prison bakery. It's a bit of a way from here. But where would the money come from to buy it, eh? It's all pretend." Alan waved his fingers through the air like a magician.

What a help Alan was. "Have y' been to the bank?" Tom asked.

"No, not me. I'm not too far from finishing my time with Sam. I can almost touch it... Keep out of trouble, do as I'm told, and I hope when the time's up, the Governor will do it. Says he's Christian. Let him prove it. Gellibrand says he pays into the bank for good work; I think he's a fair man. Bit pompous, but fair.

"I've learned, too. Not to do as I did to get me here, but to do something else with the money in the bank. I might hope for a different life. No-one gets back to England. So you do what you can here."

Tom wondered what his different life would be. The same, if Sam was right, but he, Tom, was not one to lie down and take whatever was thrown at him. What of Alan?

"What will you do?" he asked him.

"Dunno yet," Alan replied. "But reckon something will turn up. I'm not afraid of hard work. Specially after this."

Alan turned and resumed his slow walk, with Tom a yard or so behind, as they went to their rooms, if such they could be described. Tom slumped his weary body on his wooden slats and under his rough blanket, which welcomed its carpet cousin. He now understood his sisters' love of good clothes.

Breakfast was in a communal setting, like the barracks. Eight Magpies were perched along two opposing benches. In silence. Talking was punishable. Samuel supervised hominy, and then, as if in tandem with the stretching sun, he announced where each worker would toil that day. Another rule was that each settler was required to have a convict assigned to him for every one hundred acres he had. A rule of which Tom was unaware, but of fledgling Magpies there were plenty.

Tom trudged to a different field with another newcomer, again under the eye of Samuel, this time in a horse and cart. At the field, the cart stopped and Samuel went to the back and produced a pick and a shovel. Tom took the pick, the other man took a shovel and Samuel hoicked out an old wheelbarrow to share.

"Dig a trench. There's a spring seeping from the soggy ground over there, and we want it joined down to that slope there, to make a stream to fill up that hollow."

He pointed to a point in the field about twenty yards away. He went back inside the cart and produced a hammer and a post, and walked with both to a point he had determined, and whacked the post in.

"There!" he said, pointing at the post, then returned the hammer to the cart, climbed into the seat, shook the reins and off he went.

While not particularly forthcoming of his history, this convict, introducing himself as Jeffrey, seemed to acquiesce in his lot. They took it in turns to change between pick and shovel into the barrow. No direction being given on where to deposit the soil, heavy from springwater, they saw a pile of rocks some yards to the side of the post. Jeffery pointed to it, Tom shrugged and the barrow began the first of many short trips to the rocks. It gave them a sense of achievement, like a child's game; satisfaction in seeing their little unstable castle rise among a rocky foundation.

Dinner duly arrived and Tom retrieved his fork from his left boot and ate. Jeffrey watched. Tom, flushed with a little knowledge from Alan, passed on the culinary assistance, and felt he had climbed off the tiniest bottom rung of ignorance.

Resuming their labours, they became aware of Samuel's approach.

"You, Scrimshaw. Come with me. Leave your shovel." Jeffrey was left with all.

Walking behind the horse and on his bitter feet, an irony not lost on a shoemaker, he was taken to the field he recognised from yesterday. Alan was still there, working on his section of wall, which did not appear much changed from yesterday. Samuel stopped, and pointed to the section of wall where Tom had laboured. It had vanished, as if Tom had never been there. Rocks and stones were scattered as he had found them. How? Why?

"You didn't do it well," Samuel scoffed. "Do it again. Better." With that, he rode off.

Tom stood, stunned. He knew stonewalling was a skill, he had seen it back in Lincolnshire. But his work was not that bad, not so bad as to be taken down.

When Samuel was out of sight, he turned to Alan.

"What happened? This was good yesterday."

Alan stood up.

"I took it down."

"You *what*!" Tom's temper catapulted, fingers tightening into fists. He started towards Alan.

"I'll punch the shit out of you!"

"Sam ordered me to do it," Sam said evenly.

"What? Sam?"

"His little joke, he thinks. I said you had to watch out for him. I think all new workers get this treatment. I did, too. He wants to see how you, we, all of us react, and how we work."

"React! I'll punch him so hard he'll think a bash with rocks would be better. I'll shove his arse up his throat!"

"Every man says that, yes. But he has more power than you think. We all want to beat him up, put a rock up his arse. But there's a price. Not enough to get you hanged. Probably..." He paused to let that sink in. "But life would be a lot worse for you, even worse than this. They have lots of ways to make you wish you hadn't reacted. Believe me."

Tom subsided. The desire to spread parts of Sam over the field drained away. Even young and inexperienced in this new, alien world as he was, he sensed that survival took whatever was needed. Beating up Sam was not the answer. Bastard. There were other ways to survive. He would have to find them out.

CHAPTER 2

Hobart, October 1830

Marianne Wainwright almost lurched off the deck of the *Southworth*, the temporary home of herself, her husband Francis, and other officers and their wives over the long and tedious months to His Majesty's far-flung Colony of Van-Diemen's Land.

Lurching had been her mode of locomotion on the voyage, when she was not seasick, heaving and rough in both senses. Her husband assured her his was a temporary commission and they would soon enough be back in England with further advancement. She dreaded having to go through the return journey. Francis was already chafing over the delay. He saw it as his entitlement. He longed for some military action, born too late to fight the French. He complained about it so often she wondered whether he held the man Napoleon solely responsible for depriving him of that opportunity.

She looked at her husband on the increasingly crowned deck. Everyone complimented her on her choice of husband, with his good height, slim and well-proportioned bearing, and handsome features. She hoped she was approved as his choice of a wife.

His brown eyes turned towards her and she could admire again the correctness of his deportment as an officer, his hair clipped and level, which accentuated the long fashionable sideburns, shaped into precise deltas on his lower cheeks. He dressed carefully, anticipating meeting Lieutenant Governor Arthur, once a distinguished soldier who had seen the action Francis craved, but was now a career administrator and in charge here, in this place. It was, at least, land.

"Come," Francis commanded, "our possessions will be brought to us."

They had become friendly with three other officers and their wives on board, all on similar career advancement. The Morgans, Andrew and Rebecca; the Bells, Stuart and Annabel; and Henry and Sara Lynch. Closeness emerged on the voyage over shared seasickness; there was rarely a full complement at mealtimes. Sailing too, Marianne recalled, were lesser ranks and civilians to assist in the administration of the increasing number of criminals banished from dear England. She had no doubt the banishments were thoroughly just.

When well enough to venture on deck in calmer seas to take the bracing sea air (which, it was asserted, was good for her although it generally reinforced her queasiness), she had seen some of these outcasts who filled the ship's complement.

She was surprised to find these evildoers seemed to inhabit human shape and behaved as ordinary men, too. She saw one, perhaps a little older than herself, glance at her from a task he was undertaking. He was certainly sound enough in mind and body, yet had evidently done something awful to get himself put on this boat. She, at least, could look forward to returning to her beloved England and the green and... was it pleasant land?, on which a London writer had written not so long ago.

Marianne sighed. She promised herself, with urgings from her dear family, that she would keep a diary of her travels and thoughts to entertain them with on her return. Perhaps write some poetry, too. Not write like her beloved Jane, but she could put her thoughts down.

Now, her feet unsteady on the quayside, she grasped her husband's elbow as they were guided by a uniformed man to a carriage. The door was opened, and they entered after a gesture, followed by the Morgans, the men removing their regimental headgear to do so, and the ladies checking the status of their bonnets once seated.

"Well, here we are," said Andrew, "so much to see and learn."

"I am not so sure that there is anything here which a person of taste and sensitivity will learn, other than a reinforcement of understandable repugnance." Rebecca grimaced as she spoke.

Francis simply looked out of the carriage as it swayed along the rutted road, as did Andrew and Marianne. Rebecca looked ahead in the carriage. It was a short journey, but enough for Marianne to see houses, some in honeyed stone, some from rough-hewn wood which looked as if they exuded their own anxiety at a short existence. People seemed purposeful in these surroundings. There was something in the air, about the air too, so unlike Hampshire... an air which both sucked at her and blew upon her, oddly vital. She could not say more.

The carriage stopped. The door opened. The ladies were careful with their bonnets at the door top, and careful with their bright silk dresses, slightly incongruous in the setting, which they lifted slightly to permit their stockinged feet encased in delicate shoes to search for a sensible landing. One lady first, then the other. The men were more confident in their Wellington boots; good enough for Waterloo, too good for these ruts and puddles.

The Bells and Lynches similarly unloaded, the four couples were directed into Anglesea Barracks, for Officers, on the south-west slope of Hobart Town. There, each couple were directed into separate areas.

Marianne surveyed her new quarters. A bedroom with a brass bed with pillows and a thick quilt; a dressing table with a circular looking-glass in a mahogany frame, and a sturdy rather than elegant chair in front of the table. Also, another broader chair that she expected was for her husband's use, some clothes hooks behind the door, a wardrobe with drawers, bedside tables with candles in holders and in the bathroom, a bath, several jugs and a chamber pot. What a joy to see the bath she sighed, hoping someone would fill it for her. Ah, a bath, meal and bed... a bed without rocking.

She murmured about a filled bath to Francis. He left, and returned with a female servant carrying a bucket of hot water. She tossed it into the bath, left, returned a few minutes later and tossed another in. This process was repeated and then cold water added, tempering the heat. Marianne was transfixed. She remembered to check the temperature, nodded with satisfaction, thanked the woman and looked longingly at the bath.

Francis appeared with food. She hoped she could enjoy it after the privations of the boat. Bread, fresh-cooked beef, potatoes with onions, a smell of herbs she could not immediately recognise, and two apples. Were the apples to protect against scurvy? She cared not a jot.

As they ate this feast when compared with that at sea, Francis spoke.

"We are to meet the Lieutenant Governor at nine o'clock in the morning. We will need to rise at seven for breakfast. After breakfast, we as officers will proceed to Ordnance for new uniforms and pertinent outlay. We will return with our regimental clothing to be stored. We will be collected at quarter to nine to be driven to and presented to the Lieutenant Governor."

"How ought we address him?"

This was a point which concerned the punctilious Francis. The Governor was no longer a soldier, which would have been easy, but he was now an administrator.

"I will make enquiries while you bathe."

After eating, Francis excused himself and left. Marianne undressed and gingerly lowered herself into the water; not too hot, not too cold. She sighed. The servant had brought soap. She used it with easy strokes along her body. It slipped from her grasp. It was insignificant as she searched for it to resume her bathing. Her towel was on the floor. She was thinking of getting out of the cooling water when Francis returned.

"Governor Arthur is to be titled 'His Excellency,' and he is most particular that his recognition is attended to," he announced.

With this practicality resolved, Marianne pointed at the towel. Her husband picked it up and handed it to her as she carefully stepped out. She was astonishingly beautiful, a condition which Francis took, in his self-absorption, as a matter of fact, and his rightful due.

When she had dried herself, she moved towards the bedroom, turned to kiss her husband, smiled, went into the bedroom, pulled back into the covers, slipped between the sheets and was asleep under the quilt before he had retrieved the servant to empty the bath and remove their dirty clothes for attention.

They were called for breakfast after Francis's instructions. A night of intermittent sleep after months on irascible waves. A breakfast of ham and eggs and tea, which delighted them both. Francis then left in his full regimental uniform for his Ordnance rendezvous.

What shall I do with myself while he is away? Marianne thought. Perhaps I can explore a little? Uncertain how long Francis would be gone, and where she was, and that, she realised, she would have to dress for His Excellency, it would be better to dress now for that event and not risk appearing flustered if time was of the essence. She chose a silken dress of pale blue with a bodice of English flowers. She piled her rich blonde hair, which had not yet recovered its lustre, under a bonnet with matching flowers, put on long blue gloves and a pair of white leather shoes with a delicate heel.

Satisfied with her reasonable presentability, Marianne ventured out of the small apartment, went down the communal stairs to a large door at the bottom through which they had all entered, opened it, with more effort than she expected, and stepped outside. She recoiled from the brightness of the light and then the cooling breeze which poked at her. She stopped to look around. The expanse of dark water, never seen in her pastoral part of Hampshire, the sullen and implacable hills and – especially strange to her – on her left, mountains.

It was as if God had decided to create another world as different from the land she knew as He could and directed it be inhabited by those as different from Hampshire as could possibly be. This thought was given credence by the sheer energy and purpose she saw before her. Nothing at all like the gently ordered bucolic ways of her county.

The motley vessels bobbed on the water, or moored on the land's edge, all being serviced by men on deck and men in smaller boats. On land, men moved with intent, sometimes on horse, some with carts and carriages, some on foot, some in ludicrous outfits of black and yellow who laboured with uniformed soldiers looking at or after them. Shops and stores she could make out. She saw inns, with signs hanging and flapping in the breeze. A few women were mostly active, some with baskets, a few engaged in chat, or perhaps negotiation. Perhaps the Almighty decreed that this new Creation must be a hive of business. A strange perfume seemed stirred from the weird trees she saw about her, nary a solid English oak to be seen. All so peculiar!

As she looked around to take in these trees and bunches of shrubs underneath, and the cleared plots around the honey houses, her eye caught, swinging gently in the breeze, a gibbet, on which two downcast men, clothed in the eccentric garments she had seen, had their own dances. This was not God's doing. She shuddered on this imposition into her thoughts. It was time to return to her quarters.

Marianne had not long been at her desk awaiting Francis when he arrived, now resplendent in a red jacket and wearing duck trousers of blue-grey which would be changed, he said, to white as the seasons changed. They were apparently approaching the warmer months at year's end; the opposite from England. His boots remained regulation black, with gaiters and his shako, a tall cylindrical hat requiring regular removal in carriages and rooms and made of felt and leather, sported a metal plate and a plume on top to add a dash of colour. He also sported a sheathed sword and he looked very pleased with himself. He had a bag containing his old uniform which he took into the bedroom and tucked into a corner.

"You look very handsome, dear," Marianne said.

"We will be collected in five minutes." He gave no recognition of his wife's compliment.

Marianne collected herself and her purse, checked herself again in the looking-glass and stood, ready.

They were soon collected and joined the others to be allocated to two carriages, two couples in each. Bonnets and shakos dealt with, they were off – past the activities Marianne noted and, in a short space, turned left off the main road up a more substantial road which climbed a hill to stop outside on a flat piece of land before the most impressive house they had seen in their admittedly short time in the Colony. Leaving the carriages revealed a spectacular view across the river, or lake or sea, whatever it should prove to be.

It was clear they should move to the impressive front door of this palatial establishment and, having done so, the door was opened for their arrival. Although their modest barracks furnishings were on the edge of luxury after the voyage, this house had taste and refinement: Wedgwood porcelain, mahogany in a fine sideboard, drop-side table and well-carved chairs. They were ushered by a servant into a room at the end of the entrance corridor.

There, before them, stood Lieutenant Governor George Arthur and his wife, Eliza, both in their mid-forties. The Governor, of average size and height, with receding brown hair, strong black eyebrows and brown eyes, had ensured sunlight snuck through the large side window, glinting on the decorations he wore befitting a man of his stature. A man self-confident in his record and abilities and in his mastery and control of his brief as Lieutenant Governor of the Colony. His wife stood quietly by him, not as resplendent as the male, but tastefully and expensively dressed as the consort of such a man.

The officers, having removed their shakos, tucked them awkwardly under their left arms, stood to attention and saluted Arthur.

"Your Excellency," Francis began, being more advanced in protocol – a relief to the other young officers, now they had the address. Their wives resorted to uncoordinated curtsies, uncertain as to whom they should address. Eliza Arthur allowed herself a small smile.

"Ladies," the Governor started. "Would you be so kind as to accompany my wife into an adjoining room where she will apprise you of various matters pertaining to life in this Colony? I have matters to discuss with your husbands, and we will gladly have you join us at an appropriate time."

He remained standing while his wife led the young wives into a room off the corridor and the door closed behind them.

"At ease." He motioned to a large mahogany table in the room and the officers moved to sit, two on each side, placing their heavy shakos on the floor by their chairs, while the Governor moved to sit at the head.

He continued. "You are here in the hope of furthering your careers, an ambition both most worthy and desirable. Indeed, after my career in assisting the defeat of the French and making Europe safe from tyranny, it behoved me to consider how best to continue to serve our great country and Empire. I was always implacable against the different duplicities which can befall a man, and in so doing I was recommended to administer the tropic Colony of Honduras, our British Honduras, for good order and the promotion of the welfare of the settlers. How was that achieved? I must say that promotion is my idol."

"Your Excellency," interjected Francis, "May I be so bold as to say that precept is worthy of the great Socrates himself."

The governor's eyebrows raised slightly and he looked at the interrupter.

He continued.

"A principle to be borne in mind, and it has served me well in His Majesty's service. As you may know from sources which are on occasion impenetrable, His Majesty George IV has gone to meet The Divine Being whom I am certain will judge him most favourably, and we are now in allegiance to His Majesty William of the Fourth accord." He allowed himself a little smile, too. "While you were enjoying yourselves on the Empire's seas in old last-century ships, newer, faster boats brought us the news."

There was a general nodding of heads; knowledge or lack of it notwithstanding.

"But let me impress upon you, in your pursuit of such noble aspirations, that in negotiating the waters of ambition, many falter and are lost. This here is a prison, it is the reason for it. How you manage your duties here, supporting the courts, police, free settlers in their troubles with the natives, savages who live in this place, as they know no better of civilised society, you will be assessed and judged. The heart of man is desperately wicked."

He fixed a penetrating gaze on the young officers. "But I can reassure myself that in His Majesty's service, your hearts and steadfastness will lead you forth with honourable intent and success in the achievement of excellence as a beacon of light to all others.

"Such an example cannot be attributed to our late if not constant enemy, the French, hopping about the territory of Australia with intent to spawn here – and we are here to ensure they do not. We therefore have and encourage free settlers from our island and our duty is to support and encourage their endeavours on this, the end of the known world.

"Support, I must tell you, through the assignment system. These felons, upon whom you would have had the regrettable gaze to see on your voyage, have been too wretched to even commit crimes worthy of execution. As some recompense for being alive, I can put them to work on public works, such as wharves and roads, and exercise such skills as they may have had for community benefit or be assigned to work for a free settler. There are terms and an incentive is that with diligence and good behaviour they may be allowed to work for themselves in whatever capacity they can achieve. I set the terms. Some delude themselves that they can return to the source of enlightenment that is England.

"I note some furrowed brow. It is not slavery, so recently disgorged from our old history. This is expiation for grievous acts against our fellows. Pay your dues, as is said in some areas, and you can go forth to a greater or lesser extent. It is cheaper for a felon to feed and look after himself than for His Majesty to use us and those who sent them here. The savings can be used for the greater expansion of the Empire and its benefits." He paused.

"A better life than that from which they came. You will note gibbets around the Town. I have that power. Some irritant felons who commit felony again, I leave dangling for months. A lesson to behold. Keep upwind if you have occasion to be by.

"You will familiarise yourself with the Town and no doubt your wives will initiate you into areas you would not have known, or may I add, wish to."

A small, uncertain laugh sputtered for recognition from the officers who shifted uneasily in their chairs on what more might be forthcoming.

"What a prison needs is discipline. As the Army, as the Navy. Consistency in an eye for detail to ensure the regulations work. They exist to make them work. They exist to make them work for the Empire. I cannot impress upon you enough that these convicts suffer from mental delirium which is seen through a false medium, and I – we –

must sniff the scent, without being caught by it, to monitor the delirium and contain it. I am constantly engaged with London on the deficiencies I uncover, particularly the delirium which they do not understand.

"I am empowered to, and do, grant rewards. But man is evil, a rot within. Only our Creator can redeem them; we can but put these dregs on the true path to Him."

He paused, and started drumming the table with the fingers of his left hand. The officers looked furtively at each other, wondering where this was going.

"It is my duty and yours under my direction to ensure these principles are understood, rewarded and punished as determined by the particular event. To aid in the proper administration of the Colony, I have instructed the following."

He then dictated what was to all intents and purposes, a list imprinted on his memory. The stand-easy officers could only try and remember them as they were uttered, and discuss them later between themselves or in making discreet inquiries of more long-settled officers.

"I keep records of all activities of both settlers and prisoners. Some settlers are so lax in supervision of their assigned workers, they may as well invite them for dinner with the family; others scarcely less brutal than the acts of those who I sent to labour for them.

"I closed an inadequate settlement at Maria Island on the East Coast a few years ago, and this year I instructed the commencement of a new prison further south from here for incorrigibles, those resistant to accepting the wisdom and grace of Our Lord."

The officers continued their furtive looks. They were not expecting a distinguished former soldier to discourse, almost preach, on religious matters, especially with such evident fervour.

The governor was not deflected from his rigour.

"Those sent to the new settlement who refuse to learn the error of their ways will find their path strewn with punishments justified by their waywardness. I have not given it a title, although I am given to understand it is already known as Port Arthur, no doubt until a more appropriate name is decided upon."

He paused to let this sink in and he betrayed by a shift in his position that he was pleased with this swift recognition of his efforts. His drumming also ceased.

"I appointed a Police Magistrate and Assistant Police Magistrate, legally qualified in England to administer justice on the various offences which many of our charges are, regrettably, addicted to. While I do not believe the practice of flogging has any particular benefit, I do not interfere in the judicial process, except for considering and approving capital punishment for extreme malefactors. Otherwise, there would be little justification in the appointments were I to do it myself. I have enough to do."

His fingers started drumming again.

"This judicial process is most satisfactory, despite attempted interference by a legal officer appointed in London, who argued against me in league with a local newspaper of scurrilous dimension. This individual, whom I have now, after correspondence with London, had removed from his position, had the effrontery to propose, nay insist, on trial by jury for all accused. Here in this Colony; a prison!

"He waved Magna Carta and other documents at me. I cannot run a settlement of some free men and a prison on documents. If all the freemen eligible to be jurymen for all felonious acts were summoned, they would do nothing else but be in court, and the whole economy of the Town would collapse. Such a lack of thought by that individual. No enlightenment there. He would not make an officer!"

The officers all nodded in agreement, although bereft of guidance on whether this was a lecture, a statement of intent, an admonishment, or even a warning.

The drumming stopped. The governor's agitation over this individual had now subsided, and he left the officers to digest it all. Then, with a parting homily.

"Control. Discipline. God's Will. That is the necessity for your futures."

He paused.

"Time to summon the ladies to join us. I expect my wife will have arranged a social event for you to meet fellow officers, and appropriate others who can appraise you further of the needs, requirements and, may I say," (he allowed himself another faint smile) "the delights and pleasures of Hobart Town."

✳

Eliza Arthur led the young wives into a large room with damask curtains framing large windows, which allowed a view to the side of Government House. A large mahogany table was set with a tea service and plates. There were five chairs, one at the end furthest from the door and two on each side, but close to the end chair.

Mrs Arthur went to the end chair, turned to the young women, pointed to both sides of the table, indicating to sit. The young women were grateful to bypass the dilemma on how to address Mrs Arthur: Her Excellency? Madam? Ma'am?

They sat. She surveyed them. As the Governor's wife, it was her duty to introduce both herself and the arcane mysteries of these wholly raw and jolting surroundings to each set of officers' wives freshly disgorged from England. It had happened to her as a young wife with George, and she was grateful for the advice and guidance she had received.

Here the new group; a generation younger than herself. They were, in a sense, all of a piece. She, too, was the daughter of a Lieutenant General. She would warrant that these young women, scarcely but twenty years old, were the daughters of senior Army or even Naval Officers.

It reminded her of a structure, a caste system she had heard existed in India, but a peculiarly British caste. These officers begat children with wives who were also begat by an earlier generation of officers. The Bible flashed through her mind. A son to further the expansion and protection of the Empire. A daughter to marry another officer's son.

She could also rely on the young ladies being attractive; it was good to be seen in the furthest corners of the Empire, as here; an example of the exemplary virtue and breeding that the Empire sent forth. It was true here. All four of these women were attractive, would have been sought after, and make the husband who gained the prize very proud of the fact. Each wife must be pleased to have made such a well-regarded marriage.

Not without its hazards, she knew. Officers she had known over the years had died in the Empire's service, leaving the grief and despair of widows and children. It was not all pomp, circumstance and finery. But, almost as part of the caste system, these young ladies presented themselves in their finest dresses, taken, she knew, out of storage after such a long voyage and hurriedly aired. It was both appropriate in indicating respect to her, yet inappropriate in a prison setting where they would soon learn that special occasions for such showing would be rare indeed.

"You may call me Ma'am in our relations in Hobart Town. May I ask each of you in turn your names, your husband's name and, if you are minded to, and I say this without any expectation that you should consider yourselves obliged to, to tell me something of yourselves."

She looked at the girl furthest from her on the right side of the table, and nodded at her.

"Ma'am, I am Sara Lynch, née Croft," the girl said. "My husband is Henry Lynch. My father was a Colonel and my mother herself the daughter of a Colonel."

Mrs Arthur nodded, noting a girl of perhaps some twenty years with a full buxom figure, with bright eyes and fine, curly chestnut hair peeping from her bonnet. An eager, attractive face and personality, she judged. Her face bore the well disguised, through powder, of pox scars, the affliction by The Almighty on his earthy brood irrespective of age, and some of which were transported to Him, young or old. The girl acknowledged her skin blemishes as demonstrated by her acceptable nature.

She looked at the girl closer to her on the right side.

"I am, Ma'am, Annabel Bell, née Jones, and my husband is Stuart. It has been observed that we are three bells, taking my own name into account."

Mrs Arthur noted the little joke, and that the girl had the confidence to make such an aside. A girl of good figure, sparkling blue eyes with brown hair, a little of it straggling from her bonnet. She had quite dark eyebrows which were at variance with her lighter hair, but clearly of a lively disposition.

"My father was a naval officer, sadly no longer with us as a casualty of the war against the French. His valour is well remembered and appreciated with great pride by his bereft family."

Mrs Arthur responded. "We are so sorry to learn of your family's misfortune in losing such an honourable man."

The other wives, who had not had occasion to delve into each other's more secret histories, nodded in agreement.

Her attention switched to the left side of the table where her eye alighted on a strikingly attractive dark-haired girl who she saw exuded self-confidence. This young woman had a mole on her lower right cheek which was a source of great irritation to her. Her family asserted it was a beauty spot and to be much treasured, and had been much desired by ladies of the previous century. Rebecca referred to it as a fly with glue on it's legs and she refused to be mollified. A hint to seek surgical removal was brushed aside. It would still leave her with the blemish of a scar, and she had, on the boat, seen Sara's scars which although of a different cause, confirmed her determination. Her father wished those under his command had as much fire as his daughter. She was already sitting forward eager for communication.

"Ma'am, I am Rebecca Morgan, daughter of Lieutenant General Thompson, of renown in the battles against Napoleon. My mother was herself the daughter of an officer of high repute. My husband is Andrew Morgan and it is an honour to be of service to His Majesty, His Excellency and yourself."

Ah yes, thought Mrs Arthur, a confident girl of ambition, which is no bad thing.

She then looked at the young woman closest to her on the left. If the other three women fitted her expectation in being attractive and accomplished, this fourth girl was in a different category. A category of one, she saw.

This young lady was taller than average. Her blonde hair was almost kept under her bonnet, hence she could see the blonde of it. The bonnet was decorated with a ribbon of sewn silk English spring flowers. Her skin was flawless, pale and so English, though it should be in one so young, Mrs Arthur thought. Her eyes, grey or blue; it was hard to be sure, her nose seemed slightly retrousse, yet on another look was perfectly formed. Her lips a deep pink and almost, but not quite, voluptuous. Such of her figure as could be determined was exquisite. She sat calmly, without affectation and was comfortable with herself. If there was a striving towards perfection, this girl was the apogee.

"Ma'am, I am Marianne Wainwright, a daughter of General Barratt. My mother, too, was of a military family. We are of Winchester, the city of the late and much-lamented Miss Austen, whose books have given myself and my family so much pleasure."

Mrs Arthur noted that this girl had said something about herself and her interests. Reading was such a desirable pastime, especially in a place with so little to do. She smiled, herself an avid reader of Miss Austen's works.

"My husband is Francis and we are very much looking forward to serving our King and Country and being of assistance to His Excellency and yourself in this enterprise."

Nicely said, thought Mrs Arthur, and she replied.

"A pleasure to make your acquaintance, ladies. Now, some tea and cakes. Martha!"

She addressed a middle-aged woman, who had been standing unobtrusively in the room since the ladies entered.

"Please arrange for the tea and cakes for these young ladies and myself."

Martha left as instructed, and the young ladies waited expectantly on their hostess. She, in turn, knew what was expected of her. So many such wives had she seen. What to do here?

She had reflected upon this question. In many ways the answer was the same as what they would do as officers' wives in England, without the hazard of being a widow. It was best to couch her reply in such a way with added exotica of the strangeness of the climate and the land, to make the fleshing out of existence more exciting.

"Ladies. You are most welcome to this outpost... no, I should say this part of His Majesty's domain, so different from the sweet breezes and familiarity of Mother England. There is therefore much to explore beyond the confines of your lives so far, and of your husbands' too. I do

49

not dwell on the privations you have endured on your long voyage to reach this shore. Suffice to say it was a testament to your maturity as young women that you undertook such rigours and were triumphant.

"You know from your upbringing in military families of the demands and duties in your position. Those functions will continue here, in providing support for your husbands in their duties and responsibilities. You will have opportunities to continue your skills in embroidery, sewing and the preparation of the table and in of course the pleasures of being a wife and mother, to which I can most confidently attest.

"I may say there are other benefits. You can become familiar with a strange and peculiar land. The free settlers here say there are no forests that you can walk through as in England. These strange trees permit light through to the ground where it encourages the growth of thick vegetation like a brush. It causes great labour among the settlers and their convict workers in clearing it for pasture, and it is now generally becoming known as the bush, or Bush, not 'forest'.

"I must warn you that one can easily become lost in it, even just a few yards from a track... I entreat you not to venture from the track. There are limits to your adventures. There are natives, Blacks, in these huge, dark bush-infested mountains. It is rumoured that they will eat human flesh."

The young women gasped and shuddered, went pale, grabbed the table-edge in apparent horror, and reacted as Mrs Arthur hoped, thus alleviating the possibility of search parties having to search for stray young women in the bush where a successful outcome could not be guaranteed.

As reassurance, she went on: "His Excellency is most mindful of the needs and requirements of the citizens – the freemen and women of the Colony – and is attentive to their demands to ensure the Blacks are apprised of the civilising influences of our people and that ignorance of those benefits will be severely punished. Even so, there is a risk a husband may leave a widow after an expedition to punish the Blacks."

Each lady now added to her imagination the thought of her own husband being devoured by these savages. This had not been mentioned in England.

"You can delight in examining some of the extraordinary bush creatures in our little museum and zoo. Many instructive hours can be spent in study, particularly if you have young children to entertain."

This comment jolted Rebecca. She was not expecting to stay long enough in this place to have children – much less one old enough to be carted off to look at this stuff, whatever it was.

"There is also a new gallery of the arts where you will find exhibits of many talented artists in the Colony. You must disabuse yourselves of any notion that any of the inhabitants, whether freemen or convicts, or I dare say military, are without artistic skill.

"You will also have the assistance of servants. Most, although not all, are of former servitude in the other sense. They have received Tickets of Leave through His Excellency for trustworthy and good behaviour and work towards a proper rehabilitation and contribution. They are fully apprised of the nature of reprisals for serious infringements while providing assistance to yourselves or your families. It does not relieve you from close and careful monitoring of such activities as they undertake, and His Excellency is most particular in keeping his finger on the pulse of the Colony, if I may put it that way."

Mrs Arthur stopped. She watched the reactions of these young women as they digested her words and, she hoped, stored them away.

Martha returned with a large teapot, together with a generous plate of cakes – timely as there were a lot of non-comestibles to digest. Tea was poured in accordance with individual preferences and cakes taken. The party sat in silence, each young lady hoping her attempts at elegance and good manners would find favour with Mrs Arthur.

When Martha cleared the remnants away and left, Annabel spoke, tentatively.

"Ma'am, may I ask how many girls and women are there in the Colony and where are they kept?"

"His Excellency has particular details of the number of females, a word which I would prefer to use rather than make an arbitrary designation. However, I am aware they reside in a purpose-built facility ordered by His Excellency and completed a few years ago at Cascade, on the edge of the hills as they climb. It is far enough away for there to be no temptation between the females and the settlers and other ranks in the Colony. Some of the females may have been sent for persistent immorality. Accordingly, it is wise to separate males from females.

"It is unfortunate that many females are young – very young; and have little to occupy themselves, save cleaning, scrubbing, patching and prayer to aid in their repentance. To some, near the end of their sentence and thought possible of redemption, there is a lady with a respectable house in the Town who gives further shelter – and I understand has some success in reconciling them to society.

"I am fully apprised of your good and caring natures from your histories and our brief acquaintance. Before, therefore, you wish most delicately to importune me to allow you to visit Cascade to offer assistance to these females – it can be arranged. His Excellency has continuous contact and congress between here and the barracks where you reside and any communications to me can be made at the barracks. I will have your names sent to the Cascade supervisor. If you do wish to see for yourselves how these unfortunates have fallen so low, then an appointment can be made through the contact at the barracks for a visit."

There was so much for the ladies to consider, and barely off the boat.

There was a knock on the door.

"Come in."

A servant entered. "His Excellency asked if the ladies would join him and the officers."

The ladies stood up, composed themselves as much as they could or needed to and, waiting for Mrs Arthur to lead, followed her to join the men. Additional chairs had been brought in and placed around the table, one for each woman, and one placed next to the Lieutenant Governor for his wife.

"I have been apprising these young officers of the structure and administration of the Colony, of the need for strong discipline, routine so certain that no complaint will be tolerated of not knowing the obligations." Lieutenant-Governor Arthur said.

"I know my wife has similarly elaborated on how you can support your husbands in their duties. This is indeed the other side of the world, and you might easily conclude you are on another world entirely. But we are doing God's work among those who suffer from a delirium and it is our duty to control it and bring the malefactors to The Almighty in seeking repentance.

"I am aware you are not long in the Colony and will need time to settle and recuperate. My wife will assist in that measure by organising a social gathering which will provide an opportunity for friendships and advice. You will be notified of that gathering in due course.

"In the meantime, your carriages await outside to return you to your barracks. Your husbands will have their orders there. We wish you good day, and a fruitful and successful time in the Colony."

With a small and not quite imperceptible nod, the young party was dismissed.

When both carriages arrived back at the barracks and the occupants were disgorged, Andrew Morgan remarked: "Where, Francis, from out of the depths of your soul, did you dredge the reference to Socrates? He never wrote anything."

"Did he not?" Francis's face darkened, then quickly recovered. "I do not recall actually saying he wrote."

The other officers looked at each other. Francis had galloped ahead in the race to impress the Governor. Henry wondered whether the raised eyebrows were a sign of approval or of a disagreeable showing-off. He kept his wonder to himself.

"Did you see how his fingers drummed when he became agitated on recollection of a matter which displeased him?" Francis was determined to regain some ground.

"On thinking upon it, you may be right." Stuart thought he should make a contribution.

The wives could not comment, not having been present, and were immersed in their own thoughts. They were suddenly overcome with fatigue. His Excellency was right on recovery. It had been such a long day, no matter that its length had not reached noon. The ladies excused themselves to each other and to the men, and hurried to collapse on their respective beds.

The men's alternative was following instructions and reporting for duty; a test of stamina and resolve.

CHAPTER 3

Hobart, 1830-31

Derwent Park was a substantial property, befitting a man of the stature of Joseph Gellibrand in the Colony, despite the mutual antagonism between himself and the Governor, and it needed the number of assigned convicts to work the property, or properties, subsumed under the heading of Derwent Park.

Cattle and sheep grazed its lands, grain was grown and harvested, produce not consumed on the Park was sold within the Town. Samuel was an assiduous supervisor who had arrived as a free settler, but found working on this property congenial and secure enough. The land was undulating and hilly, enough to accommodate a quarry, where contents were dug by convict labour and transported onto carts by that labour to build the Gellibrand house, outbuildings, stables, barns and stonewalls. Tom found himself directed to the quarry and to wall building and general hard labouring, as he was larger than most, and young, and although there was a family history of farming, this was forgotten and he saw himself as a shoemaker if anything at all.

He therefore spent time in Alan's company on wall building, and Samuel appeared to accept Tom's efforts on stonewalling as satisfactory. Working with Alan, who certainly had a skill, developed in Tom a determination that he would not be disgraced in comparison.

About two weeks into his labouring, quarrying, wall building, fence-mending and a dawning that this was stretching into a disappearing future, Tom heeded the siren call of a break. He was young, fit and not a man to submit meekly to anyone. He recalled the Convict Bank on the road to Gellibrand. Now he knew he could get some money from the Bank. His feet and his boots had agreed to a mutually grudging disharmony. Sacrificing dinner to get some money would get him started. Quite where, was not certain – but his eye for an inn recalled the sign of The Red Lion between the bank and here.

He could ask Alan to keep aside his dinner. Ah, he suddenly saw two problems. The first was that there was no honour among thieves. Food was precise and rationed. Why would Alan not eat it? Would he if Alan asked him? Um, how could he not?

The second problem was bowl collection. If untouched, there would be a search. Being late back, or found, equalled punishment. Just be truthful. He sacrificed dinner to get to the Convict Bank.

Hmm. No. Third problem. Can't mention the bank. A look around the place, then? Hadn't seen much of it. A normal thing to do. He could slip off after dinner. Maybe Sam would skip inspection. Fat chance. If he left he could sacrifice dinner to Alan in hope he might return the favour one day. Or Alan might get punished too, if found to have eaten two dinners, and be angry even if he ate it. Lord, there was too much to think about.

At the sight of the dinner cart that late, very wet October day, Tom impulsively put down his shovel and said to Alan, as water slid down the side of his nose from a flattened soggy head:

"I'm going to the Convict Bank. Saw it on the way here. You have my dinner if you can get away with eating two... reckon I can get there and back by collect."

Alan thought about it. He was working towards a Ticket of Leave for uncomplaining work and behaviour. Not far off, he believed. It was not worth the risk.

"Nah. I'll put it aside if you reckon you can get back before collect, and eat it. Won't taste any different."

Tom thought about it too. A sacrifice if he failed to return in time, and he reckoned he would. He'd just say who he was. They had his money; Sam said so, and he would have some cash.

The cart struggled across the saturated field, dropped off the food, which quickly embraced the rain, and left. As soon as it was nearly out of sight, going towards another field, off Tom went. He had minimal education and lacked proper reading and writing skills but, as with human ingenuity, other skills and strategies had developed instead.

It was fortunate, too, that most of the Bank's customers were similarly illiterate and had optimistic expectations. It was in the staff's own interests to devise a simple but effective system of identification, aided by ships' ledgers delivered on arrival, recording convicts' names, ship, financial possessions and Master.

The desire to have one's own money overrode the desire to swipe someone else's from the same place. A theft infringement could expect a rope welcome. Tom listened for the warning Alan had advised on theft or attempted theft. It came.

Thus it was that Tom found himself at last with a very small sum of money. The Bank had a cut-off limit for withdrawals, and was severe on attempts to circumnavigate it. It still left the little matter on how to spend it, and where. There were shops and stores, and excess bread could be bought at the prisoners' barracks, although Tom as a new arrival had been unaware of it. He saw the Red Lion, and it was closer to Gellibrand's.

He ran, stumbled, sliding, in his hurry back to his shovel. Samuel was standing over it, holding his bowl.

"See we're feeding you too much,"Samuel said, dryly.

"Went to see a bit of this place."

"What did you say?"

"Sir... sir."

"Oh? Why?"

"To see what it looks like, Sir. "

"Did you like what you saw?"

"Yes, A bit different to what I knew. Sir."

"What else have you learned?"

"Dunno Sir, maybe a bit early to say."

Well, Samuel thought, at least a try. He'd given up dinner for it, whatever entered his probably very empty head. With Tom's answer, Sam turned around and left with Tom's bowl. Then he stopped, turned the bowl upside down, and they both watched the contents plop and spread on the soil where Tom had been working. For good measure, Samuel kicked the sodden earth over the mush until it was merged into the ground. Holding the empty bowl, he went to his horse, mounted and trotted away.

Alan continued working through it all, and now Tom resumed his own scratchy toil. At sundown, one devoid of any sun, suffering with the pain of gnawing hunger, he asked himself whether it was worth it. Despite the hunger, yes – he had learned something. He had never been in a bank before, and now he was a customer.

*

Marianne Wainwright had also been busy, although it was a busyness different from that of Thomas Scrimshaw. The busyness of recovering, acclimatising and seeking out new friends with other wives, older in years and experience in this so terrifying place, and with Eliza Arthur's description of native habits cemented in their minds, those young and old.

It was accepted that wives from military families adjusted to this life more readily than others, but there was still a gap between those who had sailed out together in forged friendships, compared with others who bonded on their own particular voyages. But tentacles reached out across the groups exploring mutual interests. There was, therefore, busyness.

Rebecca Morgan was a little more acerbic on the need for female coterie. She did not communicate her thoughts to Marianne, who showed much enjoyment in these communications with ladies sharing their lot in this place. Rebecca had no need to be told what was what, and what lay ahead. She was proud to be her father's daughter as well as her mother's, and she was ambitious. If that were a fault, she would stand and let others fall around her.

She had niggles about whether Andrew, delightful and affable husband as he was, had the ambition to be a leader of men as she had grown up with and expected to share in. Did he have the iron forged in the heat of ambition to achieve the position she expected, and was entitled to?

Marianne, she thought, was too pretty by half. She talked incessantly of "dear Jane" as if they played and wrote together. This place, which Andrew had enthusiastically promoted in England, demanded a mind like a rabbit trap in order to survive and prosper.

Marianne's husband Francis, she had observed, repelled all attempts to board the good ship *Frank*. Any attempt was sharply squashed. A man altogether serious and focused. An Officer. Andrew had laughed in bed that Francis had said something like "... promotion is my passion" as a principle to be followed. They'd heard it from the Governor.

What, she thought, was there to laugh about? From their voyage together she foresaw Stuart and Henry as decent, fine officers of high regard who would follow orders which Andrew would give them. The trouble was, she saw her own Andrew getting orders from Francis, and wives following this pecking order. Accordingly, she did not see her

interests as being obedient to Marianne when it was clear that, frankly –
she pardoned herself her joke – this place was littered with corpses, and
Marianne had no interest in Francis's place in the Empire – or much
beyond making this place habitable for herself while here. Lots of laughs
and giggles, and the odd sinful glass of sack. Had the French got here,
she would not have done so well.

Marianne found Rebecca congenial and accepted her rebuff of walking
together around the Town with grace. Rebecca was more reserved, and
had some depth which Marianne sensed, but she was unconcerned
about delving for it. It made her more interesting than Sara and
Annabel who were as delightful as they should be, while she hoped she
was not seen as such. However, as the only person of importance who
could judge her was Ma'am, who gave no indication of disapproval she
hoped she was safe.

Adjusting to the weather as best she could, and taking the advice of
wives longer in the Colony, as a newcomer Marianne dressed in her
lesser finery, bonnet and shoes, and walked as elegantly as she could
around the rough port of Hobart Town, unaware of the glances, sniggers
and sighs, of those who had time to lift heads up from their labours in
building a prosperous settlement, to see her.

Aside from some trips to Southampton as a little girl, she had no
recollection of the sea, except that it was what it was. It was enough
working out her own mind and body and its quirks, some explained to
her, some she still puzzled over. But she knew she was safe here in the
Town. Any infraction against her would be severely dealt with. Her
mind moved from cannibalism to the gallows dance. She wanted that
none could be laid at her feet. Horrible, so horrible.

On one of these perambulations, she found an art gallery and went
inside. Works hung by free settler artists or by convicts, delicately
described as "from training in a previous life." Good they were, too.
Well, mostly, she thought. But the majority were pastoral scenes

remarkably like the South Downs from home; vague wishy-washy skies and soft gentle grass. She could almost feel the indolent breezes and share the scene with the happy men and women sitting, eating and drinking picnics with children playing and boats almost indulgently calm.

But this was not right, despite the skills. These were memory paintings. What she saw when she looked out of the window was a different world; a land of something else denied to her. A darkness shown but even more felt from the bowels of this earth. She could not call it soul, but whatever it was, it was there. The mighty black mountain rising up behind the town was its repository. No artist had painted it as it was, but as a South Downs slumber in fond imagining.

She left and hurried back to the barracks, keeping upwind of a rotting corpse on a gibbet. She was disturbed but excited. This place was a prison. But whose?

*

Tom Scrimshaw was not a serious thinker. Life had not found it necessary to visit that skill to bear upon him. Even so, the desires and practicalities which life did distribute, had been bestowed on him to some extent in amelioration.

They were exerted from time to time, and consequently Tom considered further adventures after the sun had set on the day's toil. Not for him the rest of his hard bed and blanket of little comfort. Not day after day, night after night. His mornings were announced with the punctuating harsh warble of a strange bird, which became a call to breakfast. How he hated that bird as the harbinger of harsh labour to come. Alan told him it was a magpie, and it taunted him with its free range during the day as well. A lot bigger than the ones in Lincolnshire, and these ones were becoming aggressive. Mating season, Alan told him. Lucky them, thought Tom.

Time to flit like a magpie in the dark. He was one, after all. He had spied the sign of the Red Lion on arrival, and on his visit to his bank he fondly thought of it. Just like home, and now, after his secret trip, he had a little money. A glass or two of local ale would ease the aches and pains of work. Always a solace after a hard day, though it had brought him here, indirectly.

When darkness arrived and was well set, and he imagined the Big House and Sam had settled for the night, he left his small room and headed for the entrance to the property, keeping as close to the trees as he could. It still rained, but it was nothing to him, after his labours in it, and the excitement of promising ale. After about ten minutes, he was at the inn door. He opened it. To his surprise he was the only person in the bar area. Were other customers still home eating, or too tired to come out tonight? He saw a woman behind the bar. In her forties, he guessed, a full figure with large breasts kept apart by a deep cleavage. A kind face, although worn in making a living in this place. She smiled, briefly, and he saw there was a gap in her upper mouth.

She in turn was surprised to see a customer at this time. Her regulars had headed back to their modest homes, after the succour she supplied, to prepare for another day's hard toil on the morrow. She kept the inn open because there was nothing else to do and she could potter about awhile. She was, however, tidying up to close at this stage of the night. She looked the customer over. A Magpie; young, mid-twenties maybe, well-muscled and quite good-looking, although he had a prominent nose. He had an animal sense about him, she intuited. Young, still raw in more than one way, and fresh off a boat, she guessed.

"Welcome to the Red Lion."

"Why is it always The Red Lion," he found himself asking, "not the White Lion, or Black Lion, or Blue Lion? Never seen any other."

"Used to be called The Abandon Hope, but the guv'nor didn't like it so it became the Red Lion, boring though it is. Though if you know me properly it's the Red *Loin*." She let forth a little laugh. "Well, what will you be having?"

He surveyed the back of the bar. A choice of two barrels. Pointing at one he said, "Glass of that."

She turned and went to the barrel with a glass. She bent to fill it. He saw her copious shape, her skirt lifting slightly to show her ankles. She returned with a foaming glass, which delighted him. He asked how much. She told him, and he held out his clenched fist holding his precious coins. She took the required sum, plus a little more, anticipating he might be after another. She was right. The first glass went down without a pause.

"Ah... that's been a long time coming. Not had a beer since January."

"Been on a boat?"

"Yep." He pointed to the other barrel. She went, filled the glass and returned. Again, he tackled the beer with vim, but a little slower this time, and they went through the payment routine. She contemplated him again. Quite a handsome lad, in his own way. She cast her eyes down his body. A lot going on there, she surmised. Even wet as he was.

He suddenly looked slightly anxious and put down the empty glass.

"Better be going."

"Where are you?"

"Down t'road." He pointed in the direction from which he came. "Ten minutes thereabouts. Big house. Trees to it."

"Mr Gellibrand?"

"Didn't catch the name, but might be. Was a big wig lawyer. Fell out with guv'nor."

"Heard that."

He turned to the door.

"Come again. This is a good time."

"I will, I will."

He felt internally happy on the walk back. With a couple of beers in his belly the world had improved, even if the reality was different. He was not here for his health, but to die, preferably painfully, and the time taken over it did not matter. But he was not a rabbit and not so easy to kill off.

He negotiated the walk back to his bed and blanket safely, took off his boots and was soon asleep and snoring the snore of an apparently contented man.

Aware that his money supply was limited he did not go to the Red Lion the following night, but the night after decided he would. Excellent ale and some female company, although not something he was used to, were a welcome distraction.

Using the same after-dark routine, now in intermittent showers, he arrived at the sign of the Red Lion or Red *Loin*, as he remembered her labelling it, tantalisingly.

"Hullo," Tom said to her behind the bar.

"Hullo," she smiled. "Thought you'd forgotten me."

"Nah. Liked it here. Better than where I am."

He pointed to a barrel and off she went with a glass. He saw her ankles again and when she returned his gaze fell down her cleavage. She saw it and smiled.

"When you've had the glass, I've something to show you."

She came from behind the bar to the front door and he heard a locking sound.

He drained the glass quickly and she came to him, took the glass and put it on the counter. She took his hand, extinguished the light in the bar and led him behind the bar wall to a room behind.

"Well, saw you looking." She lowered her eyes to her bosom. "Like what you see?"

"Yeah." He saw she had some pox scars, but that was common enough.

"I like what I see, too."

She moved towards him. Her hand slid down his rough trousers. Unexpected, he was unsure – then, as his pulse quickened, her hands quickly undid the buttons on his trousers and moved inside.

"My, you are a big boy, aren't you?"

She undid his belt and pulled his trousers down, not without difficulty, but a difficulty she enjoyed.

"You lot, all you know is blood and shit. Here's a red loin."

She turned around, bent low and lifted her skirt up over her back.

He saw she was right. A sweet smell of ripe flesh flowed into his nostrils.

"C'mon Magpie, peck yer spot. Peck away with yer big beak. Poke yer pecker." She giggled at her little joke.

He did as demanded. Her groans became louder and ended in howls. No sooner had they finished when she dropped her skirt, went back to the bar and returned with a beer.

"Here. Reward yer pecker. Thought it was coming out me mouth. Let's have some more. Loved it. Like it hard and strong and lots."

The night wore on, with the double pleasure of this woman's demanding desire and free beer to boot.

In a moment of conversation, she said, "What's your name?"

"Tom. Tom Scrimshaw. Yours?"

"Cox. Jenny Cox. Widow. My hubby died an' left me with the pub. It's a living, in a way. Get the occasional extra like you.

"I got a friend. A good friend. She'd like you. Mrs Jane Taylor. I'll take you to her. She wants to make men better at this, she reckons they're not much good, an' it's not fair on women who need it. We all do. She likes to train young men and make them better at it. Teaches new tricks. Not for me, haven't the time or interest. Lots of hard and fast and long for me, no fancy stuff. She'll see you right, though. She'll like what she sees." She sniggered.

"C'mon big boy. Beat my drum."

In the haze of his beer-drenched brain and satiated body was an alert that whatever the time was, it was doubtless time to find his way back to his room ready for the morning. He finally broke away, and with last kisses and fondling at the door, he staggered into the night.

He had not gone far, weaving an unsteady path as a dishevelled Magpie, when he stopped, involuntarily. He realised his arms were seized, and blearily saw two men dressed in grey uniforms, one on each side of him, one arm of each firmly on an arm, the other holding a musket. Swords were sheathed at their sides.

"Whassa matter?"

"Where do you think you are, lad? Why isn't a Magpie in its nest? Don't think you can fly there. Where are you going?"

Tom vaguely waved his arm ahead.

"Up there."

"Where?"

"Big house. Very big."

"Don't think they'll let you in, Magpie. You come with us. We'll get you a bed. Sort you out tomorrow."

This was a very good night, thought Tom. This woman, free beer and now a bed. This place got better. He nodded and was led gently but firmly away. He found himself in a building with some warmth, which bode well. Then a door opened, he was pushed inside, the door closed and locked, and there he was, in a small room with a small barred window, a pot in the corner, a bed with a blanket. Too tired to explore or argue, he fell on the bed with his boots on and slept.

*

Tom woke to the sound of a door clanging and a loud voice ordering him up. Staggering to his feet and out of the door, another arm grabbed his arm and propelled him towards another door some ten yards away. It was opened on his arrival and he was part shoved inside as he stumbled. Another small room he saw, with benches and in front of them, a raised bench behind which was a single high-backed chair. In the chair sat a man of perhaps fifty.

"This is your first case, Your Honour. Found drunk on the street last night."

"What is your name?"

"Umm. Tom."

"Tom what!"

Tom had to think.

"Come on man. Surely you know your own name. Even you must have one."

"Scrimshaw."

"Scrimshaw what!"

"Umm..."

"What!"

"Umm. Sir."

"You should mind yourself young man. Insolence will get you into trouble. Who is your master?"

"Sam. Samuel says he's my real Master. Sir."

"Who are you assigned to?"

"Don't know his name. Big house along the road. Lots of trees up to it. I build, build lots of fences, walls – dig a lot. Sir."

"Don't know his name? When did you arrive in Hobart Town?"

Tom thought, slowly. "One, maybe two week ago."

"Not a good start, lad. I think your master is Mr Gellibrand. Does that ring a bell in your so far empty head?"

"A bit. Sir."

"You are not here to enjoy yourself. What is your sentence?"

"Here for life. Sir. Wherever it is. Sir."

"Make a contribution, boy, or you will be here before me or the other magistrate and you will wish you were not. Bread and water for fourteen days, and take him to the Gellibrand property for his sentence."

Tom was roughly grabbed, taken out of the building and forced to walk with his guards along the road in front of industrious workers, and ladies taking the airs, to be taken to the Gellibrand house, where Samuel waited.

"Thank you for returning him," Sam said, glancing at Tom with a withering look. "We found him missing this morning."

"Got two weeks' bread and water for drunkenness last night," the guard said, and left.

"Not doing well are you?" Sam chided. "Only just got here and just off to the magistrate. 'Tis a good day to work on big stones. Very big."

Tom looked up. Heavy clouds were piling up again with certain rain. Everything has its price, he recalled from somewhere. Last night had been a surprise, and well worth it then. He was not so sure now.

"Over there." Samuel pointed to a far paddock. "I marked out two sticks. Take down the wall between them, to ground level. Then rebuild it to where it was by sundown. If you do, bread and water. If not, not." He rode off.

An interminable day he saw it as. A throbbing head and the euphoria of last night was long gone. Rain lashed him. Rocks were slippery, and bleeding hands. His fellows kept their distance and pointedly enjoyed eating their dinners in front of him.

He determined that he would finish the task, no matter what physical cost, to show Samuel and the others that he was not a man to be broken.

He did it, as the sun gave up for the day. Samuel rode up, both irritated that it had been done and a respect of sorts that this young man actually had finished it, short of food.

"Hmm. Here's your bread," said Sam. "Water is in your room." He swung the horse and left.

Tom licked his face in the rain, scooped up water from puddles and staggered back to his bed and jug. Two weeks of this under Sam as he was called politely by the workers (and less politely with other names) – two weeks? No.

As he lay there just before sleep hit him, he thought of Jenny Cox and her enthusiasm for him, whatever her own reasons were, and it was in her own interest to help him. Not tonight though; sleep claimed him.

The new day was as promised and feared. Wet, colder than he expected and another punishment day, this time now taking down and rebuilding a wall. Samuel was indeed the master. Did Gellibrand know or care?

Hungry and spent as he was, he was spurred to go to The Red Loin and see if rain had washed Jenny Cox's ardour away. He arrived at the time he estimated he'd arrived before. He opened the door and his hope was there, behind the bar. She saw him and, quickly bearing a grin and cleavage tipped towards him, she added a hastily poured foaming glass. The welcome relieved him.

"Heard about you. The only excitement round here, official anyway, is what newspapers dig out from courts. We get to know."

"Could do with some food. Fourteen days of bread and water. Tough, it is."

"I can do something. We need to have you fit strong and," she paused, "big. Don't I?"

She went on: "We need to kick you out earlier. The guv'nor's a stickler for routine and discipline. Guards and police go on routine at same time and same places, at same speed, every night. He doesn't see – bless him – that you get around by knowing the routine. You get here. I can get you out before they come past here and on their route. I know the time and route, and you'll have time to get back. I'll get you back."

Tom nodded. Sounded like a plan.

"Now let's get you started," she smiled. "Us started."

She led him out the back. Him first, food and ale after. When they had sufficient satisfaction, she found him some ham and eggs, mutton and bread washed down with a few glasses of beer, before resuming her chosen path. Reluctantly, they parted, she reminding him that being caught again would mean even worse punishment. She drew her hand across her throat. He understood the possibilities and left, careful in his return.

The next two weeks were very satisfactory for both Jenny Cox and Tom Scrimshaw.

Samuel was constrained to report to his titular master that the new young wretch Scrimshaw showed remarkable resilience and stamina on the frugality of bread and water and a diet of rocks and stones in the fields.

Mr Gellibrand was slightly conflicted. Impressive work under harsh conditions merited some bank contribution – but out, and drunk?

CHAPTER 4

Hobart, 1831

Marianne Wainwright was bored. Rebecca Morgan was bored. Annabel Bell was bored, and Sara Lynch was bored.

What to do? There was a limit to amusements, or even industry. Books all read. Practising the skills acquired through their mothers only took them so far in this enclosing place. There were neither shops nor friends' houses requiring a carriage to visit. No parties to dress up for or show off, no new acquaintances to turn into friends. Even household duties had servants. A bit of desultory dusting and sweeping alleviated ennui. Walks were weather dependent, and in any case they had become boring too; the same old routes, not too close to the edge of settlement.

As educated and literate women, all excitedly awaited vessels from Britain docking and bringing – along with new literate passengers – the latest news, books, papers, magazines, games and gossip, to be swapped and added to the ad-hoc collection in the Colony.

Presentable and attractive young ladies also benefitted from musical attainments, depending on aptitude and application. Annabel had a lovely, rich soprano voice, and Marianne had been complimented back in Winchester for her playing of harpsichord and the new fortepiano, as well as her light, lyric soprano. In Hobart Town, musical qualities were overshadowed by one of the older established wives who was gifted to a higher level. She was well-taught by her mother who herself, as a child prodigy, had played in London for the great Haydn. The others in Hobart acknowledged and accepted her pre-eminence.

There was a snag. A fortepiano had been floated out with the founding of the Colony as some comfort for the officers and their families. With the passage of time, the instrument fell more and more out of tune. The star performer finally announced she would not and could not perform "on such a cacophonous monstrosity," and consequently soirées fell away, leaving traditional and light popular songs that did not need accompaniment. The musical fraternity had two hopes; one, that a transportation ship would disgorge a dishonest tuner equipped with his tools of trade, and the other that the Colonial Office would respond favourably to their entreaties for a new instrument.

London was fully aware of the parlous state of the nation's finances after the enormous cost of the Napoleonic wars, some disastrous harvests and a monarch with a great propensity for spending huge pots of other people's money. Both hopes had so far remained optimistic.

But it helped explain boredom sitting at their table.

The men were active as officers. Escorting prisoners, normally the job of other ranks, was tedious, but it had a chance of unpredictability if hunting an escapee, a two-legged Magpie as an officer commented. The ladies thought an escapee unfathomable; why would one escape, and where to? The risk of death in the hostile bush was certain, either from the wild terrain, its wildlife or from the feared natives lurking there.

Not the Blacks cowering on the outskirts of the Town, but wild forest and mountain-dwellers craving human flesh. Out There. Or hunting those savages at the urging of settlers complaining of interference with their proprietorial lives. Punitive expeditions to uphold those rights, and the Governor was very keen to authorise them. Laying waste to the native population was a necessary price for the growth of the Colony. The men therefore had active distractions.

Not so the women. There was the distraction of the marital bed to relieve monotony. The young wives had different expectations of their marital obligations gleaned from their mothers and female relatives, and occasionally friends. A duty sometimes pleasurable, depending on mood and distractions.

Marianne blended her duty as a wife with her sense of self as a woman. Not defined but fuzzy and tantalising because it was inchoate. As a wife she knew of and accepted her husband's pleasure. The rising excitement she had as he continued until he grunted, relaxed and turned away was expected. She might hope to experience more but a wise woman would neither expect nor seek more elsewhere. That way was the whiff of damnation's fire. Still, burgeoning within her, was a release into a new world of womanhood. There was a lot to be going on with, with a nagging sense of more to come.

Rebecca was also drumming her fingers on her husband, as it were. He was more attentive to his wife and her need for pleasure but lacked intuition and exploration of possible delights. She saw it as thoughtful ignorance.

Sara and Annabel had more complicated problems. Both had become pregnant, and this was not a place to deliver and raise babies when compared to what was expected in the Mother Country. There were no midwives at Home to reduce the hazards of childbirth for mother and baby. Or, God forbid, have a criminal midwife in Hobart Town. But their mothers had done it, and as daughters of strong mothers they were optimistic. Sadly, both suffered the anguish of miscarriages. All the women walked the tightrope of boredom and pregnancy risk.

As the group of wives worked through one of their lunches and their fears of a pregnancy a long way from home, with the sad experiences of Sara and Annabel, and boredom grumbling away within them, Marianne had an idea.

"Remember when Ma'am talked about a place called... what was it?" She said one languid afternoon. "Reminded me of a waterfall... a... Cascade...yes, that was it! Young women like us, no, not like us but our age, or girls even – fallen into crime and such wickedness they ended here. Ma'am said she could arrange that we could see these sad wretches ourselves and perhaps offer solace and some comfort as an example, if they seek redemption."

Marianne's Christian enthusiasm was embraced by Sara and Annabel after their own experiences, and as something to do. Rebecca saw the relief of boredom, but doing good to girls who had sinned and offended under the implacable law which sent them here was to reinforce their bitterness against her and her little group. Them and us. A sort of war. Still, the boredom won out.

"What a lovely idea." Rebecca announced.

"Ooh yes," the other two cooed, "Oh let us do it."

"I shall make inquiries as Ma'am advised." Marianne announced with a slight sense of triumph, especially over Rebecca, who seemed to look down on her, not by anything she said, but by her demeanour; a look of slight amusement, a small twitch of her shoulders, a study of her shoes when Marianne spoke.

She continued to cement her lead. "I will speak to the person at the barracks who communicates with Ma'am and request, if she would be so kind, to implement our visit through her good offices."

There was a general murmur of approval and a nod from Rebecca. There was some excitement to be had.

While the wives languished in refinement, Tom's rough education continued apace.

*

Tom Scrimshaw was not bored. Samuel devised more labours during daylight to test this young man who seemed unaccountably able to cope with whatever he was pressed into doing. Tom and Jenny continued to disport themselves in uncomplicated and mutually enjoyable ways, aided and abetted by extra food and ale, which, unbeknown to Samuel, helped his stamina and built his strength in his toil for Mr Gellibrand.

Tom also went on occasion to other pubs to try the ales and have a rest from Jenny. He had become more proficient at evading the guards and police on their rounds. But not always. Both these occupations were punctuated by Tom's appearances before one or other of the magistrates and resultant penalties which interfered with these contrasting pursuits.

"See from the paper you got another session on the treadwheel. Drunk and fighting in the street this time. A Magpie?" Jenny looked at him during a lull.

"Yeah." Tom replied. "Little bastard pushed me outside a pub. Dunno why. It gets a bit rough and tough. Was too, back in Lincoln. I pushed him back. He threw a punch. I whacked him a couple of times. He fell over and I was to finish him off but guards came. Took us away. Got fourteen days this time; gone up. Bloody hard work, the treadwheel. Little bastard only got a week on the wheel. Sam's not pleased, as there's no work done. 'Tis tough on him too." He came out with a bitter laugh.

"They know you too well at the court." Jenny paused. "I spoke to my friend Jane. She's been busy, but looks forward to meeting you. 'Tis time for you to meet up. I'll take you there if you want."

"What? Now?"

"Yep. When you're ready. 'Tis a five minute walk away, or a bit more."

While he readied himself, she regarded this strong young man who shrugged off these punishments. He would never leave these shores, as ordered. Lots thought they would, when the sentence was up. It did not happen. It would not for her, either.

Off they went, her in her long brown dress with lace trimming, now a brownish hue in sympathy with the dress. A plain bonnet with bedraggled lace. She took him along a back street, and then left, and then right. The ground was sloppy from recent rain, with a pool caught in a hollow on the sloping hillside. Some thirty yards along on the right was a large, three-storied house. Jenny Cox stopped.

Tom was impressed, believing he was going to a modest abode in keeping with those sited in Hobart Town. He looked around to get his bearings and familiarise himself with the surroundings and alleys lest he may need to use them in a hurry. The houses fell away as the mountain rose up to his left; it was too much struggle to go further.

The widow Cox rapped on a substantial door knob. Perhaps half a minute later the door opened and a modestly dressed young woman in her twenties ushered them in. She led them into a parlour on the left, and departed. Almost immediately a woman entered. A woman in her forties. Her red hair hit his senses first, then the rest of her. She was as striking as her hair. The privations of the Colony had not dimmed her beauty. Her green eyes coolly appraised this tallish young man with a strong body. Even with his Magpie garb, meant to humiliate, he was impressive. Jenny Cox was usually astute in assessing and then recommending young males. This one had an animal aura and presence although he was unconscious of it. A canvas to design and paint on. She smiled.

He in turn was transfixed by her. Her whole being invited his gaze and he lapped it all up. A figure of full breasts accentuated by a small waist and a dress in a material he did not know but he knew enough to see it was expensive. Underneath the dress he imagined her feet were elegantly covered, maybe of the quality he saw occasionally in his days as a youthful shoemaker.

"Ah. What is your name?"

"Tom." He added, "Ma'am."

"Tom what?"

"Not Tom Watt, ma'am, Tom Scrimshaw."

Hmm, she thought, is this wit, or stupidity? She expected some level of intelligence in the young men she considered her duty to take in hand, literally and metaphorically, otherwise she would lose interest were there nothing but blankness within. She had learned from Jenny that he was transported for life. No return, then, and how to improve his life? Not under the gaze of authority with punishment, but an alternative way to expand and offer some help or comfort to those also trapped in the Colony, and an expiation for the crime which brought him here.

"Thank you, Jenny. I see and appreciate what you told me."

Jenny laughed. "Well Tom, I'll leave you in the capable hands of Mrs Taylor. We have different ways of looking at things. But you can come and see me if Jane is content."

She turned, left the room and Tom heard the front door close solidly behind her.

"Thank you for the formal address of Ma'am, but it is not necessary and would indeed be odd in our friendship as it blossoms. No more of it." Tom nodded. "Now, follow me."

She left the room to climb a staircase and lifted up the brocaded dress a little to facilitate the climb. His eyes followed her, absorbed by the sway of her hips and the swish of her dress. At the top of the first flight she turned back on herself. He saw that the stairs went up to another floor. She turned into a room he realised was above the first room they entered. It was, he saw, beautifully furnished with a large bed centrally placed, with a brass head and a trunk at and across its base.

Two bedside tables, each with a silver candlestick containing a candle. He had once got into family trouble with silver spoons and had no need of further acquaintance with the metal. The trunk was covered with a throw of elaborate decoration, and two beautifully carved chairs faced each other across the room Where was the wealth from for all this presentation?

Jane Taylor closed the door behind her. Such soft sounds as he heard disappeared. She took his hand to stand them both by the trunk. She removed her shoes and motioned him to remove his. She undid the buttons on his magpie jacket and peeled it off his arms, revealing his taut muscled body. She turned and told him to undo the back of her dress. He fumbled a little but completed her instruction and, as it slid down to the floor, she stepped out of it. He was astonished at the clear, clean body before him and the red brush lower down. He thought when in Lincoln that all female bodies he had seen were the same. He now had experience in this new world and they were different. All different. Was that because they were moulded in this new place, or he had not been observant enough in the rushed sexual efforts in the old country? He was aware how aroused he was, especially as she was carefully and slowly undoing the buttons on his trousers and her expert fingers negotiated the trousers to fall to the floor to embrace her dress.

"Oh my!" She exclaimed as she surveyed what she had uncovered. He in turn remained staring at her lower body. She watched him.

"Never seen a red bush I expect. Full of fire it is, but no blacks within. Look upon it. 'Tis a map of the island and as full of as many secrets and delights as you will find outside in the Colony or the mainland. It is for me to guide you for your benefit and those other ladies you will encounter."

He was in turmoil. His exhibited desire was set against these words; "island," "mainland." Were these words used in school? He understood the way and where she used island. School use? No.

Jane Taylor taught him how to use it. The hidden valleys, the bits and pieces he never knew existed or cared to look for. He found with her expert guidance the pleasure and delight he gave, and, he was amazed to find, her explorations and caresses went to places he did not believe existed in him, or in her. He saw the rest of her body, being the main part of her, as the mainland, working out that "main" must be the biggest. It too had mountains, crevices, valleys and caves. There was so much he did not know; he was ashamed by his ignorance when it was there all the time. Here, there and everywhere. The Lincoln girls deserved better.

In a lull in his education in the arts of love he asked her, tentatively, why she had agreed to bring him to her.

"Why me? I don't know much. Except from Jenny. Now you." He did not know what else to say.

"I feel it is my duty, and my desire, to improve the lot of men and women in their intimate relations. It is badly done, so badly done, especially by men. Most do not know, or care, what is on offer for both, and there is too much disappointment, too much rough pleasure. That too has its pleasures on occasion, and my dear friend Jenny finds it more to her taste. From what I bring to suitable young men they may go forth and provide pleasure and happiness to their wives for great mutual joy.

"I was fortunate enough to have a caring and thoughtful husband who so regrettably died not long after we settled here. He was given exposure to the arts of love when he toured Europe before the French wars. He was much older than myself and I am grateful to the women who initiated him into such sources of pleasure. I believe it is my calling to impart those skills which were passed on to him and in turn to me through my dear husband.

"It is a sadness to know that few, if any, will leave here. Many expect to and their hopes will be cruelly dashed. But there is no reason... Indeed, no, I would go further and say there is every reason why the men and women and boys and girls here should extract as much delight as is lying in wait for them within their own sensibilities."

"I did not know that girls – women – had such an interest in their bodies."

"If it were not so, no men would be born. To put it truly, if a little indelicately, although delicacy is a rare value here, if you keep a woman well fed, well clothed and well fucked she will never leave you."

Not a thought which had ever crossed his mind, but he could see the insight in her remarks. The mischievous young man in him saw the opposite; withdrawing one or other would be a way of getting rid of an unwanted girl or woman. But it was of no value to him. He was not destined to have and keep a woman well fed and well clothed, to even get to what Mrs Taylor was training him to offer.

He blurted out, "You know I can't supply the food and clothes. Ever. Why are you bothering?"

"I do have a personal interest." She conceded. "As a woman I greatly enjoy what I do for my own satisfaction. I want to see my pleasure reach women through young men like you. My messengers. I am sure you will find someone in your life whom you will delight. Jenny saw it in you and suggested you to me. I see it too. You will give and receive the gifts of love."

"Don't see too many chances, round here."

"While you cannot see them, they are here. There are girls under my roof to whom I pass on the joys of pleasure sharing."

"Where do these girls come from?"

"There is a female prison, Cascade it is called. It is a little out of town, far enough not to corrupt the citizens' morals. Is it not a tacit admission of women's desire? Our snug little cat needs stroking and feeding."

Tom thought of a house of young women. Right here.

"How do they get here?" He hoped that perhaps one could stray and he could practise the skills he'd learned so far.

"These poor girls, barely twenty, lots sent for trivial offences, do nothing all day but sweep, clean and have the Bible read to them. Which is worse, I suggest. When girls near the end of their sentences there is no prospect of return to England. No money for the fare, and to what?

"I offered to take girls the superintendent regards as suitable and trustworthy. I give them some hope. Teach them some household skills beyond the rudimentary ones learned from a mother, if they had one and were not orphans. I teach them sewing, cooking and some dressmaking skills, to give them some skills for marriage. To that end, young men from officers and other military castes attend here to converse with the girls. Communication between both genders is so beneficial and to be encouraged.

"Sometimes the officers provide the girls with a stipend in recognition of the pleasures in each other's company, and the girls, in gratitude for making the meetings possible, pass on some of the gratuities to me so that here I may continue to be of service to the community.

"I am pleased to say that there has been some success with permanent engagements leading to marriage and starting families here in Hobart. They put down roots for the future."

This exposition deflated Tom. Finding a pretty girl for a wife? He could not compete.

After her explanation it was time to resume her teaching. Instruction completed and satiation achieved, she sent Tom off, once she had advised him of the local police routine, to find his way back to his bed and blanket. She gave him another date and at that time she would give him other dates for their mutual benefit. He was aware he was a different man. He could not say why, but it was true nonetheless.

Another activity to add to his life. Even courts were worth it.

*

Marianne, Rebecca, Sara and Annabel stepped gingerly out of their carriage. It was still warm in the Colony and they were carefully dressed, as they discussed, in apparel such as not to flaunt their status and worth, not only in the Colony, but also the mother Country, but modest enough to give an incentive on what was within the grasp of the unfortunates they were about to see. Or inspect.

What they were unprepared for was the dank nature of their destination. Cascade was tucked away in a marshy area to deter any escapees in pursuit of lascivious pursuits or those of optimistic collaborators coming the other way. Poor food and conditions, if that last word had any recognition there. The only happy inhabitants were the tiny purveyors of disease buzzing and gulping whatever presented itself as food. Including the residents. If they died in consequence, or in childbirth with babies on voyage, having set out from Britain often unaware of being pregnant, then that was in the Governor's view a natural conduit of their immorality and less temptation for others. Moral turpitude had a price.

Marianne, it being her idea, looked apprehensively about the gloom descending from the great oppressive mountain. She gazed up at it as if uncertain, although she knew it was here before her, and the oppression was not the mountain but from her. From them.

She, Marianne, was therefore in charge of her band, and Rebecca was not, despite her disconcerting airs of superiority. She took a deep breath, and banged up and down on the heavy door knocker. The door slowly opened and a well-built woman in her fifties stood before them. She wore a heavy blue dress with long buttoned sleeves. A woollen jacket over the dress and in the hand which did not open the door, she held a long, heavy stick – more a club, Rebecca observed. Behind her stood a male guard with a sheathed sword.

"Good morning. I am the Supervisor for the Superintendent and this is our little party, and you are most welcome."

She turned and, with the guard, led them down a high hall, which opened into a very large, square room which had doors set into each wall, as the cells for the inmates. The inmates themselves were about forty in number and were watched by two other armed guards. They were occupied, if that is the word, in doing nothing of obvious benefit. Some desultory sweeping of debris from the earth floor, although Annabel later wondered whether the debris was simply accumulated dirt from previous sweeping. Being in a prison, sharp objects like needles were forbidden so there was no scope for improvement with sewing.

The wives were aghast, watching these listless, blank women, roughly clothed, many of them merely girls younger than themselves.

"What can they do?" Sara ventured.

"Not much more than you see. Nothing which would be dangerous to them. Or to us," the reply came. "Sweep, keep themselves clean... though some of them have little idea what that even means. The Bible gets read to them in the morning and before bed."

The inmates did have one interest, now aroused by the presence of the wives. While the bodies moved slowly, the eyes were different. They collectively sparked anger, bitterness and contempt on seeing these fine ladies come to look at them, showing an attitude of horror and distaste as if spying rats on two legs.

"Like us cons, do you?" one shouted. Another coughed up a red-flecked globule on to the floor and followed up with a heavy retch.

The wives sensed that were it not for the armed Supervisor and guards, these girls would set upon them and their husbands would lament, they hoped, being widowers. Mutual fear and loathing being established, the wives were alarmed at the possibility of any of these creatures being released into the Town.

"What happens to them?" Sara enquired.

"Some die here. Some have to go when their sentence is up. Lots here for stealing. If I say they're good enough and not likely to come back they can get a Ticket of Leave and do what they can outside. If they offend again they come back here, as sometimes happens."

She continued. "I don't know what happens to lots of them. 'Tis not my job. We have enough here to mind. If I think there are a few who might be good for something, I send them to Mrs Taylor who has a nice big house in the town and tries to teach them new skills. I believe some of the girls from here have gone on with skills in the Colony and even married some of the officers and officials. Not all bad, then."

"Oh, that is encouraging." Marianne was relieved that the Town was not going to be awash with wanton women with designs on the men, and she had a particular one in mind.

"Thank you for showing us what you have to put up with," Rebecca chipped in.

"You are most welcome any time to see the progress made." The Supervisor knew it would never happen. It never had. The wives' curiosity was always sated.

When they returned to their carriage, Marianne mused. "I wonder whether we should visit the better girls who are being looked after by Mrs Taylor? That should lift our spirits. I am sure we can find the address from the barracks."

"True," said Sara, "but I would suggest if I may that we rest awhile to think upon what we have seen before we do so."

The silence which followed confirmed this suggestion and they lurched their way back to the barracks.

Rebecca smirked at her predicted outcome. Just a little, as her triumph.

*

Tom Scrimshaw continued his tuition at the hands of Mrs Taylor and the rest of her delicious body. The subtleties she showed him could not be taught at school, she told him.

How true that was. He did not remember much schooling. He did remember being always told what to do and to always obey his betters. He really hated that. He wanted to do things his way, the way he saw things; animals, birds, the streams, trees. Even the bees. They fascinated him.

There'd been nothing of that at school so he watched it all himself. He was the youngest in his family; a mistake, an afterthought. Well, here he was, and he was buggered if anyone was going to tell him how to behave or why. There were always ways around it, and he was learning some here in the Colony – this shithole.

He never imagined he would be taught anything by a woman, especially fun and on making it work. Did his Mam know, his Dad? He shut that out. Maybe you had to be as lovely as Jane Taylor and as handsome as her husband (before he died) to understand. He was lucky. She kept saying how much she enjoyed him, teaching him and how much he had to give. It had never been said by anyone before and it made him pleased, proud and, of all things, confident with a certainty in himself. Maybe he should have a sign made to hang up in Hobart Town:

Trained by Mrs Jane Taylor, Widow.

Hobart Town.

Testimonials Available.

On one of his agreed nights with Jane Taylor she said, "I have a little visitation tomorrow morning. Nearly every boat which sails in with officers brings wives who want to inspect the poor girls who get sent here. They go off to Cascade and I get sent any promising ones finishing their sentences, to teach them some useful skills. Some do well and even marry.

"The wives come out of Cascade as if hit by a cannonball, and want to see the successes to make them feel better. I have the current crop to harvest tomorrow.

"Anyway, my sweet, let us sup at the honey and gambol with Eros."

Tom had no idea who or what Eros was, and he misunderstood gambol, but Jane's choices always worked. It proved so yet again.

After gambolling, Tom took his leave for the return to Gellibrand and the new day's work. The world, or the night part of it, felt very good.

As he pulled the door behind him, two men stepped forward, one on each side.

"Do you have leave of your Master to be out? It is near to dawn."

"What's it to you?"

"We have a duty to apprehend those out without leave. Do you have leave? We think not."

"I work all day for the bastard. The time after is mine."

"Not so. You are still his. Who is he?"

"Bastard at the big house at the end of town."

"That'll be Mr Gellibrand."

"Sounds like it."

"Do we knock him up and ask if he gave you permission to be out?"

"Y'can if you want. Don't care much. A good night to be out."

"I don't think you should be here, either. This is a respectable house; not for you."

"I'm a friend of Mrs Taylor."

"Tell that to the magistrate in the morning. You're coming with us."

The officers instinctively put hands on their swords. Tom was replete, relaxed after his sojourn inside, and had learned enough that Magpies were fair game for officials looking for trouble and equipped for it. The rest of the night was in a cell.

At 10am the court sat, and Tom was brought before the magistrate.

"Ah you again. What is the offence this time?"

"Absent all night without leave, Sir," said the officer.

"Where did you find him?"

"We took him outside Mrs Taylor's house. He said he was a friend."

The magistrate thought about this utterance. If he commented that the accused's friendship was a lie or even highly unlikely, that led to the conclusion that he, the magistrate, knew Mrs Taylor's establishment. That was better left unanswered, and to rely on him being out without leave.

"Who is his Master?"

"Believe Mr Gellibrand, Sir."

"Ah." The magistrate knew the history of Gellibrand and the Governor. The Governor appointed him as magistrate, thus his loyalties lay there and not with a fellow lawyer. There was an opportunity to punish this man, again, for this comparatively minor offence – and also Gellibrand in demonstrating he had no control over his assigned workers. Something memorable.

"Have you anything to say, Scrimshaw?"

Tom shook his head.

"A lesson must be learned and a punishment to emphasise it. I sentence you to twenty-five lashes to be administered at the barracks forthwith, after which you will be returned to your... er... Master."

Tom was jolted out of his happy memories of a few hours earlier. The lash was spoken of, but rarely used. The Governor was not in favour of it. He thought it ineffective, but would not interfere with the magistrates' decisions. It did have the advantage of not taking up a cell, which were few in number, and it was over and done with. But it was so rare that there was almost an aura over any recipient of it.

He was roughly handled straight along to the barracks. There was a whipping post. He had not noticed it before, having had just two day's work off the boat and since then worked – and played – over at the other end of the town. The post was in the shape of the St Andrew's Cross. The offender stripped to the waist, his arms were outstretched and bound to the upper limbs of the cross, and the legs to the lower.

On a crisp cold August morning, Tom had his Magpie top removed. His arms and feet were spreadeagled.

It did not take long. Pain he had never imagined seared his back, his skin howling at the insult. Then another, and another. His voice found a release, a groan, then a bellow from within. As his body adjusted to the flaying, his mind jumped. Was this a punishment for stolen pleasure he was not entitled to? Yes, he was, and he would endure. He would irritate them without any submission of fear. His body had toughened too, under the daily labour in heat, rain and occasional snow. His body would show his mind how to do it. As he flinched with each thwack, his mouth was now clenched.

The thrashing stopped. Arms and legs released, he slumped to the ground. Somebody picked him up by his forearms and tossed him roughly into a cart, his jacket was thrown on top, and blood and sweat mingled during a bumping trip back to the Gellibrand estate, the sweat salt stinging the raw flesh.

"Had twenty-five lashes for being out all night," he heard as the cart stopped sometime later. "His Excellency might think you can't look after your workers."

Tom was yanked out of the cart, dragged across to his little room and tossed on the bed.

A voice stirred above him; it sounded like Sam's but he could not focus his gaze. "Thinking about working you this afternoon; in chains, so you can't skip off again."

He did not care.

✻

Having seen their husbands off on duty after breakfast, the wives dressed themselves in some finery for their visit to Mrs Taylor. It was a rare invitation to someone who was neither military nor criminal and obviously of some regard in the community; it was also an opportunity to show off on their carriage journey. As well as to Mrs Taylor. It was however, a cold, breezy August day and they were rugged up against the chill.

As the carriage lurched off, Marianne noticed activity across at the quite separate prisoners' barracks. She only had a passing interest in the barracks, largely because by the time she left her quarters, the prisoners were already off labouring. This time, she saw a youngish man spreadeagled across a structure shaped like a St Andrew's Cross. Another man had a whip – more a flail – it looked like the cat o'nine tails of naval lore. She could hear some moaning, but despite the redding of his back, there was not the screaming she expected. A strong young man, then, and obviously he was still offending. She vaguely recalled a similar-looking convict on the voyage but, she reflected, there were lots of them and England was well rid of them.

The carriage moved on, rumbling over the ruts in the main road to turn left into a side road, then two streets up right into a road parallel with the main one, to stop before an impressive house. The wives nodded approvingly; it reminded them at last of a proper English house. The driver got down and opened the carriage door for the ladies who got out and adjusted their bonnets, and the driver went up to the house to lift and drop the heavy door knocker with a thud.

Presently the door opened, and Mrs Taylor herself opened the door. The wives were pleasantly surprised by their hostess. Aside from Mrs Arthur and other officers' wives, this woman was more as they still saw themselves. She was, or had been in her youth, a great beauty. Even now, seemingly in her forties, she deserved compliments.

Mrs Taylor smiled, and as they entered she shepherded them into the parlour. They admired the furniture and furnishings. Such refinement and taste.

"Do sit, ladies. Tea and scones will arrive to assist in your comfort."

While this expedition excited the young ladies, Mrs Taylor had not only awaited the request to visit but could rehearse the nature of the conversations they were to have.

"We have been to Cascade, which we found quite depressing with the poor souls lost and with nothing to do, each and every day." Marianne spoke first, in her capacity as instigator of this adventure.

Mrs Taylor looked at the speaker. She was a girl of remarkable beauty. She was used to sheaves, as she thought of them, of attractive officers with pretty wives, well-read and of some cultural attainments. The other guests, she saw, were in that mould. But this girl was incomparable; quite impervious to her own beauty and the compliments with which she would have grown up. She just was as she was, and thought no more about it beyond sitting comfortably in the female culture into which she had been reared.

"Yes, that is true, unfortunately," Mrs Taylor nodded. "As you were advised there, some girls, thought not to be without future hope, are referred here for my help in assisting them into the real world, and in acquiring such skills as may benefit them in that transition, to be useful as servants and in some cases as wives.

"I do encourage their interaction with better-quality young men of mainly officer class, as you yourselves have done. It is advantageous for both sets to converse and relate, and share experiences. Some very firm and affectionate friendships have developed, and I am delighted to say that in some cases matrimony has been the outcome.

"The young men who visit often feel an obligation to the young ladies they interact with, to proffer some small sums to help facilitate their subsequent development in society. The girls, in their turn, usually feel that I should have a contribution from these proffered sums towards the upkeep and maintenance of my property and myself, which is so indicative of their sweet and caring natures."

Marianne, Sara and Annabel nodded sympathetically. Rebecca looked very intently at Mrs Taylor while she spoke and quickly appraised the room again; its taste – and its cost. She was more worldly than her friends.

 The tea and scones arrived and were placed on a table within reach of the ladies.

"May I ask a question, Mrs Taylor," said Rebecca, "following on from your most interesting observations and your admirable efforts to integrate these young ladies in your care?"

"Of course," she replied, smiling at Rebecca. There was always one in the group more forward than the others.

"As the young ladies in your care have had a difficult history before arriving here, and had some regrettable experiences... human nature, as I have found it to be, must introduce some temptations, irresistible ones perforce; and with no prospect of leaving the Colony, the need to find comfort must be strong and urgent on occasion.

"If the unfortunate consequence of such a close friendship should go further, what measures may the young ladies take to prevent a further – and may I say potentially catastrophic – result?"

Mrs Taylor was impressed by the clever circumlocution this girl had used to raise this issue. She noticed the others were still grappling with what was said and what it meant, if anything at all, as she looked at the beautiful girl.

"Fortunately, there are ways to address these potentially undesirable outcomes. You may yourselves have some knowledge, perhaps experience of these ways. If not, I will explain as much as I can as a poor widow, which may assist you in your future lives."

She moved to a cupboard set in a wall in the parlour. "These I show to ladies such as yourselves who ask such a question, and I realise it is a matter of such great importance that most are too embarrassed to ask it. It is, however, important that a woman be able to enjoy that which Nature and the good Lord has endowed her with, and which I regard as being of the utmost importance in the education of the young ladies whose care is an honour entrusted to me."

Opening the cupboard, she invited the women over to view. Dangling down there appeared to be sausage skins, although not entirely smooth and also devoid of any filling.

"These are called condoms." She pointed at these objects. "They are made of sheeps' intestines securely sewn tight at one end, the other end pulled by a man over his manhood. These are very effective in preventing pregnancy, although I have to say that no method is absolutely without failure. After each use, it is properly cleaned and dried for subsequent re-use."

Three of the wives, hitherto unaware of the device, turned greenish pale at the thought of a piece of dead sheep regularly inside them; once would be too much.

As usual, thought Jane Taylor.

She continued regardless. "In England, you may be fortunate to find the citrus fruit lemon. Do you know of it?"

There was a collective nod, a relief from intestines.

"Cut the lemon in half, scoop out the flesh and seeds and rinse the inside with vinegar. Place it deep inside you. Usually very effective. Unfortunately, lemons are in short supply here, though they occasionally arrive in Sydney where they are taken by the ladies there."

Mrs Taylor paused to let the girls recover from these shocks.

"There is another which is available here. Soak a sponge in vinegar and insert it when you are expecting, or even better, desiring intimacy with your husband. Again, very effective. There is a fisherman here who finds fishing for sponges more lucrative than competing with others for fish. If you believe such an arrangement as I have outlined would be beneficial, I would be most pleased to provide you with the address and details of the fisherman. It would of course be of the utmost discretion."

A general nodding of heads ensued, with some relief and a realisation that this woman was in fact a source of useful advice on a worrying subject.

"May I please have the name and address, Mrs Taylor?" asked Rebecca.

"May I too?" "And me." "And me." The little chorus sang as one.

Jane Taylor went to a bureau, took out a notebook and a pencil and wrote out the address on each of four sheets, one of which she gave to each young woman. She did not proffer any advice on how to approach the vendor. They should learn their own resourcefulness and ingenuity in the Colony.

No invitation was sought, and none offered, to meet any of the house's other residents. The wives were still mindful of the Cascade experience. This was a halfway house and their reception might not be the best.

Saying their goodbyes and bestowing their gratitude for the knowledge imparted, the wives returned to their carriage and drove away.

Jane Taylor smiled to herself and allowed a little fantasy. How would young Scrimshaw handle and delight the beautiful young blonde woman, called Marianne by one of the others over tea? Despite the chasm between their status and futures; he was a young man of hitherto hidden gifts and prowess which she had been delighted to uncover, and there was a young girl who would attain a whole new life with the right opportunity. All these potentials are so dormant. She amused herself on and off imagining this ill-matched couple in different circumstances, and a different world.

Finally, her imaginings gave way to the reality of the world she inhabited. It was, she understood, time to move on with her mission.

✳

It was some two weeks before Tom felt able to visit Jenny again. Healing was compromised, deliberately, by the additionally onerous and heavy workload piled on him by Samuel. Payment for the pleasures they did not know about. When he saw her, he complained to Jenny about the events which befell him after leaving Jane. Was it all planned that he was to fall foul of the police?

Jenny Cox laughed: "Men, young and old, think of themselves in the world. Women, young and old, *are* the world. If you want to know what's going on, ask a woman."

"You're one. You tell me."

"After we learned of your latest in court, Jane wanted to know why you were taken. One of her girls told her officer friend that she, Jane, had a regular friend at the same time usually for a few hours, and her friend was a Magpie. He was disgusted at the thought of a Magpie nesting there, and said he would do something about it - therefore he informed the police. That girl broke the confidence of the house, and Jane threw her out. Told the officer when he turned up to seek her, that there was to be no more friendship at the house.

"Jane is sure nothing more will be heard on it. Officials do attend for companionship and it is in no-one's interests to advertise the fact. The Governor is probably the only one who does not know, despite him thinking he knows everything which goes on, and which promotes good fellowship among the citizens of Hobart Town.

"Jane thinks it prudent that you not visit her in the short and middling term at least. She will let me know if and when you should return. You might find a willing recipient of what you have learned in the Town. In the meantime, there is me. Not so bad."

CHAPTER 5

Hobart, 1833

The young wives' discovery of the efficacious sponges had mixed results. Annabel and Marianne both found themselves pregnant; whether from a misplaced sponge, insufficient vinegar, indifference, or the natural desire of the organism to reproduce and bypass barriers to doing so was not explored. But there it was.

"I am with child, dearest," Marianne happily announced to her husband. The condition suited her, and she radiated health.

"Wonderful news! If it is a boy we shall call him Arthur, if a girl, Eliza."

Marianne paused in her felicitation. "Is that not reminiscent of His Excellency and his good lady?" She was a little deflated by his prompt and unexpected response.

"I see it as a reminder to him of our value to his enterprise and one which will be rewarded in the fullness of time," Francis replied. "I anticipate that the fullness will hurry along."

There was nothing more Marianne felt she could add. Francis was determined to point up his indebtedness to the Governor, although the Governor showed no indication of any favouritism towards Francis, nor his wife towards her other than a general civility and kindness which was the least that could be expected from such a lady.

That was not quite true. Mrs Arthur had numerous children and pregnancy was a consequence of routine lives in the Colony. There were midwives, some sent for various misdemeanours. Some were settlers' wives who found practising their skills personally rewarding and a welcome intrusion on their wifely duties. Accordingly, Mrs Arthur, military and settler's wives were quite well served.

Annabel and Marianne were both recipients of midwifery input, and in due course were both delivered of their babies, Annabel of Joshua, and Marianne inevitably of Arthur, and there was general rejoicing at the success of the events.

Marianne recorded her pregnancy and delivery in her diary, and wrote a letter back to her family in Hampshire about the good news, although there was naturally a lengthy delay between handing it in for despatch to a vessel returning to England and its receipt in the hands of the delighted grandparents.

Another bonus was the provision of extra help for mother and infant. As well as having trusted convict servants, there was now a nursemaid to cope with all the less convenient and less enjoyable aspects of parenthood, enabling the parents to get on with their lives if they chose.

A couple of years later, Marianne found herself pregnant again. It is possible that, in retrospect, she enjoyed her previous experience and, aided by the human capacity to recall having pain but not the experience of the pain itself, she was indifferent to the sponge and its rationale.

This discovery coincided with an order from His Excellency to each of the four officers transferring them to his special establishment at Port Arthur, as it was still called, much to the Governor's satisfaction. There was a burgeoning increase in inmates, whether from increased lawlessness in England or in Hobart Town was not examined, but the Governor determined that additional staffing was required. He was concerned to curb any further outbreaks of mental delirium during his administration.

The new appointment was a mixed blessing for Francis Wainwright. He was bored by the repetitive duties in Hobart, relieved by the occasional hunting of errant convicts or the despatch of natives at the behest of settlers for incursions on their land, where the natives found spearing sheep easier than wallabies and relished a change of diet.

Where, thought Francis, were the French when you needed them for real action? This was, however, a real opportunity – and the Governor would see the real value of his work, especially in discipline with this new regime.

When the time came, and he was sure it would be soon, the Governor would sign an order for his return to England with a recommendation for promotion, so dear to both their hearts. He chafed at lacking a real war. He also had the small matter of a wife, a son and another on the way.

"I thought it probable that my endeavours would have earned His Excellency's recognition with a promotion," he confessed to Marianne.

"I am sure your qualities will shortly be recognised." Marianne tried soothing him, although he appeared to be talking to himself.

"I would venture, however, that this movement to the Port is a test of character – and I will not fail it. The wretches there will soon understand proper discipline."

Andrew Morgan was more relaxed. He felt no need to assert himself against the settlers, the convicts or the rapidly decreasing number of natives. Duty was to be done as required of a good officer, who should make the most of what was offered professionally and personally in whatever location the officer was. There was a lot to be gained in these foreign postings. He enjoyed this odd country. He could feel himself changing from the person he thought he was... and that was all to the good, certainly in recognising that change.

It was odd that it was a written Order, and not the consequence of a meeting with His Excellency. Still, this was a civilian administration by former military and this hydra had different heads.

Rebecca had not become pregnant, and she was grateful for that and for Mrs Taylor's possible part in it. There was no place for children here. Servants were tainted with criminality, unlike those in England. This posting was to be endured, and she longed for the sophistications of London. Van Diemen's Land might as well be the Moon with trees and savages.

She was vaguely irritated by Andrew's affable acceptance of the situation. He almost seemed to enjoy it; the strangeness, dirt, squalor, and the contrast with the discipline. Francis was determined to be elsewhere, and she understood and shared that desire.

Marianne did not reveal much. True, she was pregnant with her second child and withdrawn even more into herself. However, she was thinking and acting.

She was worried about giving birth in the Port; its reputation did not suggest help was forthcoming. She therefore wrote to Mrs Arthur using the barracks network about available assistance when in labour at Port Arthur. Aware of her husband's obsession with good administration, Eliza Arthur had persuaded him to send one midwife to his Port, and that one from Hobart should be persuaded with a carrot dangled, rather than be subject to one of his Orders.

A reluctant one was riskier. Mrs Arthur offered to interview candidates. An advertisement was circulated with some unspecified benefits. Her arguments won favour; she interviewed those who showed interest, and one agreed to relocation. She was promised, and received, a newly constructed cottage built from convict labour for herself, along with the professional equipment she required and a generous allowance of medicines and sustenance. This woman was already in place by the time Francis and Marianne were to travel, and the system had been working well.

Marianne received a reply from Mrs Arthur detailing the midwife's particulars, with a covering letter to the midwife setting out Marianne's details. The reply added that she fervently hoped nothing would go amiss and The Lord would protect her.

His Excellency came to the ship as it finished loading its passengers and supplies for the Port.

"You will be doing The Lord's bidding," he shouted across the quay. "The Colonial Office will be pleased to receive details of your findings and duties at Port Arthur." Ever mindful of keeping control at all times, he added, "All reports will be sent through me. We wish you well."

With that he turned to his carriage, entered and left. To him, the officers were less valuable than the settlers. Settlers were to make the Colony viable and a credit to his administration. Officers were functionaries to that end. He was most particular in dispatches to the Colonial Office in London to set out obstacles he had to surmount and justifications for his efforts in doing so. He knew there were Colonial Inspectors who reported independently on their findings in the Colonies. He always sought to get in first with the realities.

The crew sailed their passengers in their modest boat down the Derwent, and off to Port Arthur.

Other moves were also in train to expand the Colony's activities in an opposite direction.

*

Joseph Gellibrand, former Attorney General for the Colony of Van-Diemen's Land, removed – he said – after the machinations of the Governor, was still a successful barrister in Hobart.

He was a substantial landowner too, and a particular gripe was that the Governor also bought land and doubtless on advantageous terms. While Mr Gellibrand had done well, assisted by the assignment system, he and other substantial free settlers had been refused further land by the Governor in the Colony. But there were vast tracts of land in the Port

Phillip District across the Strait on the mainland, and that was not part of the Governor's jurisdiction. The Port Phillip Association had been founded to explore possibilities.

Gellibrand was speaking to his supervisor, Samuel.

"I have drawn up a treaty, an agreement if you will, Samuel, on behalf of the Association. I, and some other members of the Association, are to venture to the District and obtain land in that virgin territory.

"As a fair Association, we will treat over all land extending ten miles of the western coast line of the bay with the local tribe there, who I believe are called the Warundjeri, or some such similar pronunciation.

"In return we will provide them with a yearly handout of provisions plus items which they may find useful such as axes and beads, and trinkets which their wives and children may safely enjoy.

"In joint company with my wife, who will of course be much devoted to our children, I appoint you to manage my properties and supervise the assigned men and women with assistance if necessary from the police and courts, although I am sure you can manage well enough without such recourse." Gellibrand was mindful that Samuel's dealings on his behalf with those authorities may not be even-handed.

"I would expect, as the results of our endeavours, there will be considerable advantages for us all – and by that I include you."

Samuel was pleased to hear such words, and resolved to do all necessary to ensure the properties in and around Hobart were fruitful and productive in his master's absence.

"We will shortly take sail towards Port Phillip Bay, together with a cargo of sheep to start our settlement. It is our intention to make land at Western Port and make our way from there towards the pinnacle of the bay and negotiate the land and commence settlement before I and some others return."

"Very good, Sir. I wish you all well and God Speed for a safe and profitable voyage and return."

Shortly afterwards and upon taking due and affectionate leave of his family, Mr Gellibrand was gone.

Some months later, he returned to his home, and after enjoying the welcome of his family, sought out Samuel.

"The expedition I must account for was a success. We entered a treaty with the natives, who seemed pleased with our offerings and the promise of a yearly contribution to their sustenance. As neither party spoke the other's language, negotiations were difficult – but I am satisfied that they understood their legal obligations under the treaty. I am pleased to say I acquired an area of land of some miles along the north west foreshore of the bay for a distance inland. The land is flat and most suitable for grazing. The sheep were very appreciative.

"It is my intention to return in a year or so to assess progress and to explore further to the west. It is heavy bush, but I am confident there is profit to be made."

"I am very pleased to hear it, Sir, very pleased."

"I take it there were no insurmountable issues in my absence?"

"Generally speaking, all went very well," Samuel replied. "The livestock are fat and content, the land rich and the crops have flourished. The workers satisfactory, except for Scrimshaw who works well when it suits him. He is indolent though, Sir; insolent, and drunk far too often. It is a matter of concern and of wonder that he is able to function at all. The smell of stale beer in his room after his sojourns is painful to experience. It is a conjecture that he has lived this long such is his recklessness as to his demeanour and actions."

"Hmm. What you say does suggest we may have to re-assign him. I do not like to acknowledge a defeat. It is not in my nature. I have not done so to date." Mr Gellibrand paused for a minute, thinking.

"There is a possibility of redemption for him. I will need to have a letter delivered to one of our Port Phillip associates who is up country, setting out our adventures, our plans and recommendations for his consideration. He is aware I will be communicating with him on these matters and is pregnant with expectation. A journey may illustrate to Scrimshaw that there are options in this Colony if he has the wit to see and accept them. When I have put together the contents of the letter, I will have you bring him to me for that purpose."

"I trust he will appreciate your concern and generosity, Sir."

CHAPTER 6

Hobart, 1835-1836

"Scrimshaw. Pick up your things and come with me."

Tom looked up in finishing the last of his hominy. Samuel stood beside him.

Arising, Tom did as ordered, then followed his superior to the front of the Master's house. A knock on the door was acknowledged by the housekeeper, and shortly afterwards Mr Gellibrand came out. It was a bright morning but the wind was edging south and Tom felt a shiver. Gellibrand was clothed in a silk dressing gown. He was not intending to stay long over his instructions.

"We have been monitoring your work and performance under, may I say, my beneficence, and the conclusion is that there is a lot to be desired, and no evidence that desire is forthcoming. It is rendered further away by your habitual drunkenness, and after speaking with Samuel on the matter I made enquiries on your too-frequent absences from your duties to discover you appear to prefer the company of the court to work on my properties. Sporadic achievements of serious work show what you are capable of in the Colony. But these efforts are undermined by indolence and insolence.

"It is within my gift and competence to have you re-assigned if you do not avail yourself of the opportunity of redemption which I am about to offer you. I can assure you that any other Master will not be as indulgent as am I.

"I have a letter of the utmost importance to be delivered to Mr Davidson at the township of New Brighton. I am assured that reading is not a skill in which you are proficient, and thus I have no concern of you perusing the contents, much less understanding their import. The letter also states that he may retain you for the purpose of preparing a reply to my missive.

"Samuel will give you a small sum to feed yourself, so that you will not be a financial encumbrance on Mr Davidson while he considers his response and returns you to the coach station for return to Hobart Town. Samuel will collect you and bring you back to me with his reply. Is that understood?"

Tom nodded.

"What?"

"Emm... yes, Sir."

"Now, as the first part of this journey, you will be conveyed by Samuel to the Coach Station here for the coach to New Brighton. When you alight at your destination, ask at the nearest venue for Mr Davidson's address and how to get there. If the person to whom you speak for directions says they can read, you may show them the front of the letter which has the address, which will help you with the location. Is that understood?"

"Yes... Sir."

"Repeat it to me!"

"I get on a coach to New Brighton and ask for Mr Davidson when I get off."

"No. You ask how to get to Mr Davidson. I do not expect him to be there to greet you, a mere convict. I have no more time to talk to you. See to it for your future's sake."

Gellibrand turned, and with a swish of his dressing-gown, went inside and closed the door.

"Come," said Samuel, "I do not think you will stray. Where would you go? These are brutal hills, though some are tamed in New Brighton.

Neither do I think you will do as bidden. It is not in your nature. The devils which brought you here are with you still. Yet, here is the money from the Master."

They trudged in silence to the Coach Station. Timing was calculated for them to arrive as the passengers and luggage were being loaded. The settler passengers looked at each other, feeding on each other's unease at the prospect of sharing the coach with this uncouth, slightly smelly young man in convict garb.

Samuel spoke to the driver. Tom watched him pass a purse. The driver nodded. Tom was puzzled. Even on his own assessment, he was not a model or even desirable assigned worker, so why had he been singled out for the benefit of a trip out of town? He did not know, but frankly, did not care. Here he was on something different, and he would enjoy it.

He was jolted by both Samuel and the driver shouting and repeating. "Hey! Up here. Be quick!"

He followed their gaze. He was to sit up with the driver, to the relief of the passengers. It was cold, but he was used to all weathers and it would be a better view. Up he climbed, and tucked the precious letter into his small bag. With a tug of the reins off they went, four horses straining to get motion.

The breeze behind subsided as it met wind resistance from their progress. Tom was exhilarated. All he had seen in his years here was limited to a few places with, for him, such contrasting experiences. Now there was this massive dark shimmering river, huge trees with languid bark and hills all around. Were these actually mountains? Definitely bigger than anything he saw in the confines of his earlier life in Lincolnshire, where he had expected to stay like his parents and grandparents; to marry, have children, work and die. Now it was just work and die.

There were grassy patches hacked out of the Bush, as he knew it was called; no easy forests here. Clearings clinging to hillsides with rough-cut houses plonked on them, smoke flicking upwards from roof pots. How long had it been since the first boats stopped in The Town and people decided that up here was the spot to work and die?

Then, as if it rooted firmly to stop further progress, a settlement. A bridge, some more substantial houses on plots, and the coach stopped. Two-storied houses, stables; the coach station.

The coachman grunted, looked across at Tom and pointed at some large buildings and a rutted track alongside those buildings. The driver got down, went around the side of the coach, opened the door and assisted hesitant ladies to get out, followed by male passengers.

Tom was now ignored and on his own, which was nothing new. He climbed down with his bag. The passengers and driver walked off to these more impressive buildings, leaving Tom alone with the horses. The day had warmed up, and the dusty road had left him thirsty. He looked behind him and across to where the passengers had gone. It did not look like a place for him. Then, closer, he spied the tell-tale sign of an inn, a crudely drawn blue bird – which, on closer inspection, was a duck. The sign of the Blue Duck. That was new. And much more like it. A glass there would slake his thirst. He had some of his own Bank money which he always kept in his boot, and could also ask there for directions to Mr Davidson. Keep your money close by; there were thieves about.

Into the Blue Duck he went. A woman of about forty was behind the bar, beer barrels behind her and a shelf with different-coloured bottles. There were two tables, each with four chairs, in what was a surprisingly large bar area. An optimistic landlady in such a small settlement, especially if there were competition. It was the nature of women working in inns, in his experience, to show off their figures to best advantage and be seen by potential customers. It was so here and very inviting too, though he was focused on his thirst and his travels.

"Glass of best beer, thanks."

She looked at him. A Magpie had flown in. Obviously not escaped, but also unescorted. Very odd. Young, too; barely thirty, well-built and with an air of mischief, of edge, which explained the uniform. It had been a long time since she had that feeling.

She poured a glass as requested and the requisite sum changed hands. He gulped it down. It was so good.

"Another, ta."

She complied, and he sat at one of the tables, savouring the contents more. She disappeared.

"Emma! Sophie! Come quick!" Girls of about fourteen and seventeen looked up.

"Got a young Magpie in t' bar. Don't know how or why. Off the coach I think. We don't see much of them... have a look. Maybe he can take a room."

The girls got up, brushed and smoothed their skirts and followed their mother to gaze at this strange customer. They looked and then looked at each other.

Tom finished his glass. This was so good. Another one, please. Now there were three fetching females. Were there more out the back? This was good business all round.

*

Two days later, Mr Gellibrand was handed a letter via the New Brighton coach to Hobart Town.

   "Dear Joseph,

Where is the letter you promised me? Nothing has arrived.

Yours sincerely,

James Davidson."

Mr Gellibrand's visage visibly darkened. What could have gone wrong? The wretch understood the clear instructions and knew it was in his interests to do so. Samuel saw him get up by the coachman and the coach depart. There was no indication that he had not arrived at the other end. It was too much. He went searching for Samuel and found him in a nearby field.

"Samuel! That idiot we sent to New Brighton is just that. He and the letter have gone missing. Mr Davidson has not seen either. He surely cannot have gone native. Take two men on the next coach you can to New Brighton to find him and bring him back. I will draft another letter."

Samuel snorted, nodded his head, in acknowledgement of both his instructions and in proof of his prediction. He put in train those instructions, and as soon as places were available, with some financial inducement at the Coaching Station, the trio travelled to their destination. He was armed with the coachman's evidence on the errant Magpie's departure from the coach.

"Morning," Samuel said to the man behind the desk, "We are looking for a youngish man in official convict garment who we believe arrived here some three days ago on an errand for his Master. The due recipient of the errand has seen neither hide nor hair of him. Have you seen or heard of such a man?"

"Ah yes, indeed, Sir. Over there at the Blue Duck Public House, owned by Mrs Wootten and her daughters. It's said a young man went there from the coach and hasn't been seen since."

"I am most grateful to you, as is my Master. We shall attend that establishment."

Over the road the three went to the Blue Duck. Samuel opened the door. There, on the floor of the public bar, was Thomas Scrimshaw, semi-attired and comatose with the snore of a man who has drunk too much and too often.

"Oi! Get up, Scrimshaw!" Samuel shouted, angry and a little confused.

The other two bent, one on each side, grabbed Tom and pulled him to his feet. When they released their grip he slumped to the floor again, and the process was repeated.

The commotion brought Mrs Wootten and her daughters into the bar.

"What is this? Who are you?"

"We're taking this miserable bastard back where he came from. Has he left a letter here? Have you seen one? Quick!"

"He has stayed with us some days and nights," the landlady said. "He has been a right royal guest, the like of which we have not seen in these parts. Would there were more like him. We do not want him to go."

"Go he will. Where is the letter?"

Mrs Wootten went out back and returned with a letter, somewhat crumpled and grubby. She handed it to Samuel.

"Where is Mr Davidson?"

She thought for a moment. She went to the door, and he followed. She pointed to a track across the road beside the property they had first entered.

"Up there. About quarter mile. Big house."

"You two hold him firm here. I will deliver the letter myself. When I return, I will seek a special coach to take us back. I warrant the Master will meet the cost."

In Samuel's absence Tom was carefully guarded, with his silly smile upon the distraught females pleading that their guest should remain and they would look after him and he after them. Their entreaties were ignored.

On Samuel's return, he said. "I delivered the letter and apologised most profusely to Mr Davidson for the shortcomings of our messenger. I have also arranged a special coach to return us. It awaits us. Pick him up, drag him if needs be – and throw him in. He can sober up on the journey. His punishment will be justified and severe."

Tom was manhandled out of the pub, with Mrs Wootten and her daughters, having failed to persuade his captors to let him remain, shouting out. "Come again, Tom. Any time, any time. We'll look after you well. Don't forget us. Come again."

There was much excitement among the inhabitants who watched the spectacle until the coach set off.

On the return trip Tom wet himself, but seemed oblivious to it. As he sobered up he hazily relived the events he could recall over the last few days.

"Beauties, beds, board and beer. Jane and Jenny. Nothing more wanted for a man," he muttered, then snorted a giggle. By the time the party reached Hobart he had largely sobered up. The coach was directed to the Gellibrand property for the coachman to be paid, and Tom was hauled off to be slung on his bed.

"You'll keep till the morrow. We'll see what the Magistrate does. Reckon you'll go from here. A waste of time, you are."

Tom slept on, fortified by the attention lavished upon him by the Woottens. The prospect of punishment at Gellibrand's did not bother him.

However, at dawn he was roused for breakfast, then escorted into the town to the police office and cells, one waiting for him. He sat on the bed and did not feel as lively as he hoped.

"Scrimshaw. Get up!"

He did, and was escorted into court and into the Accused box, which he knew well enough. He looked across at the Assistant Magistrate, a thin, balding man with an unpleasant face and a smile which, when it occurred, was not really a smile at all – more a threat.

"The charge, Your Worship, is that this man was found drunk in town, New Brighton to be precise, when in charge of a letter to convey to a person in New Brighton. He was found after three days on the floor of Mrs Wootten's Public House."

"What do you say to that, Scrimshaw?" The Assistant Police Magistrate asked.

"T'was like a birthday. Never had such a good time here."

"Insolent as well. As ever. You are too well known here. We shall see whether you still have happiness in recall. I sentence you to twenty-five lashes. Take him away for it.

"I will supervise this myself. Round up four wretches from the barracks, or the wharves if necessary. On my orders. Take them to the triangle. They can learn lessons which this... er... gentleman is incapable of learning."

Tom was taken steely-faced to the triangle, the cross, stripped to the waist and his arms stretched and tied to the triangle arms. Four apprehensive prisoners were brought in, uncertain why they were there.

The Assistant Police Magistrate stepped forward and addressed the strapped man.

"How I would relish seeing your body scarlet and bloody on the rope weighed with ball and chain, drop, to loosen your head from your body quicker than a shark's bite. But this will have to do.

"Your friends here," he waved at the four spectators, "should there be any, will watch and revel in fear, yours and theirs."

"An accursed place this is," came Tom's muffled reply.

The magistrate stood to the side, together with the Medical Officer, who was required to attend this form of punishment.

"Ah, I see criss-crossed bulges. Pussy's pearly fingers have tattooed this stinking hide afore. Flailing tails tell many tales." He laughed to himself at his little witticism.

He turned to the flogger. "Twenty-five of your finest, man!"

The flogger nodded and started. Each lash of the cat brought forth flinching and grunts. After ten lashes, the flogger paused.

"Flog, flog away. We must hear more of his tunes."

The flogger re-started. Tom's groans grew louder.

"You see how it is. No floor of Mrs Wootten's Public House here. My hungry cat laps up your insolence. She does my bidding. So you shall!"

"You do not own me. Never will," Tom groaned amid the lashing. "M' body's scarred, holed like a ship on a reef, but harbour's in m' head."

"Your back's in bloom; scarlet, watery, new little blossoms, nourished by the law!" The magistrate was overheated. "Such pleasure to see you in my power."

He turned to the flogger. "Harder man, harder. Let me see, do the sums. Mm. Twenty-five lashes by nine tails. Ah…that be two hundred and twenty-five scratches and scrapes of my cat's claws, feeding herself on such bloody scraps."

Tom struggled to articulate in the pain, but he knew that though he wanted to die, he would not buckle. His hatred of this man was a forge furnishing life's fire.

"What satisfaction, seeing such a man torn." The magistrate was excited.

"No surrender. Ever. Blood and shit wash away."

The flogger paused. "Twenty-five done."

"So soon? Pity. He will be back as a moth needs the flame. Take him off. Take him to the hospital, where this Officer will attend to whatever he thinks necessary to keep him alive until the next instalment back at this cat's cradle."

He turned to the aghast spectators, two of whom were staring fixedly at the pooling blood in the dust. "I trust you prisoners enjoyed the session? Very few of you have the pleasure of the lash, and this may encourage you not to seek its embrace, although this vermin seems to like it. You take him with the Officer."

Tom slumped to the ground, and was half dragged to what passed as a hospital for a cursory inspection of his bloody torso, with some liniment applied. After that he was carted to his room at Gellibrand's.

"It is clear to me that continuing with this man Scrimshaw is a waste of our time and my money," Gellibrand said to Samuel after inspecting the damage.

"There are others to fill the gap. You have my authority to seek his re-assignment and get a replacement. Please attend to it."

"It will be done," Samuel replied, pleased. "He will be discharged from your office."

A wound healing in Hobart. One other reckoning there was being mirrored by another, far away. A change.

✳

Across the world in London, Officials in the Colonial Office contemplated yet another lengthy report from Lieutenant Governor Arthur in the Hobart Town Colony. The Chairman stood and addressed the table.

"We have a complete drawer of the Governor's complaints and justifications for his actions as administrator of the Colony. Fortunately, the Colonial Inspectors have different evidence from their inquiries. It must be said and acknowledged that his reputation as an administrator was and remains excellent, although he is determined to support free settlers over all others. While of itself admirable, it has unacceptable outcomes.

"It is deeply unfortunate that he continually calls the Aborigines 'savages', as well as naming the convicts we send to assist in the development of the Colony, as suffering from a delirium requiring severe and firm discipline.

"While we may send some criminals who might conceivably have peculiarities which manifest themselves from strange eccentricities, it cannot be the case that all of them do. He exhibits an evangelical strain which is not within the philosophy we now espouse, and there is an inflexibility in believing in his own rightness.

"It has led, and let us be frank here, to a policy which is one of extermination of the Aborigines, the 'savages' or 'Blacks' as they are also known in the Colony. The Governor has not called it extermination and now refers to it as 'conciliation,' however, the inspectors' reports concur that it is too late for that aim.

"There is an irony, too. The Lieutenant Governor was an enthusiastic supporter of the abolition of slavery. Yet his practice of an effective extermination of the native population, at the behest of settlers for interfering with their property rights – rights of which it is doubtful the original inhabitants attain any concept – is an indelible stain on the English Government. That stain must be obliterated as much as is possible.

"Are we agreed that Lieutenant Governor George Arthur should be recalled, and replaced with an official more sympathetic and in tune with the philosophy and enlightenment of The Empire's progress?"

The group nodded assent without demur, adding mutterings of their great concern.

"Thank you. I shall draft an Order of Recall and arrange for its transport to the Colony on the next available vessel to sail there for delivery personally to His Excellency. I shall be mindful to commend his excellent administrative abilities, but suggest it is time to consider a further use of these skills with another appointment within the Colonial administration."

The Chairman mused to himself whether His Excellency was still the man to shine the light of the Empire into the dark corners of the earth. Perhaps a few quiet words with him on his return might be of benefit. He had his doubts. Administrative efficiency and righteousness were uncomfortable bedfellows.

CHAPTER 7

Hobart to Port Arthur, 1836

"It is most satisfactory that Scrimshaw is discharged from my service," Mr Gellibrand told Samuel. "Mr Cochrane must indeed be desperate to take him on. Learning about court attendances, such as his, is light relief for the populace from the daily skirmishing with survival here. There is, to be true, little by way of distraction unless one is fortunate in having a loving family."

"It is very much so, Sir," Samuel said, agreeably. "I have no doubt the standard of work will improve substantially with his reassignment."

*

The new officer contingent surveyed their new surroundings at Port Arthur. On the short voyage from Hobart, it had been impressed upon them that there was nothing south of the entrance to the Port but the terrifying expanse of the Southern Ocean, and beyond that the Antarctic, where no man dared venture.

This was not quite true, as the settlement itself was tucked away in a cove to the left of the entrance into the inlet, and therefore, there was some protection from the incessant wind hunting for them. There was a small island in the inlet. On arrival at the Port, older settled officers explained that there was a whaleboat with a crew of trusted convicts who practised in the inlet for the occasional important visitors, either accompanying His Excellency from the Town, or on their own volition from further afield; Sydney or as inspectors from London.

It was a place harsher than Hobart, and it was meant to be, working hard the convicts sent from England, from other penal settlements in the Pacific, and the more intractable convicts from Hobart Town thought unlikely to contribute to the development of the settlement.

Port Arthur was not a settlement, but a prison; a prison open and confident that prisoners were not going anywhere. Hard labour; so hard to be too tired to escape, quarrying, road building, digging coal, felling giant trees, dragging them to the cove and cutting for timber, boat building and building structures for officers, officials, other ranks and the cells for the prisoners; a long, narrow building on the south side of the cove. Many prisoners were in chains, outside the prison confines of cleared land were hostile natives and rumours of fierce creatures unlike anywhere else on Earth. Where would anyone go?

Human nature, however, determined that there were attempts to escape, and recapture was a welcome diversion, as was confrontation with the original inhabitants to their disadvantage. It was rumoured the natives set fire to the Bush, as alarming palls of smoke were seen in the summer months both in the Town and the Port. It was thought they were attempts to terrify the settlers into leaving, although another view, from a former convict, was that the fires were used to flush out prey. Whatever the explanation, the only escape was to death itself. No escapee not recaptured had ever been seen again; victims of hateful bush, snakes, natives, wild creatures, fire, or the sea, if they got that far.

What, though, was there to do? The old enemy was boredom, without any of the modest social outlets of Hobart. A store stocked mainly from Hobart, occasionally from other vessels; a butcher, a brewery and not much else to occupy anyone. Some hunting by officers yielded fresh meat from wallabies, and there was some fishing. There was nothing for the wives but their own resources; for the men, impressive amounts of alcohol from the brewery, from Hobart, and spirits from the Northern Hemisphere.

A welcoming dinner was organised in the Mess in the Officers' Barracks. After they had all settled with the ladies, old and new, glad for an opportunity to wear their finery, one of the host officers rose to speak.

"Officers and ladies, you are most welcome to this little part of... er... paradise. It does have charm and interest but you will need to commit long and hard to find it. The search itself may be your outcome. We do not lack for much in creature comforts, certainly compared to those we watch. It is sobering to realise that some of these inmates are of good education and were of professional standing before their character defects brought them so low to be here."

"But," interrupted Stuart Bell, "there is no incentive to desire any improvement in bettering themselves here, nor to believe that they can. Where would anyone escape to for a new life?"

"Yes. We are impregnable." He paused. "Or nearly so. Shall we tell our new friends the little saga of Eaglehawk Neck?"

"Ah yes." Another longer-standing officer replied. There were snorts from the officers and titters from their wives.

"What on this part of Earth is Eaglehawk Neck?" Henry Lynch queried.

"We are on a peninsula. The bottom of it. Nothing below it you would want to go to. I am sure you recall from school that a peninsula is an area of land jutting into water, joined or linked to a bigger piece by a narrower piece. We are joined to the main part of the island by a piece of land barely fifty yards wide. Cold sea on either side. Not a place to get into, with sharks and other monsters. It's the same on the land, in the Bush. No sharks there, but tigers and devils aplenty, and they will eat anything, including us. This narrow piece of land connecting us is called Eaglehawk Neck."

The new wives shuddered.

He continued. "Prisoners have built a road from here to Hobart Town to serve the little farms and settlements between us. They feel safer and get supplies from us and Hobart, and they also sell their own produce. It is rough and ready, and some prisoners come down the road too, rather than by sail. As a used road, there is a need for protection. We have sentries at the entrance into this peninsula from the Town. Nothing much for them to do, besides some fishing. They get relieved from short-term duties.

"But a month ago, one of the sentries saw a large wallaby hopping very strangely across the Neck towards Hobart. He thought it was injured. When he got back here, he told us that a bit of fresh wallaby would be a change from the rations he got from here, and fish. So he raised his musket to shoot it, and the cock was heard by the wallaby.

"'Don't shoot!' the wallaby shouted. The sentry nearly fell over with shock, he said. It turned out to be one of ours who had got that far despite the hazards of bush and water, and nearly got eaten by one of us."

There was a general collapse into laughter and table slapping by the men and giggles from the ladies.

"What happened?" Andrew asked.

"He was kept by the guards until the next handover. Kept warm in his new skin. He'd caught a wallaby, ate it as he moved, and kept its skin for warmth. He stank beyond measure, so they let him wash in the sea while they had muskets at ready. He had warnings about what was in the water that was hungry too."

"Is he back here now?"

"Yes. It must be said, he is regarded as something of a hero by the other convicts, and he has to be given respect for getting as far as he did with such resourcefulness."

"I would hang him as an example," Francis interjected.

Marianne looked at her husband, surprised by his vehemence. Rebecca looked at him too, but saw him differently; a man of decision and action, so necessary in the recent war; not such a nation of shopkeepers. She admired his moral and physical stance. A man destined for a future in the echelons of the military.

The officer continued. "It showed the determination which makes our country a beacon to the world."

Rebecca was not so sure about this statement of optimism. Firmness of purpose, as Francis demonstrated, was more her way.

As Francis had popped up, an officer asked him, "How did you come by such French names with the recent wars?"

This was a source of irritation to Francis. Both he and Marianne were born during the Napoleonic war. She was unconcerned about her identity with the symbol of France and that irritated him too, as a proud Englishman.

"I understand there was a French ancestor, a Huguenot who escaped persecution by coming to England, as a good Protestant. A trickle of the French since. I have a sister named Amelie. It is most unfortunate. A shortening of my name does not assist. I turn my face firmly against that shortening."

"A rose by any other name would smell as sweet," said Andrew.

The group laughed at the interjection. Not Francis, who darkened and retorted, "May we ask how you came to be a combination of Scot and Welsh, not English?"

"I have no idea. I surmise that one Scot and one Welsh greatly enjoyed each other's company. I have the best of all worlds, being born in England. I merely lack the luck of the Irish."

"And you, madame?" The officer spoke directly at Marianne, the deliberate French usage annoying Francis.

"My mother loved the sound of the name as most mellifluous, and its association with flowers, bees and honey."

The officer's wife spoke up, with a synchronising nod. "Such a delightful association then, and no connection with war or politics. There is more to life than eternal conquest."

There was a murmur of appreciation, except from an unmollified Francis, and the party continued until the time came to separate the men from the ladies.

When the ladies retired, the men indulged in cigars, a delight picked up by officers from the Spanish campaign, and in Madeira.

"Madeira? Where is the Port?" Stuart was alarmed at the prospect of a lack of that particular tipple.

An officer raised his glass. "Madeira sails the world. Some magic in doing so makes it invincible. It never fails. Here, at the end of the world, it is perfect for us. Port, though, is less certain," he advised. "Certainty is a necessity. Enjoy."

"I would much prefer the certainty of knowing how long I will be here." Francis said, after savouring his first sip.

The officer drained his glass. "Some make it back to glory, some to oblivion. Some like it here, as a new world fit for exploration, to stamp their mark on it now for the future. Some think being here is being tainted. It takes time to decide where you are in this maelstrom of possibilities."

"I am quite certain, quite clear. I know my way forward." Francis's firmness precluded further discussion on the matter, and left the focus on cigars and Madeira until it was time to seek the ladies and depart.

The ladies, having retired, turned to the matters occupying them, utilising their joint and several intelligences to create a sense of wellbeing in their restricted community. One of the more established ladies sat forward in her chair to announce.

"I find that artistic pursuits are most conducive to comfort and pleasure. I have arranged for artistic supplies to come from London, sometimes through the Town. There is such scope for endeavour in these surroundings; such landscapes, such flowers and sky. I am most amenable to introducing you to such pleasures if you wish to avail yourselves."

Annabel and Sara murmured appreciatively, although Rebecca and Marianne remained silent. Marianne suspected the local efforts would closely resemble those in Hobart, transposing the settlement to the South Downs, not the forbidding darkness of the land and the almost luminous sky when cloudless. She was interested in sketching and painting, when she was more sure of herself and more in tune with the rhythms and melodies of this land. She had, in any case, a much more pressing matter to attend to, and reminded herself to make the acquaintance of the resident midwife.

The topics moved to fashion and concern that their own chosen apparel would be outdated in London in particular, and there was frustration that they could do nothing about it. Warnings were given on not walking too far into the blackness of the Bush and its hidden terrors. The young wives took this advice to heart. Being listless and bored from lack of opportunities was preferable to being adventurous and dead.

Nor was Hobart in danger of somnolence while Tom was present.

*

Tom Scrimshaw again found himself in the police offices. If the court was busy, as it usually was, he contented himself with counting the boards in the ceiling and the number of knots in the boards and which had the most. It gave him something to do and at least his brain was flexed, if not much more.

"Scrimshaw!" His name was called.

In he went to the senior magistrate, and into the box doubling as accused for criminal cases, and defendant for civil skirmishes. He also entertained himself with surreptitious looks to see whether there were more scratched initials in the box from others like him since he was last in it.

This occasion was at the behest of his new master, Mr Cochrane, who had a smaller property and a number of other assigned workers. He was a devout complainer and without fear or favour in doing so, not only about his workforce but against authority and administration unless it suited him, or on the available food, the weather, his wife – for whom Tom had some sympathy, although she scurried away on seeing a Magpie, as if fearful of being pecked to death. Whether that imaginary end would have been ultimately better than death by a thousand miseries at the hands and voice of her spouse was still to be determined.

Having taken the oath, Mr Cochrane began. "This criminal, who I took as a reassignment from Mr Gellibrand, gives me great cause for complaint."

The magistrate stirred. Both accuser and accused were well known to the court, although this was their first appearance together – although he thought, glumly, probably not the last. There were more important matters for his court, and he was stuck with this irrelevance.

Mr Cochrane continued. "The day before last, I went as usual to supervise the labour I had given this wastrel to perform. He was to repair a fence and gate. I saw from his efforts that the gate squeaked, which I found intolerable, and I told him so. He replied, and I forthwith went to my home and made a note of his utterance while it was fresh in my mind. It was thus:

'Stick yer head up yer arse and take a breath.'"

The magistrate allowed himself a slight smile. There was a little more humour or imagination in this convict than he had thought was contained in his skull.

"This was insolence, gross insolence, Your Honour."

The magistrate turned to the Magpie. "Anything to say, Scrimshaw?"

"Thought his head needed a change of scenery and refreshment." Tom said boldly.

To his surprise, the magistrate found he was enjoying this little exchange. However, he had a long list of cases to get through, and it was important to be seen to be supporting the settlers of which this awful man was one, against troublemakers, of which Scrimshaw was a prime example. He would therefore have to satisfy Cochrane, whom he did not much care for, with a punishment Cochrane would see as sufficient punishment for the damage to his sense of self-importance.

On the other hand, Scrimshaw was apparently impervious to punishment, no matter how inventive, and would not be unduly concerned by whatever was meted out. A reasonable solution, then.

"I find the accused guilty of insolence," (Cochrane was disappointed it was not gross insolence), "to a reputable member of the settlement. I therefore sentence Scrimshaw to the chain gang on a hulk in the harbour for one month."

Tom was taken away to be placed in chains and a different type of labour. He would at least learn more about boat construction and have rest from Cochrane's incessant whining. Mr Cochrane had to face the prospect of Scrimshaw's return in a month. He was regretting taking on this man.

*

His Excellency stared at the official communication handed him from its transit on the latest Transportation vessel from London. The missive bore the official seal of His Majesty's Colonial Office. This was unusual. The established routine was that he would keep the Office fully and carefully apprised of matters pertaining to the Colony. There was consequently no reason for them to write to him; the silence to date indicated approval of his actions.

Nevertheless, the letter needed opening. He had almost forgotten how to break a seal, but having done so, prised out the contents and read it. He read it again, and again. It was an appreciation of his work in the Colony, which he had set out in such detail, and His Majesty, fully approving of his most able administration, had reached the conclusion on the advice of his learned officials that his abilities would be better utilised in other Colonies needing fine and sympathetic discipline and direction. His Majesty therefore commanded him to return with his family to the Colonial Office in London to discuss the future, for the mutual benefit of The Empire and himself.

"Eliza! Eliza!"

She heard his unaccustomed roar and hurried towards the sound.

"Eliza! Look!"

He handed the letter to her. She read it, and suppressed her own feelings of relief. A return to London after more than a decade away at the end of the world was a prayer answered. She and her children would benefit so much from exposure to proper schooling and a different, real, world. She could not say so though, directly.

"Oh dear... but I do recall you saying, years ago, that promotion was your passion. The letter can only be read as an appreciation of your work here by His Majesty and the Colonial Office. It must mean a promotion! And it will be so good for the children to experience life in London and our dear country. That must surely be good."

George Arthur had to agree with her words. It was the way to interpret the Order, even though there was so much more he wanted to do in conjunction with the settlers to make sure the Colony was self-supporting, Christian and a model for the Empire. The dice was cast. They would go as required by His Majesty to attend to greater challenges and attainments. They would leave before the year was out.

*

Joseph Gellibrand was similarly on the move. He sent a servant out to find Samuel and bring him into the drawing-room.

As Samuel was ushered in, Gellibrand had news for him. "Samuel, I have a billet from Governor Bourke in Sydney. He has failed our Contract, the contract I drew for the purchases of Port Phillip lands at our expedition. His *Excellency*" – he spat out the word – "writes that under the principle of *terra nullis* no one owns the land in Australia; the Aborigines can neither sell or assign it, and we settlers cannot buy it. Only The Crown, through him, can distribute it, although I cannot see how he can, in effect, claim ownership to do so any more than we can.

"I am, shall we say, most grateful that he was not Governor here, else how would we have bought this land we have; nor could the Lieutenant Governor himself, as an assiduous purchaser of land here.

"Governor Bourke is prepared to recompense us with compensation for our trouble. Nevertheless, it is my firm conviction that the Association members would have profited more had our proposals and plans met with approval. How the Governor will exercise his discretion we do not know at present.

"I am minded to go again to the District and explore other possibilities. It is possible that with development there, even on the present terms, the District will warrant its own Governor, as here; and that may be a more amenable route to what we desire."

CHAPTER 8

Port Arthur, 1836

In late May, after her arrival in Port Arthur, Marianne was delivered of a baby girl after careful monitoring and assistance from the resident midwife. Both mother and daughter were doing well; a major hurdle surmounted in the Port.

Francis peered at this new adjunct as the fruit of his loins. "Ah, Eliza."

Although exhausted by her labour, Marianne reacted to the announcement of her daughter's name.

"Eliza? Why do you insist on the same name as Mrs Arthur? Do you not think it slavish and productive of a laugh from our friends? We already have Arthur."

"I do not relish hearing these words from you," Francis admonished. "It is my duty to seek promotion for the greater glory and enhancement of the Empire with such abilities as have been bestowed upon me. In doing so I am confident my efforts will be rewarded and that you, as my wife and mother of my children, will come to bask in the benefits of my achievements."

"I do understand your reasoning, dearest, but is it not compatible with a less overt demonstration of a desire for promotion through His Excellency? It will be noticed."

"I believe His Excellency is fully apprised of the execution of my duties and will make due recommendation."

"Can we not properly name our daughter Elizabeth? If she is known as Eliza or wishes to be called by it, or some other variation, it will still be open to her. That way, you maintain your step to promotion without being so transparent, or thought to be. I must insist on Elizabeth as her birth name, howsoever she is addressed in person."

Francis stared at her. This was unexpected from an officer's dutiful wife. Nevertheless, he felt an unease which led him to consider it. "Very well. Elizabeth it shall be, but Eliza she shall become." He looked down at them both.

Marianne looked up at him. "Now leave us, please, my dear. We have had a long journey." And she pulled the bundled baby Elizabeth snugly to her breast. She felt her husband had tightened his grip on life; a life which seemed not to be shared as it once had been.

*

In Hobart,The Assistant Police Magistrate flopped morosely into his chair at the police office, which often doubled as a court as it was this week. Before him lay the list of cases due this Session, prepared by court clerks. It was going to be a long week. His mood was not improved by the dousing he received from the storm still hammering down on the roof. It was not so much the cold as the unseasonably miserable weather. His fine English leather boots were not up to the job, and his feet were wet.

Listlessly he flicked down the first of the many pages, and groaned. His thoughts tumbled over each other. 'Yet more wretches with which to spend my life. Am I no better? I read, I write, more than this lot can, or nearly all. Yet we are stuck together in this place. Why should God not sit in Judgment, not me? He has Heaven. I have Hobart. He must have laughed when He created this place, and in uproar when I came here. What an experience in the application of the law I was assured. These little ants building their little nests. Need a Magistrate, they said. Need God for the law, say I, and long may He enjoy it.'

His ruminations, if such they were, ended reluctantly as the entrance opened into the court. His clerk entered to sit at the side of his bench, to announce the cases and take notes. He was followed by members of the local papers, ready to regale their eager readers with tales of vice, crime and human misery about which they could feel exceedingly pleased with themselves.

Better not read these tales of iniquity in advance, he thought, and preserve the modicum of surprise. When the spectators were seated, he nodded to the clerk to commence the rigmarole on which judgments would in due course be handed down. His, not God's, alas.

The clerk read out the parties to the first case and the nature of the charge; one of petty pilfering, it appeared. The Complainant gave evidence while the bored magistrate drew little pencil sketches on his notebook.

"Does the Accused admit the charge?"

"No, Your Worship."

"Any witnesses?"

"Yes, Your Worship."

"Call the witness." At least he would be unbiased compared to the to and fro-ing between the parties.

"Call Thomas Scrimshaw."

A surprise he had not expected, and the magistrate sat upright. Scrimshaw's appearances before him or the senior magistrate were usually quick. He was insolent, rarely disputed anything said against him, made little jokes (always bad), and did not care what the punishment was. Now it seemed he had witnessed a crime. Was this another of The Almighty's jokes?

There he was, a clothed Magpie, not bared and bloody to the waist as the magistrate fondly recalled. Here they were, face to face in the higher witness box and the bench.

"Take the Oath." The clerk handed him the Bible.

"Why?" Tom asked, a defiant tilt to his unshaven chin. "What has God done for me? What fear or threats of death after what's already been done to me? I can say what I like, when I like it or not. God and you can't change that."

The magistrate was shocked.

"Are you refusing the Oath to your God, your King? Are you indifferent to the truth – prepared to lie, I say, prepared to lie?"

"I don't know what you're talking about with 'truth', Tom said. "You don't need it; at best a guess, at worst what you want. God alone knows what happened, and He's not talking. You just guess, to help your settler friends and to bang us up. Say what you like; enough of us sink in this shithole without you poking more in."

"I must warn you. I have power to make you regret what you have already said. Will you take the Oath?"

"Ask your bloody God. He knows everything."

"This is blasphemous!"

The pair looked at each other with contempt.

The Assistant Police Magistrate took a deep breath, sat back in his chair, and thought for several minutes while others in court were agog with what would come next.

The magistrate sat forward.

"By your refusal to take the Oath, by your utterances, you have committed the crime of Prevarication. Justice demands truthful testimony in evidence from witnesses sworn to tell the truth without which this court – any court – cannot function. You have demonstrated your contempt for truth and justice in what you have said."

He paused again, to gather his thoughts in his anger.

"I have before me a long list of matters on which I must adjudicate in this week's Session. I do not wish to delay the justice they seek, even if you do, Scrimshaw. I will deal with you at the weekend.

"Clerk! I want the record of this man Scrimshaw which is filed here in the records section upon my desk, on Saturday by 10am. I regret the imposition this man has caused but it has to be done. Guard! Take him to the cells for bread and water until Saturday then bring him before me at 10am. Notify his Master of the situation. I will deal with the present case on the evidence we have, and then continue with the list."

There was such excitement in the court. The guard seized a calm Scrimshaw and hustled him out of the court into a nearby cell, door open, as if already ordered.

The magistrate was unsurprisingly in a foul mood on Saturday morning. An arduous week making some people unhappy in varying degrees, and still no input from God. It afflicted his normal solace at the weekend, the clerk's too, and even the newspapers, although the titbits would be worth it. The clerk had brought in the records after the court rose on Friday, and accordingly when the magistrate arrived ten minutes before time, he had further time to irritate himself.

On the dot of ten, Tom was brought in, and roughly pushed into the Accused box, with the clerk present and then a rushing of the entrance by the papers' representatives.

The two men stared at each other once more. The Associate Police Magistrate fixed his spectacles more firmly to emphasise the seriousness of the situation, and regarded the record before him.

"Hmm." Tom saw him run his fingers down a page and his lips move in counting the entries. He stopped, and announced.

"There are thirteen entries; thirteen entries under your name. In five years and some months since you arrived. It is obvious you like it here; that appearing in our courts is a sport relieving you of your labours. Let me see. Drunkenness, fighting, insolence, away without permission, frequenting the houses of women, given a letter to deliver and being found three days later drunk on the floor of a public house. It is astonishing you are still alive, with alcohol for blood. Punishments: Bread and water, treadwheel, chain gang, the hulks, solitary confinement, the lash... the lash... ah... three lots... twenty-five, twenty-five, another of thirty! Adds to eighty of the cat o' nine tails. And it has taught you nothing. Nothing.

"You are indeed a pest. A blot on the manuscript of this Colony. How I would greatly enjoy seeing your carcass swing in the breeze, the debris of Man, a wreck to founder the Colony. A wanton waste."

"A cursed place, a shithole and you swim in it!" Tom retorted.

The magistrate continued over the interruption.

"I am sworn to uphold the law, and the law does not permit me, alas, pleasure though it would be, to have you hanged and rot for these persistent offences.

"However, you have added the crime of Prevarication to your litany, and I have raised the matter with His Excellency. Nothing here has turned you into treading the true path His Excellency ordains." He paused again to show his importance.

"I therefore sentence you to hard labour in chains for two years, and with a recommendation that you be removed to Port Arthur. It is a settlement close to His Excellency's heart, and he will make the final decision. You come within his category of incorrigibles I believe, and Port Arthur would indeed be most fitting.

"You will be removed to your Master's property and remain under his supervision until the decision is made. As you remain an assignee of your Master, he is to provide for you in accordance with the Rules until that decision. Guard! Take this reprobate to Ordnance for temporary shackles to minimise further mischief, and thence to his Master's forthwith."

Tom was taken out for the Order to be met, and the newspapers' representatives rushed out.

Mr Cochrane was aghast to find this dreadful convict was marched haphazardly along the roads to his property, in full view of passersby and others, and had ended up back with him. It was worse to learn what the possible sentence was hanging over this demonic individual and why. He harangued his wife over the iniquity of how a caring, hard-working man as himself should be so burdened. She immediately closed and locked all shutters, windows and doors to protect them against this monster, until the seeping knowledge materialised that she had locked her devoted spouse in with her, too.

Tom had no such cares on his stumble through the streets. Known or unknown to those who saw him, did not matter to him. Here was a possible hole better than this one. The Port was spoken of in hushed tones, largely because nobody known, or rumoured, to have gone there, had ever returned to say what it was.

As he trudged the roads to Mr Cochrane's abode he realised that nothing Cochrane could complain about him engendered any interest or significance over the magistrate's sentence and Governor's decision, which was to be made very shortly. In the meantime he could, basically, ignore any instructions from Cochrane, whom he understood had no real support in the Colony. By the time Cochrane lodged yet another complaint about him, he was probably off to this Port wherever it was. But he could complain himself about Cochrane not meeting his obligations to *him*, and the Governor was said to be particular about that. A small rest. Pity no comfort inside it was available.

So it proved. New levels of insolence were conjured up. Mr Cochrane was beside himself with anger, frustration, a raised heart rate and impotence at his situation. Enough rage indeed to engender two

Cochranes. His wife opened the shutters, carefully and quietly, for chinks of light she fervently prayed were from The Lord, hearing her entreaties and planning her deliverance.

*

At daybreak three days later, the door opened to his cramped room at Cochrane's.

"Hey you! Up! Boat's waiting for you. Get your bag!"

In the chilly morning sun, Tom shuffled as best he could under escort towards the quay. He saw he was not alone. Other Magpies were shivering there, too. Where was this boat going out of Hobart? It hit him that the Governor had made his decision. It was to be Port Arthur. The Port Arthur. No-one came back to talk about it.

Hustled into the bow of the ship along with his misdemeaning fellows they found no bunks, just the hull to find rest on, with the irritation of shackles, bones and flesh against the bare bones of the boat. When the vessel was complete with its human and inanimate cargo it slipped its mooring and headed out into the Southern Ocean that rushed forward to assail them.

A few hours later, in the enforced silence in the hull, the vessel tossed and bucked less in calmer waters, then they felt the lapping of shallower water, and then a sense of halting and muffled voices. There was new noise aboard the vessel as well, and then a barked 'Up and Out'!

Although Marianne had arrived in the Port before Tom had exhausted the anger of authority, the speed of response, once determined, expelled him into the Port a couple of months before she was delivered of Elizabeth.

Tom looked around him. The vessel was moored in a small port, like a cove, tucked off an inlet; a small island within the inlet. Here there was no mighty threatening mountain, but plenty of lesser ones... and the inevitable wild Bush. Did this land have nothing else but dark, dank, lurking Bush?

Clearings had been hacked out by convict labour. Buildings huddled along the more protected sides. There was a long, large one... to accommodate what? Must be for inmates. Lesser, better-looking buildings he assumed were for officers and administrators. And there were others; were they stores, an inn maybe (though not he imagined for the likes of him), a brewery to go with it? A bakery perhaps, and a building with animal pens attached and movement within.

Animals? Slaughterhouse and butchery? Amid and beyond were some cleared fields with crops and vegetables, by the look of it. And there were other buildings and structures of unknown origin or purpose. The Port was trying hard to be self-sufficient.

And activity. A lot of it. Men labouring in quarries, felling and hauling huge logs, erecting more structures, building boats and wharves. It was designed to be hard labour. Well, he was not afraid of it, even if the ways around it were narrower than in The Town.

An immediate personal activity, along with all prisoners, was being shepherded roughly off the boat and directed to a large building. Inside it had the familiar look of ordnance. Off with the Magpie garb, which was almost a personality itself, and on with a new, all-yellow outfit bearing stencilled P A arrows. Before he had pulled it on, the official looked at his torso with its raised latticework.

"See you were friends with the magistrates in Hobart. They're keen on the lash there – your back's a picture. Not a picture-book here, though, to show off in. And I see you have irons to wear. You're in the right place."

He half turned and shouted over his shoulder. "Hey Jim! Out here, another customer."

Tom had not noticed, in the dubious excitement of a new set of clothes, a door at the back, through which a man appeared in an apron. A blacksmith. With a cursory glance at Tom he took a pair of iron rings linked by a chain about four feet in length. "Stay!" The only word he uttered, as he moved to Tom, bent to put a ring around the ankle of each foot, adjusted it, disappeared briefly and returned with two bolts and hot tongs. He put a bolt through the two ends of each ring to tighten it further and seared each bolt with hot tongs. A rush of heat, smell of singed hair and it was done.

"Go into that room."

Tom followed the pointed digit, and shuffled off clutching the chain to allow him to do so, and with unfamiliarity struggled to open the door. When managed, he found a man dressed in grey sitting at a desk, with a sheaf of papers before him.

"Name."

"Scrimshaw."

The papers were shuffled.

"Right, Scrimshaw. What can you do, aside from being pest enough to earn your trip here? I see you had a trade as a shoemaker, which might be useful here sometime. Anything else?"

"I did some work on boats." This was partly true, having been pressed into helping the carpenter aboard the transportation ship.

"Anything else?"

Tom shook his head. Moving stones wasn't something he dearly wished to return to.

"Through that door, across the cobbles. There is a guard by the large door at the end. Large structure. He will take you in." He was awaiting the next interviewee.

Tom did as bidden, slowly, and in crossing on the cobbles he noticed across the water in the cove, a gibbet; occupied. He closed his eyes briefly.

The guard had a large key which he inserted into a heavy wooden door, turned it, and with a very strong press pushed the door open to reveal a long narrow corridor with doors set into the wall on the left side. Some twenty yards along stood a sentry, musket at the ready, and by him a narrow door was open. Tom edged his way slowly along to it.

"Get in. Welcome to Paradise Gardens." The sentry laughed and pushed him in roughly, so that he stumbled. The door closed and a turn of a key locked it behind him. Tom grabbed the bed end to steady himself, looked up and around. 'So this is *home* for life? We'll see'.

A room; no, a cell, perhaps ten feet long and five or six wide. Enough to have a bed, blanket, stool and a bucket. There was a small, high window for some begrudged light and air, pushed in by wind eddying always, always. It was usually cold and wet. The walls, floor and ceiling were of stone and all seemed damp. Was there another floor above? He was, at least, used to privation and punishment, unlike some of the inmates who had come directly from England. They'd have a real shock.

He wondered what they'd get him to do, then decided he was too tired to think about it. He would find out soon enough. He lay on the bed as comfortably as he could, closed his eyes and waited for the turn of the key. He would adapt to whatever came; that was how to survive.

*

Francis Wainwright came into his quarters, slamming the door behind him. Marianne looked up from feeding Elizabeth. Ann, the maidservant who came with them from Hobart, had charge of feeding Arthur, with soft meat from the butcher, potatoes and peas grown in the local soil. Marianne noticed he had flushed cheeks.

"There's a boat in from Hobart, from England with some wretches, some from Hobart." Francis was animated. "Captain said he had news from the Colonial Office for His Excellency. He has been recalled. Recalled to London!

"Has he orders to bring us back as well, perhaps? We have done enough here! I am most anxious for promotion, after all my endeavours in following orders punctiliously. We can but hope – nay, certainly expect – to hear from His Excellency very shortly on his plans for his officers."

"That is exciting news. I am so glad for you – for us!" Marianne corrected herself. She was still adjusting to this new world, and found new discoveries popped into view and demanded her attention. She saw, if not necessarily for her, how people could settle here and make a living; hard but rewarding on what was virgin land. Was that not what The Empire did? The native people showed no interest in cultivating the land or its animals, nor any interest in the warmth the blanket of Christianity brought to the Empire. Here, forging it would accord great satisfaction.

Her husband barely heard her correction. His mind was already planning on ways to emphasise his achievements to His Excellency's attention, such that he could not fail to recommend his return to England for promotion. He mused aloud, although she was not sure she heard it all, with Elizabeth absorbing her time as well.

"The Governor brings visitors here from time to time; some are Inspectors of Colonial matters. He likes to take them around the Port to show what has been achieved in taming this wilderness. There is a whaleboat he uses, crewed by experienced, trusted sailor convicts. They practise here."

He raised his voice, as she had made no comment.

"Have you seen a boat, called a whaleboat, in the water? Seen rowing around the island?"

She shook her head. Different types of ships meant nothing to her, except they made her sick. Whaleboat? Were there whales here?

"The crew needs supervision. The officer doing it so far said he was bored. I shall offer to take it over; make it ship-shape as they say, when His Excellency uses it – and that he knows it." He reverted to the Governor's full title when expecting to be heard formally.

Francis went to a cupboard, took out a bottle of rum and poured a measure. This was a signal, designed for him to be fed. He awaited that outcome with some impatience while he brewed his plan. Marianne, with guidance from Ann, had developed her cooking as a refinement to the rudimentary skills learned in Hampshire, and juggled her maternal duties with culinary exploration.

*

"Out!" The shout through the open door. Sunlight? Darkness was still in charge. Tom stumbled to his feet, chains clanking.

"Breakfast's down there." The guard pointed down the long corridor. Tom staggered up then fell over, forgetting the impediments to movement, and worked his way down the passageway. The Governor's feeding routine he knew.

Then, after breakfast, a shouted voice. "You! On boats. Building, not sailing. There!"

There was no shortage of yellow clad workers, some in irons, nor of guards with muskets. All had allotted roles. Tom was given his tools for boat construction, and continued building boats day after day, new light to gone light, in Sun, rain, gale, chill. He knew the routines of old. Rules were rules, but there were always around or through them, especially when lacking daily supervision from Hobart.

Boat building came from logging the great Mountain Ash, which was dangerous with axes and saws and in dragging the logs. But men were expendable in the great goal of making the Colony, in all its settlements, self-sufficient.

Days blurred into weeks of axe, saw, rope and splinters - logging, hailing, wind, rain and ceaseless labour. It took Tom some time to realise, as he shuffled about in his heavy chained irons, that there was a togetherness among the loggers, the coal miners, the haulers, the boat and quay-builders, a camaraderie shown in a general murmur, a noise he could not initially tune into. Water lapping in the breezes, he thought, although it was still around on calm days.

He began to focus on his closest workers and what seemed to be a tuneless tune; there was a general purpose somewhere inside it, and words too, although made more indistinct by the various accents and dialects in which it was couched.

During a lull in activity while waiting for more supplies, he whispered to a man wielding a hammer. A guard was nearby with a primed musket, and the prospect of this man hammering anyone was reduced, even if thought about.

"What's that noise?"

"Noise?" He chuckled. "Na. Our little song. Keeps us amused. Something to occupy heads as well as hands."

"How does it go?"

> "This is the arsehole of the world
>
> We're what's spat out to rot;
>
> We be the vermin of the world
>
> Never leave this stinking spot."

He sang it low, in a singsong voice.

"Not cheerful, is it?" Tom's verdict.

"Sometimes we sing it like a kids' round. Bit different. Extra noise."

"What about the guards?"

"They join in."

"What!"

"They're out of Earth's bum too. There's not so much between us. Only irons and blisters. It keeps 'em occupied."

Tom saw the need to keep the guards occupied. Bored guards were much more dangerous for random cruelty and spite. Petty irritations had to be dealt with within the rules. Going outside the rules led to unpredictability. Better that the guards shared their breaking.

His adviser continued: "We share little ditties. We're all stuck like fleas on dogs. All dogs here scratch together."

Sound was forbidden in Hobart. But here, facing nothing but the frozen south and expected death sooner or later, spirit was alive and – if not exactly well – not dead either. The words were not difficult, and Tom found himself contributing to this informal howling. Other ditties were also in use, and as a measure of resigned content it helped protect everyone. "Stops us goin' mad. Guards too."

*

Contentment was not a friend of Francis Wainwright. Insinuating himself as the new superintendent, as he announced himself, of the whaleboat and its attachments, particularly the crew, he introduced a harsher training regime to improve stamina and technique, although the crew as experienced sailors needed no advice on technique from an army officer, and he generated ill-feeling.

Francis was convinced His Excellency could not fail to be impressed when he made his anticipated final tour of his Port. It stood to reason that he would either announce openly or draw up an Order leaving Francis in no doubt that His Excellency applauded Francis's shared passion for promotion. Promotion would follow as surely as sun crept over the mountains to warm, slightly, this small settlement.

The Governor did indeed come, along with wife and children. It was now inconceivable that the name would ever change and that was gratifying. The family were met by a welcoming party in which Francis ensured he, his beautiful wife and their young children had to be seen. Francis introduced himself and the family, which produced a cursory raising of the gubernatorial eyebrow. The Governor's wife was more friendly. Marianne bowed her head slightly, watched intently by her husband, but with a perceptible touch of embarrassment. Mrs Arthur was a sensitive woman and understood the privations and distances of an army wife's world. She wished Marianne and the children well and looked forward to hearing of their future lives. Marianne smiled her wonderful smile, and Francis was pleased at the exchange. Was that a sign that a change was in the offing?

George Arthur requested a tour around the Port and inlet in the whaleboat, a vessel well able to handle heavy seas if required. It was, however, a bright day with a light breeze which permitted a sail and tiller. The boat was rigged in anticipation and the family boarded, along with Francis, leaving Marianne and her children on the quayside with the rest of the welcoming party.

After a couple of hours' sailing the boat returned the Arthur family and Francis to dry land. The Governor turned to face the group.

"I am most pleased, most pleased with what I have seen and what has been achieved at this settlement. It will aid the self-sufficiency and the independence of the Colony as a whole, even if the prisoners here are sadly of the sort who are in such grip of delirium to be of not much value other than in what can be managed under tight discipline."

Francis waited, holding his breath.

"Now I must return to Hobart to prepare for our departure." Governor Arthur continued. "I wish all of you well and to be safe in the Hands of Our Lord. Farewell."

With that his party returned to the boat which brought them, boarded and set sail.

Francis was deeply disappointed. There were words of praise for what the Governor had achieved but nothing on the rigours Francis had imposed, the success of the tour or even the crew who had put the boat to bed, as it were. He drummed his fingers on the dining-room table as he contemplated the day's events.

He could expect an Order on the next boat from Hobart, or at least some indication... Mrs Arthur hoped to hear of their future; that was reassuring. He poured himself another rum. There were some compensations in this Godforsaken place. Spirits for the officers, an inn for lesser ranks which brewed its own beer. He was astute enough to recognise there had to be consolation and distraction to make life bearable, stuck here because of human dregs sent from an England glad to be rid of them. Sent here, to share with Blacks, sharks, snakes, peculiar wild animals. There it was. He would have to wait for the call to return to England, however that call manifested itself.

A few days later, Henry came into the Officers' Mess and encountered Francis sitting at the table.

"There's a new boat in. Usual disgorgement. They came through the Town. Governor Arthur has sailed from Hobart. There's been much cheering from the settlers, for all he did for them."

"Nothing else? No messages or instructions from Hobart?"

"Nothing said, nor offered. More hungry mouths, more of everything... Fortunately, more spirits will cheer us up." Henry placed a full bottle of rum on the table.

Francis was not cheered. Was something overlooked on the boat? Should he not go and check?

He remembered Marianne saying he should not be overt. It could be a missive from London for recall. But that could take months, perhaps a year to get the Governor's recommendation, have it approved through official channels and communicate it to him. Another year here. Good God! What more could he do? His fingers drummed frantically on the table.

"Do you have to do that?" Henry asked. "You do it often, and it is irritating."

"Francis stopped, himself irritated by the request. He got up from the table and went without a word to his quarters. There he could drum his frustrations as he pleased, and have some more rum.

Marianne was out, probably walking somewhere with the children and with her friends. He could see that she had little to do aside from the children. No good works to do, except looking after him. No one was happy, although at least she was calm. Why was hard to fathom, in this hole.

CHAPTER 9

Port Arthur, 1837

Tom surprised himself by adapting better to life at Port Arthur than he expected. His cell was deliberately small, damp, dim and designed for a life indifferent at best or brutal and short at worst. Work was harder and heavier than in Hobart. Stone, coal, wood all risked life, limb and a man's internal workings. The weather seemed determined to trip a worker into added hazards.

While focused on humiliation and insignificance, conversely it induced both ingenuity and stoicism. Anger and frustration made no difference to the aimed arrow of no future. Life had to be made bearable within prison constraints. Understanding what it is, living with what cannot be avoided, avoiding what can be, adapting what could be, and turning to advantage what must be.

There was also a recognition by the inmates, intuitively or by murmur, that despite the constraints and rigours of Hobart imposed by Lieutenant-Governor Arthur, things were more relaxed here, out of his sight. That was a bonus, but it risked unpredictability, and knowledge conquers uncertainty.

Brian, a thoughtful man in his early fifties, worked on boatbuilding, turning huge logs into manageable timber to shape for the demands of hulls, beams, masts and decks. There was an unspoken understanding between prisoners that a man's reason for being in Port Arthur was no one else's business. Prying was not tolerated. Nevertheless, a man's intelligence could be recognised with the ability to winkle out useful information.

Consequently, Tom came to learn about the Ticket of Leave. A prisoner who had served a proportion of his or her sentence – the proportion to be determined at the Governor's discretion – who had demonstrated contrition and had not caused the authorities any concern, could be permitted to work for a wage. There were conditions, and the happy recipient was still His Majesty's property and could summarily be recalled to continue sentence. While the system operated in Hobart, Tom had been too busy irritating authority to hear about it, and with a life sentence such a thing would have seemed out of reach in any case.

But now there was... something. It suckled that fickle and unruly baby: hope. A clever ploy by authority, to allow hope to peer through the keyholes of their cells, to get them up at dawn and down again after dusk. Be good, and who knows? Not a return to the Mother Country. Few had any attachment to England any more, even to think about it; there was no guarantee of a welcome there, and many were relieved to leave behind a miserable life, which may have been responsible for their crime. There was also the little matter of finding the fare back.

For all serious and practical purposes, leaving Australia was not a realistic prospect, or even entertained as an idea. Moving to another Colony was possible, but Van-Diemen's Land had claimed them, and the Ticket of Leave barb pointed there. Thus, Tom settled into a routine with a range of possibilities that began to kindle hope of a better future.

*

Acquiescence also took root in the collective mind of the wives. There was nothing much to do, with servants on tap, and they relied on native intelligence and creativity to stimulate some enjoyment. Gossip petered out until the arrival of each new boat to perk them up. Mrs Arthur's advice, reinforced on their arrival here, kept them firmly cemented within the boundaries of the settlement, and the weather was not conducive to lunching on the local grass.

Marianne and her two small children, with Elizabeth not yet walking, and Annabel, who had a son a little younger than Elizabeth (as Marianne called her when Francis was out of hearing) had a shared interest as mothers, an interest to an extent shared by the fathers, and underpinned by servant help.

"The dear Lord must have been here to do nothing. Did he come before he went to Jerusalem and then died? There is nothing to do. What a place to prepare to die... Breathe clear air and die? Like us, really."

This was from Sara, not normally given to rumination. "Why he would come and go, except for boredom, and to do the Almighty's bidding I do not know."

Her friends were not clear on her meaning, but the references to clear air and boredom, they understood.

More recent arrivals cleared the air, in a manner of speaking, about the lack of it now in dear England. "We grope around in fog and soot. It is good for us, the government says. Clears out our lungs," remarked a new wife, out of earshot of her officer husband. She coughed, and coughed again.

Exercise was better than being stuck inside with desultory piano tinkering, fiddling and sewing. It allowed sketching outside, and all agreed that the air was bracing when one dressed for its vagaries and, although not yet ready to try sketching herself, Marianne remarked how astonished she was by the sheer blue of the sky, as if all air between her and the Sun had evaporated and it was as God intended; sky so clear it almost sparkled. Rebecca remarked that without air, sparkle would not come. She was not of poetic caste of mind.

Elizabeth being born on the cusp of Winter, and with Arthur still very young, bracing walks were out of the question, not only for young mothers Marianne and Annabel, but for wives generally.

Rebecca's dilemma was that she had no desire to see any more of this frozen waste, with its added human and animal contributions, than those absolutely unavoidable, and the winter months with howling winds hurtling up from the very realm of death further south, gave an excuse not to do more. The trouble was, being stuck inside quarters with fires blazing risked being smoked like an English haddock, as well as coughing in the gloom, and with the inhabitants trying not to reveal their frustration and irritation with everything and everyone, themselves included.

The weather warmed up in the last few months of the year, which made some little trips possible, although an irony from the God so glumly assessed by the Assistant Police Magistrate in Hobart decreed that these were usually the wettest months of the year and not conducive to English shoes or prams, The finest, driest weather was in the first few months of the year, and those inhabitants of the settlement able to hibernate or been frustrated by rain were able to venture out. The yellow wearers had no choice, nor their guards, with their simple contrapuntal ditties as some token amelioration.

When out, the wives walked around well-trod paths in the Port area. They could not fail to be aware of the constant, unrelenting activity as a counterpoint to their serene progress; the yellow-garbed prisoners, the officers, officials, guards, some others in grey, or was it blue? The ladies took it as obvious that they should ignore this male activity when they paraded in fashion carefully selected from their wardrobe; an opportunity to display, oh so safely, and of no consequence for themselves.

There were complaints that the clothing and footwear, their own as well as that sent from the Colonial Office, did not last long in this climate. Scrutiny suggested the Colonies got lesser quality of materials and tailoring. The men, too, grumbled over the poor quality received from London.

Nor could the women ignore the noises, shouts and screams that occasionally erupted. Naturally, their solution was to ignore it. Or, more subtly, a matter of looking but not looking. Pretending not to. These were criminals after all, and to get where they were they must have done unspeakable acts deserving banishment from decent people. The ladies nevertheless paraded to be admired as unattainable beauties, and therefore a lesson for the prisoners on what their iniquities had cost them as spectators.

The prisoners certainly noticed the women. It was unavoidable, and a distraction from toil. The guards, too, enjoyed the promenade of ladies picking their way over ruts, lifting their dresses or sloshing through partly set mud, wearing the *de rigeur* bonnet. They were (guards and toilers agreed, with shared glances and asides) all beautiful, desirable women, and so indeed they appeared, to varying levels – although for the men, any female would receive the accolade. Such visitations enriched their dreams.

Marianne wondered whether each of the prisoners in their yellow were so different, or so much the same? They had criminality in common, although different crimes. They had different sizes and shapes within their common yellow. There must, she mused, be thoughts in their heads as we have, though certainly not the same thoughts as us. She shivered momentarily at the fleeting image of what could settle in the rough, criminal mind. Perhaps she should entertain herself by comparing and contrasting these human beings with herself, or more realistically with her husband. She would be careful to watch unobserved.

Formulating these thoughts gave Marianne reason to embark on her perambulations, in the balmier months when it was acceptable, and which gave so much enjoyment to these groups of men. While the first year in the Port, and the demands and ages of her children prevented any meaningful wandering, aside from weather constraints, she was keen to observe discreetly what she thought worth observing.

Initially, she tried taking the children along with Ann to help, and on walks away from noise. But it was hard work, more than she expected with the children's demands, the condition of the roads or tracks, and the general rubbish she saw. She could not concentrate on her self-appointed task, and after a few efforts she abandoned it. Ann was relieved too, and there was an unspoken accord between them. The walks with the children had not gone unnoticed, nor the walks she took without them.

She waited for a fine day and for Francis to be off on his duties, grumbling again, which she now accepted as part of their life together. The children were fed and occupied by Ann, who entertained them as best she could, telling stories and playing games with Elizabeth now beginning to walk, and Arthur more boisterous. So Marianne set off that balmy day dressed modestly, she thought, and suitable for whatever the weather might surprise her with. It did happen. She decided she would walk down to and along the track by the water. Freshly launched boats bobbed in the little harbour; along the track on the shore men in yellow, some in chained irons, worked on a boat construction, with guards nearby. It was important to peek surreptitiously from under her bonnet.

Peering as she gracefully glided past, she was puzzled to think she recognised a yellow-clad man. How? She watched him with the interest she would watch a tiger in a zoo, wondering what it thought, what it could do if unrestrained. So too with this man, a little older than herself, perhaps though roughened by his time in the Colony.

In the Colony, is that where she had seen him? Was that Hobart Town? She had never spoken to a criminal. Could it be from the ship to Hobart, so full of them, all those years ago? This man, a little taller than Francis and bigger framed – did he stand out, or was this a usual convict size? It nagged at her. Something impossible disturbed her. Had she in her mind's eye, and her enthusiasm for something to stimulate her, decided this man was a true example of the convict body – on the ship, in Hobart, here, in Sydney, in Winchester for that matter – of what a man was?

She had very little knowledge of men in her family, and the concept of what a man was had not troubled her. Francis had been introduced to her, and they went on from there. Were there men like Francis but also another type represented by this man, this man in irons? She absorbed as much as she could and, in her struggle to make sense of it, she cut short her walk.

Marianne Wainwright had not gone unnoticed. Prisoners were used to being ignored by the wives, who usually walked in pairs or a group and clearly saw them as vermin. This one was out alone; odd enough, but also so lovely it was almost an affront to their senses.

Tom Scrimshaw stood up too, briefly as she gracefully passed by, to feast upon her loveliness. He, too, was disconcerted, although he could not think why. This young woman was far away, far above any woman he had ever seen, nor had there ever been or could be imagined to be a contact or connection. Yet there was, somehow. She had *seen* him. He was dragged from these thoughts by a shout from a guard to get back to his labour.

That night, she lay in her warm bed, her husband snoring beside her; and across the settlement Tom lay on his rough, narrow bed with a coarse, hairy blanket for company, aside from the scurrying of rats also shipped from England. Each of them was wondering what had made her journey that day so unsettling.

So disconcerted was Marianne that she determined to continue the walks to put to rest the cause of her anxiety. The walks continued but it was difficult with the uneven ground and, although she would not admit it to herself, she wanted to be alone on this walk, was glad to be alone on this visitation, as it became. She walked in a circular route she made to return to her quarters.

Sometimes she found herself with the company of a friend who fancied a walk, but it became known that this was Marianne's Walk and she was generally left to it. It became boring for the others. Her walks tended to be almost a timepiece for the men. When she appeared after organising her domestic day, the labourers could calculate where in the day they were in relation to dinner.

Marianne's Walk became a specific track worn by her feet. It did not help her resolve her quest. It was worse. She agonised why her feet took her to the same place every day, as if they had a life independent of the rest of her. 'Why do they hurry me to the boats, to sneak a look at him, and dig themselves in to stay, when my mind says it is time to leave? I cannot say why or help it, but I must go and see what I want to see, need to see and be near. I have my dear husband and my children, but still I come and tear myself away as if there are hot stones in my shoes – not to stop me coming, but going.'

She did not know what to do in her confusion. She decided she must have a fever; fevers either took you off or you recovered. This fever was relentless. The rest of her, too, was detached from her will. She felt an urging, a sighing she had never had before. Why had her mother never spoken of this, this nagging within her? Had her mother not felt it? She knew this was sinful. She was wild within, and evil. She knew her thoughts could not go in the diary she hoped to leave for Elizabeth. Her daughter would be appalled at her sinful, wayward mother.

One day he was not there. She panicked. Had he done something terrible? He was in the Port for a reason, or for many reasons. Terrified to look at the gibbet, she had to. Empty. Relief cascaded through her. He was not there the next day, nor the next, but on the next the gibbet had a swinging guest. No! Surely no! She hollowed inside. A closer look:

it was not him. She cried under her bonnet, went home and straight into her bedroom.

Tom, too, suffered the agony of not seeing her occasionally. Was she sick? Had she died in this unforgiving place? Did he see children once or twice? Were they sick or dying, dead even? Then she reappeared and his internal churn subsided.

The puzzle of the recognition of each other in the other intensified, even accepting the impossibility of it, although dreams and desires filled their nights.

Tom lay in his scratchy bed, muttering to himself in frustration, excitement and bitterness. Looking but not looking, she knows she is safe with me in irons. She knows I know; she knows I would give her one; lots and lots and lots of ones, different ones like what Jane taught me. I see her hungry fingers twitch in the pale blue gloves she loves so much, and I will feed them and her me. I bet when she's flat in bed after her humping husband has had his hurrah, she aches as I ache inside this lousy blanket, and she thinks about *what if*. Me too. Will she think of big, strong and dirty kids with me and not that spindly brood with him, and ache more?

Long months wore the path to the shore from a tormented Marianne, unable and unwilling to change her course. Was it this wild land which deranged her, made her a sinner with sinful thoughts which never leave her alone and sustain her? May God preserve her from herself. In her confusion of duty and desire, she turned to dear Jane. What would *she* do? What would she say? Did she feel the all-embracing sighing as I do inside me, did she write on desire? I read so much of her. I cannot remember whether she did. I am so confused. But she must know of these things, and the helplessness. She at least had an end. Her books, too. I do not. She does not help me, she cannot. This is a different world with unnatural laws. I am alone and with him and not. We are together and never. Joined and apart.

An idea spurted into her mind as she lay in bed. *Yes! Yes! Why did I not see that, do that!* Her eyes closed, her breast pounded as she awaited the day.

The next day, which threatened a shower of two, she left for her walk, with her small umbrella in case of rain. Down to the wharf she went, with her secret look primed to see him, toiling, and knowing he knew her. Down past him she went, with her feet itching to stay. But she urged them on, and she moved out of sight as ever, while each of them ached. Tom knew the routine, and it would be until tomorrow before this slow, elaborate, wanton dance stepped and ground its way in the stubborn soil of Port Arthur.

Then, one of his fellow labourers whispered, *"Look!"*

There she was, walking back to go past them, again. The men could gaze upon her twice, and two people could rejoice in their shared gaze and longing, unacknowledged by the others. She could retrace her steps, instead of going in a circle to where she lived her ordinary life. So simple, so obvious, and yet she had not thought of it until that last night in bed. Her feet hastened to leave, so they could return her, slowly. Nor had her thought occurred to him; one view of this unattainable beauty was all he could expect in reality, if not in his nightly realm.

Now a double helping of their feast; one way, then the other, stretching over many, many months, even in some inclement weather. Though she ached to walk in all weathers to see him, prudence nagged that she could catch a chill in the vicious winter months, and die, and that was not to be countenanced in her having young children. Still, there was any other excuse for the walk, her walk, to and back. Both ways, with the two Janes as Janus.

There was also Rebecca, who on occasional walks with Marianne along the worn track past the boat constructions, noticed a faltering in Marianne's steps as she arrived by the boat skeletons. Rebecca, as an acute observer, noted a weird correspondence between the hesitancy and a particular man in yellow. Some walks were the circular walk, then, later, Rebecca noticed steps were retraced. To Rebecca, all convicts were alike, though clearly not to Marianne, as the pace picked up after a slow progression, almost as if there were a reluctance to leave the scene. Rebecca cast a glance at this one and he was nothing special to look at; a bit bigger, a bit older, probably, than themselves; and certainly would be terribly smelly. Revolting. It was inconceivable that there could be any meeting or recognition. Marianne had been with her in the boat, in Hobart and now here. Very odd.

*

Mr Gellibrand called his numerous children to him in his comfortable Hobart house.

"Your father – me, I am delighted to say – is going on an adventure."

"Ooow!" came squeals from the assembled small Gellibrands." Can we come too, Papa?"

"Not on this occasion." He smiled indulgently, the smile of a father of confident importance. "But when I come back with my discoveries, I am sure you will want to come on more explorations."

"Where are you going?" asked his second son.

"Do you remember when I went to the Port Phillip District, across the Strait to the mainland? Well, there is a lot more land to explore in such a huge place; land for sheep and cows and wheat and good happiness to be taken, and I am going with a friend to whom I have been writing letters to find more of that special land."

"Will it make us rich?" shouted another son.

"Well, it could – but it will take much work, and you will have to do it too. Will you?"

"Ooh yes," came the chorus; the thought of riches, however each child saw it, was enough.

"Your mother and your helpers here will look after you while I am away, and Mr Samuel will look after our sheep and lambs and all that. Will you be good and help them too, while I am gone?"

"Yes, papa!" was the shout.

He bent to give each child a hug and kiss, and sent them off to their schooling and attendances from the servants.

"Where are you going, do you know?" Mrs Gellibrand asked, looking up at her husband.

"Just inside Port Phillip there is a small area off to the west. There is a river to explore, which appears to run west and south. A lot of Bush, but from what is known there is ample rainfall and good soil. Clearance will be needed, but it sounds ideal for grazing, and it is not as cool as here. I have been corresponding with Jasper Scholtz, who knows a little more than I do, but there is much yet to explore. Others will be trying too, so we must take any advantage of opportunity. He has found and retained a native guide for the area, so we will be in good hands."

"It sounds fine and safe enough, dear, and I can see your enthusiasm and the possibilities. We will miss you very much however, so you must return to us very soon. Do you know how long you expect to be gone?"

"Hmm. I would expect about three months. It will all go well, my dear."

"May The Lord be with you."

He bent to her. Their arms wrapped around each other from their different heights. They kissed happily, affectionately. Gellibrand broke away, went to the waiting carriage already loaded for the expedition, entered it, waved to his wife and Samuel waiting outside, the horses tugged him towards the moored and waiting boat, and he was gone.

*

"There really is something obsessive about Francis," said Andrew Morgan to his wife as he entered their quarters.

"Why?" Rebecca replied. "How so?"

"He took over – well, really took it upon himself – to supervise the whaleboat crew. They are trusted men with marine experience who practise for the arrival of any important visitors as well as the Governor. He hoped his efforts would impress our late Governor. It did not, or not obviously.

"Undeterred, he is convinced the crew are not working hard enough and that is why the former Governor made no comment. He has increased their working, and they are complaining that his treatment is unfair and unnecessary. The complaints only make him angrier, having his beliefs and methods challenged. Just like Governor Arthur, really. He therefore increases it further and they are now saying they would rather labour on logging or digging coal. Francis is obsessed with wanting to leave here, and with working out ploys to get promoted."

"Nothing wrong with that," Rebecca mused. "I want to get out of here, too. There's nothing to do, nowhere to go. I wish *you* exhibited more desire to leave."

His bright blue eyes stared at her. "I do. I *do*. I want to resume my career as an officer. It will come when the situation demands it."

"Well then, I wish you showed as much effort as does Francis. I believe you would have been better suited to Marianne. She seems content enough in this dreadful place. She even seems to be a favourite with the convicts, or at least one of them, in irons though he be. The convicts are very keen to see her parading past."

"Rebecca! This is nonsense at best, and disrespectful of our friend. How do you come by this slur on Marianne?"

"I walk with her sometimes for something to do on a pleasant day around the Port. I have seen her reaction in walking in a certain way in a certain place. *Their* reaction can be easily imagined."

"You are there, too. You could be the recipient of their admiration. You are a very attractive woman, my wife, and these men rarely see a woman of any description. Is it not possible that you are the source of their enthusiasm? Let us hear no more of these untoward rumours and speculations."

With that, he went into the bedroom to change for dinner.

*

Five months elapsed, yet nothing was heard from or of Joseph Gellibrand. No exceptional weather storms were reported in any known relevant areas to explain the silence.

Mrs Gellibrand could wait no longer. She organised a search party with local men more than willing for some adventure outside the confines of the glorified prison that was Hobart, and of mainland men found from contacts in the mainland District after letters going to and from. A native guide was obtained from the tribal area where the missing men had been heading, along with suitable provisions to anticipate the unexpected in virgin territory.

"May God be with you!" Mrs Gellibrand cried out to the party as they set out. Then she cried for herself and her children. She hoped she could show the fortitude her husband would expect of her in consoling her children over their absent father. Then she cried again.

*

"Francis is showing great ill temper. To us all." Andrew slumped at the table in his quarters, and pulled his boots off.

"Remember the whaleboat? It has gone missing. Instead of returning to mooring after one of Francis's punishment sessions, as the crew call it, they have left the port and inlet. They usually go around the island, but they straightened up and went down the inlet. No one thought it was other than part of the punishment.

"But look out the window. It is dark outside. The weather is clement and expected to remain so. There is no reason for a boat to shelter from a storm."

"Where are they, then?" Rebecca wondered.

Andrew shrugged. "Francis can barely control himself from sending boats out tonight to look for them. He will organise a little flotilla at daybreak."

A man of action, murmured Rebecca to herself. Very softly.

Marianne was shocked to hear her husband use profanities that night. She understood the general tenor of what had happened and the anger at the betrayal he felt of the trust he had placed in these so-called men of honour. She went to bed, heard him pacing in the dining room, and the increasingly common sound of gurgling into a glass before she fell asleep.

He was gone by the time she awoke, and she set about her domestic routine before she could hasten on her longed-for walk, trying to look as casual as she could. A prisoner had the advantage of being in the same spot. She wrestled with herself over her obsession, or fever as she preferred to see it, and the Why, and secretly so happy that Why was always vanquished by the Yes!

But before she could leave, Francis returned.

Oh, dear dear... what would the man, *her* man, in yellow think when she did not come at the expected time?

"I sent out boats for this scum. I will keel-haul them when they are brought back. The net is cast wide, and I *will* have them." He sat, and continued: "I found out that they were buying supplies from the store, individually. No suspicions arose. Food, water, repairs useful for a boat, extra sail. They planned all this after all the trust I put in them. They will pay dearly for this ingratitude."

But there was no news, either of the missing whaleboat or of Mr Gellibrand. Then, five days after the disappearance, the search flotilla limped into port from various fruitless scouring of the seas. Francis demanded an account of the voyage from one of the captains, who replied.

"We saw nothing but a whaleboat. When I asked what they were doing, they replied they were looking for the missing boat too. We both continued our search. I hope they had better luck."

Francis was apoplectic, his face puce.

"You idiots! That *was* the missing boat! Is the world full of imbeciles and sons of whores? Or only here? How did the French lose the Wars with you wandering around the seas? Get out, get out before I put you all in irons!"

He stormed home.

"Are you all right?" Marianne asked gently.

Her question vexed him greatly. He neither felt nor looked alright.

"Stupid woman! Do I look like I am alright! I am surrounded by idiots, fucking idiots!"

She recoiled. She had never heard him use such awful language before. It was most unbecoming. She had seen his behaviour change with his sense of being trapped and cornered in the settlement. She did not know how she could help him regain his old poise, but she felt she should offer him something.

She moved towards him and put her arm upon his. He looked at her with wild hatred and suddenly punched her left cheek. She staggered back, a hand to her cheek, feeling the pain of her injury, already swelling. He seemed not to have registered, but turned abruptly and ran out, slamming the door behind him.

Marianne fell back into a chair and wept. Her world was a spinning spiral she could neither control or stop. She was bereft of all guideposts.

Dazed, she gathered herself and walked slowly into the room where the wives gathered after their morning duties and to chat. There was great excitement. Stuart had been up early. A new boat had arrived, and one of his duties was to supervise unloading.

He had learned from the master that Britain and the Colonies had a new monarch. A Queen! News travelled slowly to the end of the Empire, but there it was. A young Queen. Younger than the wives. So much to speculate about!

Marianne slowly approached her friends, Sara and Annabel, who were surprised to see her at all. Their chatter stopped when they saw her, not only with her unlikely presence but her inflamed face.

The women gasped. A bruise had developed on her left cheek, her eyes were glistening from tears, and she was clearly dazed.

"What happened, dear Marianne, what happened? This is awful!" Sara almost shrieked her shock.

"Oh... I must have walked into the door... sorry... so sorry."

This explanation was so implausible that the wives were of one mind of the cause. It was unimaginable that an officer's wife could be so ill-treated. They were very aware as officers' wives that in unguarded moments, the men could let slip that the wives were mere extensions of themselves and could be lopped off if necessary. That belief came with a contrary understanding of correct behaviour in marriage.

Sara and Annabel did think Francis was somewhat rigid and humourless and imbued with self-importance, and even more so in recent years; an impression reinforced by occasional comments let slip by their own spouses. But this behaviour was beyond all acceptable limits. Yet individually and instinctively, they knew they were helpless.

This was outside their experiences and there was no practical help or advice they could offer. The settled response was to ignore it and offer a generalised sympathy, making a mental note to watch for any recurrence. Relief, too, that their own husbands were not prone to such horrible outbursts.

The new Queen was, temporarily, forgotten.

CHAPTER 10

Port Arthur, 1838-39

"Scrimshaw!" The voice shouted outside his cell, disturbing the rat which had adopted Tom. A surprising shout; usually it was a large bell that woke the inmates, clanging loudly for the day ahead.

Tom stirred, and as was his routine, rolled out of bed, still with his clothes on for warmth, and wrestled on his boots. Although changed every six months as the rules demanded, no-one from the officers down had any confidence in the longevity of the items sent from England. They received extra wear from his irons, which was allowed for, but chafed ankles were the norm.

Out in the corridor, he was pointed in another direction than usual, and he set off with the guard following behind.

"Straight ahead. Open the door at the end. Out and turn right and go into the building across the yard."

It was a small building he had not really noticed because it did not fit with his habit. What, and why? In he went, and saw an official and near him a blacksmith.

"Scrimshaw, your two years in irons is up. Your time here, while not ideal, has allowed removal of your shackles. As only a blacksmith can lock them on, a blacksmith must remove them. Here is the man."

The blacksmith looked disinterestedly at Scrimshaw, came to him and within a short space of time, and with some discomfort, his reluctant bedfellows for the past two years were free to clamp on another.

"Now, breakfast and work as usual."

Marching was not yet the right word to describe his gait, as he had to quickly retrain his lower body and balance with this new freedom. Understandably, there was a spring in his mental makeup, followed by a spring in his liberated legs which suddenly felt impossibly light, as if he may become airborne at any moment.

Back at work, he was desperate to see the woman, *his* woman, as he thought of her, while accepting the reality... and for her to see him, with her surreptitious glances.

She came. He saw her. He needed her to see that he was free of irons. Dancing was hardly his forté, but as she drew close, he exaggerated his movements, which amused his fellows a little, though they recognised his joy. It was not every day a man lost his irons while keeping his sanity.

Marianne saw him too, and her day blossomed, like seeing the sunrise after a cold night. There was something odd. She could not fathom what it was and she stopped. He looked at her, looked down at his feet and repeated the little gesture twice. What is going on? She was confused. Had he injured his head, his neck, with his head going up and down, or something with his legs? Then, following his eyes, she suddenly saw there was a difference. He was iron-free!

Marianne smiled a huge smile. A laugh was out of the question from a lady to a convict, and she suppressed the urge. Immediate practicalities tapped on their respective shoulders. With a last look and grin, he resumed his work on the current boat, and she resumed her walk.

She felt she floated over the muddled piles of earth. So dazed by the sight, she reverted to her circular walk. When she reached her quarters, she allowed herself a squeal. It was so bizarre, this beautiful, well-born woman and the hard-skinned, hard-boiled man, with nothing in common at all. It was indefinable except that each defined themselves through the other; a new profound sense of who they were. Her two lives; one a wife and mother and the other; this woman and this man. I no longer know who I am, she thought, but I am new. She hummed to herself as she prepared for the rest of the day.

The Senior Officer in Port Arthur stood up in the Officers' Mess.

"I required you to attend, as I have news of some import. As you know, I regularly sail to Hobart to report on and discuss matters with the new Governor Sir John Franklin, and I am pleased to say he is content to rely on our good sense to administer this settlement without undue interference from Hobart, save for any necessary action from my reports and carrying out inspections from time to time.

"I am also pleased to say that a matter which so vexes us is one which also greatly troubles the inhabitants of Hobart; from His Excellency to convicts, just as here. I refer to the inferior quality of apparel which is sent to us from the Colonial Office, and which proves manifestly unsuitable for this climate.

"It is a principle that the Colonies should be self-sufficient, and Sir John has pondered whether it may be a ploy of the Office to send out inferior products to encourage settlements to do better themselves, with a concomitant eagle eye on the costs saved.

"He has therefore taken action to remedy the situation, and I am likewise instructed. We will collate and analyse all records of the prisoners here to determine what skills are recorded, or professed to exist, at the examination on their arrival. When grouped into skills, individual groups are to be asked for their requirements. When that has been considered, I will return to Sir John with the evidence. He has assured me that he will direct what can reasonably be spared from Hobart for our use, pending the response from London, which he is confident will be favourable.

"I will direct our officials here to undertake this work forthwith, and report to me in a fortnight for consideration. I may invite assistance from among you. I will consider another meeting like this to report the findings before I see Sir John.

"I will report the outcome of my further report to Sir John in due course, but we may commence work on structures while awaiting London. That is all, but the news is encouraging."

There was a general murmur of assent and head-nodding, but no questions were asked, before the officers resumed their duties.

The work was undertaken and presented to the Senior Officer and two other officers he selected.

Francis hoped for the call to take his place among them, but in vain.

The Senior Officer, as promised, called a follow-up Mess meeting.

"We received and analysed the work undertaken by the junior officials. I can say it was revelatory.

"When we looked at what was revealed, with the impetus of self-sufficiency not merely as guardians of wretched specimens, this settlement in truth has artisans with the skills and trades to successfully run a small town.

"We have forgers and thieves here who were previously architects and draughtsmen, accountants and even, or especially, lawyers!

"We knew of some masons and carpenters among their number, but there are others such as tailors, weavers and shearers, butchers, skinners and dyers, tanners and shoemakers, painters and carvers, plumbers and chandlers. Even a medical man.

"The Sydney settlement is flourishing and Hobart is heading that way. So too should we. I too am confident that London will agree, and gather appropriate equipment which can be sent directly to us. We must assume, even with Sir John's support, that it will take the best part of a year before we can take the road to self-sufficiency. Until that time, we can clear our paths to that road.

"The clerks will provide you with a list of prisoners' names and the particular skills and trades that they each possess. I suggest an announcement at breakfast, then reinforce the message to the groups you guard, explaining what is to happen and why. I do not anticipate any difficulty at all.

"We share the same view, and I expect there will be a marked increase in the amount and quality of work undertaken once they rediscover their trade and purpose.

"Drawings and plans will be drawn up by those we discovered, to give guidance; and it would be sensible to have particular groups involved in constructing any new buildings required for their future activities. They have an interest in it. It needs to be no more than wind and water-tight, with a floor and roof. Shutters for window openings when not in use or in inclement weather, where the chandlers will be useful. While logging and quarrying must continue, and coal mining for the warmth we all need, I will switch our carpenters from boat building to land building. We have built enough boats. Some techniques in building a boat skeleton and a land one must be interchangeable.

"I will report to Sir John with our findings and the plans and action I have initiated. I am sure there will be a complete accord, and I will press him for such equipment and materials as can be spared – or more probably wrenched – from Hobart for our use in the meantime."

Such a major rethinking and planning by authority meant a reallocation of labour among convicts.

"Scrimshaw! We are determined to make this colony self-sufficient. That means better boots and shoes than those coming from the Mother Country."

Tom nodded to the Officer. There was no disagreement. His boots had always been a source of pain.

"It is noted you are a shoemaker."

"Long time ago, I was, Sir."

"How much time was it?"

"I left school at about ten, learned trade till I was here."

"That was over ten years ago."

"Think so, Sir."

"Hmm. Long enough, though. I think you can be put to your trade again. Can't be worse than the rubbish we get sent."

"Yeah, Sir. Agreed, Sir."

"We will take you off boat-making for shoe-making. We have tanners and dyers here and butchers for skins, and we will have some help from Hobart with basic equipment to get you started while we await more from London. You might have to help build your new workshop; there are a few of you. It will be a future for you if you are good."

Tom nodded again. This was good news; a sniff of a better future.

It was not an overnight change. The number of shoemakers uncovered meant a new building needed construction, whereupon they might produce footwear efficiently. Tom found himself quite happily involved in its erection, with his useful ship-building experience. With others, including labourers and carpenters, a wooden structure was built on plans allowing both for expansion, and alternatively the natural wastage of injury and death. Then such internal fixtures and fittings for their trade, as could be made or scrounged from Hobart while awaiting equipment from England.

It came to pass.

*

Marianne was aghast. Her walk took her to an abandoned boat skeleton. No one there at all. Was there a contagion, a disease which took them all off? She repeated her walk over several days. No change. She could not raise it with her group. Could she ask Francis, uncertain as she was about him? The assault was cemented in her mind. She continued as wife and mother, now playing wife more by duty than love. The man she married was not this one. She had her joyous, secret distraction, impossible though it was. He could be ill; dear Lord, please not dead, just somewhere else in the Port.

Her group knew about the developments and were enthused about it. Finally, at their meetings, Marianne learned what was happening and was equally excited at the prospect of better materials locally sourced, and locally made. Newly resurrected artisans were inundated with demands. The irony was not lost on them; if working for themselves, there was so much eager money proffered they would need guards to protect their new riches.

As the laws of supply and demand operated, there was a burgeoning intensity with shoe and boot-making. Skins were available, initially from Hobart then from the Port itself, with tanners and dyers, although dyes were more difficult, requiring input from Hobart and London. The shoemakers were very busy. Shoes brought out from England were now largely unwearable; on special occasions the ladies nurtured them to totter about.

There were racks of shoes made up in different sizes for men, women and children, to cover the usual sizes and styles. Marianne's little group, having delightedly run the gauntlet of finding new dresses and other essential clothing items, considered it time to tackle footwear.

Entering into a large, newly constructed wooden building, the smell of leather permeated the air and their nostrils. A couple of bored guards were inside by the door, although there was no expectation that any of the inhabitants would flee, and they were guarding a number of men clad in yellow, either working at lathes brought from Hobart or sitting, shaping and cutting or stitching.

Rebecca nudged Marianne who turned to her, startled. Rebecca's eyes swerved right. Marianne's followed.

There he was, right there; sitting at a bench, absorbed in shaping leather. Her heart raced, her stomach fell. He was alive, whoever he actually was, whatever name he had. She took a deep breath, her breasts heaving. Rebecca noted it all.

"Come, let's look at the shoes, perhaps there are slippers too, something for the children."

The mention of children brought her back to reality, but not her inner life.

"Yes, yes." But he was alive.

"Look, look, Marianne. Over there. There may be something." Rebecca pointed to a shelf of paired shoes for women and girls, with another shelf designated for men. She hoped her raised voice would alert this man who so fixated Marianne and she, Rebecca, could enjoy the reaction. She forgot that there was no conventional communication aside from Marianne's fixation. He knew nothing of Marianne, not even her name, nor she his. There was nothing to alert him. He remained absorbed in his trade.

Despite mooching around and noisily trying ways to gain his attention, he remained impassive. Sadly, for all her efforts, she had to console herself with buying two pairs for herself and a tiny pair for her daughter.

Purchasing done, they moved to the door. Tom lifted his head from concentration and stretched his arms. His gaze at last caught her retreating back, her beautiful hair swept up and tied to her head. Lucky head, he muttered, cursing his inattention. If she bought, there was no reason for her to return. No reason at all.

Suddenly, he realised the promise of shoemaking came with a disadvantage. They had been able to see each other in their own way at the boatyard, but now he was here. No point in unfairness, that was one of life's rules. He was gutted; this was worse than the lash; this was something over which he had some control and he had failed.

"He was very busy with his work," Rebecca tried consoling Marianne.

"Yes," was all the response she got, but it told her what she sensed. It was beyond comprehension – an incorrigible convict and her friend; refined and beautiful and slightly otherworldly. How could it be?

Tom and Marianne's mutual despondency enveloped their lives.

Marianne went about her life, her outside life. Rebecca suggested little walks, waiting to see if detours past the shoemakers would eventuate with little hints about a visit to see how it operated. Then again, Rebecca had her own life and husband, although no child. She did not believe this fetid place, ideal in her eyes for human depravity, was fit for children whether by accident or design. She remembered the advice on avoiding pregnancy from Mrs Taylor in Hobart and was assiduous in following it.

Marianne was capable of her own walks alone, and Rebecca saw that she could have managed many ways to gaze upon this curious specimen. There was, she conceded, a sense – more a vague allure – in this man. Was it that which Marianne, sweet Marianne, swallowed as a contrast to Francis? An odd choice if so, to be sure, but each to their own, as the saying went. Perhaps there was no harm in a passing fancy. There was nevertheless uncertainty in Rebecca's mind on what was going on, and what would come of it. Impossible though it seemed, it tiptoed through her mind, rearranging her mental furniture.

Marianne had her clear, ordained, observable life, although that had been shaken by Francis's attack on her. The other life howled inside her. So much pain to wish away. She prayed to God to take it away. Was she in the grip of Satan, the seducer of maids? She was not a maid in the usual sense, but she must be in the Devil's clutches to be in so much pain, an ache, a torment she had when she thought of this man, someone she had never spoken to, a possible murderer who might, given the chance, do the same to her.

She wished, needed and desired a meeting with this man whatever then befell her. She would expiate her guilt, earn her passage back to God; a price she must pay. Everything had cost, in money or morality. But no resolution beckoned. Her parents had not told her how to live two lives, or what to do. What would dear Jane do? No, she mumbled, I do not want to know. What would she know of what haunts, gnaws at me? She turned away, and I am drowning.

Tom's God was survival. Do what is needed to survive, and build on the blocks of that survival. Like those blasted stone fences in Hobart. This woman was a fateful block. He could only think and dream and desire. She was far beyond him. Someone else was a lucky bastard. But she is there, always, teasing me. Bitch... no... that is not her, or her fault that I feel what I do. Her eyes, too, her smile, so warm, almost melting, when I shed my irons. Can't say more than those eyes, her mouth was not of a bitch, but warm and into my head and seeping down. I think words differently when I dream, and I am not the man I was. Dad said I would grow up, but like this? A slow horse pulling a heavy cart. That is what I am. But she makes me go faster and the cart lighter.

Such reveries occupied his restless nights and his long days with shoes and boots.

*

Stuart came bounding into the Officers' Mess post-breakfast for the deliberations of the day. He was supervisor of new maritime arrivals, unloading the contents and bearer of new news.

"Remember that disappearing whaleboat? When was it? No matter."

Henry sat forward. Francis went pale and his fingers twitched. Any news of that boat was not going to be good.

"Well, the master down from Sydney to Hobart had a letter from the Governor there to Sir John. Apparently, the whaleboat and crew, minus one who died, made it to a port called Eden, south of Sydney. Not Eden for them; they got caught there. The note said Sir John could have his boat back if he paid for the cost of its return.

"Sir John is not happy, not one bit. It gets worse. The letter also said he was not going to return the escapees, as we obviously could not be trusted to keep them, and they would be better off with him. To add salt, he said he was fully appreciative of their efforts to get to his Colony. They called in at Maria Island on the way for supplies, but found it abandoned. I think Governor Arthur said that.

"You have to tip your shako to the men. The Governor is not best pleased, to put it mildly, seeing it as a slur on his administration. Not sure what he will do."

Hammer blows rained on Francis's brain. He had made sure beyond doubt that he was in charge of all matters whaleboat, and his efforts had not only failed in the objective, but were now laughed at, and costly. His calculation on how to get out of Van-Diemen's Land with a promotion had blown away in the winds of the east coast. Rather than admiring the men's maritime skills, he saw himself sinking as they rose on the swells.

There was merriment, but not from Francis, only his drumming fingers.

"Francis, stop that bloody drumming, for God's sake as well as ours. God alone knows why you do it. I recall Governor Arthur was prone to similarly exercising his digits. Did you take lessons?"

Stuart spoke, full of cheer on this development. The men were fully aware of Francis's capture of the whaleboat activities, and it was only right he shared in the news, although his fellow officers were acute enough to see a light mockery was better than a serious confrontation over the diminished reputation of the Port.

However presented, it was beyond Francis to cope with it. Short of ideas and with no support from his fellows, he could but await the wrath of Sir John Franklin. He stood up abruptly from his chair and walked stiffly out of the Mess and into his quarters.

"You are back early," Marianne greeted him. "The day's orders and plans must be clear."

"Shut up."

Marianne stopped. She was mending a small tear in Arthur's trousers. "There is no need for such language, even to your wife," she said evenly. "Especially to your wife. I asked because you are back now, which was unusual. What is wrong?"

"I will be stuck in this hole forever!" He started drumming his fingers.

"Why do you say that? There are pleasures and opportunities here."

"Are you mad, woman! Opportunities? Pleasures? Festering, it is. You have no idea, no comprehension of anything. You live in fantasies."

"Am I mad?" Marianne put down her sewing and rose, stretching her hand towards him beseechingly. "Do I have fantasies? Are they the same? I know enough that you should not say these things to me, even if they were true. You are being most unkind and unfair. I asked out of concern for you. You seem to teeter on the edge of an imaginary cliff. What would your mother say if she heard you speaking as you are?"

She paused, frowning. "Could you please desist from drumming? It is most distressing."

This was outrageous. Not only was this woman, his wife, interfering with his knowledge of this putrid place, but invoking his mother, too. Intolerable. He stopped his drumming, but only to take sudden steps forward to punch her again, once on the breast, and again on the left side of her face.

Marianne staggered back, out of range of any further assault. As she recoiled, so did he. Both stared at the other; horror from her, hatred from him. He turned and left the room, slamming the door.

She slumped into a chair to gather what thoughts she could. How has it all gone so wrong? Is it me? Am I truly mad? Is this place a madhouse, a devil riding the winds? Am I alone?

'I do not know what I am. Did I ever? I stare into a chasm. From both sides. I jump back and forth. I peer into it. Is it the Devil in the darkness? Is he calling me? I fear I will fall. That I know. Who will save me from my desperate sin, my repugnant desires, awash in me? I cannot write these things, these feelings, this willingness in my diary of him. It will show me to be mad.'

Her eye fell again on the little pair of trousers. No more indulgent madness; there was work to do. She winced from a short stab which drew a pinprick of blood. It was no matter, in her troubled state.

Ann came in for her morning duties. Marianne sat calmly in her chair as usual, but with a bruise swelling on her face and, with intakes of breath, she spoke.

"Elizabeth is not so well today. I think she has a chill. I must stay with her to aid her recovery. Would you be so kind as to call into my friends and say I am indisposed from Elizabeth, and I will join them when she recovers."

Ann nodded, bowed, and left.

Having been jolted into the Port reality, as she sat she decided she needed a proper lovely pair of shoes. Not the sort to traipse around the local mud in, and have Ann scrape off the crust. A pair to dazzle on special occasions, rare though they were. She could go to the shoemakers and order a pair of her choice and design. The stunning blue light of the Colony inspired her. A pair of bright blue shoes, the colour of the sky. It must be possible. And why could she not choose who would make her shoes? As she was an officer's wife, Francis could not refuse the cost; it emphasised his importance in having a well-maintained and well-shod wife.

The thoughts crystallised into a resolution. The weather was turning autumnal with April in this topsy-turvy place, which would restrict outdoor activities. But she had a purpose, and the new shoes were for internal use.

Finishing her routine activities, and with Francis off on his duties, Marianne carefully prepared her toilet, put on her best new dress from the local tailor and set her hair carefully under her bonnet. Her eyes sparkled in anticipation of seeing him. Ah, suppose he was not there; sickness, other duties, a punishment. Such awful thoughts. The only way to find out was to go. She did.

Marianne arrived at the entrance. With a deep breath, she opened the door and stepped inside. The men at work were supervised, or rather idly watched by two guards, rotated during the day to relieve the boredom of having nothing to do. One guard was posted just inside the door, to catch an improbable escapee.

"Yes, ma'am, have you come to buy?" This lady certainly banished boredom. He pointed to the rack of women's shoes, and that would give him the pleasure of looking at her.

"No, thank you. I have come to commission a pair for my own use. A very special pair." She looked around. "I would like to choose a shoemaker to make them for me."

"I am not sure about that, ma'am."

"Why not?" Marianne was not going to be thwarted when so close to her plan.

The guard could not say; never had such a request been made to have a ready answer. He was also aware of this beautiful woman, as was every man who had seen her, and his instinct would be to do as she wished. Further, her husband was a very senior officer with a reputation for being hard and difficult, and he would certainly act on his wife's complaint, which could be very uncomfortable for him. It was therefore hard for him to say no without a reason, and there were reasons to agree.

"Very well, ma'am."

She smiled sweetly at him. "Thank you, guard." She searched the factory floor. "Hmmm." She looked around as if unsure, but her gaze was absolutely focussed.

"I shall choose that man over there." She pointed straight at Tom. "Please ask him to come so I can explain what I want."

"Scrimshaw!"

Tom looked up at the voice. What now? Then he froze. Next to the guard, inexplicably, was her. *Her.*

"Here!"

His legs were like jelly. He steadied himself on his work bench. He walked as if again clamped in irons. The closer he got, the more flawless this woman became. She was probably a few years younger than him in human years, but timeless and ageless. He could smell her personal unique fragrance. Their eyes locked. He saw hers grey, she his, blue-grey, near enough to merge as one. As he closed on her and the guard she could smell him, an animal waft which unnerved and excited her. She was stirred and warming. Once that would have been foreign and hateful; not now. She wanted to grab him. What was his name? There was an arm's length between them, and tentacles of tension bound them.

"Scrimshaw, this lady is a senior officer's wife. She wishes to order a special pair of shoes to be made here and she has selected you to do it."

"I'm truly honoured, ma'am," Tom mumbled.

"Thank you. I am sure you will make me a pair of such exquisite beauty it will stand the test of time, or in Paris at least. What is your name, Scrimshaw?"

"Yes ma'am."

"You have another name, a Christian name?"

"Thomas, ma'am, known as Tom."

"Ah, Tom Scrimshaw." She felt triumphant.

"Yes, ma'am."

She was uncertain whether she should tell him her name with the guard present, aching though she was to add to their minuscule store of knowledge. Such a time would surely arise.

"I wish to have such a pair that the Colony has never seen, of the colour of the sky, the dazzling blue sky, to fit me perfectly. I think it is called 'bespoke', is it not?"

"I think so, ma'am." Tom had never been asked to make a pair of individually ordered shoes in Lincoln. If it was called bespoke, then that is what it was.

"How long do you think it will take?"

He pondered it. A bright, sky-blue dye was unheard of to him, but there was no reason why one could not be developed in skilful hands. Somewhere.

"It is very unusual, ma'am. I'll ask the dyer here if he can supply the dye for the leather and dye it. He may well need to order it from Hobart or even Sydney. I cannot say. The time to fashion it for you will depend on its availability."

"How long once you have the dye? I want your undivided attention to the exclusion of all other work once the dye is available. I am able to pay appropriately and I can assure you that with a most satisfactory outcome, I will make recommendations to friends and you will have employment for your future life. For the benefit of you all."

At this, all work stopped. What was this woman saying? Was there a crack in the penal structure?

Marianne was amazed at the coolness emanating from her lips when she was aflame inside. The words came from a mannequin not her essence, unhinged though it was.

"I think about three weeks to reach the standard I hope is satisfactory for you. You may find some of my fellows here will serve you better." He dreaded saying these words, but could not say otherwise to this woman in a different world to any he had known or imagined being within a touch of.

She took the initiative, seeing their relative social positions made him reticent.

"Being bespoke, you will need to take precise measurements and details of my feet to ensure a perfect fit. I will tell you my style requirements while you do."

He froze again. Touch her! Was it five, ten minutes ago he was working on a pair of men's working boots, in a different world? Touch this blessed girl! He was unworthy. Nothing he had done gave him credit to do so. He thought of the Catholics back in Lincoln who were said to touch bits of statues of the Virgin Mary for blessings. Here was a live one, inviting him.

"Do you wish to take measurements now?" she asked, again astounded at her calmness with turmoil raging within her.

"Er... yes, very well, ma'am."

"Good. I shall sit over there." She gazed at a rather forlorn chair away from most activity, and from the guards. Over she went, sat down, composed herself externally, smoothed her elegant new dress, then raised it to reveal her ankles encased in a pair of still just-serviceable shoes from a far-off land.

Tom went to pick up a measure, with a shaky hand, and when he returned with a measuring tape, still with his odd gait, she had removed her shoes and placed them side by side at one side of her, so her feet were unimpeded, except from his gaze as she wanted. There were these beautifully shaped feet, pale and with a perfect arch, and toes which she wriggled with a girlish giggle, which surprised him, thinking of the calm formality to date, or was she nervous too? Measuring was a recognised shoemaking practice, but had never been called upon in the rougher situation of Port Arthur. Until now.

Kneeling before her, tape in hand, he marvelled again at her feet. She held her breath as he opened the tape and ran it along her right foot from tip toe to heel. She was gripped as was he.

She recalled the men talking about magnetism and how it enabled one thing, a metal, to stick to another, even if you held it upside down and shook it. Did it apply to people too? Yes, she concluded. Yes! It was here, his calloused fingers on her smooth delicate skin. A tingle which exploded as he moved and cradled her foot. She could not find the words.

He touched her big toe in measuring the other side of her foot, and she had such a surge she was alarmed she would embarrass herself; not now please, God. Within this magnetism she could feel his fingers trembling. Not the dreadful drumming she hated, but this was a sort of song and her little foot sang along. She heard him muttering measurements to himself. Then the other foot. More of the same. She hated spiders, but now wished she were one, with all those legs with feet to be locked to his fingers.

He, too, wanted to measure and measure again and again for the joy and pleasure of touching her. But he did not know how she would react in her calm business way, and the risk of ruining this treasure together was too great. The feeling of a paradise attained after years of privation and punishment would have to do. Survival. And joy.

The measurements imprinted forever on his mind, he stood up and moved away, watching as she replaced her shoes. These humble shoes, not what he would give her; the shoes she wanted would be a gift of love from him, a life sentenced as incorrigible, and she knew it.

When she had become the wife of a senior officer again, taming a pounding heart and flooding desire, she calmly said. "When shall I call again to see progress?"

"A week maybe, to see if the dyer can do it. If not, what the delay is."

"Thank you." She was delighted about delays, choosing what she thought would be a difficult colour even if she wanted it gave more excuses to come and hear of more hurdles and delays to give cause to bring her back. She then remembered to explain what she had in mind, removed her shoes, drawing patterns using them as a model. He nodded as she spoke, revelling in hearing her clear voice, staring at her feet.

She replaced her shoes and stood up, smoothing herself, with his heart, eyes and brain arguing where to look. Hers trying not to search any more into this man, this Tom. Not here.

"Thank you for your concern and attention, Tom. I shall return in a week to hear of progress."

She turned and went to the door, the guard opened the door and she left with unconscious poise, every man's eyes willing her to stay, and their mixed hatred and envy that this man had been chosen, when each of them believed they were better. At least she said she would come back.

It was not lost on him, either. He trembled, stirred all day, and had to repeat work. Optimistic dreams rampaged his nights.

Marianne's bright mood was not missed by Rebecca. Marianne had been subdued in the wives' group, contributing little. Now she had more to say; nothing of singular importance, merely more chatty. She also disappeared on her walks again, destination, if any, not revealed. Rebecca suspected the shoemakers' workplace was the key, although there was no reason, as she and the children were well shod and the shoes well regarded. The men looked after themselves. Where was she going, and why? As her absences were unannounced, Rebecca could not attach herself. It was most frustrating.

Marianne yearned for progress with the dye. It was elusive, being such an unusual colour. The sky was one thing, translating it to leather quite another. Being such a unique request added a frisson of excitement to this bond now between her and Tom, Thomas, Scrimshaw. She teased him by not revealing her name in her regular visits. She tried to limit herself to weekly visits but her disobedient feet took her there. "I was just passing by and wondered..." Guards and artisans soon accepted this stunning woman's regular presence, and were naturally in favour of it. Puzzled inquiries of Tom on how and why he had been selected, only brought a shrug and a shake of his head, which was partly true.

Delays were secretly desired too as an excuse for more "passing by" calls. But what was to be the end of it all she could not say. The realist in her said it would be nothing; it was an indulgence between two people not destined by class or future to be together, and meeting as they did was merely eccentric. The romantic in her, nurtured by her exposure to dear Jane, sat on the realist and saw wonderful possibilities dressed as Fate. The tension between the two states helped drive her on.

Unsurprisingly, Tom's similar thoughts were from a less romantic position, but his imagination had free rein in his cell when under his blanket and with a life enriched by Jane Taylor. He imagined the ways in which he could pleasure her and how her officer husband could not, which allowed him to narrow the status gap between them. If he could not provide her with a future except for making new shoes, then he would be her equal in joy and delight. It was a great comfort to him in the cold and damp nights. He was strong enough to absorb and endure the chills and diseases which took so many prisoners to the cemetery. Here he was, making boots and shoes again. Life had gone in a rough and haggard circle.

"Have you any news of the dyes, Tom?" She asked on one of her trips.

"Yeah, ma'am. One has been made in Hobart and will come on the next boat. The tanners will use it, and it will need a few goes to get good depth. They know it must be the best quality leather they can get; they know of your husband and tell me your request will be done. Once they are satisfied with the depth they will pass leather to me. You must look at it. You must be happy."

"Oh yes, I must be happy." She looked squarely at him. She saw what she wanted to see in this man, not the depredations etched on his face and hands a realist would, but the man dear Jane would find for her. He saw she was happy, as he was. He could now show off his skills as a shoemaker.

In her happiness she spoke. "You must call me Marianne, Tom, when we are together as now and separate from the business arrangement," as the romantic in her bobbed up to say.

"Yes Marianne, I will."

There it was. A name, and such a sweet name. His brain ran it around in his skull in celebration.

"I will call in again soon, Tom, to see progress."

"I look forward to it, Marianne." It was a start on their road.

A few weeks later, on one of her visits, when the guard called Tom and left this odd couple to it.

"Any news?"

"Yes, I have the leather, now dyed. It is beautiful I think, but you must say."

"Oh, do let me see, please, Tom."

He returned to his bench and came back with a furled leather. Her heart beat faster. He unfurled it. She stepped back involuntarily with the brightness, the brilliance, as if the sky had come down, kissed the leather, and bathed it in a richness worthy of the gods she had read about in the stories she heard as a young girl.

"Ooh..." she gushed, "It is beautiful. It is... never have I seen anything or expected to see anything as radiant as luminous before Heaven if I am fortunate. This is such a wonderful place where the Sun's light radiates from dawn to capture and bathe us. It makes being here forever worthwhile."

"I am glad you like it. We do too, but it is yours."

"When can you start, Tom?"

"I will need to take another measurement of your feet; there may be an adjustment of this particular leather; 'tis top quality, too."

He pointed to the chair. She felt she weaved her way to the chair, her heart almost straining to get free. He went to his bench and returned to measure her feet again. Her feet were ready, old shoes pulled off and parked alongside the chair, her dress lifted enough to show her feet and ankles, all she could show here, although she longed to offer him, give him, more.

His calloused hands trembled giving her a tiny tingling tremor as they ran around and along each foot, the tremor seemed to her to make feet and hands indivisible, that magnetism again. She closed her eyes to close distractions. Where else could life take them, she cried inside with anticipation.

He, too, knew his own stirrings were forbidden to even hint at. He finished with a last touch as if fingers and feet had taken root, and stood.

"I'll start tomorrow."

"So late?" She then corrected herself. "That is such excellent news. When shall I call in?"

"Next week." He wanted and hoped she would call by as ever during this age, as it was. Oh God! So long... she thought, but that was his word. Back to work for him and back for her with her bubbling secret.

Marianne could no longer contain her secret. The next morning with the wives, she announced on arrival.

"I found out we can order bespoke, I believe it is called, our very own personal shoes made especially for us. You decide what you want, shape and colour whatever you wish. Your feet are measured to ensure the fit, and you alone have the reward. I have ordered a pair of blue shoes to match this special sky. It took ages to get the dye made in Hobart, but it is here and the shoemaker starts tomorrow. It is so wonderful."

Annabel and Sara's initial surprise quickly melted into excited possibilities. They chattered away. Rebecca, too, saw possibilities.

"I would like to see them being made." She watched for a reaction.

"Oh yes, yes most certainly!" Marianne was awash with excitement. They fixed a date, although with Marianne's peripatetic nature, pinning her down was difficult. Rebecca seized on a promise to call her when she was going. That would have to do.

When it came, Rebecca noted that progress had indeed been made. A routine seemed developed between Marianne, the workers and even the guards taking her presence as matter of fact. There was one worker too, as she knew there would be, and when Marianne moved to her chair, and he was called by the guard, he walked to her chair without any challenge.

Rebecca was introduced to Tom by her first name, and he to her. Marianne had clearly lost all sense of proportion and balance. It was bad enough allowing some phantasms with this man to permit first names between them, she as the woman she was, and he as a very serious criminal, otherwise he would not be here. Worse, it sucked her in as an accomplice to this breach of all propriety. This horrible place did horrible things and needed to be expunged.

The leather was produced.

"What do you think of it?"

Rebecca took her own involuntary breath. It was dazzling. She could only see the colour as the shape was still unfinished. Seeing it, however produced, raised a little roil of envy.

"I concede, dear Marianne, you will be the envy of the Colony. Oh, to think of it and to choose such a skilful shoemaker."

There was a last look, but a head shake from Tom at pleas to feel the developing shoes. No contamination risk can be allowed. While feeling miffed at the hint that their fingers were inadequate, they left. The building's inhabitants now had two attractive women to ogle. Things were looking up.

Rebecca clocked other visits. Marianne's flutterings were pointers and Marianne was too excited to worry. She wanted to share her pleasure, although to outsiders it was linked to her new shoes. Rebecca insinuated herself into these visits.

"The next time you come it will be ready."

"Not now?"

"Two days polishing and buffing."

"I cannot wait. I will be there."

"As will I," added Rebecca.

The day came. Marianne vaguely saw Rebecca as a lady-in-waiting as they went to the day; Shoe Day. Her sleep was disturbed and her domestic routine a little disorganised.

"Can I see them?" Her voice almost strangled itself.

"Yeah, Marianne. You can."

This familiarity grated with Rebecca. At best it was inappropriate or worse; at least unseemly. The guard was no help in reestablishing correctness.

Tom went back to his bench and returned with a parcel. He held it out in his arms.

"For you."

Marianne took and almost dropped it in her nervous excitement. Their hands touching so briefly, a new discovery, an urge flitting back and forth between them. She tore it open.

Rebecca gasped. What regaled her was beyond her expectation. These men did have surprising abilities, whatever rank offences brought them here. These shoes; she had never seen such a colour, or only in the sky above when a nudge in her mind prompted the thought. The style was beautiful, elegant as if guided by the ancient gods to this woman, to fuse perfection.

Marianne fought back tears. She knew the gift of love. She had never been so happy. The other shoemakers stopped work to see her reaction to these shoes, conceded by them all as a pair each of them would be proud to acknowledge. They watched her, seeming paralysed as she stared at the work with what the workers closest to her later described with a noise like a whimper. Then she rushed to her chair with her gift, plopped into it and wrenched off her old shoes.

Tom moved with her and as she removed the shoes, he lowered himself. Taking the shoe she held out to him, for her right foot, he manoeuvred her foot into it aided by his finger in the heel to ensure the fit. With his touch and the beauty she beheld she feared she would faint. He took the other shoe and fitted it the same way. Could any woman be as happy as she was! A wave ran through her from toe to head, her mind swamped with pleasure.

Rebecca saw Marianne's eyes close, entranced, as her lips parted. What was in her mind could only be guessed at, and those guesses sat uneasily in Rebecca's mind.

Marianne moved her feet from side to side. The fit was perfect as she knew it would be. She stood to test whether she still had two legs; one tethered to this Earth, the other floating and waving to the heavens in gratitude. It was such joy from such a mundane object; shoes but so much more than shoes. She handed over her husband's signed authority to deduct the price of the shoes from his Bank, and the price would be determined, not by Tom himself but by those overseeing production. It was his gift to her, but others saw it reasonably as a commercial transaction with a value of importance to them all.

"I do not know what to say, Tom. I can never thank you enough. I shall always remember this day, this work, your great skill and your kindness."

Rebecca ran this through her mind. What other meanings could there be in this utterance? It was not mere words, there was the palpable tension, the long looks, touches, a link. Now she was complicit even as a spectator, and wished she were not.

"I promise I will come back for more of your beautiful shoes, Tom, and no-one else shall make them."

"Your pleasure is always my reward, Marianne."

This little exchange reinforced Rebecca's unease. With a radiant smile, Marianne took off her new purchase, wrapped them in the parcel, put on her old shoes and left, with Rebecca who, with a backward glance, saw this man, Tom, standing as if rooted, while the other workers resumed their efforts.

Back at the Officers' Mess, Rebecca knew these wonderful shoes would be exhibited at dinner. Most nights their little group ate together as the years had blended their personalities. It was noticeable that Francis had become more withdrawn and frequently expressed his disappointment and evident frustration that his efforts in both parts of this Colony had been unappreciated. His reputation was of being difficult to work with and unnecessarily harsh with the convicts. He consoled himself with a great liking for Madeira, which made him unpredictable as either good-humoured or, more often, aggressively assertive.

The ladies dressed well that evening, hearing that the legendary shoes would make their appearance, and they came in on the arms of their husbands. The other women knew that the evening belonged to Marianne. She came in after them, on Francis's left arm. She wore a lemon-coloured organza dress bought for her by her father in Southampton. Made in Italy, it was kept for momentous occasions. This was one. It sparkled, as did she, and she raised the dress slightly so the shoes could be seen, just a little, enough that Annabel and Sara gasped at what they saw revealed, and how such a humble item to keep feet dry and warm could be so... well... gorgeous.

They made mental notes to hurry post haste and order shoes for themselves too, and the evening went well, buoyed by the topic of footwear, unlikely though it was.

Stuart remarked that the mariners were expecting a severe storm in a few days, although currently the weather was pleasant enough, sufficiently so for the group to stretch legs and take the air outside, which it was agreed was certainly a feature of the Colony.

While Marianne was extolling the virtues of bespoke shopping, Rebecca sidled over to Francis, standing alone holding a large glass of Madeira whose contents were diminishing.

"A wonderful night. A shame there is to be a storm to disrupt it."

Francis said nothing.

"Marianne bought such beautiful shoes; thanks be to you for permitting it."

Francis grunted.

"The shoemaker is most excellent. He and Marianne get on most exceptionally well. I must confess, when I accompanied her, their familiarity bordered on what might be considered an intimacy."

Francis stopped, and turned to her.

"What do you mean?"

"They are on first name terms; 'Tom' and 'Marianne.' He is a convict, even if a shoemaker. He touched her feet, and I saw she was delighted with the contact. I am reluctant to say, but I thought you should know."

She paused and watched him, thinking.

"I am sure there is no other contact as there are guards on the premises." She hesitated again. "They will of course need to relieve themselves when out of sight."

Rebecca smiled and left to join the others.

Francis considered this information as he drank into his Madeira. He recalled there were difficulties between them. Marianne had been inappropriately assertive as a wife, particularly an officer's wife. Had this insouciance arisen from contact with a criminal? She will need to explain herself. More rigorous discipline was mandatory.

Francis returned and the group dispersed for the night, Francis helping himself to a large top-up of Madeira as he returned to their quarters, Marianne having gone just before him.

Marianne was in the kitchen preparing to tidy up china and cutlery and the children's small plates. Francis came towards her, a little unsteady as he drank more Madeira.

"I believe you have been consorting with criminals," he growled.

"What do you mean?"

"You let them play with you."

"Have you gone mad? You drink too much."

"No, I see it. You go out walking. Ha, I know what you get up to, you harlot."

"What! You are mad! The only criminal, as you call the inmates, is the man who made these beautiful shoes."

"You admit it, seeing this man!"

"He is a shoemaker. There are guards there."

"They can go for a piss. You open your legs, your whore. What is his criminal cock like, eh? You adulteress, strumpet. The bastard will hang tomorrow. You can watch. Hang you, too."

He lurched towards her with his glass in hand and raised it.

"I'll make sure no-one ever looks at you again. Cut you in slices."

He lunged at her with the glass, the remaining Madeira sloshing over her. Marianne instinctively picked up a kitchen knife near her hand and stabbed at him as he came at her, the blade piercing his chest. He staggered back, a look of amazement. Then staggered forward again. She stayed still, and plunged the knife into his chest again as he came at her.

Francis clutched the side of the table and then slid to the floor, blood bubbling from his mouth.

"Curse you, bitch. Rot in Hell."

Marianne did not see the blood on her own hand, nor on her special lemon-coloured dress. She screamed an unearthly scream, again and again. Her husband lay still on the floor, the life and blood draining out of him.

She looked down at him, heart pounding, his chest still welcoming the knife she left in him. Her mind burst into flames, inarticulate. *Husband, husband. Father of our children... dead. Me. I did it. I did not mean to, but I did. I am evil... and so I am free. And in my beautiful shoes. Tom's shoes.*

Her screams woke the children, who also screamed. Ann rushed in with the commotion and screamed, too. The officers and wives who arrived in various states of undress all shouted and screamed.

The shrieks, cries, agony and pain would remain with all adults present on that fateful night for the rest of their lives.

CHAPTER 11

Port Arthur, 1839

"We must treat this as a Court Martial."

One senior officer spoke to fellow senior officers, congregating after the extraordinary event of an officer killed by his wife.

He continued. "An officer died at the hands of his wife. It is accepted that a wife is part and parcel of the officer, not a mere adjunct, although that may be sufficient in itself, and therefore they are one and indivisible. It follows that this disaster must come within the jurisdiction of military law and regulations. I may also remind you that His Excellency relies on our good sense to regulate affairs in Port Arthur."

There were murmurs of assent.

"It cannot involve the other officers in that particular group, who are potential witnesses and too involved to be impartial."

There was a nodding of heads.

"It therefore behoves us to form the court. I shall take responsibility and select those from among the officers whom I consider able to reach an impartial judgment. I remind you also that Mrs Wainwright has explained what happened. It is the duty of the court to adjudicate on the evidence."

There were no dissenters.

Accordingly, the officer performed his self-appointed duty and selected the tribunal. It was to meet the following day to hear the case.

"Mrs Wainwright." An officer appeared at her quarters, where she was confined with a guard as required by the regulations, despite an unspoken acknowledgement that the prospect of her attempting escape was ludicrous. Her children were placed under the care of Mesdames Lynch and Bell, one each, with Ann shuttling between them as some continuity.

"Mrs Wainwright!" he repeated, louder this time.

Slowly the bedroom door opened. Marianne appeared, having dressed herself carefully to present herself as she remembered she should. Beautiful, but she was very pale and distracted.

"Yes."

"It was decided that, as an officer died under unclear circumstances involving his wife who is part of the military corps, the correct forum is a Court Martial. Do you accept the court's jurisdiction?"

Marianne nodded. Whatever it was, let it be. She had lost her husband, her children and the man who made her alive.

"The hearing will be at 10.00 hours tomorrow." He turned and left.

She sat in the nearest chair, her mind fragmented. Her children apart from her, the man who reached into her soul apart from her, her husband whom she had killed. A murderess. Tomorrow her fate. A fragment too of resignation. She sat quietly as time passed.

There were voices outside, the male voice of the guard, and female voices. The door opened. Annabel and Sara came in. Confused as they were, they were compelled to see their friend, sitting composed, but not herself, they thought. She smiled in a way that the two women took as a smile of welcome.

"We do not know what to say. It is awful, awful, awful," said Annabel repeating herself. "Francis was not an easy man, but this is awful, horrible." She found another word.

"My children?" Marianne spoke very softly.

"We are sure it will all be to the good tomorrow, and there is unnecessary worry," Sara offered encouragingly.

Marianne shook her head.

The two looked at each other. They were uneasy over their own expressed optimism.

"We will look after them."

Marianne nodded. It was enough.

It was tense, uncomfortable. There was nothing anyone could think of to say which would not sound silly.

"We will come and see you later." Marianne nodded, and they left. She roused herself and asked the guard to wake her at 09.00 in the morning so she could prepare herself, if she were not already awake.

She woke before the guard was required and prepared herself to appear as an officer's wife. She put on her most elegant dress and bonnet and reached for her shoes. She hesitated. No, not the blue, her blue, *their* blue. The best English pair, still serviceable, will do. At 09.55 there was a knock on the door. She was ready.

The court was a tribunal of three officers, plus a prosecuting officer. All introduced themselves and their function. The prosecuting officer called the prison medical officer. His evidence was that he performed a postmortem on Francis Wainwright. He found two entry points consistent with stab wounds, one on the upper chest to the right, the other into the heart. It was his opinion that the one to the heart was fatal, although he could not exclude the possibility that the other entry point might have proved fatal even with medical care.

Marianne was invited to ask any questions. She declined, not wishing to relive the catastrophe, nor was there anything to ask.

The prosecuting officer called as witnesses the Lynches, Bells and the Morgans on what they knew and what they found. The evidence was consistent; Marianne was found with a knife in her hands, blood on her hands and dress, her husband on the floor bleeding and with blood on him and on examination found to be lifeless with two wounds to the chest, one in the heart region. After each witness Marianne was asked if she wanted to ask any questions. She declined each request; there was nothing to disagree with.

The shoemakers' guard was called. Yes, he was on duty when Mrs Wainwright attended. Yes, she had ordered a pair of sky blue shoes, and very unusual they were, too. She had them made by one of the shoemakers. Name? Scrimshaw, Thomas Scrimshaw. She was very excited by the order and attended regularly to see what progress had been made. There was nothing unusual about the business except the shoes were made by a convict. No, he saw nothing untoward between Mrs Wainwright and Scrimshaw, nor were they ever out of sight of himself or anyone else. The room was always full, a hive of activity.

Marianne declined to ask any questions. What he said was true, except that her and Tom's inner lives would have told a different story and that was to stay within them.

"We considered calling the prisoner Scrimshaw to give evidence." Marianne suddenly stiffened; surely a time to see him, and he her.

"However, we considered his record. He was sent here after a long list of offences, the last being a refusal to give evidence in a Hobart case. I therefore had no confidence that any evidence he might choose to give, if at all, would be reliable. The court heard evidence from the guard, which was unchallenged. I therefore have no further evidence to put before you. There is only evidence from Mrs Wainwright."

"I have already said what happened."

"It is important to have a formal record of these proceedings of these tragic events. Please proceed."

Hesitantly, Marianne went through the events on that fatal night. When she finished, the tribunal invited questions from the prosecuting officer.

"You have told us that when your husband came at you with the glass after accusing you of adultery, you believed he wanted to disfigure you with broken glass."

"Yes. That is what he said."

"So you grabbed a nearby knife."

"Yes."

"You then stabbed him with it."

"I was protecting myself as he came at me."

"He then recoiled from that stab."

"Er... yes, he did."

"Then you stabbed him again."

"Yes."

"When you stabbed him a second time did you mean to?"

"I do not know."

"But you must have, which is why you did stab him. Do you agree?"

"Yes. I suppose so."

"Therefore it was your intention to stab him?"

"Yes."

"Do you accept that this was the stab which pierced his heart, not the first stab?"

"I think so."

"It was, therefore, this intentional stab to the heart which was responsible for your husband's demise. Do you agree?"

"Yes."

"Thank you, Mrs Wainwright."

"Is there any other evidence you wish to call, Mrs Wainwright?" Inquired the presiding officer.

Marianne shook her head.

"Then we will retire to consider our verdict on the evidence we have heard and of any matters you wish to bring to our attention."

Marianne was motioned to sit.

A very short time later the court resumed.

"It is clear from the evidence we have heard that there is a distinction to be drawn between the first stabbing, which can be explained and understood as a reaction to a fear of a very serious assault upon Mrs Wainwright.

"We accept there is no evidence that you, Mrs Wainwright, committed adultery or acted with impropriety, save perhaps for over familiarity with a prisoner, which your late husband regrettably misinterpreted. We can and do accept that your initial reaction in reaching for and using the knife was a response to a reasonably perceived threat to your wellbeing."

"However, the second stabbing, which you have accepted was intentional and which you agreed was to the heart and the cause of your husband's death, was of a quite different nature.

"This court and this settlement are bound by the laws of England. An intentional act resulting in the death of another person, whether or not an Officer of Her Majesty, is under the law of England the crime of murder.

"Accordingly, it is with great regret that we find you guilty of the murder of your husband, Captain Francis Wainwright. Do you have anything you wish to say before we pass the sentence prescribed by law for the crime of murder?"

Marianne stood, looked at the floor and the tips of her shoes under her dress, and shook her head.

"While this court, in finding guilt in a case of murder, would order execution by firing squad, we have determined this would be inappropriate for you Mrs Wainwright. For the murder of your husband, we sentence you to be hanged by the neck until you are dead, the sentence to be carried out at 09.00 hours on the day after tomorrow. May the Lord have mercy on your soul. Do you have anything to say?"

Marianne shook her head.

"Please escort this lady back to her quarters and arrange for her to be guarded until the appointed time of the sentence on the day after tomorrow."

The guard snapped to attention, touched Marianne's arm to guide her out. She only half noticed a man at the back of the court who had been watching her intently. A burly, bearded man with a balding head.

When she had gone, the presiding officer of the Court Martial announced for the purposes of the recording clerk.

"I will instruct carpenters to build a gibbet forthwith for the execution. It must not be a public hanging, as it would not be conducive to good order in a prison. It will be assembled in the garden of the Officers' Barracks, and it will be swiftly dismantled after the execution. Is that agreed?"

"Agreed."

All was recorded by the clerk.

The extraordinary events and outcome were soon transmitted throughout the officers and the lower ranks, with reactions ranging from pity and sadness to anger at the loss of an officer of repute and a just sentence. There was general recognition that the whole terrible matter be kept within the confines of officialdom.

When news of the sentence reached the Morgans, Bells and Lynches, the stunned husbands struggled to console inconsolable wives.

"I never meant this to happen… never expected this… never never," sobbed Rebecca.

Andrew paused in his attempted care and consolation, and slowly withdrew his arm from around her heaving shoulders.

"What did you not expect? What did you mean to happen?" His gaze fixed on the top of her head. "What did you do?" he pressed.

"I told Francis that Marianne was so friendly with the shoemaker they were on first-name terms. It almost bordered on intimacy, and I thought it unseemly in her position."

"You did *what*? You should know, *must* know, how unpredictable Francis is, was. He has been difficult as a fellow officer, and unnecessarily harsh on those below him who did not do as he said. He believed himself unfairly treated in remaining here. He was on a precipice."

"Do *you* not think it unfair, being here?" she interjected.

He stood up. "No. It is part of the service I signed for. All will be resolved in the fullness of time. But you sent Francis off on a trip to the madhouse. Look what you have done; one dead and another to follow. You are the link which made this chain of catastrophe!"

"Cannot something be done for poor Marianne?" Rebecca implored her husband.

"No. You should have thought of that before you set sail on such a terrible and unforgiving sea of your plans."

He paused, as she turned to face him. He thought through what he had learned, and now saw. He stared into her eyes. She saw something she would never have imagined in him, and she shuddered for herself. It was a look of contempt which speared her.

"I see it now. What your plan was. I remember you talking about you and Francis being more suited than us. You would have him reject Marianne. What had you planned for me?"

Andrew Morgan paused again, a little longer. "You have supped with the Devil, and he demands his price. I will do it for him. You craved a man of decision and action such as Francis, and you had me instead. Well, now you have your man of decision.

"Henceforth I will not sleep in the same bed as you, nor touch you, nor will you touch me, save for official duties. You are defiled to me. While you may seek to while away your days with dalliances elsewhere, you will be monitored. If it should occur, or there be reasonable suspicion, unlike your indifference to the truth, then the truth of your perfidy will be revealed and your overt reputation irretrievably besmirched. You will remain as my wife, as an officer's wife with the privileges and status the position entails and carry out such duties as the position demands, save for intimate marital obligations.

"I shall talk to Henry and Stuart about their wives taking responsibility for the soon-to-be orphans. I do not imagine Annabel and Sara resisting from that obligation. For your part, I will say your maternal instincts are insufficiently developed to be a rewarding mother, real or surrogate, a view I expect you would agree, and therefore the children would have greater benefit with the Bells and Lynches; perhaps one each, but that is a matter for them. Marianne will have a say in their future, and I suggest Sara and Annabel approach Marianne about it. See to it.

"I will also ensure a legacy for these unfortunate children, and talk to my superiors about the possibility of repatriation to England, given the horrible circumstances and the welfare of the children.

"I trust this meets with your approval and can dovetail into your schemes." His mouth turned into a sardonic smile as he finished.

Rebecca was speechless and could only nod her head. Andrew turned, and walked out of their quarters. So adrift, she could not immediately see a way through or around these all-encompassing thorns. Going to see Annabel and Sara gave her time to think.

In fact, the discussion had already taken place, but the two women braved their fears of contamination by association and went to Marianne.

"Oh, Marianne, oh, oh," Annabel sobbed, "what are we to do without you?"

Even in her befuddled state, this was an unexpected question. "You will do as you always do with your lives," Marianne murmured.

Sara was more practical. "Shall we bring Arthur and Elizabeth? You must want that?"

Marianne wrenched internally. "No, no. What is left of me unbroken will break if I see them. Their eyes will see their mother who murdered their father. It is in my eyes. It will go into theirs, to haunt their dreams and lives. It is better they know nothing when young. Arthur is easily distracted, and will have but a hazy memory of his parents. Elizabeth is too young even for that. My father, as an officer, was often posted away, and we children were looked after while he was away. Children forget in time.

"Please look after them, though, as if you were me. I have my memories in the time I have left. I am resigned to my fate. What is worse than a woman killing her husband? I accept what awaits me for my sin. I must be evil. The children can learn whatever you wish to tell them when they are older, but please be as charitable as you can. Please, please take one of my babies which best fits with you. I cannot presume to judge. I am judged and found wanting."

She erupted then into tears and, with heaving shoulders, fell back in her chair. Her friends sought to comfort her, their arms about her while feeling wretched and helpless. There was nothing they could do to assuage her anguish, save to fulfil her request to look after her children. Although neither had discussed the position with their husbands, they were good men and were unlikely to demur. A refusal would be unbecoming of an officer. All the two women could offer was immediate sympathy and copious tears in their own misery.

Exhaustion finally claimed and calmed the three women. In the silence, the realisation came that it was time to leave. Marianne got to her feet a little unsteady and the three hugged as if never to separate. The parting with reluctant arms and hands, and feet dragging desolate bodies to the door, was then brief; an opened door, a brief glance back at their friend and the sounds of disappearing feet.

The rest of the day passed in silence. Guards were changed, food and drink brought in for her, and left untouched, save for water. What was it to her, an evil woman?

Evil, yes. She thought of Tom. She outdid him for evil. He had not killed, else he would have hanged as she would. Whatever he had done to find himself in her gaze, thoughts and desires paled beside her crime. She was now free, at the cost of a murder. They were both criminals and there was now freedom together. She could not help herself smiling at the absurdity of the thoughts leading to that conclusion, factual though the circumstances were. How her feet had taken her to his boats, her looks as pretend not-looks in his presence, wanting his closeness even at a distance, was beyond her rational control. Her desire for this indescribable man was her very essence, and she was his too. She knew it like breathing.

How ironic that even Jane, so ironic a writer, had never imagined or countenanced such a situation. She, Marianne, had gone beyond dear Jane into a new land, a territory of excitement and desire. Was this not love? Even in the criminal class to which she now too briefly belonged.

What would they say? Did Tom even know? It was all so quick. What of her parents, Francis's family? Would they find out about their deaths? Would the real story come out or be hushed up, or changed for propriety's sake; both Francis and Marianne succumbed to one of the diseases so prevalent in the Colonies, and so young too? So sad. What would happen to Tom? What would his future be, now that she was free to join him as an outcast, if only in her mind; with their bodies only with fingers and feet and toes?

Her thoughts cascaded and tumbled into the darkening night until emotional exhaustion melted into physical exhaustion and she stayed sitting in her chair, too tired and indifferent to seek what little solace there was in her bed. The dark turned into night, and the wind rose presaging the promised storm.

There was a change of guard outside the quarters' door. The new guard thought how weird that a woman about to be hanged should need a guard. She would need wings to fly away, and then she would be an angel and as she was a killer she was no angel. Her thoughts briefly turned to wings too, to fly to Tom the shoemaker.

She remained in her chair as she had since her friends left, with her thoughts fighting for priority. The new guard, younger than her, opened the door to look at this condemned woman. There she was, beautiful and serene in her chair. As he looked at her, a thought formed in his mind. She was going to die anyway in the morning; would she fancy a bit of fun to be going on with or out with? She might be up for some exercise?

He went into the room. She sat motionless and quiet, barely aware of him as she was locked in her mind, piecing together the fragments.

"I was wondering, ma'am, as you was going to leave us tomorrow, to whether you might be partial to a bit of fun for both of us. No harm in it, is there?"

She made no answer, showed no response, nor looked at him. He was not there. That confused him. He was annoyed that he was ignored as if nothing; or maybe she was thinking about it. She did not say no, she was not shouting at him. Did it mean he could, they could? He did not know, but he was reassured she had not reacted badly to his suggestion. Was she just a bit shy being such a lady and would enjoy it once they started?

Emboldened by this rationale, he put down his musket, took off his belt and strode towards her. He stood before this silent, passive woman. He bent to put his arms under her armpits, stood her up, turned her around, lifted her up and carried her into the bedroom.

When he finished, he adjusted himself, returned to collect his belt and musket and resumed his guard duties outside the door. He was greatly disgruntled. She had remained silent, impassive as if he was not there; never existed.

"Not a bloody sound, not a move, not a wriggle, nothing." He fumed. "Like stuffing a piece of steak." He resumed his duty, confused and angry.

Dawn was dragged into the day, as if lamenting what it would bring, heavy clouds and wind were fore-riders for the storm. Rebecca left her quarters. True to his word, despite entreaties and as much allure and promises as she could offer, Andrew slept on the chaise longue, she in their bed, as it had been. Her guilt and situation with Andrew drove her towards an expiation with Marianne.

She approached the young guard, who seemed fidgety and nervous.

"You can't go in."

"Why not? I am Mrs Morgan. My husband is Captain Morgan and my friend is inside. If you do not know what you are doing here, she is to meet her Maker shortly. I am here to help her in any way I can. Do not stand in my way."

She said this in a voice and certainty which left him in no doubt she would pass. He stood aside, fearful of what could follow.

Rebecca noted Marianne's empty favourite chair and expected to find Marianne asleep in bed, exhausted and spent. Into the bedroom she went.

There was Marianne. Asleep on the bed, not in it, her dress up around her waist.

"Oh no, God no! Not this, not this!"

Marianne had been used. She screamed, turned, and ran back to the young guard.

"I see what you have done! You will pay for this! You will pay such a price!"

She ran back into the bedroom, the guard paralysed with fear outside the door.

"Marianne, Marianne!" Rebecca shook her. Marianne slowly resumed the world.

"I see what happened. Oh God," she sobbed, "It is horrible, horrible. Did he hurt you, too?"

"Oh, I felt nothing, nothing. I was in another world, a better world. I killed a soldier. I am punished in revenge. I expect there will be more soldiers taking revenge. It is my punishment for being evil."

Marianne is going mad, has gone mad, Rebecca realised. She has fallen into a pool of desolation and swims in it. She is mad. Rebecca herself was wild-eyed.

"Oh, I am safe," Marianne continued. "I am in the depths. Of another world. Better one. It is black with my evil. I hear the Devil's cackle. It is white. I hear the voice of my Lord. It is blue. I feel the fingers caress my feet. It is Tom, my Tom, to meet him again. My love, my love. I am everywhere and nowhere. It is more than I can imagine. The colours, the luminous light. Fighting over me, me, Marianne. Silent centre of it all. Let it be, let me be there."

Rebecca was convinced that Marianne had truly lost her reason. Was that all to the good, with what would shortly befall her? But her own sanity was being sucked into Marianne's maelstrom.

"You must dress, you must."

"Why? Am I not better as this, showing soldiers what I have; they can sin with a sinner."

Rebecca did something unexpected, even for her, and which always remained with her. She slapped Marianne.

"Stop it! Here, pull down your dress!"

Marianne recovered some poise. "Take my soiled clothes away and have them burned," she instructed. "Take the rest of my clothes. Send them to Hobart Town. Someone will wear them. Say the owner died suddenly." Marianne snorted.

"I will keep my blue shoes, however. I will wear them. My Lord will see them in his Heaven. He may show me mercy as a poor sinner.

"Give my diary to my daughter. She may wish to read it when she is older. Not all my thoughts are there. I could not bear to put them all in, and I carry them with me to my grave.

"I have sinned greatly and I am ready to meet my Lord in the next life if I cannot meet my lord in this one."

Rebecca hurriedly ensured Marianne was dressed, helping her into a brown dress with a floral bodice. The blue shoes Marianne took from a drawer and carefully put on. They fitted perfectly, although the day was not conducive to a blazing blue sky. She giggled when they were on and wiggled her feet.

She has gone already, thought Rebecca. To Marianne she said, "I will walk with you. It is nearly time."

Marianne seemed not to hear.

CHAPTER 12

Port Arthur, 1839

Captain Jolly, an officer with firm views on the position of women, and particularly in an area on which he claimed great authority, namely that of officers' wives, offered to supervise the execution. There was no rush of enthusiasm to make the selection difficult, and accordingly the responsibility was his, to his great satisfaction.

"I have selected three prisoners as a detachment to deal with the body of the murderess. Carter, Rogers and Scrimshaw. Have them bring a pick and two spades. Under guard. They are to stand by the gallows and await my orders."

The gallows, hastily built, would be hastily dismantled after its grim work. It sat tall as a stripped and leafless tree badly lopped, in the grounds of the Officers' Barracks, by a walled garden – away from the eyes of anyone not involved in this process, as much as thought possible at such short notice.

The three men were rounded up, taken to stores, issued with two spades and a pick, Tom taking a spade, and escorted to the scaffold.

"Stand there until I give you orders," barked Captain Jolly. He was particularly upset at a wife killing an officer husband. The men stood as ordered, resting on their individual tools. They exchanged glances, puzzled. It was an execution, but not at the general gibbet. What was going on?

Jolly called out to a young officer. "Bring out the woman." He could not bring himself to refer to the condemned with anything more personal, and fought off the urge to say "husband slayer." The young officer turned smartly, went into the barracks and shortly Marianne, escorted by the young guard from the previous night, came slowly across to the foot of the scaffold with Rebecca at her side, carefully guiding her. Marianne had refused the ministrations of the Gaol Chaplain. She would face the Lord without any intercession.

The young guard was walking as slowly as he dared. The sight of the gallows now churned his stomach. The other officer's wife knew what had happened and said he would pay a heavy price for it. The officer's wife walked with them.

What could he say? He could not deny it had happened. All the other ways of looking at it flashing through his mind had bad – very bad – outcomes. Even if he could convince anyone she consented, he could imagine their looks of disgust. On none of the possibilities he came up with did he want any of the outcomes. These women, especially she who was heading for her fate, were so calm, while he could barely walk from fear and panic.

The base of the scaffold was out of the direct sight line of the detachment. Marianne stopped for about half a minute. She raised her eyes to the heavy clouds as rain began to fall, thrust by a gusting wind. Rebecca swore to Annabel and Sara later that Marianne's lips moved. She assumed it was a prayer, and her friends earnestly prayed it was so.

Then Marianne set off up the steps, carefully looking where to place her blue-clad feet. She reached the platform. There was the burly, balding man who had watched her intently at her trial. She vaguely remembered him. No matter. As she reached the platform her blonde hair tossed around in the wind. The bonnet was unnecessary.

She came into the view of the detachment group. Tom Scrimshaw's hand gripped his spade as if it were separately alive and savaging his gut; his mind and body exploding from attack. The spade alone stopped him falling, even as it ate into him. A drop into a Hell beyond him.

It could not be her. Could not be. A few days ago she was happy, feverish in joy, and so was he. This must be someone else dressed like her? But these were the blue shoes. No others ever existed. She would never, ever give them up. She would be buried in them. That thought caved and hollowed him. Nothing done to him from the ingenuities of Hobart or here all put together could remove him from being a man more than this sight. He wanted to be expunged from misery. Survival was devils' work.

On the scaffold he saw that Marianne was windblown, wet and calm; she was poised and unconcerned. What had she done, what could such a gentle, loving woman have done to end up under these crowding, crowing heavens which taunted him too? Was the world mad, even madder than he understood? What monster decided they should be together at her hanging? Is this the God they preach, as they did to him as a boy?

The hangman moved towards her with his noose. She had not seen him, as if already gone above for judgment she must have for what she did. Then, as she heard the executioner, she turned her head.

She saw Tom. He saw her seeing him. Had he been sent to witness her passing? They both thought this, as their eyes never deviated from the other. While time stopped for them, Marianne automatically smoothed and held down her turbulent dress as much as she could and as decorum demanded. The executioner went about his business. He positioned her to stand amid a trapdoor and reached for the knotted rope which he directed over her head to her neck to tighten it.

"Where is the hood, man?" shouted Jolly. "I do not want her to see this world yet again."

The hangman left her briefly to rummage in a bag for a black hood. Returning, he slowly lowered it over her. As she became aware of an object over her hair, her face became a strange visage, a look he, Tom, did not recognise as ever seen. This look, never wavering, at him, plunged through him. It was almost a smile, or a glow of calm contentment, a desired end – all at the same time, all locked in his mind and relived for the rest of his days, short though he now wanted those days to be. A memory to be churned over and over for its meaning.

The hood found its rest over the rope. The wind grew into a howl, the rain tumultuous. The executioner moved to a lever, lifted it, and the trapdoor fell. The rope stiffened with Marianne's slight weight as she dropped. There she was, dangling, her delicate feet wriggling in her beloved sky blue shoes in the darkness of the storm. Finally she stopped moving; just hung, hanged – swinging slightly in the gathering wind.

"You, Scrimshaw. You had some interest in all this somehow. You will bury her yourself. Bury this woman against the west wall, facing it and standing up so she will never have any rest or see the light of a new day."

"Sir. She can't stand," Tom managed to utter in his horror.

Jolly considered this. It was true. "Very well. Carter, Rogers. Fetch a coffin from the stores to fit this woman and bring it here."

Pleased to be relieved of an onerous and grim task, the two moved quickly to obey, returning in a few minutes with a basic flimsy coffin.

"Right. The three of you bring her down. Give her to Scrimshaw, and you two return to where you were. You!" He turned to the young guard. "You watch that my orders are met." Jolly looked at the sky; the storm was well set and roaring into the inlet. "Everyone else go." With that, he too hurried out of the tempest.

The clerk there to record every minutiae, could not, with the rain pelting on his papers and washing his penmanship into unintelligibility, perform his duty, and he hurried off to record later in the dry from memory.

Marianne was brought down, the rope and hood having been removed. She was placed on the ground by the open coffin, and the other two hurriedly left. Just Marianne, Tom and the young guard remained, and the storm.

Tom gently lifted her body into the coffin and half-dragged the coffin to the wall, placing her as close as he could to it to give some protection from the rain for the dead woman. But she was his now. He would look after her. He now had both pick and spade to work into the heavy soil, rapidly turning into a quagmire as he heaved and dug in his heavy boots. When he had almost finished preparing a deep, vertical, sloping trench, the guard, already paralysed over his likely terminated future, said to Tom.

"Had enough of this. Too bloody wet. You finish off. I'll come out later and check." He left to seek shelter in the barracks some fifty yards away.

Tom looked around. He and Marianne were alone. He was not going to have her face a wall away from the rising sun. He had to dig a vertical grave with the guard present. He packed the base of the coffin with extra earth to give an angle for her to lie in. Whatever the cost to him, he would turn her around to face daylight.

He moved the coffin against the wall, holding her in with one hand as he struggled with the effort. He looked at her face, with the hateful hood off. There she was, head down over her mottled neck and with now-wet hair. It was too much to bear. He was burying himself in and with her. Mud under his fingernails now mingled with rain and streaked her hair. His hands cushioned her as best he could. Standing at a slight angle in her shoes, her shoes still reflected the light just as she wanted, despite the mounting mud over them. He saw her slumping. How could he help her see?

He looked around him. The wind had caused some damage. There were pieces of tree, different sizes, twigs and small branches. His work on the boats had trained him to estimate size. He looked and found a small branch, green and flexible. A bit long, he guessed. He grabbed the spade and hacked at the wood until the right size approximated. He bent it with the strength his anguish and passion demanded to press each end into each side of the coffin so it jammed and bent slightly under the strain and with the suppleness of the wood. He tenderly raised the mid of the wood under her chin to lift her face so she could see more light. But her mottled neck needed care, too. Grabbing the discarded hood he wrapped it around the twig to take the rough edge away. She now had some soft protection. It was a sort of triumph. Her head was raised a little and she could taste the sun through her glazed eyes. What else could he do for her?

Tom Scrimshaw bent to kiss her forehead. He could think of nothing else. Kissing those lips with the enigmatic smile, that he could not bring himself to do. It was not blasphemous to give a farewell kiss as he had, and would comfort his distress over however long he had left, but kissing her lips did not feel right, even with his love for her. The rain cascaded into the coffin off her hair and down over her partly uplifted face, down to her shoes, *their* shoes and it raced with his tears.

He stood up, put the lid on the coffin and screwed it down. He lifted it to its resting place and covered it with earth as the rain poked and prodded him. He damped down the earth at ground level. There she was, and here he was. Can he confess to breaking orders and be punished and hanged too? He stood in the deluge, indifferent to it.

The guard suddenly reappeared, and saw it was done. He was relieved that the evidence of the happening was now covered and she could not be asked. This man had done him a favour.

Tom interposed the guard's thoughts. "What happened to her? Why this?"

"Not sure. She killed her husband, an officer. It's said another man was involved, so she killed him."

Even exhausted as he was, Tom staggered back with another blow from a hidden source. Another man? Could not be him, could it? Nothing had happened between them except fingers and feet and an imagination he did not know he had. She was so beautiful and lovely that men would fall at her feet, even without the blue shoes. Maybe she wanted them to impress this lover. Strings of lovers to play on her fiddle.

The worm of jealousy wriggled less with his realisation of the gaps between them. Whatever it was or whoever it was, it was wonderful he was now a different man and he loved her, and was still sure she loved him, even if there were rivals for her affection. It cannot be wrong to be consumed like this, when every hair on your body stands at the mere thought of her, and you die for a glance and are reborn for the next.

"Leave the tools. I'll sort them out when this bloody storm stops. Go back to where you should be. Cell in this, I expect."

Tom was grateful. He could not remember any act of kindness by any man since he left Lincolnshire. Jenny and Jane were different, but they were women. It took the execution of the woman he loved to produce an act of kindness by another man.

Back in his damp cell with his dry rodent companion, feeling drowned like the proverbial rat, and he smiled, feeling a new bond with the creature, and before oblivion took him for the night, he muttered; Let God take me, or the Devil; whoever has Marianne.

Rebecca left as Marianne mounted the steps. She could not go further. There was nothing she could do except wrap herself in the losses she created. Going back to her quarters she thought about the guard. It was not as simple as first thought. If she accused the guard – and he made no effort to deny it – the consequences for the guard would be for him to follow Marianne. It had consequences for her, too. Andrew would add this act, only possible because Marianne had a guard for the crime she committed, of which she, Rebecca, was the prime mover. Another iniquity for her list. It would not aid her attempts to rehabilitate herself in his eyes.

It was safer not to mention the happening. Marianne had not suffered, or was beyond suffering. She thought it revenge for her act and accepted it as such. Better to let the sleeping dog lie, like Marianne herself. Rebecca just realised what she thought, and muttered a prayer to Marianne to forgive her for the awful slur. There was too much misery all round.

CHAPTER 13

Port Arthur, 1839-45

Tom Scrimshaw opened his eyes, slowly, blinking and adjusting. Focussing. He looked around. Clean, honey-coloured walls. Here in Heaven too? He was in bed. In Heaven. Nothing was said about beds in Heaven when a boy. Strange bed covering, too; must be Heaven's way.

But silent. Where were the angels forever singing praises of the Almighty? Where were the harps he'd been told about when he was sent to the parish church as a boy? He had made it to Heaven.

Or, as he was a criminal, was this more cunning punishment? Was this Hell? Here? Where was the terrible heat, the horrible furnace, the shrieks of the damned such as him?

Where was Marianne in it all? He was newly judged, and she must already have been judged by the Almighty. Could she say a few words for him?

In his confused ponderings, he failed to notice the entry of a uniformed man older than himself, who entered quietly and noted that Tom had stirred, and his eyes betrayed an awakening. Then as Tom squinted and this blur came into focus, he blurted.

"Are you God?"

The man smiled and shook his head.

"The Devil, then. Can't see your horns and tail."

"Not Satan either."

"One of his devils." Tom was persistent in making sense of this alien place.

"No."

"Isn't this Heaven or Hell? Where am I, then?"

"Hospital. Port Hospital."

"Huh?"

"You were found in your cell when you did not respond for breakfast and work. You were very unwell. Captain Morgan took charge. He thought you had unwarranted extra suffering in the recent disaster of the killing. He asked me to tend to you if I could."

"You?"

"I am the doctor here. Despite the rumours, it is neither my intention nor my function to try and kill those who live here, by choice or otherwise. As a doctor, I am sworn to preserve life not to take it; to try and heal the sick. You were very sick when you were brought here, but with God's help you have recovered well enough.

"You were fed by spoonfuls of food and water, not without difficulty I may say, but you will shortly be able to resume your tasks. One more day with a decent dinner and a breakfast on the morrow, and you will be discharged from here.

"Captain Morgan considered your uniform was beyond useful repair after your work in the deluge. After you leave he ordered you to go to ordnance to get a new uniform and boots."

Something good had come out of all that was unspeakable. Tom could even make his own boots, or be given a pair he could make. Or made.

This man was a doctor. The only knowledge he had of doctors was being seen by one as required after the lash. What they did after the lashings in the Town bloody hurt too, and he was sceptical of doctors' benefits. Yet he could not but be grateful to this one, even if the benefits had not included joining Marianne.

Tom nodded and grunted. The doctor took that as recognition and left, for the events of the day and the next to take their course.

His Excellency Sir John Franklin sat at his capacious desk in
Government House, Hobart. His Private Secretary sat opposite him, and
he had handed the Governor a sheaf of documents. Both men had read
them and all emanated from Port Arthur.

"Well, what a rum business. What on Earth has been happening in the
Port for these catastrophes to occur? I will need to attend to the Port
quite shortly and more regularly, for further inquiries and investigation
into the behaviour of the administration. But for now, we must deal
with what we have before us.

"We had a murder, an execution and the death of a young guard found
dead by his own hand near the grave of a woman executed for killing her
husband, one of our officers. A tragic tale: it appears beyond doubt the
wife and young soldier are lovers; the husband finds out, she kills him
and is hanged for it. The young guard, broken-hearted and grief
stricken, cannot live without her and takes his own life to be near her. I
am sure the Bard wrote on this tragedy in one of his plays.

"Such strange love, if so. Things happen to people who believe they are
in a prison, even if not official prisoners. Perhaps we all are prisoners
adrift from the familiar. Very curious. As those involved are no longer
with us, we shall never get to the bottom of it. Ah well, very sad losses
all round."

Sir John picked up another separate bundle.

"We have a letter from Major Campbell, my delegated officer for
administration in the Port. I shall have to see him over the tragedy.
There is also a Letter of Request from a Captain Morgan, arguing for the
return of himself, his wife and the remaining two officers and their
families who arrived together with the murdered officer some nine or so
years ago, to the Mother Country.

"It is submitted that morale in the Port is very low after these awful events. There are two children of the deceased couple to be looked after by the wives of the other two officers, Bell and Lynch, one child apiece. Their education is greatly to be preferred in England, particularly far from the stigma of learning in due course of the circumstances of their parents' deaths.

"I am inclined to agree with Captain Morgan and with Major Campbell who wrote in support for the same reasons. The Major added that the officers had performed their respective duties as befitting their rank over the years in both parts of this Colony, that their morale and that of other officers and ranks would greatly improve when reminders of the dark deeds were removed. The position of the children is particularly untenable in that regard. I have no doubt that our beloved young Queen would want these children back in the bosom of her England. Do you have any alternative suggestions for my consideration?"

"No, Sir John. I believe you have summarised the position and your proposals are most excellently constructed."

"Very well. I leave it to you to draft an Order for each of the officers and families involved to have free passage for themselves and their possessions to take ship from Port Arthur to England, either direct from here or via Sydney, whichever should prove the shortest in time. In the Order they are to present themselves to the Colonial Office in London for further instructions and allocation, whether in the Colonial Service or in Her Majesty's Army, on which they can make their own representations.

"You may also draft appropriate replies to Major Campbell and Captain Morgan acknowledging their missives and setting out my decision and in the cases of the Captains, including Captain Morgan, a letter setting out my decision and that they should investigate the shortest sail to England and pack for the voyage in the direction nominated. These letters should accompany the formal Order for each officer.

"Please present each document to me for approval and I anticipate in tribute to your most excellent skills, for my immediate signature."

The secretary flushed with pleasure at this accolade and excused himself to devote time to these instructions.

And so it was that Marianne's friends; her circle of officers and wives, along with her children, were soon packing their trunks and ending the traumatic chapter of their years in Van Diemen's Land.

✳

Officialdom continued grinding its mill of convicts over the next few years; Tom among them as the dark void of Marianne's loss sometimes smashed around within him, spurring him through more outbursts, more punishments.

Nonetheless, in February 1841 Thomas Scrimshaw was considered for a Ticket of Leave.

"Here, Mr Foster, are the latest batch of convicts to be considered for Ticket of Leave under the regulations and the exercise of your discretion."

The official handed a bundle of records to Mr Foster, a more senior administrator with the power to recommend or reject Tickets of Leave, a freedom under certain conditions. Mr Foster adjusted his reading glasses and waded through the documents punctuated by occasional comments, sighs, grunts and head shaking and flourishes of his ink-dipped quill to indicate success or failure and any conditions attached to success.

"What of this Scrimshaw? This is a notoriously long list of offences in Hobart and here. I see one here for twenty-five lashes for something and drunkenness. I cannot read the – something – whatever it is."

"Nor can I, Mr Foster. It is almost certainly by a lawyer."

"Typical," opined Mr Foster. They both laughed.

The junior official volunteered. "The offence, whatever it was, was not long after the infamous husband murder and wife's execution a few years ago, in which it was rumoured Scrimshaw had a part, although no one knew why. It may have been a reaction on his part. Drunkenness is a feature of his misdemeanours. It is a wonder he is still alive, much less functioning. Still, he seems to have quietened down and works well as a shoemaker with some earnings going into the Convict Bank."

"Should give him some encouragement, I suppose." The Foster quill made a recommendation.

*

"Scrimshaw." The official addressed Thomas Scrimshaw standing before him. "I should say that four years ago you were recommended for Ticket of Leave. You know what that is, do you not?"

Tom nodded.

"However, before the happy news was communicated to you, as I am now doing, you went on to commit further irritations here in the Port for which you received due punishments. Accordingly, the ticket was deferred time and again.

"I will not go into the litany of all your offences here and in Hobart, but my count puts it at twenty-six. There is nothing in the imaginative punishments devised in the Colony which you have not tried, save for the ultimate one of execution, as none of your offences allowed for it in law. Or perhaps it was not imaginative enough to attract your attention as it did not allow further explorations.

"It could fairly be said that the recurrences before the magistrates suggested you enjoyed them as devised adventures. Even a total in Hobart and here of one hundred and five lashes over four punishments via the cat was like water off a duck's back." He laughed at his self-assessed witticism.

"Even your most recent appearance for exposing your person, a new trick, elicited a defence that your clothing had recently been stolen by another prisoner shortly before, for which he was punished, and therefore you had nothing with which to cover your person. That at least, Scrimshaw, was imaginative."

The official continued, "Nevertheless, it has been decided that the Ticket of Leave should be granted and I am presenting it to you now. You will see that it entitles you to earn wages on employment and is authorised by His Excellency. He retains authority over you and you can be recalled to resume your life sentence for any infringement which His Excellency in his sole discretion decides warrants such recall. Do you understand?"

Tom nodded. While the contents of the written document was beyond his scholastic level he was aware of the general conditions.

"Keep it safe. You need to present it to any prospective employer who is not bound to employ you. We have, I believe, had enough of each other with your fifteen or so years here and there. Whether you can survive is up to you, even with your resilience. You are now on to your own. How you get to Hobart is up to you."

The official handed over a document scrolled into a case, and motioned Tom to leave the office.

Tom nodded, turned, and left. His old, yellow uniform was discarded and his old clothes were returned to him, although would they still fit him still after fifteen years? He doubted it. Still, he had also been given a new pair of twill trousers and a shirt. He had a pair of his own boots and a pair of socks bought from the Port store. Convict Bank money, too. He thought he could find a boat to Hobart and knew his way around the dock. It was now onwards.

He fervently hoped Marianne was with him every step of the way.

CHAPTER 14

Hobart, 1849-1852

Standing outside the Red Lion, Tom Scrimshaw took a drag on his roll-up. The weather threatened rain at any moment, and he was about to go inside once he finished his smoke, his day's toil ended. Casual work, when he could get it.

"Are you George?"

Tom turned to see a young woman at his right. Very agreeable too, he saw. Dark brown hair halfway to her shoulders, about five feet tall and with brown eyes. Her full lips and figure suggested a woman fully aware of her charms as was her confidence in approaching him, a stranger.

"Been called many names, never George."

"Said he'd meet me here. His loss. Who are you?"

"Tom will do."

A few drops of rain flopped on them both. "Raining," he continued. "You'd better wait for him inside. I'm going in." She shrugged, and followed him in.

"Ale?" She nodded in reply. He went to the bar and returned with two glasses of beer. As he handed one to her, he asked. "What's your name?"

"Mary, Mary Richardson."

"Haven't seen you here before."

"No," she said. "New pub for me. You?"

"Used to come here a long time ago. Good ale pub, and very friendly landlady. She died some years ago, I'm told. A big loss. You? Why are you in Hobart?"

"I'm come from Devon. I worked in a big house there. I found a box in a room I was cleaning and opened it; beautiful gold ribbon inside. I swear it spoke to me, told me to take it with my pretty fingers. So I did. But I got seen. Got seven years here. Seven years for a lousy ribbon. Good with my hands, I am. I'm on the *Anson*."

"Ah, the old warship turned into transportation and now moored in the river? Things have changed a bit."

He did not want to say how or why he knew. That led into darker alleys. The Town had become more conscious of its history and wanted to brush it under the carpet, or anywhere, as long as convict labour could be avoided in doing it. "They"– those who ran the place, or thought they did – couldn't avoid it, though.

The place had grown in his absence. There were new arrivals, with some convicts among them, but there were complaints about that, and talk of stopping it. They liked to forget that most of the men in the Town were freed men, just like him, who couldn't go anywhere else. Who did the work? Men like him. He worked around the docks and wharves when he could, as he knew that work. But he had, when desperate, laboured in the quarries, quarrying and crushing rocks for gravel. He thought of the gravel in the main streets; walking over himself, he wondered.

There was talk about changing the Colony's name as well. That didn't matter to him. Whatever it was called, he had to live in it and with its new fancies and airs. Less smelly; so not so many bad airs, those running the place thought. Depended on where you lived, he thought. Or what you had to do in the airs and graces. A young Queen, younger than him, changed the way of looking at things, maybe. Too much to think about in survival. Always survival. And Marianne. Marianne...

"Yeah. A doctor and his wife run it," Mary was saying. "They try and reform the likes of me with better conditions if we behave ourselves. We're given things to make. I'm good at bonnets. We make our own in the nice, fashionable funnel shape, with material sent out from England.

It's good stuff. We sell some to all the fancy ladies here." Her lips pursed over these last words.

"There's a place a couple of streets away, along the main road, turn left then right. Lovely big house. We sell from there."

"I know it," Tom said. "Used to belong to a Mrs Taylor, Jane Taylor."

"Yeah, I heard that name. She vanished. No one knows how or why. No record of her dying here, or marrying. She just went somewhere. Sydney, maybe? England? It kept the gossip going for years."

Tom had made similar inquiries when he returned to Hobart, with the same fruitless result.

"You sleep on the *Anson,* do you, and work here?"

"A bit of both."

"You'll get a Ticket of Leave then, get out and back to England."

"Get out? Do you see any wings? Do you think I can fly? Have I cash for a boat back? To what? Nah... I'm stuck here. I'll do what I can, when I can; scratch about for little pleasures or big ones. Life's not for long here. Or in England, neither. What about you?"

"Sent for life. I have problem fingers, too," Tom smiled. "I got caught; good ones don't get caught, I was told. Mine's a small brain. I do what I can here, too. I got me Ticket, but it's hard even so. Those who can give you work don't trust you, and other workers are angry. They think you're taking their work. At least gaol gave you food and a bed of sorts. Here, you fend for yourself. I was a shoemaker; I do some of that when I can. And some work around or on the boats; I know a bit about them. Or just labouring.

"Nothing more to say. Don't talk much; never told to. School, then here; don't speak unless spoken to. Maybe the fingers did the wrong talking. That's the lesson, but it pisses me off. In my head I have words, even if they don't come out right. Anyway, I've enough in the pocket for an ale or two. Another glass?"

"Yeah" Mary said. "I am partial to a beer. One of the little pleasures."

A couple more ales later, and with the non-appearance of George (although it was possible he came in out of the rain, saw this couple talking and drinking and left), it was time to leave.

"Do you live near here?" Mary asked.

"Got a room not far away."

"What's it like, a real room to yourself?"

"You can have a look."

"Got a bit more time before I'm due back to *Anson*."

They hurried back in the rain to Tom's room. It was a room in an ordinary house, the entrance at the rear. There was a bed with two rough blankets, a pillow, a table and chair, a small bureau, by the door a bucket, nearby another pair of boots, and a fire grate with some kindling and wood stacked loosely nearby.

"Where's the water?"

"Outside, we passed the pump getting in. Take the bucket; it works well enough."

Tom went into the bureau and came out with a candle which he lit from his latest roll-up and placed on a cracked saucer from another drawer in the bureau; his repository of domestic items with only him in mind. In the flickering light, her wet, dark hair glistened. She was shapely and full, and in the intermittent glow his age was disguised and she saw a younger man.

Fuelled by the ale, Mary felt desire coursing through her. She was used to men from her youth in Devon and in working in the big house of her downfall. Men were attracted to her. She knew that. She was attracted to men. They knew that, too. With the fatalism of never getting out, the normal social mores if not tossed aside were left disconsolate in the corner. She was in the mood, and knew that, too.

Mary Richardson approached Tom, and reached up to plant an ale-perfumed breath on his ale-perfumed lips. He was aware of the age difference and had not given thought to such a close contact, so was surprised by her advance. His reactions, with urging from the beer, overtook reticence very smartly.

Afterwards, as she dressed quickly to return to *Anson*, she asked if they would see each other again. "Will you be around?"

"Yair. Most nights I have a glass or two at the Red Loin."

"Ha, like it. Loved the great pleasure after the little one. Very great one. Loved it. See you there."

Mary returned to the Red Loin, where Tom was indeed a regular. In a short space of time the relationship with the inn altered as that of Tom and Mary veered off on a different trajectory. Rather than settling in for a few beers before heading to his room, Tom purchased beer in a refillable keg which went with them to his room where they indulged themselves with both little pleasures and big pleasures. It was cheaper by the keg and therefore a thoroughly satisfying arrangement for them both.

As they spent more time together, Tom noticed that Mary had an impulsive, reckless streak. She sometimes decided she wanted "forny" – it sounded more "naughty" than mere fornication and went with "horny," she giggled – in odd places with the tantalising worry of being caught. Forny up against a tree on the green when draped over him; in an empty carriage outside an Inn while its owners were imbibing inside; in the Inn stable rolling in the hay under the glassy eye of the horse. She spent much thought trying to work out a way of having forny in Mrs

Taylor's old abode, which indeed sent a roistering memory through Tom, but she had so far at least failed to exhibit the necessary ingenuity.

Tom was more alert to the consequences of being caught. Time and experience had shared many years with him. He was still on his Ticket. She had yet to qualify but should expect to after about three years, although not if caught in semi-public forny. She was more focused on beating the risk than the consequences. He wondered if her impetuosity had been part of her capture in England. There was still a frisson of the challenge in him, but making something of himself overrode the urge to scratch that itch. A thought of life with Marianne now a felon like him, albeit dead, tempered risk as well.

Mary was also impatient to get her hands on her portion of Convict Bank money which followed her from England, which was negligible, and her earnings under the guidance of the good people in charge of *Anson* as part of her rehabilitation. Under the rules she was told she would have to wait until her Ticket. In the meantime, she reluctantly had to content herself with making straw bonnets for the fashionable ladies of Hobart, and cutting and sewing cloth sent from England if not available in Hobart for the enjoyment of these ladies. She despised these women and also desperately wanted to be one. The muddle in her mind kept her work fuelled by anger and hope.

Tom in turn found himself subsidising two sets of expenses, including drink and incidentals and Mary's desire to be always alluring.

"Do you not want me to look presentable and desirable?"

"Yeah. For me."

This was not necessarily the complete answer she wanted. There was therefore some underlying tension in the dances of little pleasures and great pleasures. As it remained in the undergrowth their overall situation rattled along quite satisfactorily in their eyes. Work and play, as it was, was much improved to what had gone on before and in knowing other options were limited. Then again, their options back in England had been and would be restricted, had either of them thought about it.

Mary had been in Hobart about a year when they met at the Red Loin, and as the next year meandered with the pleasure quotient, there were rustlings in their minds on where else they might go and why. The why was easier for Tom. He felt a marked man in Hobart. He was or would be known by some of the older inhabitants; the name appeared often enough in the court reports in the local papers, and there was merit in moving away from there. Somewhere large enough to earn regular money without being known.

Mary was less keen. It would take her away from her ability to make some money, to be seen in society and also to cajole Tom into buying finery for her. Then again, if he earned more outside Hobart she could order through the mail-coach services and persuade him to take her to Hobart where she could be admired.

There was a snag from both perspectives. How to do it? Rumours being the unruly steeds they are, the *Anson* was not immune. In the zeal to have women and girls become useful citizens of the Colony, what could be seen as more stabilising than a marriage, particularly if the groom had been a prisoner? What a justification of the authorities' philosophy! A person with a Ticket of Leave could apply for permission to marry. Mary saw how this could help her get her hands on her money.

She fed this information into Tom. He was still bereft of Marianne and still wretchedly in pain, but the practicalities of life going on and how to get out of Hobart showed a path ahead.

"I will do it. I will ask the official for permission, when I find out who it is. I have the Ticket. It will bring me more work. Thinking on it, Mary, ask the gossip at *Anson,* who is the person there to ask for permission, as well as me asking about another place where we could marry, to help our lives.

"I have heard of another settlement called Hamilton, with inns and breweries, so there must be a lot of settlers. Should be good for work and fun, little ones and very big ones. Do you like the sound of it?"

She certainly did. "Oh yes. I'll ask for the man who can say we can get married."

As befitting their status and their modest contribution to society, it was a practical arrangement overlaid with basic enjoyment, which was not to be despised. The matter of love did not enter their calculations, and would have been met with incomprehension.

Officialdom, as is its wont, ground the wheels of marital grain slowly. The official made the determination as well as on the proposed location. As neither of them were literate, a personal request had to be made. The official considered their records with some distaste, disbelief too that this man was not only still alive but seeking marriage to a much younger woman who, given the shortage of females in the Colony, could have chosen better. But he saw this so often that he was inured to the fact, and had no interest in the actual outcome.

However, as usual too, it was at least a public commitment. It was an anchor in society for future good behaviour and contribution. That this now middle-aged man and this younger woman were prepared to sail on the so-called calm marital seas was to be encouraged.

So it was that official duty outweighed personal distaste, and permission was granted for Tom and Mary to marry at St Peter's Church in Hamilton. Banns needed to be proclaimed, which meant the business of visiting the town needed to be undertaken, including a visit to the vicar and asking around to see what work might be found. Inns and breweries were tempting; too much so, given their fondness for being in the hug of the hop. Tom was set against doing manual labour for someone else; he had done too much already. Was the new town ready for a shoemaker, or could he join others in the trade?

Under the terms of the Ticket, he had to notify a change of address to an home in Hamilton and he was to advise of all address changes in the Colony. Governor Arthur's beady eye remained in the sky.

The doctor and his wife on the *Anson* were pleased that one of their girls was marrying, a girl who was excellent with her hands and imparted skill to her work, although there was a reckless streak which could foretell trouble ahead. A good husband would see her right.

The couple, happy in the new adventure and finally free enough, set off on the very early coach with their few belongings to Hamilton, some forty-five miles north-west of Hobart. Mary was allowed a little access to her account, not as much as she wanted, but it was a start. A new start.

Hamilton was a small, thriving town servicing a grazing and farming area. The settlement had been hacked out of the bush and had good soil and water, general stores, inns and breweries. What more could a town want?

On arrival, and collecting their possessions, the couple headed for the nearest inn to book a room while they explored the settlement and its possibilities. The most likely opportunities shaped up as a brewery for Tom and inn work for Mary, if labouring on the land for a farmer was out, which it was for Tom. He pressed upon Mary the consequences of further light-fingered activities for which, as a convict, the penalties could be fatal. Mary heard the warnings but was not perturbed at all. On the other hand, there was a shortage of free workers, and one could be carefully monitored for dishonesty.

It was a bucolic setting; honey-coloured houses in the Georgian style, arbitrarily scattered in clearings with a foreground tributary of the Derwent hurrying to make its acquaintance with the river, a background of dense mountains forbidding further examination by crops and animals. After Port Arthur, it was paradise.

Self-sufficient but producing enough to contribute supplies to burgeoning Hobart, it was however hard, even brutal work, not so different from the gangs who laboured in the Colony. The need for labour overrode any employers' reservations about new arrivals with a Ticket, and them being married suggested permanence.

Contact was established with the vicar, and the Banns published. Tom found work in a brewery, rather like manna from heaven, and Mary was taken on as general cleaner and worker in The Queen's Head, the inn they first stayed in. There was a newly built property for rent, too. Stone around a wooden frame, with two front rooms, one on either side of a central door, along with a parlour and kitchen and a fireplace. Their precious savings went on essentials: a bed, bedding, a table and two chairs, and wood for the fireplace. Candles and holders too, and firelighters. A local store supplied hardware: axe, saw, pick, shovel, hammer and nails, screwdriver and screws. Two buckets, one to fetch water from the river for drinking and cooking, the other for waste to go to the pit that Tom had to build at the back of the cottage. Oh, and a couple of cups, mugs, plates and knives, forks and spoons.

What was not supplied was how to cook. That they would have to learn, helped by what Mary picked up from the Inn. Tom would need to build the privy and in due course, a barn and stable, as a signal of intent. They paid a weekly rent on settling in.

After a few weeks, with no challenge to the Banns, up the aisle of St Peter's they went, as Richardson and Scrimshaw, and came down as Mr and Mr Scrimshaw, ages recorded largely on guesswork, although Tom may have adjusted his age downward a little from his estimation, so not to alert his much younger bride.

A pioneering settlement with a harsh, unforgiving life and its consolation of alcohol was readily understandable, but a potential disaster for some inhabitants. Do not drink at work, on pain of the sack. Tom's employer allowed him, as an employee, a free glass at the end of the allotted day's work and to purchase a keg at a discounted price to take away. For a man with a close friendship with beer, Tom saw it was a necessary companion in the inns – but a death dealer at work.

Mary, too, found that although inn work was no strain on her abilities, she was quickly bored by the routine. Dalliance in the bar would have her "out on yer ear" as the landlord tersely told her when she started at the Queen's Head.

Life therefore set off on a satisfactory course with a regular diet of pleasures, great and small. However, the insidious creep of the small pleasures found its way into Mary. Tom noticed she was reaching for the evening keg more readily than he was, and she was becoming more erratic and assertive. Some mornings he found himself warning her.

"You smell of beer. He won't like it. Customers will notice."

"'Tis nothing. I'm fine. I work hard." She dismissed his concerns.

He wondered if any ale left over in the keg overnight was taken after he went to work in the morning, and before she went to work. What did she do in that gap of time? He realised he had someone called a wife for whom he had some responsibility; her behaviour forced the realisation upon him. Having never been responsible for anyone before (Marianne's fate precluded development there), he had little knowledge on how to exercise the duty, except to learn on the job as he had with shipbuilding.

His concern was compounded by Mary taking to spending her earnings on new clothes ordered through the mail-coach service, as other free women in Hamilton did when money permitted. Mary made sure it did.

"Why do you spend all this money on clothes?"

"I want to look nice."

"This isn't Hobart."

"Don't you care about me?"

"Yair, I do, but the money goes like water down the creek. I pay for everything. You just pay for your clothes." He had a sudden flash, recalling a saying by Jane Taylor all those years ago. He was supplying two of the three necessities. The different visions of life were starting to grate on each other.

About a year after their arrival in Hamilton, there was good news: Mary was entitled to her own Ticket of Leave, with an extra keg to celebrate. Then, within a fortnight, she had lost it.

While Tom worked longer hours at the brewery as the settlement continued to expand, Mary decided to spend some of her wages, now available, no longer on more clothes, but on visiting other inns in Hamilton after her work finished.

When Tom finished his shift and trudged towards the cottage, he was approached by a man he knew by name, but not much else.

"Scrimshaw. Your wife is pissed out of her head in the White Horse. Or was. She's been thrown out. Wanted to fight the landlady."

"Oh Christ!" Tom grunted at the man and hastened off to seek his wife. There she was, propped up against the stable by the White Horse, without the horse. He fleetingly wondered whether she fancied a go in the hay; he hoped not, as she could barely stand. There was no need to worry; she was too incensed to be interested.

"Stinkin' bloody bitch," was all she said when she saw him.

"What!"

"Stinkin' bloody bitch." She repeated, "Wouldn't give me any more beer. Who does she think she is?"

"Is she the landlady?"

"Yair."

"Then she thought you had too much."

"Yair. Said so. How would she know? She's not me." Very true, thought Tom.

"Come home," he entreated.

"Don't want to. Want to tell that bitch what she is."

Tom felt helpless. Responsibility meant sorting this out, and she was being silly and irresponsible. He was not used to argument or persuasion, or only of the more obvious sort with men. He sensed that a rough and ready approach on her would not go well with the spectators who had assembled around them.

"Come home," he asked again.

"No."

"Come on. This isn't sensible. Let's talk about it at home." He did not know what he would say when he got her there. The thought of talk registered with her. She wanted to talk, but shout really, about the outrage she had suffered, and venting her voice was a start. She twitched and shrugged, muttered another obscenity and allowed him to take her firmly by the arm and away.

She slumped in a chair by the table in the cottage. He put away and out of her sight the cask of ale he had from the brewery. She had too much already, and he had lost his enthusiasm. Instead, he found bread, cheese and milk.

"Here." She looked at it, then away.

"Eat it! Eat it!" She picked up the food, as her anger and fight was not with him. She did, but then lunged forward and her mouth turfed the mangled food to the floor. There were lessons in marriage he had not expected.

"Bed!" he barked. She staggered to her feet, gripping the table, and almost fell. He stepped to hold her up, then half-dragged her to the bedroom with the other half throwing her on the bed. Returning to the kitchen, he got a bowl, and with an old rag cleared up the acrid mess on the floor and carefully rinsed the rag. They both slept fitfully, he aware there was now a black mark against them.

In the morning, he took a hard line. He slapped the rag, wet again, on her face, and hoicked her to her unsteady feet. "Get dressed. Here. Water. Drink it. Gargle." He thrust a glass of water at her. She hesitated, but knew in her sodden depths that her position was poor, and she did as he demanded.

"Go to work. I will walk with you. We are poorly thought of now." He walked her to work, left her and went to the brewery.

Her employer gave her a warning. "I should sack you. Stupid woman. But I don't like the woman at the White Horse either, so I'll let yer off now. Never do it again." She nodded weakly and went about her work, chastened and scrutinised.

There was another consequence. She had breached her Ticket and was again subject to authority. She was permitted to work, but her wages went into the Convict Bank. While she was prevented from spending, it reminded the Queen's Head that Mary had an unreliable past. Her work became more erratic as if sympathetic with her past, and after a few more months her employer eventually lost patience and she was sacked.

In such a small community, word travelled. Who would give this woman work; unreliable and with a demonstrably excessive drink habit? Her husband worked longer hours to catch up on her lost wages. It was a struggle.

"No one wants me here," she said. "I can't even get work to sew or make bonnets. I'll have to go to Hobart to do it."

Tom heard this, and it was true. She still had a good reputation there as a worker. She would have dangerous temptations to face which could undo all her good work, but he could see there was no option. He found, too, that his own wages were being depleted, and not by his employers.

At home. It coincided with her sudden departure on the early coach to Hobart, from whence she did not return for two days.

"Where have you been?" Tom demanded a response as she walked back into the cottage.

"I bin getting work in Hobart. They like me there." She turned around, looking pleased with herself, spinning so he could admire his wife in clothes he had not seen before.

"Where did you get the money for those?"

"Oh, I did some work on bonnets. They know me. 'Tis better pay."

Her trips to Hobart continued, lasting several days at a time, and she often returned wearing new clothes and looking very happy with herself. Pleasures continued, but the line between great and little blurred. Neither raised, nor faced, the obvious change in their respective circumstances. "Need to work," was all she said when he pressed her. She no longer seemed interested in the state of marital finance. Although he continued to secrete his own wages away in case a shortfall appeared, she showed indifference to his activities.

Mary was no longer seen as part of the community, nor did she want to be. She was ignored and she ignored them when she got off the coach, which was more and more infrequently, and the months drifted into a year or so. Tom picked up noises in the little town; he was not supposed to hear them, but there they were.

"She'll be playing up. The coachman knows Hobart. She likes a good time. Sorry for the man here. He works hard, well-liked... likes his ale, but who doesn't?"

Drifting, like a boat with shattered masts towards shoals, a marriage not made in heaven but not even close enough to be one of hell. What to do? Tom could not see a way forward.

Then came the one word which drives men MAD.

"*Gold*! They've found gold on the mainland!"

A brewery worker shouted the fatal word. A gabble of workers shouted back. "What! How do you know?" It was that fount of all knowledge, the coachman. "Big heaps of it, coachman says. Fall over it. One man stumbled over a rock, he thought. Big chunk of gold. Broke his leg, it did."

This was not good news for employers. Workers downed their tools and even belongings to head off and make their fortunes – wherever it was.

Tom hurried to the cottage to take what he needed: a few extra clothes, another pair of boots and a pick and a shovel, and his little stash of wages earned and hidden from his renegade wife. Mary was down in Hobart again, and would hear of the gold before he did. Even if he found her, he doubted he had enough for two fares to the mainland; he now had a better concept of the mainland compared to the island, a different meaning to that imparted by Jane Taylor. This gold was in the Port Phillip District, the place where Gellibrand had vanished into thin air all those years ago, and men like himself would be fighting over coach and ship tickets. He hoped he had enough, even for one ticket on each.

The brewer was reluctant to pay the small amount of outstanding wages since the last payday. Tom returned packed and impatiently awaited the next coach, even although it was not due until the early morning. Mary could have whatever was left in the cottage, though he doubted she would want any of it, even if she came back now with gold fever heating the brow of the Colony.

"I have to go for it. Can you pay me till yesterday?"

"What about the work? How do I go on?"

"Dunno that. The women can keep it going."

"What? With women?"

"They're very clever when you let' em," Tom tried to reassure him. "They work hard, too. But digging is Men's business. You'd want to."

The brewer paused. It was true. His mind raced to planning an adventure, to be rich beyond his expectation as a brewer. True too that women were surprisingly hard-working and resourceful when not in the kitchen.

Tom continued: "Reckon I'll come back with bags full of this stuff, and I could go into business with you, maybe. We could put breweries, pubs all over the island. Life of luxury, eh? Sounds good?"

It did. The brewer was seduced by the prospect. Scrimshaw doing all the work, too, while he kept brewing. He was tough and hard-working, despite or perhaps because of that wife he had.

"The extra cash will help. I did the work."

That was true. With a nod, the brewer left and returned with a few coins, which he counted out into Tom's palm. That is what a man is worth; bits of metal, Tom thought. He pocketed the coins and held out his hand, which the brewer took, both hoping against realistic odds that their lives would be richer for it.

Hobart beckoned on the morning coach. He hoped that crossing the coachman's hand with metal would help secure a seat. He expected his wife would be celebrating the gold discoveries in her own way, somewhere in the town. That was her way; this was his. Hobart became to him a world to be paved with gold, not dirt.

CHAPTER 15

Hobart, 1854

"Ho! Scrimshaw, isn't it? Have not seen you for a while. Must be twenty years or more. You were known in the papers. Used to hear of your trips to the courts."

Tom turned to see the man who spoke to him. A man he recognised, although he could not immediately recall his name. A man in his late fifties, paunchy, suggesting a good life, and sporting a top hat, a fashionable floral waistcoat and, Tom noted, shiny black shoes. A man keen to impress that he had done well.

Noticing that Tom had not immediately recognised who he was, the man added. "Alan. Great wall builder. Gellibrand and bloody Sam. First one disappeared, second was murdered one night. Good riddance. Never found who did it."

"Yair," Tom said, happy to share just a bit of his experience. "Went off to the goldfields like half the town – the male half. Sailed to Melbourne, then off to Bendigo Creek. I was told you would fall over gold, there was so much. But none jumped into my pocket, I can tell you! The creek is just big yellow puddles, or even pools. Lots trying their luck in them, even though you couldn't see the bottom. Or digging hopeful holes, as I did. I even took my own pick and shovel. Pretty smelly it was, too. Miners not keen on good habits. They take up too much time, and someone else might find the gold you would have got. T'was hot, too, not like here. All I found was fool's gold, which served me right.

"It's very pricey, too. Here, you get a bed – at least something to lie on – some food and a roof. You work bloody hard and get treated like shit, but you do get bed, food and shelter. Not there. On your own. Rain?

Wet? Tired? There's only the ground, under a tree if you're lucky, or unlucky with its roots. Food? 'Where's yer money?' they say. You can come and go, but to what?

"So I found no gold and soon I had no money. The belly demands work. There's lots of boredom. Some who get gold splash it out a bit, to show off. There's games, contests, even fights. Some fights for prizes. So I got myself a couple of prize fights. A few fancy themselves after a few beers, they found some gold and think they're lucky all round. A couple of weeks digging and sifting and they think they are hard men. But they're soft. I won both of them. And I got good money. So they wanted me to fight more. But I'm too old now. The prize money got me out.

"I headed for Geelong on the coach. Melbourne is too clever, pricey, noisy and full of thieves. Geelong is closer to Bendigo Creek, as the crow flies. I went through the goldfields at Ballarat. More wasted time by others, but not me. The coach took me to Corio Bay as they call it, and with lots of empty boats.

"I found plenty of work there, in Melbourne too. Boats come in, then the crew always jump ship and head for the gold. So who sails the ships back again? Shipowners and merchants have produce and animals to sell or buy, or rot or die. Desperate for crew, they are, from here and the north of the island to the mainland. Back and forth. They'll pay anything.

"So I made good money, bloody good money. I know something of boats and got work as ship's carpenter. I'm still doing that. They know me, and I don't jump ship. So I go back and forth here to the islands and mainland."

"Sounds good," his old fieldmate responded, now hoping for an inroad so he could elaborate at similar length on how well he had done; certainly better and more stable than sailing from here to there and back again. Ah, he'd ask about Tom's wife, that should do it.

"Your wife go with you?"

"Na. Not enough cash for two. We were in Hamilton. She came and went between there and here. When I came back here, I went looking for her. Everywhere I went she had been, but no one knew where she had gone after. I never caught up with her."

"Ah, she's been around all right. Got into trouble with the courts. Going round the pubs, chatting the men; know what I mean?" Alan paused to let it sink in. "She got time in hard labour. I'm not sure where she is now."

He waited expectantly for the response to lead him into his own successes.

"Hmm, that sounds like her," Tom nodded. "She always said a girl, or woman, does what she needs to do to live. She's plenty of spirit there, and clever. Sort it out, she will."

This was not the anticipated reply. A silence descended upon them.

"Well," Tom said, to close the conversation, "that boat over there." He pointed to a ship moored at the quay, busy loading freight and with a few cattle waiting to be loaded. "Just about ready to sail. I will do the last checks. There'll be plenty of work at the other end, either a return on this one, or another. I have places to stay wherever I dock. 'Tis peaceful; good and fine wages and my own man. Good to see you, Alan. Hope all well. God speed." With that, Tom left with his bag of possessions and his bag of trade tools, and went to the vessel.

While not exactly a friend, this old wall builder stood frustrated and disconcerted on the quay, watching this man walk steadily back to the ship and then board her.

He, too, had been a Ticket of Leave man, and had been denied the opportunity to show his ascent of the mountain of respectability, with a good wife in tow. A man whose wall-building prowess got him work after his Ticket was granted. More work kept coming in, and then he had branched out as a building contractor employing a good number of men in and around the Town. A man of wealth and importance, of good reputation in the Town with a doting wife and five children to continue the family business. He had a lot to be justifiably proud of. Alan had found a man who knew his beginnings, and somehow the moment to compare his success had slipped past.

He went home and snapped with irritation at his younger wife.

CHAPTER 16

Geelong, 1862

Late afternoon. A gentle breeze blew off Corio Bay. Across the light blue expanse of Port Phillip Bay, the lump of Arthur's Seat kept a surly eye upon the craft sailing up and down the waters of the bay in their pursuit of trade or fish.

Tom Scrimshaw noticed a few clouds above his head as he stood smoking a roll-up before going into a nearby pub he frequented as it was close to his lodgings.

Into his uninterested vision came a young lady, struggling a little under the weight and bulk of two large bags and a basket, all full of goods. A pretty girl he saw, not much more than twenty, with brown curly hair and a neat bonnet covering most of it, in a dark brown dress with a pink bodice. She had obviously been shopping nearby with considerable success.

As she approached the Black Dog Inn on her walk, a young man came out of the pub, who seemed a little unsteady, as if excessive time was spent patting the black dog within. He lurched towards the girl.

"C'm here girl. H'about a good time?"

She ignored him as she went to go past with her load.

"Don't be like that. Here." He came close to the girl and pushed her, laughing. She dropped her bags and basket, scattering her purchases. Distressed, she bent to pick up the bags and basket to collect her goods. As she bent, the young man put his hand up her dress. She screamed, dropping the bag she had retrieved and started crying.

Tom dropped the roll-up from his lips.

"Leave her alone, lad. She's a working girl, not your toy to play with. Too much drink in you."

The young man, temporarily distracted, turned to him.

"What's it to you, old fart? You after a swift smack? My fist will do for you." He turned back to the struggling girl, his hand seeking her again under her dress.

Tom moved swiftly to him, spun him and punched him hard in the solar plexus. The recipient, badly winded, dropped his hands and his head. Tom grabbed the youth's ears and drove the head down to meet his raised knee. There was a crack, a groan, blood coming from his nose, followed by a punch to the side of the head as he dropped to the ground. There, he received a kick to the ribs to aid his journey into a temporary, painful oblivion. The groaning ceased.

Keeping an eye on the prostrate man, in case he managed an aggressive move, Tom gathered the bags and basket, found their scattered contents and restored them to the containers. The girl stood and watched, sobbing. When he'd finished putting her things back in order, Tom motioned to her to sit on a bench, which she did slowly, and eventually calmed down and the young man on the ground managed a twitch.

"Thank you, sir, thank you. He was horrible..."

"What are you doing here?"

"Shopping for my lady. From Colac, we came. She bid me buy these," she pointed to the basket and bags, "and return to her hotel."

"Where you stay, too?"

"No, sir. I room nearby when I am not needed. Yesterday we came here. And tomorrow we must go."

"Your voice sounds familiar. There's a sound in it. Where are you from, and who are you?"

"Grace, sir, like my mother, a Grace from Devon, too. Grace Hall, I am. I came here with other girls like me, we're to work as servants."

She paused thoughtfully. "In Devon, I was nothing. There was no paid work. Even if I found a fair man to marry, he'd still be a one that we'd still struggle for food and lodging. Seen people dying from want of it."

That was the sound, Tom realised. Mary, wherever she was now, had hailed from Devon too, in the old country.

"Here in the Colonies, my mam and dad hoped I would do better. Could I do worse?" She managed a rueful smile, then frowned, a crinkle appearing in her slightly tanned brow. "I did not expect this."

She rose slowly from the bench with a sigh, and held her arms out for the shopping-basket. "I must get back, sir. Thank you for your kindness, though. "

Tom stood, too, bending to check the condition of the fellow on the ground, who was gradually stirring. "I will take you, Grace, to this hotel. You are not safe here. Some girls fight hard, but I fear for you, in Devon or here." With a glance at the still-horizontal man, they left in the direction she indicated.

The hotel was as he anticipated; very grand, as one of the finest. He had seen it in passing, but expected no other contact. Walking up the steps into the foyer, they were met by a woman dressed in what he could only assume was the latest fashion stood straight and confident. A woman younger than himself, but with the impatient air of a woman unfamiliar with having any orders unmet.

"What kept you, girl?" she demanded, her arched eyebrows looking directly at Grace.

"This very kind sir, my lady," Grace replied. "He averted me from an awful fate. I was returning with what you ordered, but a terrible man came at me. This man here came to my aid; he fought and beat him till he lay very still."

"Most commendable, sir."

"Here is not safe, ma'am, for ladies young or older," Tom said; "working girls, respectable girls. There is unwanted attention."

"Would there were more men like you," the lady said. "Live you here? You have a name?"

"Tom will do, ma'am. The other can confuse, though sturdy as English oak. I lodge nearby. A ship's carpenter I be, for the past ten years or so. Back and forth I go, twixt here and Melbourne to the island, to Hobart and Launceston, on different ships. I am between sails presently."

"If you may find your way to Colac," the lady said, "some forty or so miles from here, we shall be pleased to offer you a short respite in one of our buildings in recognition of preserving our goods. And our servant."

Tom thought. "'Tis ten days till my next sail. I do not know Colac... a few days there might do me well. Thank you, ma'am, I would be glad of it. If I have your address, I will find a passage in the next day or two, and for my collection a few days later."

"That is quite acceptable," the lady affirmed. "I will instruct my coachman to furnish you with some directions, too." She looked at Grace, pointed to where she wanted the goods deposited, and swept off. Tom and Grace looked briefly at each other before she hurriedly left with her orders. The coachman arrived.

Tom walked slowly back to his lodgings, avoiding the route past The Black Dog in case that young man had recovered sufficiently to seek revenge, unlikely though he thought it was. As he walked, he thought about this unexpected adventure. She is sweet and trembling. Pretty, too. Unwed girls are as rare as hen's teeth in the Colonies, and there are so many men to choose from. Still, I will stretch my old, iron-cropped legs in this new place, Colac.

✻

The station was based around Lake Colac where the settlers' tentacles snaked into the south and west of the new district as clearances continued. The township was soon awash with news of poor Grace's ordeal. She was too ashamed to recount the day's events in detail in her recall to the other young female servants: Molly, Kate, Ruth and Florence, a number thought necessary to help manage a large agricultural and grazing station, not long hacked from the bush and now thriving well enough with an edging of the civilising stamp of the Mother Country upon it. The other servants heard from her the statement from the rescuer that she had suffered "unwanted attention." That pinged excitedly around their young febrile imaginations.

The girls were friendly with the men of various ages, working to make the station profitable, helped by fertile soils and adequate water, with the lake dominating the landscape. There were varying degrees of flirtation and intimacy among them; all discreet, as discovery could end in the sack.

By the time the news had spread, Grace's saviour had become over six feet tall and had thrashed, nay pulverised, was it one, two or three oafs in protecting Grace's honour? It had to be acknowledged that Grace's honour was the focus of a couple of the workers not otherwise engaged in real or hoped-for dalliances with Molly, Kate, Ruth and Flo, depending on the degree of boredom either side felt. She was not as yet, however, amenable to any invitations.

But now, here was a new man, a hero who had saved her reputation; which yet endured for the men to aim to remove, and he had saved ma'am's bits and pieces as well.

Tom took the directions, both verbal and written, and when he arrived in Colac presented himself to the contact. He was advised to wait for transport to the property which would be dispatched once informed, as they now would be, of his arrival in the town. A cart duly arrived. Just him and his bag on board. When he entered the farm there was no welcome as such, just curiosity at this man, smaller and much older than his hero status demanded. Broad and weathered, yes – but beating up three oafs? They must have been mere boys. The older farmhands sensed this was a man who would not say much, and did not need to. A man who had been in and through it, and kept it covered.

"Over there. In with this lot." The cart driver nodded towards a barn. The men looked at him, and he, at them. Whatever his physical shortcomings, he was invited by ma'am and there were risks in challenging him, if the younger men were thinking about it. Tom walked past them all to the barn.

Ruth had been detailed to prepare a bed therein for him, and stood by the door, excitedly awaiting this mighty saviour of Grace. Well, she said to her friends later, if that's what Grace got, she's welcome to him. In her disappointment, she directed him to the bed and hurriedly left. He put his bag down. There were a few men still in the barn. One put out a feeler of curiosity to this man.

"Where y' from?"

"None of your business."

This was enough. As this abrupt conversation passed between him and his interlocutor, the other workers decided he was a man from The Island, which meant, in the notoriety of the Colony, that Port Arthur was the place. There was no evidence other than this intuition of his history, but that satisfied them. No one ever escaped; most were believed to have died a terrible death in the Jaws of Hell and the clutches of the Devil. The more superstitious of the group feared he might be the Devil himself come among them for their sins. If he was from the abyss, he was best left alone.

Added to that circumspection was Grace. Pretty enough and though naïve and a bit silly, the young men wanted a piece of her. But she had the ear of ma'am and anything which happened to him, or her, would get back to ma'am and pillow talk with her husband. The girls said the pillows are of the finest softest linen. How they knew this was beyond the men's ken… but if her husband knew his wife was unhappy by her mutters on the linen, and knew the cause, then a man could be picking up his sack to seek work elsewhere, without a reference from this best of all workplaces. Safer to leave Grace and this weird old man alone, it was tacitly agreed.

In the morning, the men in the barn prepared for work. The days of orders up at sunup now gone, there was no cause for Tom to follow suit. He was also sensitive about exhibiting any glimpse of his bare body, with its criss-cross evidence of his past. He was master of his own (admittedly minuscule) realm.

When he was alone, he washed himself and his clothes, which he hung out to dry, no longer at risk of thievery being too old and worn, though he was pleased with different soaps to try on them. Although the seasons were soon changing it was warm, and his clothes would soon dry.

Then there was breakfast. Ma'am was fully cognisant of her duties as hostess, albeit in unforeseen circumstances with a guest she would never have imagined. However, she appreciated the effort he made on behalf of herself and her servant. She instructed her female servants to accommodate his presence, even if outside the station routine, such as his being late for breakfast. She also needed to oversee Grace, a sweet young girl. She had her duties, and this man was not invited to interfere with those responsibilities, nor should it be so. He could enjoy a strange area, the clear air, and explore the station and its organisation.

Tom found his way to the breakfast area pointed out the night before. Flo and Kate, on kitchen duties, watched him with great disappointment; this old man with a big nose to match his age. Later, they gossiped about him; how his manners were no better than the rest they daily served. There was an oddity with him, an untamed waft which was attractive, if you liked that sort of thing.

Oblivious, Tom enjoyed a hearty breakfast of mutton, eggs, mugs of tea and large gulps of milk fresh from the herd; it was all delicious. Then he went outside.

The light was so clear, he swore he could see two flies crawling up the wall across the yard. The gold gamblers in Bendigo Creek would bet on them in a race. He decided to walk around the property. The fenced paddocks were enormous, they would have dwarfed old Gellibrand's in comparison. He could enter through a gate and walk until he came to another fence, and follow until he found either another gate, or if a corner then re-trace to go in the opposite direction. In all his years in the Colonies, he had never had any freedom to explore this land in this way. Days doing just this could not be expected to come ever again.

There were probably Blacks lurking in the dark, forested hills, but he had never had cause to think about them and would not start now. They were there in Tasmania, as it was now called, though not many left now, as they were hunted like foxes by the military and settlers. Wouldn't give a convict a gun, would they? Enough now to go to this horizon; that was freedom.

*

Ma'am, Mistress, my lady, whatever name she was called by her staff, was aware that as head of the station (subject to her husband of course), her duty was to promote and exhibit hard work and Christian values to all within her orbit. It is what made the station what it was: an example of what Christian teaching can achieve.

The Matriarch; a term she thought she had picked up from Biblical study, or had someone just said that about her? Either way, she rather liked it. She knew her junior charges would note any shortfall in her example. Her personal feelings about this new guest, who was only passing through after all, were confused by two points of reference: one of distaste for an obvious unsavoury past, the other an exoticism for the same reason. She thought it important her values should be demonstrated in such an unusual situation.

"Today," she announced at her morning gathering of those under her domestic control, "I will have Grace tending to my requirements in place of Molly from five o'clock in the evening, and Molly will undertake Grace's duties until then. Is that clear?" She repeated it as a command, not a question. "Is that clear!"

The household had nothing to say, save curtsey in their little linen caps, unfortunately not topped with the grand chiffon-draped headgear of their mistress, and shuffle off.

"Grace. Stay. You may go and show our visitor the charms and workings of our station. I am sure he will be outside, wondering where and how to appreciate what is opened before him. Do what you can, girl, to sustain his interest."

Molly and the girls overheard this command and left with pinched faces, even though the work involved was simply rearranged, not changed, and the day rolled itself across western Victoria (as it was now called) like a slightly worn nobbled carpet.

Grace felt ashamed. She was now with this man, her earthly saviour, without any warning as a servant girl. How could she thank him further as a mere servant? Her orders were clear. Off into the bright sky she went, and found him wandering around the perimeter, unsure what to do, just as she was. He was not a young man, nor handsome, but she thought, neither was she. He was clean, bewhiskered, with a little grey starting through the hair.

Tom heard her footsteps crunching on the gravel with the edge of walking on eggshells. She turned towards him, looking clearly nervous, not sure what to say or do, and probably unsure about men. Then again, he knew not much more about women, overall.

Did it matter? No, an awkward girl and an awkward old man, old enough to be her father, maybe even her grandfather. He would be proud to see her as a granddaughter, had there been any children. That had passed him by as far as he knew, definitely after that terrible day in the Port strangled all his longings and imaginings.

He turned to see her. Grace in a dress. Was it brown? Was it grey? Simple and adequate for her role. She wore a tight bodice; he often wondered how women breathed in these things. Her cloth bonnet, tightly strapped against her head, protected against the quixotic breezes. She was, despite the formal attempts to hide it, a pretty girl with brown eyes and very comely, a word he had heard about the female figure. What he wondered, did they say about men's figures? She was of a decent height, a good hard-working girl from a hard home. She expected life to be hard while she had it, and was uncomplaining of her lot until then. Even then. She looked down at her shoes, betraying her uncertainty. His shoemaker's eye pronounced her working shoes as ill-fitting as she approached.

Grace watched him too. Not so heroic, but not unheroic, either. Taller than most of the men, bigger nose than most too, but somehow in keeping with the rest of his face. She took in his bushy eyebrows and blue-grey eyes (or were they blue?) when he raised them from studying his boots to look at her. A man also nervous out of his routine. He had a lined, tanned face from exposure to the elements, both natural and manmade.

When he moved, there was a slight limp. Was that, she wondered, from the fight in Geelong? She knew even from her limited experience, that he was not a man to be trifled with. Whatever he was, wherever he had been, or why or how, or where he would go, he would have more control of himself than other men did or would. She halted before him.

"Hullo, sir."

"Hullo, miss. Miss Grace. Call me Tom, please. 'Sir' is too strange to me."

"Yes, sir," she hastily corrected herself, "I mean Tom. Please call me Grace. Everyone does. My mistress allowed me time to take you around the property to see what we do."

She lowered her voice. "I do not know myself how much land we have here, nor can I tell you much of the family who tamed this land, it is said. I am just a servant girl and I am grateful for her leaving me off my work today.

"She also gives us help for our lives, the mistress. I never had much schooling. I had to work for the family. We all did. I cannot read and write much, but I can add and do sums. The lady has lots of us who can't do much reading and writing, but she has someone who can. We can send messages on what we say, and make little marks on them to prove it is us. She thinks we need to learn more to be good girls and women in this new country. I like it here. Do you? It is very exciting.

She continued: "Every day a man goes into Colac for the post and sends ours from here. I have not, so far. Who would I send to? My mam and dad, may God preserve them, would not know how to receive it, if they are still alive. But I can do it."

Tom reflected on his communication channels. He had never thought of attempting to send a message back to England.

"I have rooms in the ports I sail to," he said. "I can get messages there; need to for the boats I work, to know when they are to sail. A man I drink with reads and writes. So I get him a glass or two and he reads to me, and writes out what I say, and then I send it to the Post if I need to. I never did much at school either. No need to, I was told."

She nodded. Not knowing what to do, she impulsively put out her hand, and he instinctively took it, although it was an unfamiliar gesture for them both. Her hand still soft from domestic toil, his hardened by hard labour.

When parted, she asked, "Where would you like to go?"

"Over there?" He pointed to a dark mass of bush which looked about three miles distant.

Grace looked unhappy. She looked again at the ground. "That would be nice. But, I don't know how much land we have. I have never been much beyond the homestead, so I do not know what there is there, or..." she faltered, "anywhere."

He heard her voice falter and her feet scruff the earth. He looked down; these were domestic shoes, not for tramping across fields into what she saw as going towards darkness with a man, even this one. He had experienced enough monsters to know her fear of the unknown was real.

"Nah... too hot," he said encouragingly. "Let's just walk about in these paddocks... fields." He corrected himself with a more English word. "They're huge."

She nodded, grateful. Two people, an old man, by the life expectancy of the time, seasoned by experience; and a young girl, neither with any real social or verbal skills to help steer them through life. Or through moments like this.

Into, around and through the seemingly endless paddocks they walked, with cattle and sheep and wheat and the silent grass for mute company, comfortable and at peace with themselves, each other and this piece of the world.

"I'm happy we met," she started, eventually.

"Me too. Meeting you. Not so nice there." He meant Geelong.

"Where are you from?" she asked.

This was more difficult. Lincolnshire? Hobart? Port Arthur? What would she think? Did it matter?

"Like you, from the Old Country. Even older now. Came from Lincolnshire, many many years ago now. I made boots and shoes. Came here for the climate," he smiled. She giggled.

"I – well – I did lots of things, and got used to the place", Tom continued. "Strange it is, but it's a comfort when you get to know it, or some of it. There's lots of nasties, snakes and so on, but some are people. Both can kill you."

Grace shuddered. As she suspected, this man knew more than she wanted to know, about things she wanted to know about. She could not ask more; her shudder told her so.

"You?" he asked, peremptorily.

"Just a bunch of kids in a Devon village. It was awful. Dad got caught pinching some turnips."

"Turnips?"

"Yes. We were hungry." This stopped Tom. He, at least, was sent down for greed; taking stuff to enjoy or sell. Mary, too, wherever she was, had been, got her seven years for stealing some ribbon. But a few muddy turnips to feed starving kids – turnips! Bloody Mother Country! It could go to Hell – or already was there.

His voice cut in on his thoughts.

"Silly kids, all silly kids, doing silly things, all end up here if not strung up first. 'Tis a big price for being silly. Out of sight here, out of mind, rot or die. Not all do though... not all."

They walked on, occasionally commenting on a bird, a sound or something odd. As conversation had never been part of their lives, they were comfortable with silence and each other. Grace was able to keep time from the little timepiece she had, and the moving hands reminded her of her debt to Molly and that she had to take over.

When homing in on the homestead, Grace turned to her companion. "It's been lovely. I never get the chance to wander. You've done it for me, in being here."

"Yair. Loved it too. Same thing. Never really had time to look and listen. Or just be with someone like that, too."

It was true. Lovely Marianne's walks had been hers alone, and he had never taken one with Mary, nor with the voracious women back in Hobart.

Grace turned full to him and gave him such a smile that her teeth slightly parted. "Will I see you tomorrow, if my lady lets me?"

"Yair. Reckon I'll stay another day, unless I'm told something different."

Grace turned back and half-skipped to the outbuilding to start work. Tom turned, too, and walked to the fence enclosing the homestead and outbuildings. He looked in all directions, this bush now tamed. Men could make a green and pleasant land out of wilderness; he had heard that said. He was not sure that 'pleasant' was the right word here; there was a ridge of enormous, craggy rock with bush clambering wildly over it for thousands of miles northwards, it was said. Even here, Victoria, the smallest Colony, was bigger than England, Scotland and Wales put together, and much of it was yet unexplored.

With a sigh, he turned to his temporary bed and prepared for the evening meal when the men returned from their labours. He sat alone at dinner, the other men making no effort to engage with him, but he was content with that and his memories of the day to mull over. Peace had never been a close friend, barely an acquaintance – but now he had been touched by it.

Next day dawned bright, dry and warm, promising much, especially if Tom stayed another day and snatched a little more peace with this lovely girl. He finished breakfast alone, and the men went to work wherever they were required. As he rose, one of the girls – was it Flo? – came to him.

"The Mistress wishes to see you. Go to the house, press the bell at the side of the front door. Someone will come for you."

Was he about to get his marching orders? He could not complain, it had all been far better than he had hoped. He went to the door, amazed again how this elegant, very large house had been built and crafted in place of bush, snakes and wild creatures, but looking like it had been there forever. Pressing the bell, he was surprised to find the door frame was almost immediately filled by a shape, which opened the door and came out.

The Mistress herself, dressed soberly in black. There was none of the bright, gay colours of early Hobart, or even the Port. She was however, reflecting fashion and social mores as they filtered to the Colonies, on account of news of the death of the Consort.

She motioned Tom to sit in a chair on the veranda and she took a comfortably well-cherished seat at an angle to him.

"I trust you have enjoyed your time here... er... Tom."

"Yes ma'am. Time and peace are usually strangers to me."

"You had some time on the Island?" Both knew that meant Tasmania, as the Colony was now to be known.

"Yes."

"Did you know a man called Gellibrand?"

264

Tom stiffened. He hoped she would not notice. But she did. There was no profit in explaining how and why he knew Mr Gellibrand, but a simple acknowledgement would have to do.

He nodded. "Yes, ma'am. I knew of him. He was said to have disappeared on an expedition over here in this Colony? It must have been nigh on twenty-five, thirty year ago. Time flies so fast."

"He disappeared not far from here," she affirmed. "There were many searches for him, unsuccessful, alas. Until a gentleman from further west than here, on the coast, organised a search about twenty years ago.

"He found a tribe of Blacks, who told him that Mr Gellibrand found his way, nearly dead, into the tribe. They had looked after him for some two months. He said his companion had died. But then, another lot of Blacks came and murdered him! The poor gentleman was taken to his grave. Mr Gellibrand was buried here, on our land, before it was cleared. The gentleman searching for him was shown the grave, and took his skull away. It sounds like that Shakespearean play where the hero talks to the skull. Was it Hamlet?"

Who? What? Talking skull? What things happen in this land? "A talking skull, ma'am?"

"No, no," she laughed. "He spoke to the skull."

Tom was unsure whether this was worse. He had a vague memory of a name something like Shakespeare. Unusual name, but what's in a name? This was all beyond him.

"Er... What happened to the skull?"

"It was taken back, and identified as being Mr Gellibrand's."

This was certainly worse. How would anyone know, unless Mr Gellibrand had two skulls and they could be compared, one to the other? When he had last seen Mr Gellibrand, he was certainly in possession of only one skull, hidden under his face as is usual. Did funny things happen here? Really strange.

He asked, hesitantly, "What happened then?"

"The expedition went out and punished the murderers. The whole tribe was wiped out."

Blacks never did well anywhere, thought Tom. Nor did Marianne. A short silence.

Then she said, "We have noticed in this short time that you seem to fit in here very well and the men have respect for you."

It flashed through Tom's mind that respect was probably not the right word. Where was this going?

"I, too, have emphasised to my husband your qualities in preserving my goods and items and protecting my servant Grace, who is a fine, gentle girl."

Tom nodded. "She is."

"He asked me to offer you work on the station. You will be handsomely rewarded."

This was completely unexpected. Various thoughts popped up in his mind. Aside from a life with Marianne that he never could have won, this was as close to Paradise as he could imagine, and yes, there was a lovely young girl he found peace and contentment with.

Yet, and yet. He had vowed, after his years of blood and sweat on the Island, that he would never labour on the land for any man, only for himself. It was a promise to himself that sustained him in his sense of self-worth. To accept this offer would be going backwards. He had achieved a measure of respect and worth, both self and financial, as a ship's carpenter, working when he chose. He could not surrender that.

The lady was surprised he had not, in effect, kissed her hand in gratitude. Then, he spoke.

"I am very surprised and honoured by your offer," Tom said slowly, mustering all the delicacy and refinement he could. "Please forgive my silence while I thought about it. Over many years of work on the Island, I vowed I would never again work the land for another man. I would only work for myself, if the chance came. I would not be true to myself to overturn that promise. I work for myself, a free man, as ship's carpenter. I am well-known in shipping and, thank God, I have never been short of work. I have breaks between sails, which is how Grace and me met.

"Sadly, therefore, I have to say no to your generous offer. I am, however, eager to remain in contact through young Grace. I sail into Geelong from time to time, and I would hope to see you and her on your trips to the town. It depends on the times linking like a chain.

"My reading and writing is not good, but I have someone in Geelong who does it for me when I need it. I can send a message from Geelong to Colac on when I will next be there. Or how long I will be there. If it fits in with your expectations, it would be very welcome."

The lady was a little put out by this refusal, an act which was foreign to her. No one had ever refused to work for her husband or herself. But she could see his point, and it was consistent with the decency she had witnessed. Very well, sobeit.

"I am sorry to hear what you say," she replied, "but I appreciate your stated principle. We have a facility here for staff who have the misfortune of lacking reading and writing skills. If our working people need to make contact away from here, a letter will be prepared and delivered by our daily cart to Colac, which delivers and collects mail, among other requirements.

"It will therefore be possible for Grace to send and receive letters from you, which will be written and read in strictest confidence. Now, on practical matters, when were you thinking of departing?"

"I thought tomorrow, ma'am, if I may take the cart to Colac, where I will stay until the next coach to Geelong for my next sail."

"That is acceptable. I will arrange a seat for you. I will also arrange for Grace to finish her duties early so you can see her before you go. She will finish at four o'clock and there will still be enough light in which to walk about." She stood up, nodded to indicate the conversation was over, and went inside.

Tom, with a mixture of confusion and relief, rose, went down the steps and walked aimlessly around the property, checking on the clock from time to time as the hands seemed reluctant to move towards four. Then at four precisely, Grace skipped out of a side building in a skirt and top, both dark brown, her bonnet tied under her chin, feet crunching on the gravel.

"Here I am!" she announced excitedly. She held out her hand and he took it, but not too firmly.

"Where will we go?" he asked.

"Oh, let's go down to the creek. Down over there." She pointed to a shallow valley which appeared about ten minutes' walk away, with telltale trees marking a water course. They went through a gate, closed it and walked across two paddocks until they reached the stream. There was a small, grassy area surrounded by stringy gum trees, with some light flickering through the leaves in the late-afternoon sun. The weather was dry, and she sat down and took off her bonnet. Her brown hair was tied tight to her head with braids and pins.

"Oh, this is so lovely," she sighed.

"Yes." He paused. "I am going tomorrow. Had my few days and it is very good here, but it's time for me to go. We can keep in touch, though. I saw the Mistress today, and she said we can send letters. We might even meet in Geelong when she goes, if she takes you along."

Grace was devastated. When the Mistress said she could leave at four to see Tom, she did not know there had been a meeting, much less that he was leaving. She felt vulnerable again. She had built a new confidence, a feeling she could cope with anything so long as he was here to watch for her. Now he was going. She felt restless, a pain, a need to be close to touch and be touched. A connection. There was something different going on within her she did not recognise, but an experience was to be taken.

She realised, to her own great surprise, that she wanted him, this grizzled old man. Whatever anyone else would say or think, did not affect her desire. The girls gossiped about the men and being with them. When they "did it" it hurt. Or could. Or did not. It was nothing special. It was. You had to keep at it, like a habit, to get the hang of it. So many contrary opinions. She did not know what it would be like. She was apprehensive, scared but excited, and it was time, it was time.

He did not seem to notice. How could she let him know what she wanted and needed? She tentatively reached down and lifted her skirt up to reveal her lower legs, nicely shaped they were, she thought immodestly, and then lifted the skirt higher to just above her knees, with her feet in her work boots pointing to the sky. She looked at him and then at her raised skirt, not with an attempt to cover herself but raised as an invitation to explore.

Yes, he was puzzled given the age chasm, and she had a wide range of eligible men at her disposal, yet his training from Jane Taylor on women's needs and wants was not wasted. This young girl was showing him what she wanted. From him. He started touching her slowly and gently on parts of her body she had almost not known she had. Her desire rose and exploded as he explored her. It was so good.

Afterwards, she was surprised how gentle he had been with her. How wonderful and caring he was with her vulnerability. She was on the side of when it is wonderful you radiate confidence, not the disappointing side. Did she imagine in the joy of receiving him that he shed years, his face smooth and line-free, a young man again?

They lay there, his arm around her and enjoying each other, as the light started to drop and fade, as if their little darting beams had done their work and a breeze was becoming cooler. Time to return, and eat, so prosaic after this shared time.

"Will I see you tomorrow?"

"I take the cart to Colac. I will be told when. But I will give and leave you my address in Geelong. You will remember it." There was no doubt that each of them would hold these addresses tight within their minds.

"I have a man in Geelong who will write for me and tell you of my movements. And he will read me what you say. Ma'am said you have someone here too?"

"Yes, she helps our education," Grace said. "I will write to you as Tom, and I will add three crosses as kisses so you will know it is from me."

"That is good. I will send the envelope to Grace with three kisses, too. I hope we can meet. I am sure we will."

When they thought they were out of sight, he bent and with his stubbled face he kissed her lips. She thought she would faint and clung to him. She never imagined it happening, and it happened so quickly. He gave her confidence, whatever happened, although she decided not to think about that. They parted, with a lingering releasing of fingers as he went to his dinner and she to hers with her friends. She avoided their gaze and the furtive looks exchanged between them. Did they notice her slight smile? She cared not. They would dismiss the thought as too awful to contemplate.

They returned to their shared rooms and Grace slept happy, re-living what would have been less likely than the sun falling from the sky a week earlier.

When Grace came on duty in the morning, the Mistress knew. Women always do.

"It happened," she mused. Grace had a new spring and self-confidence. Grace had left the girls' field of gentle pale flowers and balmy sun and crossed, never to return, into the field of women, so much bigger and wilder with great joyous blooms of red, yellow, purple, orange, blue, of luminous greens. There were nettles and brambles to negotiate, predators, vipers, poisons for the unwary and at the field's end withering and decay into which all must pass.

CHAPTER 17

Colac, 1863

Grace continued her duties. From Geelong, Tom returned to Hobart and immediately sought vessels due to sail to Geelong rather than Melbourne. His inquiries found sailings from Launceston to Geelong, and in juggling coach routes he made those voyages.

The little system of exchanges worked, with three crosses of erratic sizes and someone to write and read the contents. Yes, Grace went to Geelong with the Mistress for additional necessities, but Poseidon did not command the waves to match the horses' hooves, and frustration and disappointment bubbled away.

Then, some months after their parting, Tom arrived at his Geelong lodging and found a "Tom xxx." Dropping off his bags he hurried with his envelope to his source, the publican at his regular inn.

"Got this one, Fred. A glass for you for your trouble."

"Let's see." Fred went to a barrel and returned with two glasses of golden ale, their little white baby heads glistening in the sunbeams hunting in the inn's darker room. Tom grasped the beer, waiting for the contents to be revealed. Fred pushed his fingers under the envelope and, with a rough tug, prised the seal and reached inside to withdraw two folded pages which he unfolded. He reached for his spectacles and read out.

"Dear Tom, I hope you are well. I am missing you very much. I am fine here, although I am having a baby."

Fred paused and raised his eyebrows at Tom, who felt a very peculiar sensation in his stomach but said nothing. Fred continued reading: "It came from when we were by the creek the day before you left. I have not been with anyone else. I would hate it.

"I have not been feeling very well for some time and it was only when I was sick a few times and my tummy did not feel like it did before, that My Lady asked me some questions. I am due to have the baby about July, she says.

"I am very happy knowing it is yours. I do not expect you, as an experienced man, to do anything more, but I thought you should know. My Lady said so, too. She said I can work while I am able, but I will have to go to Colac for the baby and must then leave my work. She does not want to encourage the other girls, she has more than enough with her own children, she says. There is a little hospital in Colac with a doctor, so I will be alright at first.

"Your special friend,

Grace."

Fred took off his glasses and looked at Tom. "Well, you were busy there. Didn't think you had kids."

"Didn't think I did either."

"What will you do?"

"Dunno. Think about it." Tom gulped down his ale. "Better have another. You too." He had several more glasses as he sat, pondering this unexpected news. He was responsible for this child. While he had a sense of responsibility for Grace that was different from life with Mary – and what happened there – and Grace was young and innocent, which Mary certainly was not, when did responsibility start and end? Did it ever end with a kid, even when grown up?

His parents had washed themselves of responsibility for him, and he thought he did not need them as he was adult. Well, that was a bit of a laugh. His responsibility for Grace had surely stopped when he took her back to her lady. But now, now there was a baby. His! And in his fifties!

He believed her when she said so. He had never thought about making life before. Not true. Ached for it with Marianne, but where did that go? A dream, a fantasy chopped... no, hung. Mary had never mentioned any interest in children. True, they were only together for a couple of years, but they were always at it when they were, and she seemed to have her body under control, whatever she did with it. Grace was, however, real in this real world.

"I'll come back tomorrow to say more. Think on it," he told Fred. He weaved to the door, partly from rapid ale consumption, partly from the shock of the revelation, and pulled the door behind him.

In the morning, he was back, waiting for the door to open.

"A hard night?" Fred said, when he opened.

Did some thinking. I'm not used to it. If you're not too busy?"

"No, not at this time."

"If you get your paper and pen, I will say what to take down when I think of it, and it can go on the Colac coach. They collect each day."

Tom entered the pub and sat at a brown table. Fred went behind his bar and reappeared with some white paper, quill and an inkwell. He went back for an ink bottle, unscrewed it and topped up the well with some flourish. Fred enjoyed these little sessions. He had few opportunities as a publican to show his reading and writing skills, of which he was rightly proud. Tom was a good customer, so it worked well for them both.

Fred sat opposite Tom, and waited and waited. It would take time, as he had to keep dipping his pen to record the words, and if Tom changed his mind on what he wanted to say, it would look like no one was any good at this letter business. Best to leave the words as first thoughts.

"Dear Grace, (Fred then left a gap)

Thank you for your letter. I am very well thank you, and even better on hearing your news. I never thought of me being a father. I like it very much, especially knowing it is your baby and mine. Thank you for telling me. It was a shock, but one I much like. A shock for you, too, I expect, but I am glad you are happy about it also.

I will be sure to be in Colac about July to help look after you and the baby. I am told they can come early, or even a bit late. I hope not, but I will work to be there. I hope you are well, and not being sick. Please thank your Mistress for letting you work on.

I will keep looking for your letters and your situation.

Your very happy, special friend,

Tom."

Fred stopped. "Is that all?"

"Yair, that's enough." Fred nodded; yes, it was.

A celebratory few glasses followed.

When he travelled back to the Island, Tom focussed even more on Geelong. He had savings, good savings now, from his work. And nothing much to spend it on, having had his enthusiasm for spending money, especially other people's, rudely stamped out in Lincoln. He was well paid, very well paid, from the time he stepped in to help crew ships whose crews had abandoned them for gold. It stood him well in negotiations. His reputation, he heard, was being very good at what he did; he knew his stuff and was a hard worker.

The little missives pinged back and forth across the Strait, and even between Geelong and Colac. There was still no meeting. There was an itch for them both; the worry of his not being there when it happened. And another for Grace; would he come, truly, or was he just being kind while really turning away?

Tom put himself into an inn in Colac. It was rough and ready, but what was that? He was a good customer for the inn as well. Coaches arrived daily, and carts from the homestead. Contents disgorged from both vehicles and replaced. He watched the routine every day, as the weather turned wet, windy and cold. But there was no Grace to grace him.

Then, there she was. In the cart. On another wet and windy day, she was rugged up against the weather in various versions of spun or woven cloth. Grace, with her few possessions, some tied up bits of family memories and her own favourites; gifts from the other girls with their efforts at sewing, knitting and crocheting for not only the baby to come, but practice for their own, although with a stern warning from the Mistress that pregnancy would cost them their job; a discouragement, at least in the short term.

He was shocked to see her fatter than he remembered. Was this part of having babies? He had been the youngest in his family and had no experience of the requirement, in Lincoln or on the other side of this world. But she was here. He helped her down from the cart. She was in warm clothes for the weather, but he saw the swelling. She would have directions to the hospital whenever she needed to find it, and he had also found it while in Colac.

"It is good to see you." He grasped her instinctively.

"Thank you, you too." That was all. She winced.

"Did the trip shake you up? Very wet and muddy."

"Can I go to the doctor please?"

His practical side switched in. He picked up her bags in one hand, took her hand with the other, and they picked their way carefully across, around and through the Colac mud to the little hospital, where the doctor resided as well as having his practice. The doctor was alerted by the homestead of a delivery in the offing. On rapping on the door, an older woman opened the door and on Grace giving her name, she was ushered inside.

"Come back tomorrow," the woman said to Tom. With that, the door closed and he, left stranded with the peremptory command, went back to the inn for an anxious night founded on uncertainty, as ever.

But tomorrow it was. There was Grace, Grace tired and pale, and with her a tiny pink thing. Nothing like a human, but alive, and theirs. He stumbled to a chair beside her little bed, a bed with two lives.

Grace turned slowly to look at him. "I was never sure you would be here to see me, and our baby, our little boy."

"A boy!" He digested it as much as he could with the confrontation of it.

"I said I would come. I have stayed here so long that I am nearly a native. I wanted to see you, like at the house. You came off the cart, so fat and round with what was inside. Now you are not. New life from us, of us! My slate is wiped clean from the old country, and 'tis not known here on the mainland. A slate fresh marked with a child and you, and I am here to stay!"

"You showed me love in not abandoning me," Grace smiled. "Being here and now is enough for me. I do not expect you to say you love me, a man from a world I can never know. But you left off your adventures to be here. You said this is mine. Mine too. I trust in your protection. No one can pass without you."

He nodded. "When you are fit and able, we'll go from here with our little boy. I earn good money on the boats. An' I haven't spent much, except in pubs. There's not much else to spend on. I'm well known on the boats. Some take passengers; families, too. I reckon I can get us from Geelong to Hobart and start again there. Somewhere different. I can keep on the boats, but it will be harder. I am older. They have these strange new ships now, iron-clad with steam and noise. They're beyond me. Our son won't know what a ship's carpenter was."

"I have a little money too, from my work." Grace was eager to offer.

"I will be in the pub until you are fit to go, and I will call in every day when I am allowed."

"The doctor said we have to register the birth. I do not know what that means or how to do it, but it will make him a Victorian. A new birth in this new country, not old like us. We will do it. We will call him Thomas, after you."

Thomas, after me. What a girl! What a thought, he had never thought of it. These thoughts made Thomas senior a very happy man.

CHAPTER 18

Brighton, Tasmania, 1869

Late in the day, the sun had had enough exercise warming the inhabitants of the Island and was drawing away into the west. Outside the general store in Brighton, a little town north of Hobart Town, a horse stood patiently harnessed to a cart. The store was impressive, reflecting its importance in the community as a stockist of whatever a small community might want. There was a central entrance, flanked by large windows on either side, partly obscured by sacks of grain and other merchandise, resting on a raised platform with a tin roof propped up by rough-hewn timber, with two steps down to the earth.

The coach from Hobart had disgorged its contents, human and otherwise, and moved on up the valley.

"Thanks, Mrs Scrimshaw. See you again soon," a voice called from within the store as Grace came out carrying two large bags, which she lifted into the cart. She returned into the store and emerged with another large bag for the cart.

"Heard your name called out there." Grace stopped and turned towards this female voice. Seated, more slumped, on the platform, and resting against a grain sack, was a gaunt, dishevelled woman, grimy in garment and body. She did not look well.

"I had a name like that," the woman continued, "Had a husband too. Might still have a husband; names don't change much. Tom, a Lincoln man."

Grace put down her bag. "Lots of husbands in Lincoln. Lots of Toms, too." She retorted.

"You from Devon. I can hear it. Our Tom likes Devon girls, I see."

"*Our* Tom?"

"A Devonshire Mary, me. I married a Tom of your name years ago, maybe twenty years, I dunno. The bastard upped and left me alone. Sailed for his fortune, I was told. Looks like he found you instead."

"I came out a servant," Grace explained. "Met my Tom in Geelong. He was a ship's carpenter."

"Was he in Hobart Town? Port Arthur, too?" This Mary asked.

"Err... yes." Grace felt unease spreading through her. She continued. "In Geelong... I was shopping for my lady, buying for our station. There was a drunk young man... I still shiver, with nasty wet red eyes, smell on his breath, wanton hands. My Tom came and stopped him so he could not move. I knew that even old and scarred, he was scared of nothing. Everybody knew it. Sly as they were near me, no man went for me, knowing of him. No man ever has or will. But yet he is a kind man, very kindly man."

"You have kids?"

"Three. They're six, four and my dear little girl is two."

"D'you think Tom, your Tom, my Tom, might have more in Hobart Town? Did you see faces, hands, eyes there, familiar if strange to you? Will he move on from you like from me? Snap his fingers, snap, snap, gone?"

"Nothing, I saw nothing, nobody like that," Grace scowled.

"Wanton hands, you said. I seen lots of that. My brother's friend forced me when I were a maid. He pressed hard, pained me, then it was nice. So I learned to live with it and what it could do for men, and for me. Easy then to have more."

"Us village girls," Grace's memories sidled into her mind, "remembered what went into the cow, ewe, the sow... but it was not for us young girls. Here though, where I worked, fingers were pleading, but I would have none. My Tom saved me."

"Fingers do good, fingers do bad," Mary muttered. "Make boots, steal ribbon, make pretty things, petting, pulling, punching, destroying, make guns and quills. All of us, too; good and bad. Chance is what you get when you want better and get the worst."

"I must go," said Grace shortly, picking up her bag again, although upset by this so unexpected conversation.

"Nearby?"

 Grace nodded.

"I go too."

"Nearby?"

"Did life send me here to find him, find you? Do I go further?" Mary lamented. "I have gorged on too many bitter pills. I hear death's fingers drum on my winter's broken door."

Grace was suddenly stirred. "Come with me. We will see if your Tom and mine are the same. We will see what he says. Let me help you." Grace put her last bag in the cart and returned to the woman, who had staggered to her feet. Besides her dirty dress, spattered with mud, she wore a once-elegant lace shawl, now a lacklustre grey, a bonnet once light green (now dusky), and old, battered shoes. She had with her a small velvet bag.

Grace put an arm around her to guide and half push her to the cart, and to the side to get her up on the bench to sit beside her, while fearing she might topple over before she, Grace, could mount herself. Her visitor hung on to the side until Grace was in position and then clutched

Grace's free arm. Grace flicked the reins, and the horse slowly pulled the load.

"You talked of Geelong," Mary said. "Why are you here on the Island now? How long?"

"When my first, young Tom, was born in Colac, about forty miles west of Geelong," – her passenger had not heard of Colac – "we decided we would sail across between here and the mainland. He earned good money on the boats, and he could arrange for us to travel with him. I had my second boy on one of the crossings. I do not know whether he belongs to Victoria or here. With two young 'uns it got more difficult, and they were not gonna be getting any schooling. So we decided we should settle, and with our savings we rent a piece of land out here, close enough to Hobart for Tom to get some work as a bootmaker, and he brings some home to work on. We have a little cottage. We mostly feed ourselves with a few animals and some chooks, and this old horse and cart. We get by, though could do with better, who couldn't? My dear little girl was born here. Naomi.

"Over there." Grace pointed to a small house about a quarter mile away. "That's us." There was silence as the horse covered the distance to stop outside the door, painted a defiant red.

Grace got down and hurried around before her passenger exhibited any tendency to fall. She held out her hand and edged her passenger down, ushering her to the veranda, and whispered, "Stay here." The passenger held on to the frame. Grace unloaded her bags and put them by the door. Tom would bring them in later. There was something else to do first.

The cottage was typical of its type. Built of local stone, double fronted, with a bedroom on either side of the front central door, and a wooden veranda and tin roof as protection from the elements. Behind the two bedrooms and along a central passage from the door were two more rooms, one a kitchen with a stove and fireplace, a copper for boiling clothes, and two stools. And opposite it, the parlour with a solid wooden table, four chairs with planks across the arms to assist small children reaching the table, and a small high chair for the two-year-old. A sideboard with four drawers and shelves for plates, glasses and cutlery.

Two pictures hung on the wall, one of the Queen, the other a tinted print of Hobart providing a little colour in the modest room. Outside was a privy of sorts, dug by Tom; a little shelter incorporating a bench with a hole in it over the dung-pit. There was a stable for the horse and cart with a loft for animal feed, a woodshed, a hen house and a sty and pen for pigs and sheep. Vegetables were growing on part of the land, which was about four acres.

Tom sat at the table, working on a pair of boots brought back from Hobart. Some days he worked in Hobart at a shoemaker's, and sometimes he brought work back to finish it off. It worked well enough and he was more than competent at his trade.

He heard the clip-clop of the horse outside and waited for Grace to walk in. He was looking after the children while she went to the store, and young Tom had finished his day at the little school. The door opened and her footsteps echoed down the passage. She came in and looked at him with what he thought was an odd look.

"You'll never guess who I saw today, not in a dozen years."

"Not if not from these parts. You do not know the old lags I knew."

"Funny you say – old lag. More an old hag, grimy and gaunt she is. I think it be not long before her creaking door drops off and she dies. And she thinks so, too." Grace turned and went back down the passage and returned, with a slow-walking woman of that description.

"Your wife! She says. Abandoned, she says."

"Jesus! Mary!" Tom gasped, jumping up as he surveyed this woman. "Life's beaten you up... You liked risk, but this much?

"Hello, Tom," Mary grinned.

Tom looked as sheepish as he now felt."I looked for you when I was ashore, but you were never where I was. Then I heard you got into trouble with the law."

Mary shrugged. "Got the pubs, beds, grass, Cascade. Life doesn't go to plan. Not sure I ever had one anyways. We see where we are, and the tread that got us there, and a meaning for it... though you don't see it coming. I should have. And you! Look at you."

Looking at himself was not something Tom took much interest in, and physically, it was not enjoyable when he did. His back was only known to a few women, tattooed by the cat's claws. To deflect further examination of himself, he asked, "What brings you here? Where are you going?"

"Don't know. Away from Hobart. We used to live in Hamilton. Remember?"

There was now no doubt for Grace; the diminishing hope that it was chance or coincidence vanished. She had never pressed him on his past, but a wife was something she surely should have known about. She longed for marriage and had long waited for him to raise it. No wonder he had not. Well, she thought, let him have some of the pain she had and wriggle a bit, like a worm on a hook.

"We can't just let her go, Tom. She must have some food at least. We must sit her down. Is it Mary?"

"Yes."

"You must have tea with us. At least."

Mary nodded from her kitchen chair. There was palpable tension between them all in different ways, with little experience certainly by Grace and to some extent Tom on how to deal with what acknowledgements the occasion demanded.

Practicalities offered an outlet. Tom fetched in the bags and assisted with the unpacking, attended to the animals' needs and laid the table for the adult meal. The children were introduced: young Tom, Alf and Naomi, with appreciative murmurs from Mary as required in the circumstances. The children were fed and then put to bed in the spare bedroom, a single bed where the boys slept together, with a rug on the floor in case one fell out. The little girl had a cot in the parental bedroom.

As a little routine for the children, especially for Naomi, there was a singsong of nursery rhymes from Grace, who had a light, pleasant voice, especially good with Naomi's favourites; Three Blind Mice and Ring a Ring o' Roses, where the little girl could fall down at the end. To the surprise of both parents, Mary dredged her distant memory and sang along in her own creaky way, the two women unconsciously blending in Devonian accents. Tom was constrained to join in but his squawks elicited, "Shut up Tom!" as a duet from the ladies.

Instead, he contented himself with fetching wood for the fire and the copper. He had a notion that the least that could be offered to Mary was clean clothes, fire stoked in the copper, her wear soaped and soaked and dried by the fire. He realised it was late and that she, Mary, would have to stay the night, short of trying to find a bed for her at an inn in Brighton. In her present state, he imagined an innkeeper would be unenthusiastic. He could hardly turn his own newly found wife out. The stove was fired more or less continuously for cooking purposes and for its warmth to permeate the house. He set the copper aperture with wood, lit it, and filled the bowl with water from the pump outside. He did not mention his thoughts or activities to either woman, both occupied with desultory chatter which directed attention from himself, which was good.

With the singsong completed and the boys more interested in their own hobbies and back in their bedroom, it was time to eat. Grace had purchased beef from the store, some steaks for easy preparation, and it would stretch to three adults, not that it seemed Mary had much appetite. Potatoes from the plot would bulk it up as would their beans, enough for a decent humble meal. Not forgetting ale.

Dedicated as Tom was to beer, despite the misery it had caused him over the years from Lincoln onwards, he always kept a plentiful supply of kegs, refilled from his favourite inn in Brighton. At the end of a hard day a few glasses put a man to right, was his belief. Grace also took a small glass most nights, but with a wariness of excess. Tom also had some rum in the sideboard for special occasions, not that such opportunities had arisen and thus the bottle slumbered unmolested.

The little augmented domestic scene worked towards dinner, and with warmth from different sources. Grace noticed the copper was lit and getting hot, but thought no more about it. A keg was broached while the meal preparation was underway. Mary had no compunction about consumption, never had in Tom's recollection, and was advanced in holding out her glass for refills. By the time Grace served, Mary was showing the effects. While her ability to consume was undiminished, her capacity to cope with it was severely compromised. The meal went off well enough, sustaining and nicely cooked. Grace had picked up some culinary skills at Colac and her naturally inquisitive mind, save in asking pertinent questions of Tom, made her into a most satisfactory cook.

"That was good, good," Mary pronounced, slurring a little, and taking yet another swig of her glass. Tom then recognised something about her from those couple of years together. Her eyes became slightly crossed when the hops were hugging her tightly, and he recalled this was not a good sign. It was normally followed by something reckless. Mary looked at Tom, then Grace, fixing her slightly crooked gaze on them both in turn. And then the something reckless began.

"I'm yer wife, Tom. Yer real wife. Not this... umm... woman, pretend wife, this bitch. I'm the one y' married. Remember? I got rights as a wife. More than her. Yer me hus...band. Want yer to stick yer big one right up me, like yer used to. Show her how yer did it."

Grace nearly fell off her chair, and gripped the table tightly. Her insides seemed to have left her, vanished. She was speechless; no words came to her, partly because this woman was right. Mary was his lawful wife and she, Grace, was but a fallen woman, a 'bit on the side', she heard it called. Children or not, she was not his lawful wife. Why had she not thought of possible disasters in trying to give Tom a little irritable nudge? Now she had the horror of this woman taking her man, taking him as her lawful husband to bed in this, her own home. Husband and wife. How could she be so stupid? Desolation was not even a word which came close to what she felt. She saw a lopsided grin on Mary's face in keeping with the disconcerting eyes and the catastrophic utterances from her mouth. She looked desperately at Tom for support and a way out of what was staring at her.

"Well, 'tis true Mary. You are my wife. Wouldn't you want to be as beautiful as you were when we were together, to enjoy it even better?"

This was not what Grace expected. A collusion.

Tom continued. "You will have to be at your best for that. A nice, fragrant bath will help. I'll get our bath from outside in the outbuilding, fill it up with some water from the copper here, top it up with some cold from the pump, and you can enjoy a nice warm bath first."

This sounded just right to Mary as she returned in her mind to her youthful days in Hobart. She was not that old in years, mid-forties, but had crammed so much into those years. Now her husband had reclaimed her, and now she had her rights to him, too.

"While I get the bath ready, here's another glass to celebrate your arrival." He poured her another glass. "Grace, give me a hand!" Grace was shocked by the tone of this peremptory order but, too stunned by the turn of events to argue, she followed him outside.

He turned to her. "I'm going to put her in the bath, wash her and get her into the boys' bed. Get the boys out and into our bed while I'm in there. It will be a squeeze, but it will work and they will love it. I will give her clothes to you. Wash them hard in the copper with soap, then wring them and hang them by the fire to dry. I will stoke with extra wood."

Grace was a shell. She was betrayed first by her own stupidity and then by the man she loved, the father of her children. She went about the allotted tasks, got mumbling, shivering boys out of bed and herded them across the passage into her and Tom's bed. As she put them in and covered them with blankets she looked at her daughter in her cot, and her tears erupted, even though she wanted not to show her anguish, even to half-sleepy boys. She staggered out of the bedroom and down the passage, sat back in the chair opposite Mary and howled. Mary looked triumphant.

Tom brought the bath in, cold as it was, which helped cool the hot water from the copper as it adjusted the temperature. "Now the bath, Mary." He walked to her and hauled her up.

It was beyond Grace. She wanted to die, but did not know how. She could not look at what was about to happen. She put her arms across the table and rested her sobbing, heaving head on them, her body convulsed with grief, anger and self-pity.

Tom leaned Mary against the bath, warm enough not to scald her. Her lopsided grin and displaced eyes fixed on him. "Lift your arms." She obeyed. He undid the buttons holding her bodice and removed it.

She wore nothing underneath, but her breasts of which she had fairly been proud in her youth now sagged with a lesion on the left one. Mountains in the mainland with a quarry. He reached for the dress, and undid it and the stays holding it tight to her waist. He dropped it to the floor. Nothing underneath. Just a body he had once shared pleasure with, now a husk, scrawny with lesions scattered randomly across her skin. He thought of it as the mainland, the lesions as mines or quarries. He surveyed Mary's map of the island. Turned into pasture now, with a little bit of bush here and there. An awful picture of skin and flesh painted in dirt and sweat.

She was so light, he lifted her into the bath, quickly took soap from the kitchen and returned to stop her sliding under. She looked so pleased with herself, he decided she should have a celebration.

"A special treat for you. A special rum." That perked her up. She held on, unsteady, while he went to the niche and pulled out the bottle. He retrieved the empty glass from her, almost filled it with rum and handed it to her. "Here, drink this while I wash the parts I can see and reach." He was uncertain what to do about the lesions; wash them or avoid them? He doubted she knew what they were, or possibly even that she had them. He took a bucket of water, prised the glass from her under protest, although she had almost finished it, put it on the table and tipped the bucket over her head. She shrieked. Grace shuddered. What unmentionable acts were these? Her eyes remained closed on her arms. He applied soap to Mary's wet head, rubbed it vigorously until she yelped, and poured another bucket of water over her, then another. Then: "Here. Soap for what you can reach and I cannot."

He handed her the soap. She drained the last of the rum from the glass returned to her. He took it before she dropped it in the bath. The soap had already gone. It was now too much for her. He hunted for it, found it, returned it to her, she fumbled it again, the process was repeated several more times until he gave up as she was now incapable of doing anything, even staying above the water level. He reached for a towel he had brought in with the bath.

"Hold on!" Tom ordered, and one drunken arm waved in the direction of the bath's side until it found it. He reached, put an arm under each armpit and hoicked her out, almost inert. He dried her as best he could, turning her over this way and that as a piece of meat. He let her slump as she was easier to lift from the floor that way. He bent his knees, reached down and lifted her, and carried her down the passage to the bedroom. Grace almost cried out, but the sound of his feet heading for a bedroom found new sources of misery. Then, feet again. How long was it?

"I put her to bed. In the morning you will need to boil the bedclothes, they are a mess. She has been sick. We still have her clothes to wash."

Grace got to her feet, groggy from the emotion. She scooped up Mary's filthy clothes, pushed them into the copper and grimly stirred, washed and beat them with ferocity while imagining they were still occupied. When satisfied, she lifted them all out and arranged them on the clothes-horse around the re-stoked fire. Tom emptied out the dulled water in a bucket, rinsed it and took it outside. It would need a soak in boiling water.

"Off to bed. A long day." Tom muttered. Grace could have wept, had she not already exhausted her supply. They struggled to get in with their sons, and with their daughter asleep in her cot on the floor, a family of five. Five only.

Morning trundled into their lives, sunny but chill. The baby awoke first, prompting parental activity and bleary thoughts that last night was imagined. But why were the boys in bed with them? Not daring to look in the other bedroom, Grace wandered down to resurrect the fire, hoping for enough embers. She saw the drying clothes and with distaste touched them, relieved that they were dry enough to be worn. Her recollection of their owner bubbled fear through her. Would she have the same wifely desire for her Tom this morning? Was the inevitable only delayed? She felt sick. Tom followed her and saw her grey with fear.

"There is a coach coming through later. She will be on it. Are her clothes dry?" Grace nodded.

"Good. When breakfast is ready, I will fetch her." He went out for more firewood and Grace attended to breakfast, modest but nourishing, of porridge, bacon and an egg each and milk or water to wash it down. When Grace nodded that she was ready, Tom went to the boy's bedroom to rouse their unexpected guest, with her clothes over one arm. Grace heard female mutterings, then a male voice becoming more insistent, then louder.

Tom returned." I told her to be here in five minutes, though I think it will take longer for her to dress. I will see to the boys and rouse them, and look for any new eggs." He went to the boys who, still sleepy, were puzzled and fidgety with the different bed but finally, with whingeing and hunger, were ready to eat. As they left the room, the door opposite opened and the lady they saw last night appeared. She looked different; in brighter clothes and smelling a bit nicer, but she was quiet, not even acknowledging them. The boys instinctively stopped to allow her unsteady path down to the kitchen.

Grace saw Mary coming and gripped the nearest chair. What was going to happen? Tom stood by her, looking taller than she had ever seen him. He was quiet, just watching Mary, whose eyes were focussed on the floor. When those eyes found his feet in the kitchen, she lifted her face.

He saw the eyes had reverted to normal. The fire that blazed in her belly last night, her very insides, was quenched. She was, again, a woman old before her age, a woman who had gone yet another bout with life and lost. There was no risk of her asserting any rights as a wife, a lover, or any rights at all, not even much to life itself.

"Have some breakfast," Tom said, inviting her to sit. "There is a coach going north later. I will put you on it. I will pay the fare and give you, or the coachman, some money for you to stay at an inn awhile until you sort yourself.

"I am sorry we lost contact, but we were going in different directions when we were together, even if neither of us knew where, maybe still do not. I am sad we could not have tried more. Perhaps we knew inside we were finished."

Mary sat at the table, eyes down, saying nothing. It could be seething anger, but he felt she was not long for this scrubby world. Was he part of her farewell journey, a last goodbye? He was not good at answers. It was as it was. Breakfast plates came before her with desultory responses and virtually uneaten plates were later removed. Otherwise, it was the domain of noisy, fidgeting boys and a jolly small girl and adults going through politely necessary social motions. The sun warmed the front of the house.

"Mary, why not sit outside?" Tom said, kindly. "You will get the sun's warmth; better than being stuck inside." Silent, Mary stood up, walked slowly up the passage, and hesitated over which room she should enter. She went into the right one and after a few minutes came out with her small velvet bag, opened the front door and sat in the chair outside to feel the encroaching warmth of the day.

Tom went into the boys' bedroom, now vacated, and returned with bedding. Even though his years had exposed him to many of the less salubrious aspects of human existence, this example was particularly unsavoury. He walked straight through the house, out the rear door, vigorously shook off all the debris he could and returned without the bedding.

"Get the copper up and running. It stinks, the bedding. She threw up in it. Too much drink. Needs boiling twice. After I drop her off at the coach, I will go to the store. If they have bedding for this sort of bed, I will buy it. If not, I will when next in Hobart and we will have to make do with this lot until then. I will put it in when the water boils and take it out after the first boiled wash then do it again. We have to wait awhile until it is time for the coach."

The household went about its tasks and young Tom went off to the local school, a short walk away. The time came to get horse and cart ready to leave for the short journey into the centre of the small town.

"Mary. Time for your next adventure. You always were after excitement and the unknown. I will help you up."

She let herself be led. Tom got her up to sit beside him; Grace steeled herself to come to the front door. The younger children were uninterested in the adult games. Mary turned her head to look at Grace, who returned her look. Mary's head returned to look straight ahead. Tom flipped the reins, and the horse dutifully moved off with its burden.

When they were out of sight, Grace panicked. What if they stopped in one of the bushy areas on the way into town? They could do it and not be seen. She was too drunk last night. Today, has she planned this; by stealth this time, put her hands on him while he holds the reins? What if he gives in, hard not to – she thought of her own pleasure with him. They know what the other likes. Oh dear God, I wish I had gone too. No, the children; could not leave them. Oh God... She wept again, helpless in her imaginings.

A couple of hours later, although to Grace it felt like all day, her anxious gaze saw a horse and cart coming towards her, getting closer by with each stretched minute. Then it was with her. Tom jumped down, the horse quiet, went to his sobbing Grace, and put his arms about her, which made her crying louder.

"She said nothing, nothing at all on the cart," he told her. "Did she know where she was going and why? Nothing. I asked whether we could have done more, could I have done more, to find her? Had we found each other, would it have worked? I thought she might have thought about it after breakfast. Or ships passing in the night. Seen enough of those, and you still sail on and live. I felt guilty, though why? We came, and went.

"But she said nothing. Just looked ahead to where she was going wherever it was, with me as her helper holding the reins, just a while.

"She's gone. Gave the coachman a sum for the fare further on. He asked where she wanted to go. She shrugged. He said he knew an innkeeper, and he would get her in there. I paid him for her having a few nights there on what he expected the cost to be. I can do no more. We cannot.

"I doubt we will see her again. She is not well. Her island" – he corrected himself – "her body has lost its fight and her head will soon leave its thinking. We could have been kinder years ago," he shrugged. "Regrets get us nowhere."

They sat quietly at the table next to each other, with his arm around her. Finally, Grace rose to get on with dinner. The children came to see their father with attendant tickles and rumbustious play with the boys, and tensions eased. The children, fed, had a singsong and were put to bed. The parents sat with their meal, at peace, even if a different sort for each. Sadness and relief for Tom. For Grace; she has gone, but what if he had, or did, on the way back to the coach stop?

A week later, Tom returned from Hobart with more footwear to finish.

"On the coach today going into town, a man I knew a bit was on it. Comes down from further north in the valley. He said in the town there was a woman with the same name as mine – ours – and that she had died in the inn.

"She had a bit of money on her, it paid for her stay and her burial locally. Did I know her? Said I thought I did. I asked what she looked like but he did not know; had not seen her himself but from the innkeeper's description which he passed on to me it was definitely Mary. I hope she found peace at last."

CHAPTER 19

Geelong, 1875-76

Grace hummed to herself, sitting at the table in her little house in Geelong. A house design well-known, and familiar to her from Brighton. But this one was a little bigger, and it was possible to have a third bedroom, for guests or for one of the children as they spread and grew. They had a quarter acre to show a grip on God's earth, with neighbours similarly anchored. Together, they were putting roots down; the land was taking them in its grip, its people hurrying out of one building into another in the big towns and cities. It sometimes felt as if the buildings were there to sweep them up and succour them from storms and vicissitudes, and to feed on their occupants' comfort.

Grace was therefore in her little house in a street with other little houses providing shelter and comfort. It was so good to have company, someone to chat to, to have friends. The years in Tasmania had worn her down. The shadows in Hobart. That horrid Mary who tried to take her Tom away. After Mary died, that screeching brake on their lives stopped. It was time to exhale bad, stale air and think again.

It took time. Being shaken by Mary's descent upon them brought blame and guilt. She blamed herself mainly in bringing her back home, but Tom, too, was touched by a bedraggled, soiled feather of responsibility in not telling her, Grace, about his secret wife and her part in his life. But it was his life, she knew, not hers, and an old life that was over, and what would she have done had he told her of this history and she hadn't met Mary at the general store? It was not the life she had with him and their children. It was the past and worn out like a discarded boot.

Still, it was a worm, no – that was too awful to think about – but whatever it was wriggled within. What – or who – could sidle up from

Hobart, or anywhere on the island, or even here, on the mainland to gnaw at the gut she had grown to replace being gutted by that experience? Would she have to keep growing a replacement gut each time a disaster loomed? Were humans designed for it? She fervently hoped not to find out. But she would not make the same mistake again.

Grace therefore hummed away happily with a sense she had some control over her life and of those whom she loved, which she had not realised until she had to do it, and she had. This was new confidence as a woman and a mother, and independent in thought of her husband. That, though, was not quite true. She always called herself, wanted to be known as, and was called, Mrs Scrimshaw – even without the formalities of marriage.

She had to rebuild that edifice after Mary. Unofficially but a common-law wife, with no miserable piece of paper, which she would have trouble deciphering anyway. Still, it nagged at her. A *sort* of wife. Not an official one, like her mam and dad. The thought then crossed her mind that they could be the same, for she did not recall being shown any such piece of paper back in Devon. Life, she was still learning, was not in a straight line, but what its shape was she had not discovered. Yet. It was bitter as a lemon. Her status became a priority. Her desire and her three children demanded that she and their father become a real husband and wife, not pretend as Mary flung at her. The position had not been raised with the children; they can sort it out when it is done, she reassured herself.

A fresh start from Tasmania would calm the itch. Somewhere different. There were practical and financial reasons, too, besides the emotional uncertainty. Tom had expressed concern that his shoemaking work was not developing as he hoped. There had never been enough work in Brighton, and Hobart was the place to be. But there was competition, and the stigma of being once a convict. Hobart was shying away from its earlier history and promoting itself as a prosperous, open society, broken free from the tarnish of having been a prison. For twenty years now, all the new arrivals in Hobart had come of their own free will.

Still, they were acutely aware that former convicts still walked among them. There were still some who knew Tom, or of him, and that was a bar to finding work. His work, when he did it, was thought of excellent quality, he heard, but it did not cover the wariness of having a convict in employ. He and Grace had supplemented their needs from produce on their own bit of land, but the struggle would not be easier as they aged.

There was also the children's schooling. Lumping all three together in the little Brighton school was all very well, but where next? Tom and Grace were fully aware of the shortcomings in their own education in England, but they were good at sums. Just as their ancestors were usually illiterate, it did not stop them feeding themselves and entering transactions to better themselves. So too with them. How to haggle, order, buy, pay, collect, and sell, how to put money in a Bank and get money out. All were developed skills. Nevertheless, not reading and writing was a drawback. Parents wanted their children to do more, go further than they had. We were different from other animals, Grace insisted; cows wanted their calves to do as they did; no more no less. But we want more of ours.

Tom was against moving to Melbourne. He had come to know it on his travels and found it had become too big, too dear, too much competition, too many sharks; not all were in the Bay. Neither were they suited to the bustle of a city.

Geelong insinuated itself in their brains. Nostalgia and affection for where they first met, although the memory of the immediate meeting still produced a shudder in Grace. But Tom said he had a clean slate there, they knew something of the central area for work, and it had such better schooling opportunities.

It took time to make the decision to uproot themselves from Brighton, and then to leave their little home and plot, the animals and the possessions they did not want to take with them, to take those they *did* want in the horse and cart to Hobart, book passages to Geelong and find rooms in a hotel until the sail date. Then they had to sell the horse, against the tearful pleading and protest of the children, and sell the cart too, for what they thought was a poor bargain, but there was no choice.

Tom allowed himself a last walk around Hobart. The Red Loin was no more, now a family home, oblivious to its ghosts. He tipped his hat to its long-gone landlady and turned away from the building for the last time.

Then came the sail to Geelong, where they briefly stayed in the inn whose landlord, Fred, had read and written the letters that passed between them, although, sadly, they were told he had died. There they were though, with a new life and so much to look forward to.

Then, with a little coaxing from Grace, on cementing a new life and a new start... what of a new status as husband and wife? Tom was persuaded on this perceived status as a husband with a loving wife and children, and unlike with Mary, their aims were as one.

The deed was done; Grace had her victory and validation at last. They married in the District of Geelong. Tom had been a widower for the past six years. It was taken on trust; there was no document to prove it, or needed to prove it. Tasmania and Victoria were separate colonies. Were documents swapped between them? Probably not, Grace thought as she prepared for it.

It seemed that Geelong needed to know how old they were; it was part of the record-keeping for the marriage. Officials; there was no getting away from them, they lapped at your feet like icy tides.

How old were they? The registrar asked each of them. They looked at each other for answers. None came. The registrar, obviously a man of experience, took a different tack. He asked them, when were you born, and in what month you were born? Each reached into the mind's catacombs, remembering what their long-ago parents had told them, and what year it might have been when, as children, they had proudly told hazily-remembered adults how old they were. From that, they each worked out what they thought might be their birth dates. The registrar, armed with this possibly hazardous information, did some little sums on paper and pronounced;

"You sir, are 69, and you, lady, are 35."

No-one had ever told them their ages. These were new facts to store and, just as children, to proudly tell anyone who showed the slightest interest in this odd couple.

The ages, and the gap between them, meant nothing particular to them. They were together as they had been for some years. Neither was the registrar interested in that fact, even if it could be established.

A heavy, thick line had been drawn under the dreadful Mary, and Grace could not be happier and more secure.

She continued her humming as she re-lived this happiness, a year on from the marriage. She was helping with Tom's work; work that he had begun in Lincolnshire more than half a century ago. Her fingers punched holes in the leather for laces, a task with which she was content, indeed happy to do, as part of the finished product which they could sell.

Her mind wandered into seeing her laces; tightening shoes, boots; anything to ease feet. Binding and tightening... if only The Lord Jesus had Tom's boots and her binding for his wounded feet; if her little fingers could have been there to bind his feet, his wounds. His bare, wounded, red feet sorely needed their fine boots. Grace was not particularly religious, so her little reverie surprised her. But there it was, escaped from somewhere.

It passed, and she continued her wordless tune, stitching and binding, while Tom worked on shaping and cutting. The children were happy and learning at school, and had made friends, as had she in the locality, although Tom was more reticent. They were also looking at opening a little shop of their own not far away, a Bootmakers for Tom, with her helping.

Thomas Scrimshaw, Bootmaker.

She liked the sound of that. It had a ring to it, like hammering the final nail in a boot.

CHAPTER 20

Geelong, 1876

"Naomi! Get up! You'll be late for school."

"I don't feel well, mam. An' wish you'd call me Lizzie like they do at school," Grace's daughter said.

"Well, you were given the names Naomi Elizabeth because we liked the sound. Very Biblical it is. You're Naomi to me and dad. Now get up. Brekky's on the table."

"I don't want to; I don't feel well. Honestly, mama."

"You *like* school. Teacher says you're very good at it; reading writing and 'rithmatic, all things dad and I never had a go at really."

"I do. But not today. Feel awful."

The girl did look flushed. "Well, I'll see what dad thinks," Grace said gently. She left the nine-year-old in bed and went to Tom, who had eaten breakfast and was preparing for a day in their little shop in the town as a shoe and bootmaker, which was going well. The move from the island was the right one.

"Naomi says she's not well. That's not like her with school. I could imagine the boys trying it on."

"Kids go up and down quickly," Tom said. "Sick and then not. They do have days with colds; a day in bed and up and running again. I think she can have the day off if she's not well. She'll be full of beans tomorrow."

Grace returned to her daughter. "Dad thinks you've probably got a cold, and caught it at school. You can stay in bed today and get ready for tomorrow. Tom can tell the teacher."

This plan was executed, although when her older brothers Tom and Alf returned from school ready for tea, Naomi was still in bed.

"Time for tea, dearest," called Grace.

"I can't eat, mama. Got a sore throat. Don't want to eat."

"You should try," Grace coaxed. "Tell you what, I'll bring you some." Grace made up a plate and took it down the passageway to her daughter. She looked at her and thought she was surprisingly listless. The room seemed hotter than usual. This was a very bad cold, Grace thought.

"Here's some titbits you like. I'll leave it here for you, and I'll come back later and see how you are. Dad will come see you, too." Naomi smiled weakly at her mother as she left.

Grace and Tom went about their evening routine, while Tom and Alf played. Alf was keen on making things and seeing how they worked. He loved going to see the trains at Geelong station coming and going. He often played contentedly by himself, and left Naomi and her adored big brother to play together.

It was time for bed. Darkness had sneaked into Geelong, the lamps were oiled and prepared to show hesitant light to the bedrooms. While the boys readied for bed in their room, Grace tiptoed in to see Naomi, who had her own bedroom. There was no sound. Grace took the lamp closer. The food was untouched, and in the dim light she saw Naomi was asleep. That was at least good, with school tomorrow, and she would feed her a good breakfast, a big one to see her off. She tiptoed out and went back to Tom sitting in the kitchen, his face flickering in the light.

"She's asleep. Hasn't eaten." She showed the plate. "But she'll be hungry in the morning." The house and its occupants settled in for the night, and then approached the new day.

Grace went in to see her daughter, and opened the curtains for morning light. She was shocked to see a bright red face and neck, with a rash of sorts. She went straight to her, as she was still asleep, and put her hand on the girl's forehead. Oh, she was so hot! A fever of some sort. She realised, too, that in touching Naomi's forehead there was an odd feeling to it. She instinctively put her hands to her daughter's neck. It felt like sandpaper. This was not a cold. She rushed outside.

"Tom! Tom! Naomi! There's something wrong with her. It's not a cold. Come, look!" He stopped his activity and went to see his daughter.

"Good God," he muttered. "What is it? Naomi, Naomi! Speak to me, to us."

The girl opened her eyes at last, a wan smile on her face; a pink face radiating heat.

"Can you eat something?" The girl shook her head, slowly and deliberately. Her parents looked at each other. "Get the boys off to school," Grace commanded, "and go and fetch the doctor. Never needed one till now. I'll watch her."

Tom nodded. This was beyond his wide experience of life's harshness, and he was aware of his helplessness. He hurried the boys through breakfast and shooed them off to school, with an order to apologise to the teacher for their sister missing another day.

Tom set off for the doctor, a semi-mythical creature all residents knew of and vaguely where he was, and aided by some questions and answers in the area where Tom thought the medical man was, he found the address, a large house in an area of larger houses, with a small annexe which he assumed was where patients were seen. After knocking on the main door, it was opened by a woman of about forty, elegantly dressed.

"Is the doctor in, please? My daughter is very ill."

"I am afraid he is not here at the moment. He is very busy seeing patients. A number of children have gone down with what looks like Scarlatina, which is very worrying."

This was a word unknown to Tom, or to most parents, but being focussed on his daughter, he did not inquire further on its meaning, simply asking, "Do you know when he will be back?"

"No, I do not, unfortunately. He also has patients to see here during the day."

"Can I give you my address? It is not too far. We do not know what is wrong with her. We thought it was a cold, but she has gone very pink." The woman stiffened. "Which school does she go to?"

Tom told her. "I will tell him when he gets home. He will do his best..." She turned to get a pencil and sheet of paper from a bureau just inside the door and asked for the address, which was quickly given, and confirmed. "I am sure he will try and get to you sometime during the day."

Hurrying home, Tom was puzzled by the 'do his best' comment. That is what he does, although his time on the island had mixed outcomes from medical men.

"The doctor is out seeing people, some other kids, too. The woman, think she's his wife, asked which school Naomi went to. She took our address here and said she was sure he would 'do his best' to get here today. How is she?"

"Come and see."

"Dad's here." Naomi looked at her father. She was anything but pale. "Does it hurt anywhere?" She nodded, pointing to her throat. "Horrible. Can't swallow. Awful. Can I have some water? It hurts all over too. It's hard to move."

"We asked the doctor to come; he'll be here soon." Tom hoped his uncertain optimism hit the right note. The house moved through its labours, accelerated by increasingly anxious parents, restless, their helplessness a stabbing, accusing reproach upon them.

Hearing a noise outside, they rushed to the door. The boys were back from school. "School might be closed tomorrow," Tom said with some relish, "Some kids are sick, it might be something the teacher doesn't want caught at school."

Grace jumped in. "Naomi's not well. We don't know what it is, but we're waiting for the doctor. Better leave her alone, though, until we know more." The boys put down their bags and got on with their usual routine of burrowing for food, and then headed off to play with whatever interested them.

The parental tension rose as their daughter showed no sign of change back to what they saw as normal, and tears welled up in Grace. The sun was sinking.

They heard a squeak from the gate opening again and both dashed over to a front room window to look. There was a horse and cart outside, and a man in his late forties perhaps, dressed soberly in a dark suit, stiff collar and tie with a waistcoat, a hat and holding a large bag was coming up the short path to the front door. He had no need to drop his poised hand for the knocker; the door was flung open.

"We are so glad you have come, doctor," Grace twittered anxiously. "It's our little girl. We don't know what is wrong with her. She is usually so lively; she loves school... but hasn't moved for two days."

"She's in there." Tom pointed to the bedroom.

The doctor saw a girl of about nine, and even in the dimming light, a clearly flushed face. He moved to be beside her, Grace hastily rearranging a chair so he could sit.

"Hullo dear," he started, "let's see if we can get you better." He put his hand on her forehead, noting heat indicating fever, and felt the rough sandpaper effect of her red skin. "Can you open your mouth, please?" She struggled a little but obeyed. "Can you poke out your tongue?" She did.

He saw a tongue, red and bumpy with a white coating. "Strawberry tongue." He muttered to himself.

"May I look at your arms, legs and tummy?" She nodded.

He pulled back the bedclothes. He looked and moved his hands across her body and found it red and sandpapery. There were little red lines in the folds of her skin in her groin, elbows and knees of a darker red than on her face. He felt her neck and found swollen glands. He stood up.

"She has, I am afraid, Scarlatina."

"Scarlatina?" queried Grace. He added, "More commonly known as scarlet fever. Children of this age range are more prone to it. From about nine to fifteen. We do not know why these ones are more susceptible."

"What causes it?"

"We do not know yet. Medicine does not know everything. One day we will, or The Almighty will tell us why He created it, allows it and what to do about it. It seems to pass from one child to another, and sometimes happens around schools where there is close contact. I have seen a few children from the same school today. There may be more to come."

"Will she get better?"

He was thoughtful in his words. "Generally, yes. The rough skin peels off after a week or so, like having sunburn. She has the usual signs and may have difficulty swallowing."

Grace interjected. "Yes, she hasn't eaten."

He continued. "There is usually recovery after a week or so, although it can come again at another time, another attack from whatever causes it. There can be vomiting, although as she is not eating, that may not happen. Keep an eye on any shortness of breath, trouble breathing, or swallowing."

"She does have that," Tom interjected.

The doctor nodded and continued. "Keep her drinking; she must not dry out at all. We shall have to wait and see. All should be well enough in a week."

His remarks were carefully phrased. This girl was quite unwell, and there was not much medicine could do beyond diagnosing the condition and wait and see. Most children recovered, but some did not. If the family were of a religious persuasion, prayer might help, but he did not want to worry them unnecessarily. "Come for me if things become worse, but it is a case of wait and see, and the expectation is that all will be well." He stood up and moved to the door.

"How much do we owe you, doctor?" Having been told, Tom went into the parental bedroom, opened a drawer, counted out the fee and returned to hand it to the doctor who nodded. He had remarked to his wife that the more modest citizens paid his fee without demur, whereas the more wealthy ones delayed as long as they could. She retorted that was probably why they were wealthy. There was nothing more he could do or advise, and left.

Tom and Grace looked at each other. Scarlet fever, or the other name, meant nothing to Tom but he now knew it was not good. Grace recalled one of the children on the Colac station had it and recovered after a week or so, which reassured them both when she recounted it to him.

School closed the next day from the risk of contagion. That act stimulated Tom and Grace to separate the children. Naomi was watched in her room, 12-year-old Tom kept in another room and the garden while the school was closed. That left young Alf. His fascination with trains and engines offered an opportunity to keep him at a safer distance – why not take him to the station to spend the day watching trains? His father would see what could be done.

So the next day Tom took Alf to Geelong's main station, the terminus of the line from Melbourne. Alf was a happy boy, a day with no school, spent with trains and his dad.

Chatting with a railway employee led to another employee, who referred him to a more senior-sounding one, and finally to the Station Master. Yes, under all the circumstances and with the lad's enthusiasm, the station staff would be happy to look after Alf during the day and he could learn a lot about trains and railways. Trains would replace the horse one day, the Station Master told Tom. Tom was not so sure, but the men shook hands. Alf had sandwiches brought from home and the station staff would supply him with water. Father would collect him for tea.

His first day went well, so the arrangement continued. Alf was a sensible boy, and as the school remained closed, the ten year-old was trusted and able to walk to and from the station without parental help, carrying his sandwiches. The distance was not very far and the boy came home talking excitedly about trains and railways.

His parents were focused on their daughter. She was hard to interpret. Pain? Swallowing? Aches? She was very drowsy, not eating, virtually nothing in the chamber pot. They did not want to worry the doctor; he was a very busy man with all these children, and all his other patients. But she was not getting better. Grace was passing the very disturbed phase and becoming frantic.

"We must get the doctor, we must!" Tom saw there was no alternative. There was nothing he could do, nor could Grace, and that overrode their respect for the doctor's busy practice.

"I'll go for him." He got the same result. The doctor's wife said her husband was out seeing patients. It was a very busy time, but she would pass on the message of concern and he would come when he could.

The doctor came. It was getting late and he asked for a lamp to see Naomi properly. He looked at her and examined what he could with this inert girl. He stood up. Her parents heard an intake of breath.

"It is not looking good, I have to tell you. You must continue with the love and care you give your daughter, and that will encourage her fight. There is nothing I can offer. We know what it is and what it does. But not why or how to cure it. It is in God's hands and your love, I am very sorry to say."

He packed his bag and went slowly to the door, depressed by the number of ailing children he had seen and had to see. The helplessness he felt, when all these people, these good people, looked to him for a miracle. Miracles were sadly not part of his training. Both he and the parents forgot about his fee. He got on to his cart, shook the reins and moved slowly away.

He was just out of sight when:

"Mam, dad. I don't feel very good."

They turned to the noise. Young Tom stood there, with a flushed pink face.

"AAAAAAAAAAAAAAAAAAAAAAAAAAAAAAAAAAAAAAAAAAAAAAAAAAA AAAAAAAARGHNOooooooooooo" came the sound that Grace's heart sent shooting from her throat.

*

The gravedigger scraped the remaining earth from his shovel; a shovel which twice dug and turned the same soil in a week. He moved slowly away to his hut to put away this tool of his trade. Behind him, two couples, all dressed in black; the Scrimshaws with the old man's arm around his younger wife, a woman beyond tears, as she stared at the fresh earth.

The other couple were the Reverend Cyrus and Mrs Emma Carmody, in their late twenties and newly arrived from the Mother Country, as they were fond of telling their parishioners. The Reverend felt a calling to the Church and there was a family history of service to that august institution. He enthused about bringing the Gospel to those less fortunate than himself, secure as he was in God's love.

His readings brought him to the natives in Australia, ripe for the message of The Lord. His superiors gently advised him that the natives in Australia had been subjugated when necessary to the greater improvement of themselves through introduction to the Gospel. Nevertheless, it was true that the Colonies had to a considerable extent been forcibly settled by less esteemed personages than lived in England, and by Irish troublemakers. It was beyond doubt they would benefit from reminders of God's Grace, their need for redemption and spiritual guidance.

Accordingly, the Reverend Carmody transferred his allegiance from native to miscreant and communicated this desire to his young wife. As a good Christian woman anxious to please her husband, she accepted the requirement to sail to this far-off place reputed to be full of dangerous and unknown terrors. It would be a good deed in the eyes of The Lord in their final reckoning with Him.

Here they were, then, in this growing city of Geelong, big and important enough for them to become highly respected pillars of the local community. Better than the bustle of Melbourne, where the shouts of Mammon drowned out the Word.

Here they were too, more pertinently and immediately at a graveside. Cyrus told Emma of the tragic history and she saw her Christian duty to provide comfort and succour to this poor woman who had lost not just one but two children in the space of a week.

There they were, by the hastily turned earth to welcome them to share in God's embrace. Emma had not caught the name of the bereaved couple but thought her presence to comfort the woman sufficed. She looked at the woman. It was hard to judge her age; older than herself certainly, and the wear of life had etched her face and cheeks. There was not much more of her to be seen, swathed in black as she was, as they both were. On what was visible, she was a pretty woman, but her eyes were hollow when she turned to look at her, with a dullness which filled the etchings on her face. The man was quite large, motionless with grey flecked hair, but a man used to looking after himself, she judged.

Her husband turned to the parents. "God is good," he said.

"God is *good*?" The woman turned to the Reverend. Her blank eyes suffused dark, and erupted into black orbs.

"God is good! My poor babes in the earth and God is good? Hate to see Him bad. Has he not enough dead already? Not enough wars to keep Him busy? He needs to fill up, make more cemeteries? He wants my little children, too?

"What have I done to deserve this? What have my babies done to deserve such a cruel fate? How is God good? Only a wicked one would take clever, happy young children to their graves."

This outburst shocked the Reverend and his wife somewhat. Thus the Reverend spoke.

"The Lord Jesus said, 'Suffer the little children to come unto me.'"

"What!" Grace retorted. "Does He get the kiddies and the Father gets the grown-ups? What does He do with them; sing songs, tell stories? What do they do all day, every day with Him? What with a tiny baby? With a bad mam, an evil father? The baby goes down there," – Grace pointed to the disturbed earth – "Blameless with bad parents. To play, have songs and stories with Jesus? It couldn't understand them. Not enough life to learn anything, was it? Born alive then dead. Do my children go any further when suffered by Jesus? Stay? Is that all? Eternity staying as a child and never growing up?

"I imagined once I was making boots for Jesus to cover His sore feet," Grace continued with desolate fire. "My fingers punched holes in the boots for him. Fine boots, made by my Tom here. Now life's punched holes in me. You're a learned man; do the children stay forever as children? To never know a love for children of their own?"

This tirade was not what the Carmodys envisaged. A brief expression of condolence, comfort and then leave them in God's mercy. Nor could Cyrus immediately see an answer. It was true that a sermon on a child having eternal life as a child was not attractive on the goodness of God.

"How will the children recognise me if, if, I got to Heaven when I am older?" Tom lurched in with his own query. "I don't reckon I'll get to see them. They are not to blame, so why can they not have messages from their dad wherever I am? We were mostly young and silly and stupid. Does the punishment we got, get a sufferance from God to help?"

Grace was not done, either, chiming in: "What if my son asks for his father? What to tell him? Is it said he was a bad dad. He's not. What do they know up there?" She waved an arm upwards. "Does he get to see them? In these little boxes?" Her arm pointed down. "Or are they cleaned up by God and His angels, who know what to do even if medical men here don't?

"God knows everything, created everything, created the scarlet fever. So He could have stopped it. And He didn't. You tell me God is good? When He takes my children and gives them nothing, nothing but songs and stories, instead of a life!"

Before Grace flowed on in pain, anger and bewilderment, Emma was desperate to say something ameliorating. "Perhaps God allows the children to grow up and experience the joys of being an adult?"

Grace thought about this. "So Jesus gives them across to The Father to be grown up... How old do they become? Do they keep growing for ever?"

"Perhaps they get to forty?" Emma's desperation plucked a figure out of the ether.

"Can they marry, have children like we do? It would be wrong for God to let us have children here on earth, even if He takes them away like He has, but not let us have them in Heaven."

Where was this going? Cyrus was stunned, and his wife circled inside her own now convoluted mind for an escape, unsure how to answer questions she'd never considered. It brought on the thought of getting married and having marital relations in Heaven. It had to be marriage, otherwise it was Sin.

"Where do people live in Heaven?" Tom was concerned about the practicalities. "Are there houses and palaces? I've never seen any in drawings and pictures – it was all flowers and grass and trees. Everyone looked very happy. But if you make babies, does it need be out in the open with no homes, and no-one cares? Or are there palaces and big houses for more important people? The Saints?"

Emma could not recall seeing any houses in Heaven either, in the pictures she had seen. She had to concede that if it was right that you could have the joy of babies in Heaven (although she still awaited the joy of babies on terra firma), and there were no homes, it would have to be among the trees and flowers and on the grass with melodious birds and no-one watching, possibly because they were busy at it, too. The ministry had not prepared her for this. What had she started? She saw the Heavenly Finger beckoning her.

The Finger became more insistent, as Tom waded in. "If we age in Heaven to forty and have children, then we are taught everything which ages dies. So, how can we have eternal life if we must die? If we die in Heaven, where are we sent on to from there?

"We're told we are in God's likeness, otherwise if He had eight and a half heads and tentacles," (where this idea popped up from, Tom did not register), "we would not be so keen to believe. We are told, from the pictures, He has grey hair and a long, grey beard. Like us. If we are in His image, then He is in ours, and as we get old and grey like we do, and He does too, then as we must die, so will He.

"I suppose if you age in Heaven then you must be allowed to die in Heaven?" Tom continued. "So must God die too, being old and grey, so then what happens to Heaven? Even Jesus will age, too. Do we start again if He dies? Does it all close down?"

A tangental question popped into Tom's head and straight out of his mouth. "If you do bad things in Heaven, what happens to you? Do you go to another Heaven, but not as good? How many Heavens are there? How will we find our people among them?"

Emma was speechless. Her husband started up. "I should be very careful with these remarks," he said sternly. "You betray your ignorance of God's Mercy. You may compromise your soul, your immortal soul."

"I am a poor, uneducated man," Tom said, raising his palms defensively. "You are learned from books and a Man of God. God and you talk to each other. I know not much about anything, and I don't understand much about the soul. When you're dead, you're stone dead. I've seen it." He stared at the fresh earth – for a moment, he was back digging Marianne's grave in the rain – and gulped. "You can't move no more, just like our kids can't here.

"How do you get to Heaven? Is it the soul? Gets you from one place to another. How do you get from a dead body to Heaven? What's the fare?

"What if God made a mistake? We are in His likeness and we make mistakes, so does that not mean God can, too? If it was a mistake and you weren't meant to die at that time, does the soul act as a hansom-cab and bring you back here again and hang about until it is the right time, or does it go off and pick up someone who died at the right time instead?"

Cyrus was floundering under this barrage of thoughts from this ignorant man. How to explain God's Mercy when faced with such silliness?

The man was not finished. "Some men do not believe in God. Some ladies, too, I expect. If they don't, they don't need a soul to get them anywhere, do they? They just rot in the ground like any other animal. Is the soul God's invention so He gets more of us than the One down below? He uses learned men like you to tell us of God's invention, so we behave ourselves."

The Reverend was at a loss. How did the human get to Heaven if palpably dead, other than by the soul? Was it somehow like a cab? The books were silent. In his prayers to the Almighty no answer was forthcoming, although he conceded he had never thought to ask the question. Why did the young and innocent die when all manner of sinners went merrily along? The ground of faith felt slippery under his feet. He had come all this way to save souls and give strength and love. It sounded like he should have come laden with fares for Almighty destinations.

This old man was looking at him quizzically, no, expectantly, at him. These simple, foolish people were asking questions he had never thought of in reading his theology. Worse, they seemed more confident in their questions as if they had thought about them; they were more like statements than uncertainty. What could he ask God, or The Lord?

This little reverie was interrupted by the woman, whose tenacity was unnerving.

"God's Son had to die to save us from Sin, so you Men of God tell us. Well, it didn't work, did it? Awash with Sin, we are. That must be why

God is angry and does not behave good. He sent His Son to die although he would have known – as you tell us He knows everything – that it would be a waste of time and of His Son's blood.

"So maybe His Son can put in a good word for us, and our babies here... I dreamt I was putting in laces to bind shoes for His bloody feet. Please, sir, can you put in a good word for us when you next speak to Him?" Grace's eyes filled with tears, lost in despair but willing herself of hope.

"My wife is a good woman, a good wife, good mother," Tom added. "A good servant she was, and still is; a good servant to God, the God you know so well, serving two children to your God. I hope you remember that, too. Will you speak to Him? Please, Sir?"

Silence. There was nothing more anyone could say. Two couples, not looking at each other, wives clutching their husband's arms, bereft and hollowed, walked slowly away in different directions, shattered and desolate for different reasons in different lives.

*

One desolate life moved on with the seasons. Grace put down her laces as Alf came in. He was almost twelve now – nearly the age when his older brother was taken by God, or not. Alf was now sportingly fit and keen to learn about modern life, especially trains, railways and the new station now being built; things Grace did not really understand, but trains were certainly faster than horses.

Tom was sceptical of the new iron engines. "Never replace horses," he said, whenever asked about such progress."Horses been around forever. Can even eat them. Can't eat iron." They had settled in Geelong which was growing and enough for their needs. There was no reason for them to take this wretched machine to Melbourne. What for? To come back again. It cost money, too.

"School good?" she asked as Alf walked in.

"Yair. School's getting up a footy team to play against other schools, same sort of kids. Reckon because I can run and jump a bit, I could give it a go."

She understood she was being asked for permission. "Why not?" she smiled. "Better than doing nothing."

"When's tea?" Alf was never that interested in what was for tea, just when he could get at it.

"About half an hour." He nodded and ran outside. She watched him run down the lane, with mixed pride and sadness. He was hers; all she had now, aside from Tom, her Tom, old Tom compared to her dear young Tom. One Tom. She thought some more.

That night, in bed, she turned to her husband. "Tom."

"Umm."

"Been thinking."

"Umm."

"I still bleed. You're still vigorous," she flashed a smile. "Can we try for another, just one other... baby... just a little one?"

Tom had been half expecting this chat over the past few months. He greatly missed their dead children, and their shared visits to their grave emphasised their pain. They vowed that when their time came, they would join them under their patch of earth. They had never gone to the church where the Reverend Carmody preached, which was probably best for all.

As he missed them so much himself, he could only guess at the devastation Grace endured. She was not the same woman since they had lost Naomi and Tom; she was more hardened and determined, but soft with him. But now he was old by all standards and had weathered, he guessed, the Biblical threescore years and ten.

There was something in what she said, though; it would be a comfort to her when he died, which couldn't be too long now, and she had young Alf to occupy her. A good lad. She would cope, as women do.

"Umm. You bleed. I don't. I suppose we'll see what happens." He turned and kissed her cheek. She smiled at him. There was no point in asking God to help. He had done enough damage. Grace smiled again, snuggled up and went into a dreamy sleep.

CHAPTER 21

Geelong, 1887

Immersed in shaping the sole of the left boot of a pair he was making for a local dignitary, Tom did not immediately respond to the tinkling of the bell at the shop door when it opened. Most likely it was Grace, returning from buying necessities, or it was young William back from school. It was a sensed presence which made him look up.

A woman stood inside the door, looking at him. She was not a regular customer, although elegantly, even beautifully dressed; he had some sense of fashion from the ladies who came to his shop, and he was pleased to learn that it was his reputation that brought them along, for themselves, their children and even grandchildren. Their husbands and older sons were steady customers as well.

The woman was dressed in navy blue; a top buttoned to the neck, waist pulled tight, emphasising her shapely figure. Her navy skirt stretched not quite to the floor, allowing the tops of her black boots to show. Her only concession to colour were her white lace collar and cuffs. Her broad-brimmed hat was also navy, trimmed with a light-blue sash, which somehow jolted him. He thought she must be in her late forties or thereabouts, although her skin was almost – what was it called? – ah, *alabaster* – smooth and white, but not quite.

Her face was set purposefully as a woman who meant business. Whatever her age, she was remarkably attractive, and he had not, with all respect to the fine ladies of Geelong, seen one such among them. Her hair was swept up under the hat and she carried an umbrella, or was it a parasol? Protection from the sun? Whatever it was. There was something about her which disconcerted him, something familiar, though he had never set eyes on her before.

Tom stood up, not without some difficulty, to look at this woman. She must have been a beauty in her youth, a beauty moulded now by caressed years. Why was she here in his shop?

This woman also perused her surroundings. A small, rather worn sofa, two chairs and a stool, a wooden counter in front of a work desk with assorted tools of his trade set out within easy reach. A small, patterned carpet and green wallpaper embossed with white and red roses as a pretence towards some lightness. The occupant of this room was unfamiliar with frippery, and it was unadorned by any particular taste. The occupant, she saw, was an old man of about eighty, with thinning grey hair wrestling with odd flicks of a darker colour, with mutton-chop whiskers in the old style and consistent with being uninterested in fashion.

Though slightly stooped from age and experience, to which his heavy fingers attested, he was well built. As far as she could ascertain, his eyes were greyish-blue when he looked at her, with a nose which featured more prominently and added to his lined face from having been once handsome, perhaps or perhaps not, to now interesting and quite compelling.

"You are recommended to me," she announced. He nodded. "I wish to order a pair of blue shoes. The bright blue of Australian skies."

Confusion multiplied in Tom's mind. While any blue other than dark or navy for shoes was rare, there had only ever been one request for sky blue.

It may be achievable, although difficult, and the dye was not readily available. He had experience, and his experience and memory shied him away from accepting any bespoke order that could remind him of that awful day. Even with cajoling and the dangle of a handsome reward, the request merely resulted in apologies and a suggestion to try others in the city.

Accordingly, he responded to this lady. "I am sorry, Madam. But I do not make sky-blue shoes. Others in the town may do so, and I can point you towards them." He returned to shaping the sole with his knife.

"I believe you made a pair for my mother."

The knife slipped and he nicked a finger. He slumped back in his chair, not now knowing where he was.

"Oh, Marianne, Marianne," he gurgled. As he opened his mouth she saw gaps and tobacco staining on those teeth which clung on.

"You remember her?"

"Yes, yes; she is with me every day, every day. I did not know, or I forgot she had children. But you are not from here."

She was surprised at the vehemence of his reaction, not unkind or angry, but a surge from his depths. He certainly knew her mother, though how she did not know. She hoped to find out. Something between her mother, beautiful as she was always described, and this old man, when a young man. All she had so far found out pointed towards him, but no-one, no document, gave any inkling of what had happened.

"I come from England."

"So was I... once. Long time ago."

"I was born in Port Arthur as Elizabeth, born after my older brother Arthur in Hobart. When our parents died, their friends took us back with them to England, and the Bells and Lynches took one of us each. Our gratitude to them in doing so is immeasurable; we were raised along with their own children. We were also given some support as orphans by members of our parents' families, although that was painful to them. We also received most generous contributions towards our maintenance and spiritual guidance from General and Lady Morgan. Whether they saw us as the children who by-passed them, I am unable to say."

The woman, Elizabeth, perched herself on the sofa, lit by light streaming in from the window.

"After my dear brother died of his wounds in the Crimean campaign, the General passed their contribution to him across to me, and I am indebted to them for their continued assistance. I am fortunate, therefore, in having adequate means to support myself in whatever endeavours I choose. My brother's death, in odious conditions, drove me to support Miss Nightingale in her mission to improve care, and make it attractive for young ladies to enter such a noble calling as nurses, rather than endure squalor and hardship in factories – or worse, being seduced into more depraved activities."

Tom nodded. He had heard about conditions in the Crimea. "As you are needed in England," he asked slowly, "Why are you here?"

"When I was thought old enough, my family, the Bells, told me the true horror of my parents' fate. Etched in my mind was that my mother wished to die, and to be buried in her beautiful, bright blue shoes. The shoes, I was told, were made by a convict who was also a shoemaker, and this convict was somehow to blame for the subsequent misery which affected us.

"I learned, too, that the record-keeping is and was most assiduous. I embarked on my own investigation into such records as there were in England. I also sailed to Hobart, where the records of Port Arthur are retained. I cannot, at this time, bring myself to visit Port Arthur.

"I live in London. I have never married. I have seen the military life. I resolved that I would never march to the drum of being a military wife, with the extra hazards my mother found. The precedents before me of that position were, I concluded, not conducive to my good health."

Tom blurted out. "I was there. I have lived it every day since. I was told by the on-duty guard that there was another man involved. But it could not be me. A lag sent to Port Arthur as incorrigible... An adulterer? Me?

Lashes, treadmills, chains, bread and water, solitary confinement with a rat or two or three; they tried some clever ways to break me. Never did.

"Your mother was the most beautiful woman. No-one who saw her could say otherwise. All men wanted her, but were all too in awe of her. She could have had any man she wanted. She was beautiful, serene, untouchable. And they are blaming me. Ha! With my back? My back... Do you want to see it? God laughed every time the lash landed. And that was many times."

Tom suddenly jumped up, his age forgotten, pulled up his rough shirt, and turned his back to her. She recoiled from the criss-crossed mulberry furrows. Seeing them was worse than she imagined, having read about Port Arthur. Yet she was sympathetic, even warmed, to such a man who had endured so much, seen so much; ancient, but was still demonstratively alive and vital. She could glimpse what her mother saw, and understood it had been a meeting her mother rejoiced in, despite her different status. It was the source of her life's Spring, snuffed out.

"Can you see your mother with *that*? Would she have wanted to share that, a man like me?"

She looked at the mangled torso. "Yes, I can see it, yet I cannot say she would not. I see. There are matters our minds do not understand, but are real nonetheless."

She continued. "I read the records. The order in the storm; to bury her standing upright and to face her to the wall so that a woman who killed a fellow officer would never have repose nor see the sun. How meticulous cruelty is.

"But although evidence was sought – chased around, it seems to me – to justify my father's initial assault on my mother and her response to him, evidence was there none. There was evidence that my father was unpredictable and had been violent to my mother, but that did not appear to amount to much to the court of officers. The only men in her life, such as it was, were my father, and the shoemaker who made her the so-desirable shoes. And there was no evidence that the shoemaker could, even with intent, have got anywhere near her. The evidence suggests that my father was sorely mistaken, and his misunderstanding was the cause of such catastrophe. The other man in her life was her shoemaker. You."

Tom Scrimshaw howled, or that was the nearest she could put a word to, from a rumble exploding. "Some fifty year or so... the other man was another man worthy of her; it was not me!

"Half a century. Pain worse than the inventions to shut me up. Daily gnawing, nightly biting. I've known no rest, thinking it was not me. It *was*, you say? It was?" He subsided.

She was suddenly aware of a warmth, different from the outside heat. It was nothing that could be described in any words, but it washed and bathed the small room.

"She is here, she is here," Elizabeth said, lifting her eyes. "I am not particularly religious, and religion has done so much damage in the name of peace and love, but I know she is here. Now you know you are him, the other, the one... she is here, telling us. Her presence, her love, cascades onto and into us, wherever she is. Now you know, and I know."

She lowered her head from looking for her mother, forlorn though she knew it was, and saw this old man, shoulders shuddering, crying.

There was silence awhile. Then he spoke, softly at first as he gathered his words.

"I was there. I made her blue shoes for her. She wanted me to do it. She pointed me out in the workshop. She came down often to see their progress. I longed for her to come.

"She came when she didn't need to. There was always a guard there, watching. I measured her feet, she had beautiful feet. I was guided to make them, by something other than myself. Was she guiding to me to make them? We only ever touched when I measured up her feet for the shoes, helped put them on. There was a tingle, a charge…

"No," he interrupted himself, stepping out of the sea of ancient memory. "We had seen each other over the years before, now I see. She had been in Hobart before. Did she see me? T'was hard not to see her. Even on the ship that brought me to Hell, I saw her. Did she see me, there, in Hobart Town? In the Port?

"Yes. She would walk past where I laboured, as if to tease me. Well, I was happy to be teased. She looked, careful to look like she was not looking. A pretend. She came nearly every day, once I was at my shipyard. None of us knew why she walked slowly past us, but we all waited to see her. I longed for her walks, I thought of her when I was in my lousy cell. What did she think at night?

"Then I was moved to making shoes. They thought we could do better making them locally than live with the rubbish sent out to us. Right they were, too. She was particular, and interested. There was, I hoped, a feeling she had, like I had… but how could it be? The day came, the shoes were finished. She was so excited. She was so pleased with the shoes, my love, all I could give to her had gone into them. She tried them on with my help. We washed over with whatever it was, and I swore to myself that she felt it, too. She left looking so happy, so happy. Me too, me too…"

His hands covered his head. The blood from his pricked finger had stopped, but slightly stained the shoe leather. His sobs were audible.

"Next I knew, I was ordered with others to come to an execution. Bring spades and picks, they said. I swear it was only a day or two later, maybe three, since I'd put the blue shoes on her.

"We went not to the usual gibbet, but in the officers' place. We didn't see her until she got up onto the scaffold. I saw it was her. I thought they had got me to Hell at last. Fell apart inside. I grabbed the spade to stop from falling. Thought I had gone mad.

"But she was so calm, as if somewhere else. Then she saw me and our eyes locked. There was this... stream between us. It never left. Then as the hood went down over her, she smiled at me. No, it can't have been a smile, can it? Whatever it meant, it has never left me.

"Then she fell, and I saw her blue shoes." Elizabeth Wainwright closed her eyes, tears falling silently. "I went through what was ordered. I was told to bury her myself. I see I was being punished for knowing her at all. They ordered me to stand her up and face her away from the rising sun. The officer was a real bastard. It was pouring with rain.

"Everyone left, it was just one young guard and me. But he got fed up and left me to it. So I turned her around, I used the hood to lift her lovely head towards the rising sun so God could celebrate her too, though He didn't think to stop it. Pretty useless, He's been. And there she is; there she remains to my knowledge; upright and always looking towards the sunrise and Heaven. She still had that strange, serene look on her face. I left, and next thing I recall was a session in the hospital." He omitted having kissed Marianne's forehead; it might be too upsetting.

He looked at her daughter. She too was now sobbing heavily, dabbing her eyes and cheeks with a forlorn damp handkerchief. She knew something had happened or something had not happened. Suddenly, it hit her; it was both. That was the tragedy. No one saw it or cared to look. This was a kind, caring, loving man. Whatever he had done to get to Port Arthur was expunged. Her mother knew it.

There was silence. Then, when sufficiently recovered, Tom ventured. "I jumped inside when you arrived. Now I know why. I saw her in you. How did you find me?"

"The records in Hobart are so assiduous," Elizabeth said. "Her execution, evidence supporting it... although I believe had she been represented, or cared to be, the result may have been avoided. Who knows what may have happened?"

She paused briefly while the what-ifs jumbled before them. "The name of the execution party, the name of the convict singled out to bury her: Scrimshaw. There's not too many of that name. I found a Scrimshaw sailing regularly from the island across to Victoria, in the years afterwards. Why would such a man not want to start a new life away from such a scene of misery? A Scrimshaw named as the father of a girl born in Brighton in Tasmania. Back and forth. Records of a Scrimshaw family sailing to Geelong. Working again as a shoemaker in Tasmania, and here too, as I found from asking around in Melbourne. You are known in Melbourne. Tanners know you, dyers know you, some shoemakers. Go to Geelong with this address, was the advice. And here I am."

Tom sighed heavily. "Like a cuppa tea?" he said, rising to his feet – something that required a good deal more effort these days. "Not what you're used to, I expect."

Nothing like tea to breeze to a calm after the maelstrom, Elizabeth thought. "Ah, yes, thank you."

She moved to a chair at the small table while he shuffled off. After the sounds of a kettle boiling and a few curses, he returned with a mug of tea, and a small jug of milk which she declined. He disappeared again and returned with a beer. He looked at the glass as if something completely new, with an affectionate grumble.

"This has done for me and made me, me. What does that mean? Dunno. You're a clever lady. You can come and go. Not me. I'm stuck here. Nowhere else to go. I'm not allowed back to England. And why would I go, and where? The beer and this country made me. I reckon I'd be long dead if I'd stayed back in England. And I wouldn't have met her, either.

That was worth coming here for. Beer, the country and your mam made me." He stopped, still ruminating on who to add to the list of essential influences.

His visitor turned away to try and disguise her anguish. "May I ask you again; will you make me a pair of shoes, just like my mother's? Sky blue, Australia blue. For us, for her, across the years?"

He raised his wet face, only wet in the past for his dead children and for Marianne. There was a sense of expiation, a righting of the wrong he had inadvertently caused and been blamed for in the horror so long ago, now raised again with this woman sucked into it. All he could offer was to say yes to her request. He looked at her, dulled by emotional exhaustion yet also excited by this new tentacle to Marianne, as a sort of penance.

"Yes. I will," he said.

"I need to measure your feet. If you'd like me to begin, please remove your shoes." He pointed to a small cubicle she had not noticed, for privacy and new fittings. She obeyed, and returned to hand over her shoes. Nicely done, he thought. He could learn new designs in fashion. They went back into the cubicle and she presented her feet. When he touched each, there was a charge. She was her mother's girl, a phrase he had heard before. She knew too, from his touch what her mother had felt instinctively. That something as humble as a foot could be so communicative astonished her. The blue shoes would dance again.

After measuring her feet and with a space to regain mutual composure he said. "It will take time for the dye. My customers do not want to be reminded of the incessant blue sky. I will need very special leather, as your mother had, and for the exact standards. It may take a month or more before everything is in place and I am satisfied. Is that too long?"

"No, I can reside in Melbourne as long as necessary," Elizabeth replied. "I will give you an address to reach me for fittings or your requirements.

I will travel about the Colony to familiarise myself with it, but I shall be reachable." She reached into her bag, removed a small leather-bound note book and a pencil. She wrote her name and address on one page, tore it out and gave it to him.

"My son Alf often goes to Melbourne," Tom said. "He works on the railways. I will send him to your address when I am ready, and he will take a note from me to you."

She moved to the door, turned to look at this man. This was the last person to see her mother alive. The last to see her dead. Bringing her to life again in the only way he can in the external world.

"Thank you for agreeing to my request. My mother will be so happy. She is with us." Elizabeth smiled, that same, serene smile; opened the door, stepped outside and left, the bell clanging behind her.

Tom Scrimshaw sat at his work desk for some time, idly sipping at his beer, stunned. Looking at his clock, this encounter had filled no more than twenty minutes. But a lifetime was crammed into it. His mind was so overwhelmed it went blank. He was still sitting there when William arrived from school, and the demands of an eight-year-old boy ended his father's reverie. Father rose, got the lad a glass of milk, cut a slice of bread, added a smear of butter, and the boy settled down on the bench.

Presently, Grace arrived with her purchases, some for work, some for the house, and mutton chops and potatoes for the evening meal for the house, fifteen minutes' walk away. After she handed over her husband's requirements, he said. "I've just had a woman in who wants a pair of sky-blue shoes. I said I'd do it."

"What? You were always against blue shoes, for your own reasons, I suppose. Why now?"

He paused. "Thought maybe it was time to. I told the woman I'd send Alf with a message when they were ready. She gave me her address in

Melbourne. We need to get the dye from Melbourne if we can't get it here, and the finest leather, too. Can you ask our suppliers tomorrow?

"She is from the Old Country, London, and has been looking for family history in Tasmania." He said no more; the conversation was ended, and he returned to his work, now needing to replace the bloodied sole.

Grace duly carried out these instructions. She found a dyer for the dye, and the highest grade of leather available. The leather dyeing required numerous applications with drying overnight between them. Small samples were sent for scrutiny before Tom was satisfied with the richness of the dye depth. He then set to work on his last, to the exclusion of other work, which caused remonstrations with Grace, who had to pacify customers. He grudgingly diverted to complete unavoidable urgencies.

Alf, on one of his trips home, was deputised to write to the woman. Confident in his work in this labour of love, Tom did not need to see her for fittings or checks, and the silence had surprised Miss Wainwright in Melbourne. However, one balmy Melbourne day as a breeze flitted along Spring Street, she picked up a letter requesting she attend at her convenience to inspect and try on her shoes, made to her specification and design; in effect, the same as the shoes she wore when she arrived in Geelong. He hoped the fashion had not changed, although he doubted that fashion in England covered sky blue footwear.

Miss Wainwright took a seat on the train to Geelong the next day, with an early start, so she could return the same day in daylight. She took a cab from the station to the shop. It was not far, but it was not seemly, in her eyes, for a woman of her age to traipse alone around the streets of a foreign city. Rejecting the role of army wife did not mean she abdicated the trappings of her class. At the shop entrance, she paid the modest fare and opened the door to set the bell ringing.

Stepping inside, Tom sat working at his desk. Busy too with laces at a small table was a younger woman. A workmate or assistant, she thought, probably younger than herself, who stood up and went to the counter to greet her. She was a woman of medium height, with what Miss Wainwright would describe as mousy hair, with a full figure and the air of a woman who expected life to be one of uncomplaining effort and labour.

"Good morning, "said the visitor. "I am here in response to the requested attendance for the blue shoes I requested Mr Scrimshaw make for me."

At the words 'blue shoes', Tom startled and looked up at this woman. She had dressed a little more informally this time, with a dark suit and bustle decorated with white and yellow lilies on a grey background. He imagined how the bright blue shoes would match. Perhaps she just wanted them to look at and treasure, and was unconcerned by fashion.

"Ah yes, Madam. I will get them for you. I hope you like them; they were special for me to make. I have reproduced the style you wore when you were here, which I took as high London fashion, and very nice it is too. Oh – may I also present my wife, Grace, who works with me in our little enterprise."

The visitor raised an elegant eyebrow. Ah, she thought, she is much, much younger.

Grace looked at this poised woman, carrying herself with effortless grace which accentuated her beauty with flawless skin and dark hair, full lips and eyes which seemed to be hazel with long lashes. A woman secure in her standing in society. Grace had seen pictures of the sort of clothes the women wore in the fashion magazines filtering down from fashionable Melbourne. Seen, but not desired by a working woman – once a servant, now a wife and mother. These fancies never impinged on her.

Miss Wainwright appraised Grace in return. So much younger than I thought; I knew there was a family, but this age disparity? Have I misjudged him? No, he was adult at Port Arthur when I was too young to remember. Work and her life have added to her age. Her face is open and friendly, and I'd venture to say, trustworthy. He certainly has an attraction for women, whatever their age, which I acknowledge, and an attraction for trouble on which I expect he would agree.

"I'm very pleased to make your acquaintance, Mrs Scrimshaw," she said, holding out her hand. Grace, half-remembering her servant days, was uncertain whether to curtsey, but seeing the proffered gloved hand pointing at her almost accusingly, took the appendage in her own right hand. Hands withdrawn, the visitor walked to the sofa, newly vacated as Will was sent to a chair, sat and composed herself. She reached down and undid the laces on each of her shoes in turn, carefully removing each and putting them aside one at a time.

Grace studied this procedure carefully. They were a fashion technique she had not actually seen. Could Tom, she wondered, make more of these shoes' style to appeal to ladies like this in Geelong or even Melbourne?

Tom burrowed, however, into a corner cupboard and after some wrestling returned with a box, went around the counter, opened the box and brought out two shoes of stunning brightness in the blue of the sky, which almost smiled upon them in appreciation. Even in the modest gloom of the shop, they were magnificent, demanded to be seen, shown, worn.

The customer's breast heaved and she burst into tears. "Oh! Oh!" She gasped. "They are too lovely, too beautiful. More than life itself."

"Try them," he said, humbled by her reaction. She did, with shaking fingers, stumbling with the second shoe, tangling with the laces. He bent and their fingers touched as he helped her to loosen the laces and open the tongue. Their eyes met and she looked down, hurriedly, to urge her foot into the shoe; a little push and she was in. He tightened the laces to her satisfaction as she recovered, and she rose and walked about.

"Are they comfortable? Are you?"

"Yes, oh yes. More, even more than I expected. You are a man of great skill and imagination. I am so grateful, so pleased. My mother will be smiling, laughing."

Grace felt unease with this dialogue; where had it been; where was it going?

The customer paraded up and down the small shop. Tom fetched a mirror to further tickle her fancy, reflecting the delight as she moved this way and that to see, a movement from this woman which disturbed Grace. Finally, she subsided into the sofa, carefully undid the laces, removed the boots, and in a triumphant look of pleasure, passed them to Tom to re-box, which he did and passed to her.

"How much for your skill? Your care and thought is beyond price, but it is all I can give." It dawned on both that in the fraught initial meeting, cost had not been discussed, even elliptically.

"Err... nothing," he heard himself saying in a somehow different voice.

Grace was aghast. All that work and cost! Nothing? This woman had money and was prepared to pay whatever he asked!

"No, no!" The visitor replied, "I must pay you, and handsomely, for this work of shoemaker's art and may I add, love."

"No," again he heard himself saying from the heart. "It is in memory of your mother. I could not charge."

Mother? It hit Grace. *Mother*?

Tom pushed the box into the woman's hands. "You are always welcome here for my humble talents at any time, and I will gladly make you fine boots and shoes and charge you a fair price." He stopped, then started again. "But not this time."

He knew, and she knew, it would not happen. She held out her hand, now bereft of a glove. He took it in his hardened grip, though more softly than she expected. The touch was enough. She sought her other glove, and carefully put both on. "Where may I find a cab to the station?"

"That will be difficult here. I will send my son Will with you to guide you, if you do not find a cab nearby. A cab is preferable, but may not be available. It is not far."

She nodded and smiled. Tom called Will, a slight, quiet, slow boy. His father gave him careful and deliberate instructions. He looked at the lady and set off to the door; she followed outside, the bell clanging, and they set off at a pace which was congenial to her, carrying her bag and now a precious box, to which Tom had tied string to help her carry, inelegant though the method was. She did not care.

Tom watched until they were out of sight, without a cab intervening. He turned about, to be confronted by Grace. "Are you mad? Are you so old? Throwing away all that money? She *has money*. Lots, and she wanted to pay whatever you asked. And you said no, no NO!"

She wanted to fly at him with her fists, instinctively, but another instinct went elsewhere. Had he lied to her, after all these years? This man, husband, father of her kids, was he a stranger in her bed? He had never said much about his past. The scarring showed her it was dreadful, the effect if not the cause, of which she knew nothing. She knew enough that those sent to the Colonies did not talk about it. The why, what for, what happened. Any of it. Lips sealed, buttoned up. She suddenly sobbed.

Her sobbing roused him from absorbing her anger. It was real, justified. Necessary, even. It was right to explain as much as he could and hope she would understand, or at least accept there was nothing sinister, nothing for anyone to be ashamed of, even though he saw that was where she was.

"I buried her mother. In shoes I made."

"What?" Grace subsided into the sofa.

"In Port Arthur. That lady's mother killed her husband, an officer. She was sentenced to death in a court-martial. I was in a group to watch her hang and then to deal with her after. I was ordered, me, just me alone, to bury her. To bury her standing up, facing away from the sun so she would never see or feel its warmth, never rest. She was wearing blue shoes I made for her in the Port. Sky-blue she wanted, for Australian light. Our workshop made better shoes, better quality than came from England for officers, wives, kids, settlers, each other. That's what she ordered. I made them."

"Oh God, how awful," Grace gasped, "how cruel."

"I buried her. Alone. T'was a terrible day, pouring rain. The guard left to keep himself dry. So I turned her around, so she'd see and feel the sun. Even though she couldn't." There was nothing further to be gained on what he knew of her, innocent and compelling though it was.

"That lady was her daughter, who was very young when her mam died. I didn't know there were children. Why would I? Two, she said; she had an older brother, now dead. They were taken to England and looked after. She was told more as she grew up about her mother killing her father, then she made her own journey to find out the truth. We never get to the real truth; one side then the other, and truth slithers out between.

"There are records, always records. Mine was read out to me once in Hobart, before I went to the Port. The records showed her what I did there and after, you and young Tom and me in Colac, living on the Island, being here. Reckon they know all the shoe sizes. Having found

Scrimshaws over here on the mainland, she traced us in Geelong from those who know us in Melbourne. And here she came. She wanted blue shoes like her mother had from me, and which her mam died in, all she would have of her mam. How could I charge her? Can you see that?"

Grace looked through her tears and saw his, too.

All she could do was nod, get up slowly and go to the door. She turned the sign around. "Closed."

CHAPTER 22

Geelong, 1888

"Ho old Tom! Good as ever to see a man who likes a drink, knows a good beer when he takes it."

John Kane, publican of The Warwick Castle, watched as Tom Scrimshaw walked into his pub, along with a tall, young man. The pub was Tom's local, a five-minute walk from home. John Kane was a man in his mid fifties who had been publican at a number of Geelong inns, all well-run and profitable. An affable and well-liked man.

Two other men, in their thirties, sat at a table in the bar, drinking ale and listening to the chat.

"Yair, take two glasses, me and this me son, Alf. 'Tis hot out there." John Kane poured two glasses, put them on the bar, and each man picked up one.

"Here's to old times." Tom raised his glass. "Old times for old men, though not young Alf here. He's young enough to be silly, but old enough to be sensible, not like me at his age. Silly and stupid I was, maybe still am. A Lincoln man, I was. Once. Where were you?"

"A Derby man," John replied. "Came by boat; it got wrecked near here. A man died, but I got away fine, as you see. Got salvaged for better things."

"The Mother Country abandoned us," Tom replied. "Cast-off whelps we were; me anyway. Here we are in Victoria for her pleasure, mine anyway, much to her surprise." Both laughed at the thought. "Here to make your boots and your wife Mary's, and your girls' shoes and boots too, for the winter."

"The best boots," John added.

"'Tis a bit of a boomerang," Tom grinned. "Money you give me for the boots swings back for your fine ale. A bit of this for a bit of that. Good swap. How are you and the wife and kids?"

"Not too bad. Get pains though, up here." The publican pointed to his head. "In my head. Last couple of weeks or so. I tell the wife I have to take my hat for a walk. My little joke with her. I take her a morning cuppa, then walk to clear my head. Sometimes I go to the Bank on the walk, sometimes visit old friends, others like me in other pubs, see how they're doing, have a yarn. Works, so far."

"Not drinking enough of your own good ale, I think. You need more of it." The two men laughed, comfortable in their banter. "How's your son Alf?" John Kane addressed Tom, not Alf, who was standing beside his father. "Haven't seen much of him with you till today."

"He's a railwayman now. Off here and there, all over the place. 'Tis a good job to have, especially for a lad who loved trains as much as he did. Messes up his games though, for the football team."

From a door behind the bar, a girl of about eighteen entered to stand behind the bar. She had clear skin, curly hair and a slender figure, and on a hot day in a series of hot days, she wore a light fabric print dress which went below her knees and, as befitted a young lady, her arms were sleeved. She looked at the two older men on either side of the bar and then at the young man who returned her gaze.

"My eldest girl, Grace Eleanor," John Kane said. "She's usually at the back of the hotel with her mam and sisters. My wife Mary was a widow; had four sons and a girl. Then with me, three girls and another son. She reckons it's evens. Don't think you know Tom, Grace? Mr Scrimshaw. He's one of our best, if not *the* best customers." Tom laughed at that. "He makes our boots and shoes; the ones you've got on, I bet, and he gives the money I pay him to cover our feet back to me for ale. A joyful business. And this," he said, indicating Alf, "is his son, Alf."

Having received an informal introduction the young pair could scrutinise each other a little more. He was, she saw, in his early twenties, quite tall, taller than both fathers and nearly six feet, she guessed. He was clean-shaven but growing a brown moustache in the modern style, although that growth was still uncertain of the territory it should conquer. She could not see his eyes clearly but he was slim and looked athletic. Quite good-looking too, although his nose was a little large. He was dressed in a blue uniform of jacket and trousers, which she did not recognise. The jacket had epaulettes and an emblem sewn on the top left-side pocket. He wore a peaked cap of the same colour as part of the uniform, and sturdy black boots; his father's work, no doubt.

Alf thought similarly of her, phrased differently for the gender. He thought her very pretty. He moved along the bar, beer in hand. She stood on her side of the bar as if waiting for him.

"Hullo, I'm Alf. Alfred, like The Great, or the Prince, but without crown or the money." She snorted. "What do you do?" he continued.

"I help mam out here in the hotel." She gestured behind her. "Help with my little sisters and my little brother, who's a big pest." Hearing this, Tom and John laughed.

"I've a little brother, too; Will," Alf said. "He can be a pest, but he's alright. Maybe it's easier if they're the same; all boys or all girls I mean."

Grace Eleanor continued after this interruption. "I help out dad, too, if he needs it. What do you do?"

"I'm a railwayman. The coming thing, too. I've always been keen on trains and railways, even as a lad. There's plenty of work and the pay's pretty good. So I do lots of travel, there's new places to see, new railways joining up towns in the Colony."

"That sounds exciting," Grace Eleanor said. "Going even faster than a horse or lots of horses. Faster than even the best one, the fastest one!

Once I saw a train pulling away from the station. Very noisy and smelly... A bit scary. It was straining to leave, like an iron horse."

"Ah," replied Alf, "but horses jump fences, swerve, change direction, throw you off if you're not careful. On my train I can only go straight ahead, straight and true. I come to stay with dad and mam and little brother when I am able."

"Another ale, young man?" John inquired from along the bar. Alf nodded and John busied himself pouring.

While this interaction was under way, Tom mused on the common ground he and this other man shared: Mary and Grace, Mary and Grace. Strange to share a Mary and Grace.

Time has fallen out of reach, he thought. Must be nigh on forty year since I married Mary in old Hobart, twenty since she died. Petrified Grace she did, just before she died. But hers wasn't much of a life. Did I treat her well, or not? I looked for her before I left. Should I've looked harder? She haunted the pubs. She knew all the pubs I did. They knew me well. How did I miss her? Did I not care enough? Does it hang on me? The cards she'd had dealt to her, some I held. Were they too poor to help her, or badly played? Or played the way she wanted, or had to?

He sighed. Maybe it was just meant to be, and he was meant to be with his very own Grace. He looked at this young Grace, Grace Eleanor. How would the two Graces get on if she and Alf joined the family? Two families.

She was near the age our dear lost girl would be, he thought. My Grace keeps her mind on our sweet girl. Secret lives of a mam and daughter, hard cut from her heart. How would they be? How can I know, an old winnowed man in a dry month, withering years from time gone, yet still time now.

Ah, yes. Time to wet the needy parts. A beer. Wet. Ah yes. Wet wakes my old brain. Pops up in the Port, pouring wet, stirred from time to time, day to day. It did for her, too; Marianne, Marianne. I know now; she knew all those years ago. Over all these years. Here I am still and 'tis enough.

Her daughter, her lovely daughter, alive to tear my heart, but a year ago with the blue shoes, shoes of love. Enough now, he thought, closing down his reverie. John had passed Alf a beer and they were chatting, the boy distracted by this pretty girl, this Grace.

"Ah, John, t'other glass please." Hearing the request, John left the young couple, Alf with a beer, Grace Eleanor with a glass of water on this hot day, to return to help slake Tom's thirst, and for the men to return to reminiscences.

The pub door was suddenly thrust back, followed by six young men wearing railway livery, slightly boisterous from a few drinks elsewhere. One, with blond hair peeping under his cap, announced:

"Ho, Alf! Imagine that. Thought we'd find you here, in a pub you said you knew. Here we all are! Finished work today and ready to trawl the pubs and fish the alehouse brew! Glasses, publican! For us all. Cheer our thirsty bellies with your finest ale, and then some more."

The publican took down the required glasses, filled all with foaming ale, set them along the bar for anxious hands, hands also rummaging in pockets to find coins. The other two drinkers sat and watched.

"Ah, Alf." The young railwayman continued, one hand wrapped around a glass, and emboldened by what he had already consumed on his travels to date, "Been keeping quiet then, with this lovely lady? Not surprised with that; isn't that right lads?" There was a mixture of nodding heads and murmured assents from those not actually in the throes of drinking. "Here's to happy days." He raised his glass and started singing.

"We are the jolly railwaymen,"

At this point the others joined in and the cacophony made the words difficult to catch.

> *"Men so straight and true*
>
> *Get you there and back again*
>
> *Like no one else can do.*
>
> *O... wrap yer fingers round t'glass*
>
> *And raise it to yer lips*
>
> *Open wide yer great divide*
>
> *Yer 'tache will catch the drips.*
>
> *We are the jolly railwaymen*
>
> *Going places new*
>
> *Doing things beyond yer ken*
>
> *We arc ycr futurc, too.*
>
> *O... wrap yer fingers round t'glass*
>
> *And raise it to yer lips*
>
> *Open wide the great divide*
>
> *Yer 'tache will catch the drips.*
>
> *We are the jolly railwaymen*
>
> *We'll always get you home*
>
> *When you slip inside your den*
>
> *Then to the pubs we'll roam.*
>
> *O... wrap yer fingers round t'glass*
>
> *And raise it to yer lips*
>
> *Open wide the great divide*
>
> *Yer 'tache will catch the drips."*

The railwaymen sang the "O... wrap..." chorus three times as a round while Alf looked slightly uncomfortable with this exhibition by the purveyors of the coming thing in front of Grace Eleanor.

The leader held up his hand to cease the warbling. "Ah, maybe it's time to fish elsewhere and see what we can catch, like Alf here. Happy landings, Alf me lad. We'll leave these old men drinking away." With murmurs of approval, the group downed their remaining beer and left to continue their trawl and crawl.

John went to clear up the remains of the carousing. Tom resumed his musing, muttering his thoughts to himself. "Mary and Grace, unlucky for one, not t'other. One I neglect, not show respect. Mary, Mary, how does your garden grow? Not at all, not at all, withered and bare... Didn't you care? Don't ya know"?

John looked at Tom, picking up the old man's mutters, louder than Tom realised, and responded.

"I've had so many happy days with Mary at my side, wife and mother still my bride. What could man, any man, want more than a Mary in every house? A Mary born for everyone, and that would grace us all."

Alf turned to Grace Eleanor. "I have to say those were my friends, workmates more the truth. I hope you were not shocked or scared or thinking less of me."

"Oh, no, not at all. It is a pub after all, and noise and fun live here happily."

"That's very kind of you, I'm sure. It's very nice to see you... I mean to meet you, Grace." Tom and John laughed at this little slip.

"Very nice to meet you, Alf. Please do come again."

John butted in. "Better take her away Alf, get her off my hands. Too many females here bossing me about." He added a laugh. Tom followed.

Grace Eleanor suddenly looked flustered. "I forgot why I came. A message from mam. I'll have to go back and get it again." She turned and hurried through the door to the rear.

"See what you've done, Alf?" her father laughed, and slapped the bar.

No-one noticed the two other drinkers quietly leave, leaving empty glasses on the table.

"Better get Alf home before he does any more damage to your family," said Tom. "I'll take a small keg of this ale with me for tea, John; it's damn hot out there, too many days of it." John smiled, went for a small keg, filled it with the favoured ale and put it on the counter. Tom reached into a pocket for coins, counted them out and handed them to John.

"C'mon lad, pick up the keg and we'll see what yer mam has cooked for tea." Alf picked up the keg, hoisted it to his shoulder, and with a wave from Tom they left.

February continued its baleful glare on the citizens of Geelong. The following day was even hotter. Tom and Grace started work in their shop, Grace worked part-time juggling the work with her other duties. She did not stay long. "'Tis too hot. I'm going home," she told Tom. "I'll open the front and back doors for some breeze, not that there's much. I'll go. See you later."

Tom soldiered on, but finally the heat and glue exasperated him. He cleaned up, turned the sign to "Closed" on the door and left. Sensible people stayed inside and no customers were expected, or even wanted in the heat. He trudged home, changed his sticky work clothes for an outfit slightly cooler and announced, "I'll have a couple of glasses to cool off and see what John is up to." Grace nodded, though thought it odd to leave a comparatively cool home to go out again in the heat. He took with him the now-empty keg for a refill.

Opening the door of the Warwick Castle, he called out, "Glass of the usual John, thanks."

But as he looked towards the bar he saw not John, but the innkeeper's wife Mary. "Oh, hullo, Mrs Kane," Tom addressed her more formally; she rarely worked behind the bar, that was her husband's domain as hers was behind the scenes, looking after paying guests at the hotel with help from her older daughters. But there she was, behind the counter and not looking very pleased to be there.

"Glass of the best, please Mrs Kane. Where's John?"

"I don't know. We don't know," she replied, pouring the ordered ale and plonking it on the counter.

"What? Is he sick?"

"No... well, maybe... He does have these headaches, pains in his head he says, and he goes off when he has that; takes his hat for a walk, he says. He comes back when he feels better and takes over here. There's not usually much for me to do early in the day. He went off this morning, made me a cup of tea like he always does. Said he was taking the hat for a walk. But he hasn't been seen since, nor heard of.

"After midday came and went with no news, I sent Grace down to the police station to say he was missing and how unexpected it was. We are respectable people and the police said they would keep an eye out for him as they went about their business. It's not like him. We're worried sick... The little ones are crying."

"Sorry to hear that," Tom said. "I'm sure he is all right. Mebbe he could have stopped for a yarn at another pub, he told me yesterday he does that sometimes? Maybe a few too many ales in the heat and needs to come good before he comes back."

Mary Kane nodded. She was grateful for any possible explanation. Her husband was a most modest drinker; being too inebriated to walk home, while a rational explanation, was implausible; but in the worry and fear mounting within her in these unusual circumstances, implausibility was easy to ignore.

Tom sat and drank in silence. He cast around mentally for another reassuring explanation for his missing friend. He knew he was too old now to go out in the heat searching for him personally. Nobody knew which direction he'd have taken, and it would be stupid to go wandering about in this heat. Better for young policemen to be doing it. Tom finished his ale and ordered another. It gave him a sense of solidarity that he hoped Mary Kane felt too in her evident distress, he would stay here to offer what support he could. She knew him as a regular customer and it would be poor to leave her in this state. He resolved to sit awhile and hope for the balm of good news which would surely come while he was there, and they could all share it. It also occupied Mary Kane, fidgeting as she was, checking and re-checking the glasses, the stock and staring at the floor as if it had not seen soap and water for years.

Grace Eleanor appeared from the rear. "Any news, mam?"

Her mother shook her head. "No, but Mr Scrimshaw here thought dad could have stopped at another pub for a chat. Told Mr Scrimshaw last night that's what he sometimes did. Isn't that so, Mr Scrimshaw?"

 "Yes, he did. Maybe he stopped for tea and had a few too many drinks to walk home in the heat. Not easy to do. He might be waiting for it to cool a bit." He wanted to reassure this young girl who had obviously been crying. She in turn suddenly remembered yesterday, though it seemed ages ago, and in her distraction, asked, "How is Alf?"

"Ah, he's working on a train somewhere. May not be back for a few days. He gets to places I've never heard of. It all sounds important, and very fast. There was nothing like that when I was his age." He remembered that when he was Alf's age he was practising the skills of stupidity back in England, which was why, ultimately, he was here now. Had there been trains back then, what might have happened? Probably just more ways to be stupid. Better not expand on his last remark to young Grace, he thought, especially if something developed between her and Alf. His own history was best left as ancient history.

Grace Eleanor was at a loss on what to do, besides having her mother's instinct to keep busy doing nothing in particular. After a few minutes busily interfering with her mother's attempts to be busy, Grace announced, "I'll go to Elizabeth, Emily and Albert and see what they are doing." She was aware they were not doing anything, save the girls being tearful which relieved tension temporarily. She left.

Her mother and Tom were shortly joined by another customer seeking respite from the heat with a cold beer or two. Time passed, as did the stray customer, leaving the two to seek some esoteric comfort in each other's presence. Tom began to think he should return home. While his Grace knew where he was, she too could become concerned at his time away and why.

Grace Eleanor returned. "Any news from anybody?"

"No. Nothing."

Just then the door opened and a police officer entered. "We have some news, Mrs Kane." Mary and Grace Kane's agitation ceased and they were still.

"We found his hat, we believe. This one." He produced a hat – a wet one.

"It's his, it's his!" They chorused. "Where did you find it?" Mary demanded.

"In the river."

"In the river? The *river*?" The women had not fully realised when they saw the hat that it was wet. Now they had it and felt it. Wet. "The river? Well, where is he?" The policeman shrugged.

Tom ventured a question. "Was – was he not underneath it?"

"No." The policeman looked at him, then the two women. They said nothing, and finally he offered. "We will continue looking, some are out looking still, and we will continue tomorrow too." With that, he turned and left.

Grace Eleanor howled and clutched her mother, who put her arms about her daughter's convulsing body for mutual comfort. The younger children, hearing the ominous sounds, realised these were not happy sounds and burst into tears also.

Amid the sobbing, Tom thought of a suggestion. "Your dad was not under the hat. So he must be somewhere else. His hat could have fallen off if he was near the river. Hats fall off. Might have been a gust of wind. Unexpected, blew it into the river. Maybe he wandered off, maybe to sit down to rest his head pain; recover from it. And then he'll come back later. Or he found a pub to sit in without his hat till it cools down a bit. No point in trying to fish it out of the river. He can get another one tomorrow when he gets home. He's not been found in the river, only his hat. That's the main thing."

Through the sobbing, these words filtered into their minds. A gust of wind blowing the hat into the river. Stopping after for a yarn in a pub rather than walk back hatless in all this heat. It was plausible.

"Oh, I hope so. We hope so. Please, God. Thank you too for your hope and good thoughts."

"I think you should shut the door now to be together without any distractions. Just be together. If there is any news they will bang on the door and you won't have to worry about customers."

Grace Eleanor rushed to the door to lock it. "Good. But let me out first please, Grace. I will tell my wife the news we have. It is not all bad news. I believe he will be found safe and ready to be returned to his family." With that utterance he went to the door, looked at the family clinging to

349

each other and to the glimmer of hope he offered. He looked at this young girl, standing by him at the door, her wet cheeks and her pale wan smile meeting him.

*

The Coroner began: "This is the Inquest into the Death of John Kane and I will summarise the evidence I have heard and my verdict on the basis of the evidence.

"On Thursday 9 February last John Kane made his wife a morning cup of tea and said he was going for a walk to clear his head. The day before he told a witness, Mr Scrimshaw, who gave evidence, that he frequently took such a walk with his hat when he had head pain and sometimes would call into other publicans. I also heard evidence from family members that Mr Kane had been complaining about head pains for some two weeks before his death. He was otherwise in good health save for what was described as a 'bad leg' which affected his walking.

"Investigations by my officers revealed that he was on friendly terms with his wife, and examination of his financial records including his bank accounts adduced no evidence of any financial difficulties and that he was a popular and respected publican.

"In their inquiries my officers found evidence of the deceased's standing in the community. Produced before me was an extract from a Geelong paper of some years ago which recorded that John Kane was organising support for a destitute widow with six children under ten. The father was killed the previous week on a coal ship in the wharf. Mr Kane was seeking assistance in food, clothing and money even if enough for a loaf of bread, and an entertainment, presumably as a way of raising money. There is no record of the success of this endeavour although it is greatly to be hoped that there was some at least, but it is an indication of the respect in which he was held and this court might say, justifiably so.

"On this date of 9 February he left at 9am and stopped at the Belmont Hotel about half a mile away from his own establishment where the proprietor Mr J O'Keeffe gave evidence that he requested Mr Kane stop and partake dinner with him, which he refused and left at about 11.30am.

"I heard evidence from Mr Dyer that he saw the deceased walking along the banks of the Barwon River at about noon in the heat of the day and his walking gait was slightly affected, which would be consistent with his "bad leg." Mr Dyer said he saw two men who he thought were aged in their thirties following Mr Kane. Unfortunately, we do not have the identities or whereabouts of these young men to assist me further in ascertaining what befell Mr Kane.

"However, when he did not return a search was instituted and his hat was found floating in the Barwon River. A resumed search the following day, 10 February, recovered his body from the river. His pockets were empty and we have no evidence on whether he left home with money on his person although on occasion he was known to do so. An autopsy was undertaken on my instructions and from the autopsy finding I record the death of John Kane was by asphyxia by drowning.

"My condolences and that of the court to the family and friends in their sad and tragic loss."

CHAPTER 23

Geelong, 1897

"Grace took the kids off?"

"Yes." Grace looked at her husband. She sat on a chair by the bed – a bed in which a very old man lay in the front room of their double-fronted house in Geelong. Tom Scrimshaw was breathing slowly, eyes closing occasionally.

"Good enough. Said goodbye earlier. This time's different though. They won't know it. Too young and lively to be here in this miserable scene."

"Yes. Three under seven. Ours were once…" She broke off with her memory.

"Saw me as they know me. If they will at all later. Doesn't matter."

"Grace said today's the day her dad was found in the river," Grace said, changing the subject. "Same month, same day. Very upset she is. Still. Hasn't fully recovered since that awful day."

Tom sighed, and there was a slow exhalation, then a slow intake of breath. "Funny thing, life and death. Need each other. One lost without t'other. John Kane was found… was it eight, nine or ten year ago today?" He paused with his repeat breathing process. "About ten minute walk from here… in the river.

"A good man." He paused again. "Good man. Hope a pub above needs good publican. Pour a good one for me. Not too bitter… if I'm lucky." He coughed, and a little wheezy laugh snuck out.

Grace looked at her husband's lined face, his nose a beacon, wisps of grey hair, his eyes watery. Whatever she saw, she loved. She reached out and took his right hand in hers. She felt the slow pulse.

"At least being out with the children will keep her occupied." Grace paused briefly. "Alf will be back from work. Think he misses being on trains, now he's too important in the main station."

"Boy's done well," Tom wheezed.

Grace continued. "I have Will in the shop. This is time for us. Our time."

As she spoke, he turned his eyes to her. "Lying here, dying here. Had to be sometime. It's taken ages. How long?"

"Alf said you were nigh on ninety-one. Good with sums and figures. He always was."

This was not what Tom meant; more how long had he been dying, in her eyes at least, but he let it pass. No time to worry about misunderstandings. Instead, he punctured his words with silences and gasps for breath. "How did I get here... robbed a stupid man... he was robbed by a *very* stupid man... silly man... silly boy, even...

"My father... William... farmer. Ploughed all his furrows. Straight... huddled up, one next t'other. Cuddled. Knew each other. My furrows... crissed and crossed... kissed and cursed. My own way... special to me. Brought me here. With you and our two boys... now lives made."

He paused again, gathering air and thoughts. "I would be long dead, strung up and forgotten in the Old Country. Or on the island, dead from planned and damned indifference, neglect. Not planned well enough, eh... whatever done to me, right or wrong, deserved or not... I'm still here.

"Three or four lots of lashes, was it? Counted them once... got bored when in a solitary for something in Port... got to know the cat. Hundred and five. Only you and one other ever saw my back." His memory prodded him; the one other – Marianne's daughter – he'd best keep quiet.

"Once caught myself in a mirror," he continued, "saw my ploughed field there, blotched and lumpy, seeds sown in an old life... never seen by the kids... always covered over, always." A cough stopped him, he heaved.

Grace said, quietly. "As a girl I saw fishbones stripped of flesh. Your back's like herringbones, stripped and striped."

"Keep me away from the boys' sight... they're not see me w' no clothes and dead. They will ask how... when... why... you would have to explain my shameful life, awful life before we met... so jus' put me in with our dear sleeping ones... dressed as I am."

While he spoke haltingly, Grace was afraid she could not tell her sons much of the how or why, as she did not know much herself. Hearing him talk on, keeping him as he was, hidden from view, was a relief. She squeezed his hand. "You will be with our sweet babies who wait for us until my time comes to be with you too. You will go dressed as you are. No one will touch you."

He seemed to rally slightly on this news. "Put my best boots on my old feet, though. If I ever go up, more likely down... but I can hope... I can show my wares... there might be need..."

Tom Scrimshaw moved to another concern. "My good and loving wife... you must find another... make another man good as you made me... with your love... and... being you." He stopped, then gathered some remaining inner strength. "You are still young... still strong... your fingers know the pathways to good boots. No waste of tears... on an old, dry man beyond time... his time."

Grace shook her head, released his hand and stood up, a little angry despite herself, with his urgings. Then she eased, sat down again and again took his gnarled hand in hers. "I came as a servant. I became your wife." She faltered briefly. "I am always your wife. All men knew it. All men know it. All will know it.

"You looked after me, protected me. Gave me your care and your love. Though you never said it, I knew it. You gave me, give me, kindness and courage. You guide me. Lead me always until I am with you."

She looked down at him, holding his hand firmly. His breathing altered, and a noise, a gargle, arose in his throat.

He looked at her lovingly, his loving, kind and caring wife, her face lined with uncomplaining cares over these years. As his eyes dimmed and faded they found a strange transformation.

Grace's grieving face, staring intently at him, gradually metamorphosed but ineluctably into Marianne's. Marianne, with that same strange look, the peculiar, inexplicable smile he had seen before the hood lowered, and which had tormented him throughout so much of his life.

Now he saw and knew it: *I wait, my love. Welcome.* He felt enveloped in Marianne's light, and was ready.

Grace felt his hand grip lessen in her fingers. She heard a gasp, an exhale and three faint words from a half-forgotten hymn: *"Lead, kindly light."* Nothing more.

She looked at his face. Was it a miracle? The lines on his old face left him. He looked young again. Was young again. So young. Is this what happened when you die and the bad things crabbing your face drop off? Not only that. There was a smile on his face. Such a smile. Peace and happiness.

So pleased was she at this revelation that he was at peace and so happy where he was going, she muttered to herself; for me too, then. Please. She was not religious, nor he, but there was still a residual worm nudging her of a better life to come. Wherever it was. Grace sat in her chair, holding his hand and watching the light, an internal light diffusing his face, magical to her.

Time passed. Time will bring William back from the shop, and then Alf back from the station. Then Grace Eleanor and the children can come in. It was all over, and she and her man had made a good ending. Alf, practical as ever, would sort out the funeral arrangements. She rose, went into the kitchen, made a pot of tea, cut a slice of bread, buttered it, slapped a couple of dabs of apricot jam on top, put all on a tray, and took her pot, cup, covered bread back to the bedroom. She put the tray on a small bedside table, sat and waited for her sons to arrive.

✳

On a cold, wet June day, a few months after Tom's death, Grace sat alone in her living room. Will was at the shop working on tasks his mother had set for him. She was not at the shop herself as she would shortly have company. She was expectant, sad yet buoyant. She heard an approach to the front door; the door opened, with a circle of cold air preceding Alf. Now a young man in his early thirties and dressed not in the livery of a railway man, but in the fashion of a young man, he walked to his mother.

"Grace is readying the kids; packing is nearly done. I ordered a cab. Here in ten minutes. The kids are so excited. Big city, Melbourne, eh? But when promotion knocks on your door and you're told to come now, you can't say no."

"No. It's good. Dad would be so pleased. You have done so well. We are proud of you, dad and me. Sure he's looking down."

"Good to get Grace away. She still thinks about her dad. Strange to think that the day after we met in her family pub — it was almost our family's too, dad spent so much time there — and we started courting, her dad didn't come back from taking his hat for a walk. Pains in his head. I'm not a medical man, but is that it? Took his hat swimming? Fell in? Two missing men seen near him. Who were they? What happened? Thinks and thinks, she does.

"The move will distract her. A new place, there's so much to do, somewhere new to live, Schools to find. New friends to make. We can come here on the train and see you though, and Will can come to us.

"Oh, and a surprise! Grace says she's with child again, and due about Christmas. So still the year dad went. If it's a little boy we'll call him Thomas, if a girl, Grace."

"We've had three Graces, isn't that enough? Maybe Naomi after your little sister?"

"Something to think about when she is settled and occupied." Alf looked at his time piece. "Well, mam, I must be off now. The train waits for Melbourne, or other way round. I'm not in charge of it."

Grace raised herself, steadied on the table and held out her arms as her son moved towards her. She put her arms around him and lifted her face. Alf was not used to affection outside the norms of propriety and his own little family. Although affection to a mother was right and proper, the method of exhibiting it was unclear to him. He took her embrace and kissed her on the cheek. He recalled later that her cheek was wet. A kiss of sorts, a hug and a wave as he left.

That left Grace now alone again. She went into the kitchen, made herself a pot of tea and decided she should have a biscuit – no, two biscuits. She took her teapot, cup and saucer and biscuits back into the parlour, sat, poured the tea and ruminated as she crunched a biscuit.

Gone. As was right and proper. He has done well. We are poorer here with them leaving us, not being here. They have each other, and the dear children; three now to be four, if all be well. God forbid that God is good. Ha, a good laugh that is.

What will we be in a hundred years? Will these dear children begat children as we were told as little ones with Bible readings? Will our names be gone? No more than scratchings on a stone, then hard to read with the weather. Graves that no one visits. I don't visit my mam and dad's. Do any of my brothers and sisters visit them? Do they have any kids? Not important enough to visit, we are?

Will we be happy and healthy a hundred years from now? Two hundred? Any bits of us still above ground? Poor? Rich? Rich; does that mean always able to pay bills? Eat whatever we want whenever we want? Have our own carriages? Or will we stay poor? Or in the middle? Is that it? Stay as we are. Like cows. Eat grass. Chew cud, have calves, get milked, die. Calves become cows, eat grass, so it goes on. Was like that. Will be like that. We're different animals.

Want our little ones to do more. My mum and dad wanted more for me. A servant girl better than what they had; living by thieving turnips. Though dad was a shoemaker. Like Tom. Like us. But we don't have to eat turnips no more. Not unless we want to. Tom too. Shoemaker to shoemaker. Like a cow... no, bull. But a middle. Prisoner to ship carpenter. Doing different things.

Someone told me our name was someone who engraved, carved something like whale teeth. Sounds silly. Why would you do that? How does it pay to eat? Eat the whale first? Made me giggle. Will anyone carve anything about us, but a gravestone? Carve who we were, what we did? Who would be the teller of our tales?

Who would write for us? We cannot. People talk and write of battles, famous battles with great men. No one writes of us, the boots that run into those battles, the underbelly holding it up. Only the men who sent us there, the organisers, get the statues, the books.

Who writes about the battlers who fight battles every day? Every day, day after day. At night, too. Must sound boring if it's not you having to do it. We do not know how to speak, folk like us, to say what we think or put it down in words. But we keep our feet warm, have kids and we die, like cows, like the fine ladies and gentlemen who get the same size boxes as us at the end. Will one of us become a teller of tales? We all like tales. Makes the dead live. Do carvings on the grave?

Even the famous. Our dear Queen with her Jub... um... jubilee or something like that, this year. Lots of celebrations. Will I get more orders for boots to march in? Famous ladies should wear famous Geelong boots. They won't, though. Tom is dead and gone, though his boots still go on. What do I learn from that? Don't know.

I have young Will to keep an eye on. My old servant eyes are still to serve. My young Will still needs me, pottering about with bits of the boots and happy enough, and I can still sell them. He has me.

I had his father, thirty-five years a gift. Still my gentle and kind beacon. And his last words... that hymn...

The Scrimshaw carving on our grave, can it be *Lead, Kindly Light*?

Acknowledgements

This novel exists because of genealogical investigations, and I am delighted to attribute that burrowing for the truth, as close as we can get to it, to Irene Morgan and Tony Cocks and to my daughter Anna Scrivenger, who, aside from genealogical input, also provided her editing and publishing skills to bring this tale into the world.

I am also very pleased to acknowledge the support, confidence building and urging on unravelling the arcane mysteries of self-publishing to two women in San Diego, California: Liz St John and Dee. Lucky San Diego to have them. Nor forgetting Mary Anne Yarde's professional eye cast upon the work.

And of course my wife Gaynor, for her non-interfering guidance and patience while I was absorbed in the work.

Who could have imagined that the little group in the novel would be caught in such a wide net of supporters.

While it is a work of fiction, based on historical events in the three records and with plausible outcomes following on from them, any errors and solecisms are entirely mine, alas.

About the Author

Mark Scrivenger is an Australian living in England, about 62 miles (100km) from the city of Lincoln, from where the hero – or anti-hero – was banished in March 1830.

This was a tale which the author thought worth telling.

While the names of historically recognised persons remain the same, other surnames have been changed in respect of hitherto unknown historical figures referred to in the three records on which the novel is based.

There is a connection. In writing this work of fiction, the author realised he can claim to have met one of the historical characters in the novel, who was born in 1869.

If a 'contemporary' can be defined as two (or more) people who are both (or all) alive on a certain date or period of time, then the author and this person are contemporaries stretching over more than 150 years.

A lot to talk about, eh?